Wicked Women

It's much easier than you think becoming someone else. First of all, you get used to the name right away. It's not like in the movies or on TV when someone is under cover or pretending to be someone else and a guy calls them by their pretend name and they don't answer at first because they forgot that's who they now are. Someone calls me Wren, I respond immediately. Maybe even faster than I did when people used to call me Luna.

The mundane details of life swapping were pretty simple. I found Wren's birth certificate when I was packing up her files. I took it down to the DMV, told them I'd lost my driver's license, and had them reissue a new one, this one with Wren's name and my photo. After that I was able to get a passport, credit cards, and anything else I needed. Once I saw how easy it was, I was surprised more people, when their lives got too complex or disappointing, didn't just up and become someone else.

In the movies when someone wants to disappear, they fake their deaths in a flaming car crash or something. I didn't have ~~~~ far. As far as ~~~~ day Robby and ~~~~ was fake my life ~~~~

Wicked Women

Laramie Dunaway

NEW ENGLISH LIBRARY
Hodder and Stoughton

Printed and bound in Great Britain for Hodder and Stoughton Paperbacks, a division of Hodder and Stoughton Ltd, Mill Road, Dunton Green, Sevenoaks, Kent TN13 2YA. (Editorial Office: 47 Bedford Square, London WC1B 3DP) by Clays Ltd, St Ives plc. Photoset by Rowland Phototypesetting Ltd, Bury St Edmunds, Suffolk.

A CIP catalogue record for this title is available from the British Library

ISBN 0-450-55128-8

PART ONE

How to Have a Near-Death Experience

1

When I finally arrived at the police station, Wren was standing on the front steps under a bright light, a pair of blue panties balled up in her right fist. She was waving her fist around like she was about to do some sort of magic trick with her panties, turn them into a dove or something. At the same time, her flushed face was leaning into some young uniformed cop's pale face, yelling at him. The top to my Rabbit was down, so I could hear each word as crisp as snapping carrots.

'This is total bullshit!' Wren hollered.

The skinny young cop was leaning as far back as he could without flipping backward over the railing. His eyes were wide and unfocused, as if he'd just been told he was the offspring of incest. Like most men who've come face-to-face with Wren's temper, he looked both a little murderous and a little in love.

I quickly swung the Rabbit to the curb and honked twice.

Wren didn't take her fierce eyes off the young cop. She continued to glare at him as she backed down the steps toward my car without actually looking where she was going. As if she were guided by some psychic homing device. Anyone else I'd have been worried would trip and fall. But not Wren. She had never done one ungraceful thing in her entire life. She'd probably pirouetted out of her mother's womb and done the Maypole dance with the umbilical cord. Finally, Wren turned toward me. This is when I noticed the huge tan bandage the size of a business card angled across her forehead, partially covering her left eyebrow. A moist rusty spot soaked through the center of the bandage. Three drops of blood formed a teardrop constellation on her white T-shirt.

Wren had only descended two steps when she stopped abruptly and pivoted back around toward the cop. Her tennis shoes squealed against the smooth cement. The startled young cop flinched. His hand dropped to his gun.

'And you are an asshole!' Wren proclaimed, pointing her panties at him. 'You hear what I'm saying, Officer? Do you?'

She marched toward my car, climbed in, and slammed the door. 'Let's get the fuck out of here before I kill someone else.'

*   *   *   *   *

'Stop that,' Wren said, slapping my hand.

I have this nasty habit when I'm nervous of reaching inside my collar and rubbing my thumbnails back and forth against my bra strap. I do it in class, I do it at work, I do it before and after sex. During sex I rub them along the seam of the mattress edge. Both my thumbnails have deep ugly groves in them as if they'd been crushed under very thin bicycle tires. Fingernail polish only makes them look worse. A student once asked if I'd had them amputated and sewn back on again. I usually try to hide them in public.

'Loony, goddamn it,' she said, slapping my hand again, harder.

'Ow,' I said, slapping her hand back. But I stopped.

She lifted her butt off the seat and pulled out some papers she'd been sitting on. 'What's this?'

'A petition. Sign it.'

She picked up the pen that had been rolling annoyingly across the dashboard and signed the line under my name. 'What's this for?'

4

'A new law.'

'Oh.' She opened the glove compartment and stuffed the petition inside. She smiled and picked up my purse tucked next to her seat. 'Got anything interesting in here?' She started digging through it looking for a joint. She wasn't going to find one. I'd given up on that stuff after I split up with Robby two months ago. He was the one who liked to get high anyway. I never really did, not really. Not in my teens, not in my twenties, and especially after I turned thirty last year. Marijuana seemed like such a sixties thing to do, a nostalgic act, like teatime for American Anglophiles. But I'd been in diapers for a lot of the sixties and felt no nostalgia for its return. I was relieved now I didn't have to fake being hip anymore. The only good part of smoking dope was that when Robby got the munchies afterward, he'd cook us a ten-course gourmet meal. His dad was a real chef in a fancy Beverly Hills restaurant. At home, his dad had dozens of black-framed photographs on the wall of himself in his white chef's hat and white tunic that buttons up one side like a military uniform. In these photos, Robby's dad is leaning over the table between some celebrity and his or her dining companion, smiling directly at the camera. His arm is usually resting on the celebrity's shoulder. My favourite is of Jay Leno, who has a straw up his nose and is pretending to snort the freshly grated Parmesan cheese from his plate. He signed it: 'I could eat your food by the kilo.' I loved watching Robby putter around the kitchenette, naked except for his dad's white chef's apron framing his boxy buns.

'You going to tell me what happened?' I asked Wren, taking one hand off the steering wheel to tug at her tattered panties. Wren only wore one kind of panty, plain cotton, no lacy designs, cut French style, high on the hips with only a small pouch to cover the crotch and skinny string up the behind. What I called her 'butt-floss panties'.

'These old things?' Wren unfurled the panties and stretched them out between her two hands. They had a

5

hundred tear marks in them, like some hungry dog had been chewing them.

'Jesus, Wren,' I said. 'What happened?'

Wren tossed the panties up into the night air. The draft around us sucked them into the dark. She craned around to see where they landed. 'Tomorrow some bicycle-seat-sniffing brat will find them and be in horndog heaven.'

'It must be gratifying to know you've done your part to relieve his adolescent anxiety and clear up his skin to boot.'

'What can I say, I'm a humanitarian.'

'Meantime, Dr. Schweitzer, you mind telling me what the hell happened with the cops?'

Wren returned to my purse, digging until she found a lone rat-gnawed cigarette at the bottom. Smoking is another habit I no longer had since I no longer had Robby, all part of my new purification program. Like my volunteering to gather signatures for Amnesty International petitions. I said, 'So what crime did you commit?'

Wren stuck the cigarette in her mouth, punched the car lighter, and waited. I knew she wouldn't answer until the cigarette was lit. She was very theatrical that way.

'Wren, it's after midnight,' I reminded her. 'I just got home from the library twenty minutes ago after twelve butt-numbing hours studying a dozen of the ninety some doctoral dissertations that have been written about Thomas Pynchon. I got your message on my machine. I'm here. I haven't eaten since breakfast and I'm close to killing you for the food stuck between your teeth. So just tell me what the hell happened.'

'Pull over! Pull over!' She gestured frantically.

'What?'

'Pull over.' Wren grabbed the steering wheel and jerked. The Rabbit squealed across two lanes and I braked to a stop in the bicycle lane in front of the A&W fast-food place. They were closed. Even though Langston, Oregon, was a small university town, almost everything in it closed down at six o'clock. It was as if the residents didn't want to admit that most of their livelihood depended on the students who comprised half the town's population. Luckily, there was no traffic after six either.

'Jesus, Wren,' I said, clutching my pounding chest.

But Wren wasn't listening. She tossed her just-lit cigarette into the gutter and started ransacking my glove compartment. 'Paper,' she demanded. 'Paper, paper!' Then she mauled my purse again. She found an envelope and started scribbling on the back.

'Not that,' I protested, reaching for it. 'That's the letter from Robby's lawyer about our divorce.'

'I'm writing on the envelope, not the fucking letter.'

'But the letter's inside. I have to, you know, file it or something.'

Wren yanked the letter from the envelope and shoved it at me. 'Here. File it.' Then she returned to her scribbling. It was pointless to interrupt her now.

I unfolded the letter and looked at it again. Brief. Polite. Two paragraphs. Divorce proceedings were in effect. Blah, blah. No fault. Blah, blah. Sincerely yours. Blah.

The law firm's name was longer than the letter.

I looked over at Wren writing furiously in the dim glow of the streetlight. Her shoulders were hunched, her eyes squinted in concentration less than eight inches from the envelope. She appeared to be conjuring dark forces.

'Let me pull up to the streetlight,' I said. 'You could ruin your eyes.'

'Hmmm,' she muttered to herself. 'Yes, yes.'

Like a woman enjoying sex.

I refolded my letter and placed it on the dashboard. Down the street, a couple of rugged boys from the university came out of the 7-Eleven convenience store. They laughed in that raunchy way males laugh when they've just said something derogatory about women or the other guy's penis.

I yawned until I could feel my ears pop and the bones in my jaw click. I took off my glasses and rubbed my tired

7

eyes. I'd been reading small print on the fourth floor of the library for twelve hours. At some point while I was reading about Pynchon's *V.* I nodded off and dreamed I was in hell. I was surprised to discover hell was a lot like Dante described it, complete with various rings depending on the nature of the condemned's sins, only the rings were marked by round cardboard fences like at a circus. There was no fire, it wasn't even particularly warm. I had this big heavy sword I could hardly drag behind me and for some reason I was expected to battle all these hellish demons that kept rising up out of the ground. The demons had the thick scaly bodies of sea serpents and two heads. The heads had the faces of Willie Nelson and Julio Iglesias.

'Let's just pull up to that 7-Eleven,' I said to Wren. 'There's more light for you and more food for me. I'm starving.'

'Shush,' she responded.

I shushed. I didn't know what she was writing. It could be anything. She wrote poetry, plays, stories, screenplays, scholarly articles on literature, art, sculpture, philosophy. She already had masters' degrees in art history, philosophy, and English literature.

Wren was a genius. This had been documented by test scores since she was a toddler. She was also stunningly beautiful. This could be documented by observing men pretzel their necks to watch her walk by. I was neither a genius nor a beauty. I was a worker bee. Everything I did required strenuous work and long hours. In high school, I had been a B+ student who had earned As by doing extra-credit reports on Guatemala (major exports: coffee, sugar, bananas, corn). My look was milk-fed wholesome, poster girl for the Council of American Churches. For Wren, gathering knowledge and boyfriends was like walking through an apple orchard where all the ripe apples are within easy reach. She merely needed to stretch out and pluck them. In my orchard, all the branches were high, out of reach. I had to jump up and down, whack at them

8

with a stick. By the time I actually got an apple, there was nothing left but pulp.

I'd been slaving over my master's degree for four years; Wren earned hers in eighteen months. Her dissertation was already finished, two months ahead of the due date. It was a comparison of the metaphysics in the lyrics of Paul Simon and the poetry of William Blake. Some New Age publisher in New York bought the thesis last week and intended to bring it out in time for Christmas. Last Christmas the same publisher had a bestseller with *Mother Knows Best: Mother Theresa's Teaching Applied to MBA Strategies*.

My stomach gurgled. I reached across Wren and rooted through the glove compartment. I found half a roll of wintermint Breathsavers. I popped all of them into my mouth.

'Loony!' she said, annoyed. 'Sit still.'

I spit a wet Breathsaver at her. It plopped onto the envelope she was writing on. Without looking up, she picked the white ring up and sucked it into her mouth. She kept writing.

My name is Luna. It means moon. My father was a physicist with NASA since it was established way back in 1958, the year before I was born. Actually I was born exactly nine months after he started at NASA, so I imagine he and Mom had quite a celebration the night he found out he got the job. After I was born, Dad had some security clearance trouble over my name because the Soviets had a whole bunch of space shots called the Luna series. Luna 3 was the first space vehicle to photograph the far side of the moon in 1959. Anyway, they grilled poor Dad for months about the significance of naming his daughter after the Soviet lunar space program. They interviewed his college sweetheart and asked her if Dad had ever read Karl Marx to her. I suppose I was lucky to be named Luna; Mom tells me Dad's first choice was a combination name, Abby Baker, after the two monkeys, Abel and Baker, they sent 300 miles up into space in 1959.

Suddenly Wren looked up from her writing. She was smiling. 'So I'm sitting in my cell. There are two other women in there with me.'

'Hookers?'

'No, not hookers. You watch too much television.'

This was true. I never used to watch, but then Robby bought his homemade decoder box from one of his students so we wouldn't have to pay the cable company. He made it sound like screwing the cable company was a political act, but mostly I think he got off on the prankishness of it. So he hooks the box up and something in the TV explodes so that the only channel we got clearly after that was ESPN. At first, we couldn't afford to fix the TV; then Robby left me. By then I'd gotten in the habit of watching sports. Sometimes I'd breakfast over a billiard game or grade papers during a rugby match. Once I set my alarm for two A.M. so I could watch a rodeo. I'm not sure what it is I like, maybe the variety of rules and terminology. In trapshooting if they launch the target before the shooter's call, that's a 'no bird'. A face-off in field hockey is called a 'bully'. It's a little like traveling to a foreign country, only cheaper.

'So the three of us are in this cell,' Wren continued. 'This one girl is young, maybe twenty. A business major. She and her boyfriend had been stealing typewriters and computers from the secretaries' offices. They've been putting themselves through school for two years doing this. Campus cops caught her tonight but her boyfriend managed to get away.'

'So, what about her?'

'Her? Nothing about her. I was just giving you the general ambiance.'

The two boys coming down the street from the 7-Eleven were drinking beer from paper bags, punching each other in the shoulder, laughing.

I looked over at Wren. 'So what happened? What are you writing that was worth almost getting us killed?'

'I'm sitting in this prison, mentally listing famous people

10

who have also done time. Thoreau, Cervantes, Joan Baez—'

'Wren, a couple hours in a local jail is not having "done time".'

'—Gandhi, the Berrigan brothers, Galileo, Robert Mitchum—'

'Hitler,' I added.

The boys were getting closer. I could make out their features now. We were all sharing the same umbrella of weary light from the same dim street lamp. One of the boys noticed Wren. He couldn't take his eyes off of her.

'—Martin Sheen, Martin Luther, Martin Luther King—'

'Uncle Martin from *My Favorite Martian*. Wren, get to the point.'

That's when Wren lunged across the seat at me and began to tickle me. Her strong fingers teased my underarms, my waist, my neck. She plowed my pelvic bones, weeded my rib cage. She was relentless. I flailed my arms, laughing and choking, pushing at her. My glasses fell off. My elbow cracked her forehead. The rusty spot on her bandage turned bright red with fresh bleeding. She didn't seem to care.

'Stop it,' I cackled. 'Stop. I'm going to wet myself.'

Wren stopped, leaned back in her seat. 'Okay, now tickle yourself.'

I gasped for air, retrieved my glasses from my lap. 'Okay, now fuck yourself.'

'I'm serious, Loon. Tickle yourself.'

'You can't tickle yourself.'

'Try.'

I tried. I fluttered my fingers in the same spots, but nothing happened. 'Goochy goochy goo. Satisfied?'

'Did you know that the ancient Chinese used to tickle people to death? Thousands of years ago, they used it as a form of torture.'

'Hey, girls,' one of the boys said with a smirk. They stood a few feet from the car. 'Looks like fun.'

11

'Need any help?' the other boy asked. This was the one who couldn't stop staring at Wren. They were both big, athletic-looking. Teammates.

'Let's go, Loony,' Wren said. She wasn't afraid, only annoyed.

I, however, was afraid. I quickly started the car.

'Come on, girls. Don't be that way.' Wren's boy came up and leaned on Wren's side of the car. He had blond hair mildly spiked. He looked a lot like Tom Cruise and seemed to be aware of the resemblance. His friend didn't look like anybody. Tom C. smiled at Wren and winked. 'I could get interested.'

Wren laughed. 'Yeah? Well, come back when you can get interesting.'

'Oh, I'm pretty interesting right now. Once you get to know me.' He put some extra English on 'know me'.

Wren turned toward him, smiling now in an interested way. 'You mean "know" in the biblical sense?'

'Sure. Whatever.'

'Lady,' the other boy said, 'if dicks could talk, his would spout poetry.'

Both of them laughed at that. So did Wren. I twisted the flexible wire earpiece of my glasses, not looking directly at them.

'Really?' Wren said. 'Poetry?'

'With some encouragement,' Wren's boy said.

'Okay,' Wren said. 'Whip it on out.'

'What?'

'Whip your dick out and come here. I'm a poetry lover.'

'What?'

'I'm going to suck you off.'

'Really?'

'That's what you want, isn't it?'

'Well, sure. Yeah. I guess.'

'Okay. Just flop it right here on the car door.' She patted the ledge of the door. 'Careful of the paint job.'

The boys frowned. 'Here?' her boy said.

'Sure.' She pointed at the other boy. 'You too, Jack. I want both of you at once.'

'Both of us?' Wren's boy made a face.

'Don't worry, you'll fit.' She opened her mouth wide. 'See? Lots of room.'

'What about her?' Pointing at me.

'She likes to watch.'

I put my glasses back on and wheezed at them. 'Asthma.'

'Let's go, man,' Tom C.'s pal said, pulling his arm. 'She's just yanking your chain.'

Wren laughed. 'Maybe you two boys should go home and yank each other's chains.'

Wren's boy, seriously angry now, massive shoulders bunched, remembering all the tough guys he's mowed down on all those muddy football fields across the state, clamped his huge hands on the car door and leaned menacingly toward Wren. The car tilted toward him. 'I could fuck you right now, sweetheart. Fuck you in the mouth, in the ass, any place I fucking want.'

'Then fuck this,' Wren said and stabbed my pen into the back of his hand. He hollered and jumped back, holding his hand and staring at the welling blood. Wren turned calmly toward me. 'Drive.'

I pulled the car away from the curb and drove off.

'Fucking bitches!' the boy who didn't look like anybody hollered. He threw his beer can at us and it bounced off my rear bumper and clattered across the pavement.

'Lesbos,' they shouted. 'Fucking dikes!'

'Fuzz bumpers to you, boys,' Wren shouted back.

My heart was thumping from the confrontation. I slipped my thumb under my bra strap and felt relief when the strap snuggled into the groove of my thumbnail. I swallowed, took a couple deep breaths, pretended to be as calm as Wren.

'So, the point is,' Wren said, resuming our former conversation as if nothing had happened, 'you can't tickle yourself. We know that. Yet, we can be tickled by others,

tickled until we hurt, even die. But if we can't tickle ourselves, then tickling is obviously not merely a physical
reaction.'

'Freud already said all that.'

'Exactly. It has psychosexual overtones, a manifestation
of repressed emotions.'

'How many people in this car are bored? Raise your
hands.' I raised my hand.

Wren ignored me. 'So those ancient Chinese, when they
tickled a man to death, were basically helping a person
kill himself. I wonder if the suicidal implications of tickling have been researched. The *thanatos* aspects. Suicidal
tendencies as displayed by ticklishness. If we could map
the tickle zones and see which repressions they represent,
then gauge the intensities, we could recognize people who
were predisposed toward suicide. I think there might be
an article in this.' I knew that by the end of the week,
Wren would be showing me such an article. By the end of
the month some psychology journal will have sent her a
check for it. She would use the check to take me out to
dinner and I would have to act thrilled for her. It was an
annoying cycle.

'Wren, that's all very interesting,' I said, my voice suddenly tight. 'But why were you in the goddamn jail and
why were you waving your goddamn panties around and
what happened to your goddamn forehead? That's all I
want to know.'

'Byron,' she said with a sigh.

I waited. Byron Caldwell was her husband. The details
are a little sketchy because Wren didn't like to talk about
him. When she did talk about him, it was the only time I
ever saw her act uncertain, clumsy. Like he was kryp-
tonite, sapping her strength. Then she could have tripped
over anything. This much I knew: Byron and Wren were
still married, although she had walked out on him one
week after the wedding for some unspecified reason;
Wren hadn't seen Byron in almost two years; Byron was
in a federal prison somewhere.

Wren twisted the radio knob. 'Crying' came on.

'Is that Roy Orbison or Don McClean?' she asked, like it was a quiz.

'Roy Orbison,' I said. 'Wren, what about Bryon.'

'Okay, so I'm out to dinner with Geoffrey. We drive all the way into Portland to celebrate, which in his crummy car is—'

'Whoa. Slow down. Celebrate what?'

'Oh, right, I haven't told you yet. I've got a job interview at *Orange Coast Today*. They called this morning. Want me to fly down to California in two weeks.'

'Really? An interview? To be what, a reporter?'

'It's a magazine, Loony, not a newspaper. One of those thick glitzy regionals with lots of health club and plastic surgery ads. But, yeah, I'd do some writing, some editing. Mostly I want to learn the business end. You know, the technical side of running a magazine. I'm not talking First Amendment, I'm talking layout and payroll and whose palm to grease and ass to kiss to make deadline. Nuts and bolts shit.'

'You didn't tell me you were applying to magazines.'

She shrugged. 'No big secret. I didn't want to get my hopes up.'

'Wren, that's great. Really great.' A long, rickety sigh whooshed from deep inside of me, like escaping locusts knocking into each other in midflight. 'Did I sound sincere?'

'Not very.'

'Good.'

'Don't be petty.'

'Petty is my main character trait. Without petty, I might not have any personality at all.' I drove without looking at her. Sure, I felt happy about Wren's good fortune, but mostly I felt jealous. Wren had sent out only five résumés, this was her third interview. As of yesterday, I had sent out 116 résumés to various universities, colleges, high schools, and military schools and had so far been offered one lousy interview. Somewhere in Kansas. A city with

15

the word wheat in it. Wheatfield. Wheatvale. Wheatville.

Wren's dream was to study as many different disciplines as interested her and then start her own magazine, a kind of up-scale down-to-earth women's magazine that featured articles combing the esoteric and the everyday. Articles like: 'Sartre in the Workplace', 'Dating the Compulsive-Obsessive Anal Retentive Executive', 'How Would Emily Dickinson Throw that Baby Shower?' Stuff like that. Okay, maybe I was being petty again. Here's how she described it to me: 'You know what the nineties woman needs? Something that doesn't pander to her vanity or ignore her social responsibility. Something that shows her how to incorporate art and philosophy and psychology into everyday living. *Vanity Fair* without the gossip and perfume inserts; *Whole Earth Catalogue* without the granola; *Mother Jones* without knee-jerk Latin American politics; *Ms*, without the simplistic slogans. Can you see what I'm saying, Loony?'

Kind of. Well, Wren had the degrees, she had the publications. All she needed now was some hands-on magazine experience, which is why she'd applied for this job. The differences between us often discouraged me. Wren wanted to write, to create, to fill a cultural void in the lives of women all over the country. I just wanted a nice cozy teaching job somewhere where I could expose the thrills of English composition to sleepy freshmen and have a good dental plan.

My thumbnail was skating back and forth under my bra strap again. As if I were trying to generate some enthusiasm for my life.

'So, we went to dinner,' Wren said.

'What?'

'Dinner. Geoffrey and I. To celebrate.'

'Oh, yeah.' I'd forgotten about the story, about the arrest, the tattered blue panties. I realized I no longer cared. I just wanted to go home and watch television, it didn't matter what was on.

But Wren continued: 'We drive to Portland to eat.

Geoffrey's going on and on about some gorgeous guy he met at a tennis tournament.'

'Another gorgeous guy?'

'He's lonely.'

Geoffrey's real name is Jeffrey, but he had it legally changed so it would be the same as Chaucer's. I'm not sure why, since he didn't seem to have any particular affinity with or affection for the dead poet. Also, Geoffrey is gay. He confided this to Wren and me in very hushed tones one afternoon after his short story had been shredded by our Fiction Workshop. He thinks his gayness is a secret, even though all of the characters in all of his stories are gay. Nevertheless, we swore ourselves to secrecy. 'I don't want any homophobic bias to affect the others' critiquing of my work,' he'd explained seriously. 'I want their complete honesty.'

Fat chance.

Wren grabbed my hand and pulled it away from my bra strap. 'Stop that, you little mutant.'

'I'm listening.'

'Anyway, we're having dinner and Geoffrey is going on about—'

'Cut to the chase, Wren. How does Byron fit in?'

Wren reached over and started honking the horn, shouting out the car with each honk, 'PMS alert! PMS alert!' A big orange cat dove under a parked car.

I stopped the car in the middle of the street. We were still the only traffic on the street. Wren was laughing, her head back, her mouth open. Her teeth were large, something like Carly Simon's. Here's the thing: she had just returned from some sleazy adventure involving arrest, jail, a convict husband, and tattered blue panties. And she was laughing. I had done nothing more adventurous all day than turn pages and I was the emotional wreck.

I couldn't help but stare at her. I tried to see her the way men see her. As a woman who could change their lives around. That was what they all saw. I'd heard men

17

say this about her. They confided this to me. God, they'd say, Wren is the kind of woman who can change my whole life around. At thirty, I still looked pretty much the same as I did in high school: straight wheat-blond hair that without the miracle of perms would always look like the matted hairs on the hind leg of an English sheepdog; thin body with arms and legs straight as toilet-paper tubes; thick glasses because I was allergic to contact lenses; a semi-pretty face that was often referred to by adults as lovely and by my peers as sweet. I didn't turn men's lives around. I adorned their lives, enhanced them somewhat, like Sweet'n'Low in bitter coffee. But I didn't actually change anything.

'I'm going home,' I said quietly. 'I'll drop you off.' I shifted into first and began driving.

Wren leaned back in her seat and wedged her knees up against the dashboard. 'After dinner we came back to Geoffrey's apartment. He invited me to take a dip in the Jacuzzi with him, but I didn't have my bathing suit so I just went along to sit with him. There were a few other people already soaking, so we all sat around and talked and drank a few beers. Geoffrey left to call his tennis friend. I stayed. Well, I got tired of sitting at the side and watching everybody else enjoying the water, so I took off my skirt and T-shirt and climbed in. It's not like I was nude or anything. I had my bra and panties on. But some asshole in one of the apartments called the cops and they came over.'

'And they arrested you for that?'

'Not exactly. One of the guys in the Jacuzzi, big brawny type from Sweden, grad student in comp lit, started to give the cop a hard time. He was a little buzzed from the beer and hot water, so I admit he did use a few harsh terms. So the cop runs my name through his computer and comes up with Byron's name, which is excuse enough to start hassling me, asking questions, you know, being a cop. Then the Swede jumps in to protect me and there's some shoving. I get knocked to the ground and scrape my head on the lip of the Jacuzzi. The Swede knocks the cop into the hot water. Next thing I know we're both arrested.'

'You could have talked your way out of that, Wren. No one's better at that than you.'

'I could have,' she said. But she didn't continue.

'What about the panties?'

'Yeah. The smart-ass cop makes me give them over when they throw me in jail. Says he doesn't want me to hang myself with them. They gave them back when they released me, only they're all shredded. He and his pals were probably gnawing on them for dinner.'

'Christ, you could sue them.'

'Probably.' She studied her notes on tickling, no longer interested in the incident.

I drove in silence for a couple miles until we were at her apartment complex. I hit the turn signal.

'I don't want to go home yet,' Wren said, sitting up with sudden fidgety energy.

'Then don't,' I said. 'But I'm dropping you off. I'm tired.'

'One more stop,' she said. 'Come on. There'll be food there, I swear.'

'Where?' But I already knew.

'BeeGee's.'

'Damn it, Wren, it's late.'

'Come on, don't be such a rag.'

'Right now I'd eat a rag.'

'BeeGee always has food, you know that.'

I turned the car around and headed for BeeGee's house. BeeGee was Wren's abbreviation for Bat-Faced Girl.

It was after midnight and we were on our way to see the Bat-Faced Girl.

*   *   *   *   *

The Bat-Faced Girl was cleaning her gun.

'Smith & Wesson Shofield .45,' she said. 'Like the one Jessie James used.' She thumbed a cartridge into the dark chamber. 'The same one my dad used to blow his brains out. Hungry? Help yourself.'

We were standing in the kitchen. The Bat-Faced Girl sat at the table polishing the black gun barrel with some sweet-smelling oil. The refrigerator door was wide open, but the refrigerator was empty except for the television set on the metal rack. *The David Letterman Show* was on. It was disconcerting to see David Letterman's head where a head of cabbage should be, but I was almost used to it by now. If I'd opened the oven door, I'd have found her stereo system. The records and compact discs were stored in the dishwasher.

BeeGee, real name Esther, worried about thieves.

She even had a letter she wrote to herself from the County Health Department on official-looking stationery she designed on her computer. The letter was sad to inform her that her test results reveal that she has AIDS. She kept this letter in her car and when she left the car, she displayed it openly on the driver's seat. She hoped this would scare away car thieves.

'Don't you think that gun is clean enough by now?' Wren said.

'It's an antique,' BeeGee said. 'I clean it twice a week, just like my father did. I don't want someone breaking in here in the middle of the night and have the thing misfire.'

'You really think you could use that on someone?' I asked.

'A thief gets what he deserves,' she said.

Wren opened the cupboard under the sink. A mini-refrigerator squatted there next to the garbage disposal pipes. 'What do you want, Loony?' She leaned over, poked through the shelves.

'What are my choices?'

'We've got your standard two slices of Domino's pepperoni pizza, the traditional half a breast of Kentucky fried fat, a tub of macaroni salad, three Chicken McNuggets, a strawberry yogurt, and unsweetened applesauce.'

'Yogurt,' I said.

'Check the date,' BeeGee warned.

Wren looked at the bottom of the container. 'Just under the wire.' She tossed it to me. I grabbed a spoon out of the drawer and sat at the wooden table across from BeeGee. David Letterman had dozens of Ping-Pong paddles fastened to his body, up and down each leg, across his chest and back. He was wearing a motorcycle helmet with a paddle stuck to the top like an alien antenna. He gave the signal and Paul Shaffer turned on a machine that fired Ping-Pong balls at David. They bounced off at crazy angles. They played the whole thing back in slow motion.

'There's plenty of food in the cupboards,' BeeGee said.

BeeGee favored those freeze-dried meals in a pouch that Dick Cavett touted on television. You microwaved them and they were supposed to taste like a regular TV dinner. But I couldn't eat them because they reminded me too much of disaster food, the kind of stuff you store for an emergency, a nuclear war or something. I thought of the bomb shelter my dad had built in our backyard when I was a child. We spent Labor Day weekend in it once as a test of endurance and family strength. Mom beat Dad about a hundred times in gin rummy and we never did that again. Occasionally I saw them sneak down there together, giggling, and come out disheveled and flushed. When we sold the house, the new owners thought it was a marvelous place for a wine cellar.

BeeGee snapped open the pistol's cylinder and thumbed another cartridge into the chamber. I saw this out of the corner of my eye as I watched Ping-Pong balls pummel David Letterman.

Wren hopped up onto the counter across from me and began spooning applesauce into her mouth. She sat cross-legged, her denim skirt stretched tight against her thighs. With her short skirt and no panties, she was pretty well exposed.

'You mind?' I said, pointing with my spoon. 'I'm trying to eat.'

Wren laughed and flicked her tongue in a lewd way.

I laughed too.

BeeGee thumbed another cartridge into the chamber.

'What'd your new doctors say?' I asked BeeGee.

BeeGee shrugged. 'The usual crap. Mine is the most unusual case they've ever seen. They practically played patty cake at the thought of the medical papers they would write about me. They gave me more benzodiazepines and talked about stimulus control procedures. Same old bullshit.'

BeeGee had insomnia. Not just stay-awake-late-cranky-in-the-morning insomnia, but never-sleeps-a-goddamn-wink insomnia. She did not sleep. Ever. Hence the nickname Bat Girl. Which Wren changed into Bat-Faced Girl because that's a phrase from a Paul Simon song.

BeeGee, by the way, did not look like a bat. She had a round, but pretty face, though the features did seem a little squished together. The overall effect was that of a small pumpkin carved by a talented but untutored artist.

Because she never slept, BeeGee made her house available to grad students from all disciplines. Twenty-four hours a day you would find biochemistry lab rats drinking beer with lawbots. Psych nerds watching TV while journalism scabs waited for the campus newspaper to be delivered. Even a few professors dropped by to relive their old college days by pretending they didn't need sleep. BeeGee always had plenty of food and drink, though it was not unusual for a group of students to arrive with half a dozen bags of groceries to show gratitude.

I looked over at BeeGee. 'What's stimulus, uh . . '

'Stimulus control procedures. That's when they give you a set of rules to make the bedroom associated with only good feelings of sleep. For example, if I get into bed and can't fall asleep within ten minutes, I have to leave the bedroom and return only when I'm sleepy enough to go to sleep. I've been through that stuff before with the other doctors. It doesn't work.' She looked at me very intently. 'I miss the dreaming, Luna. I never get to dream.'

I thought about my dream earlier at the library, the circles of hell, the horrible two-headed demons with the faces of Willie Nelson and Julio Iglesias. Not much to miss there.

Wren hopped down from the counter and tossed the empty applesauce jar into the trash. She went to another cupboard and grabbed a jar of unsalted peanuts, funneling them into her mouth with her hand. 'I had this idea about tickling,' Wren said to BeeGee while munching. 'I want to run it by you.'

'Hypergargalesthesia,' BeeGee said. 'That's extreme sensitivity to tickling.'

Wren smiled. She had come to the right person. Running it by me had been okay for a start, the way a businessman might practice his speech in front of his dog before trying it out on a colleague. I didn't blame Wren. BeeGee was the only other person around who knew as much as she. Of course, BeeGee had the unfair advantage of never sleeping. David Letterman was her one weakness. The rest of the time she read. When she wasn't home reading, she worked at the campus library. She knew something about everything. The difference between her and Wren was that though BeeGee knew more information, had more facts stored in her brain, Wren knew how to use information, how to make connections between things and translate all that into articles that anyone could understand.

Wren and BeeGee discussed Wren's theory of tickling. BeeGee cited scientific research in the area. I watched them out of the corner of my eye because I didn't want them to feel as if they had to include me in the conversation, which would have only made me feel dumber. I'd done a pretty fair job as a teaching assistant this year, goading students into cranking out literate essays. I

23

thought I'd probably make a good teacher somewhere. But a few minutes with these two made me feel criminally incompetent, an underachiever.

David Letterman turned on his bubble maker and everyone applauded.

BeeGee's calico cat jumped onto my lap. Her left hind-quarters were shaved down to the skin. Three red scabs pocked the skin.

'Hey, Sphinx,' I said. 'What happened to you?'

'Cat fight,' BeeGee said. 'Cost me $174.' She held out her arms and I handed Sphinx to her. 'I have to give her antibiotics twice a day. Make her swallow these pills, same as me.' BeeGee began picking at the cat's biggest scab. Part of the crust broke away from the skin. She dug out the rest of it.

'Yeech,' I said, making a face. 'What are you doing?'

'You have to keep the wound open,' Wren explained. 'So it doesn't get infected.'

I took off my wire-rimmed glasses and cleaned them with the tail of my Oxford shirt. One of the wire earpieces was all chewed up. Last week I'd been studying outside the library, actually leaning up against a tree the way you see in college catalogues, my glasses lying in my lap while I rested my eyes, when some gnarled black mutt with a red bandanna tied around his neck comes running by, snatching my glasses up in his yellow teeth, and loping off across the quad. I climbed on my bike and chased after him, but by the time I caught up and wrestled the glasses away from him, the end of the earpiece was gnawed off. The stump that was left was all jagged, which I tried to bury under a hundred layers of clear fingernail polish, but which wore away leaving the jagged metal to rub against the top of my ear. I could even feel a callus starting to form up there. I put my glasses back on and turned back to watch David Letterman. 'I have to get home pretty soon, Wren,' I said. I didn't want BeeGee to think it was because I was sleepy, so I added, 'I have a lot of studying to do.'

24

'Right,' Wren said. 'A few minutes more.'

'Excuse me,' BeeGee said. She laid the gun down on the wooden table. It thumped heavily, like a bowling ball. She stood up and walked into the bathroom, closing the door behind her.

Wren and I exchanged grins. I clamped my hand to my mouth to smother a laugh.

Finally, we heard it. The low hum of the vibrator.

BeeGee was well known for her habit of getting up suddenly in the middle of a conversation and disappearing into the bathroom to use her vibrator. I think it was therapeutic more than sexual. A woman who could never sleep tended not to attract men. It made men nervous to think of her awake, walking about while they slept. One guy who had dated her briefly told me it got so he couldn't sleep either. 'How can I sleep, knowing she's in the next room doing things.' What things, I'd asked. I don't know, he'd said, *things*.

BeeGee returned a few minutes later, her face as expressionless as when she'd left. Her cheeks were a little redder. 'So, what'd I miss?'

Wren pointed at me. 'Loony wants to know the best brand of vibrator. She's in the market.'

'Well,' BeeGee said with a serious expression. 'It depends upon what kind of features you're interested in.' And she began a discussion of the merits of various types, styles, attachments, voltage. She sounded like a professor discussing species of plankton.

Wren grinned at me from over BeeGee's shoulder.

'You can go in and try mine, if you like,' BeeGee offered.

'A test drive,' Wren said.

'Thanks,' I said to BeeGee. 'Some other time.'

BeeGee shrugged, picked up her gun, and took a rag to the walnut grips. Sphinx curled up on the tabletop next to her.

'We should go,' Wren said, standing.

BeeGee nodded.

I stood up.

BeeGee cocked the hammer of her gun, placed the tip of the barrel against Sphinx's head, and pulled the trigger. The explosion made me jump. Sphinx's limp body flew off the table. A bloody clump of fur stuck to my cheek.

'Jesus, BeeG—' I screamed.

She turned the gun toward me and fired. The explosion and bullet hit me at the same time. A hot wind pulled at my face. My legs went numb and I collapsed against the table, knocking over a chair. My chest burned. I was afraid to look, afraid I'd see a hole straight into my heart. See the bullet stuck in it. Funny, when I thought about it, I didn't imagine a real heart, a fist-sized muscle, I saw one of those Valentine Day hearts, plump and red.

I saw BeeGee cock the hammer again, the gun aimed at my face.

Wren leapt at her like some hero cop on television. BeeGee didn't flinch, she calmly swung the gun around and fired into Wren's chest. Wren dropped to the kitchen floor.

I tried to crawl toward Wren, but nothing worked. The only thing moving was my heart pumping gurgling blood through the hole in my chest.

BeeGee spoke to no one in particular. 'The mistake many people make is putting the gun to their head. It is too easy to miss the vital parts of the brain, which often results in leaving the victim paralyzed, not dead. This is the proper method of disposal.' BeeGee opened her mouth, slowly lowered her head over the barrel, and pulled the trigger.

2

'I need to urinate,' I said.

'Go right ahead,' she said.

'But I'm in bed.' My eyes were closed. I had the feeling that I could open them if I really wanted, but I wasn't confident enough to test my theory. What if I was wrong? I decided instead to impress everyone with my patience.

'Go right ahead and pee, dear,' she said.

I did. I didn't feel the urine, just the relaxing of my bladder, like a fist gone slack. The sheets around me stayed dry. Stiff and dry.

'Who are you?' I asked.

'Your mother.'

'My mother is dead.'

'Sorry to hear that,' she said.

*   *   *   *   *

'How is Wren?' I asked.

This was sometime later, after one of my naps. I still didn't open my eyes. After all, what if she really was my mother. I had thought my mother was dead. Killed in an auto wreck when I was eighteen. They'd used the jaws of life to cut her out. I read that in the newspaper account. The jaws of life. Silly phrase. An oxymoron. I'd pictured a fat shark chomping open the station-wagon door. I thought I'd attended Mother's funeral, wearing a new black dress because I hadn't owned anything black. I'd settled on a velvet dress because it was summer and it was the only black dress I could find that didn't have huge white polka dots. My shoes were navy blue but no one seemed to notice. Dad gave me Mom's pearls to wear. They broke in the limo on the drive to the cemetery. I'd been rubbing my thumbnail against them. We were on our knees gathering the pearls into his linen handkerchief. He twisted the corners and tied them in a knot. For a moment he looked like a little kid holding a prized bag of marbles. That was the only time I ever remember Dad looking young. They buried Mom in the morning, the grass still wet from the lawn sprinklers.

Or maybe they didn't bury her. Maybe I dreamed all that in some etherized haze. If she were alive it must have hurt her deeply for me to pronounce her dead. Some Freudian slip, she must wonder, wishful thinking? I didn't want to see the hurt in her eyes. I kept my eyes pressed closed. 'Is Wren okay?'

'Who, dear?'

'Wren Caldwell. She was shot too.'

'I don't know her. Pretty name, though. Wren.'

My chest hurt. As if a starving rodent had gnawed through the skin and muscle and now was crunching through the bones of my rib cage. Each breath felt like another bite.

'Can you check on Wren, please?'

'Sure, dear. Now get some sleep.'

'Is it okay if I urinate again?'

'Of course, dear. Fire away.'

*   *   *   *   *

'What day is it?'

'Saturday.'

'Thank you.' I counted days. Three. Three days since the Bat-Faced Girl shot her cat and Wren and me. I was

28

unaccountably cheerful. 'Saturday. I've always relied on the kindness of Saturdays.'

'That's very funny,' she said.

Encouraged, I opened my eyes. They worked. I couldn't remember why I'd thought I'd be better off with them closed. I looked at the woman standing next to my bed. 'You're not my mother.'

'Of course I'm not. You said your mother was dead.'

'You said *you* were my mother.'

'Glover,' she said. 'Nurse Glover.'

Your mother. Nurse Glover. They did sound similar.

I stared up at her as she made the empty bed next to mine. She was a chubby woman in a rumpled white uniform. She wore a nubby blue sweater over her uniform. She had clumsily bleached hair and the vacant look of someone who'd graduated at the bottom percentage of her nursing class. But she moved around that bed like a pool hustler lining up a money shot.

'I'm sorry about the misunderstanding,' I said.

'It's the drugs, dear. You had a lot of drugs. You'll snap out of it.'

'How's Wren? Did you check?'

Her face snapped taut as the fitted sheet she was smoothing. 'I'm not allowed to discuss other patients.'

I sighed with relief. 'If she's a patient, then she's okay.'

'I can neither confirm nor deny that.'

'That doesn't make any sense. She's my friend.'

'This is a hospital,' she said by way of explanation. She turned her back and fluffed a pillow. The back of her sweater was matted with long white cat hair.

'Who can tell me about Wren?' I asked.

'You'll have to speak to your doctor. Dr. Granger.'

'Where is he?'

'She. Dr. Jennifer Granger.'

'Goddamn it, Wren's my best friend.' I tried to sit up. The hungry rodent bit into my plump heart. Sparks sizzled in my brain. I dropped back onto my pillow. 'Just tell me if she's alive.'

'I'm sorry,' she said and hurried out of the room.

*   *   *   *   *

'Hello, Mrs. Devon, I'm Officer Simmons.'

I opened my eyes. 'You're the one Wren yelled at the other night. At the police station.'

He grinned and nodded. His cheeks flushed. 'She was quite a woman.'

'Was?'

His baby face drained white. 'Well, I mean, she's uh, dead.'

My body sort of collapsed in on itself. Like time-lapse photography of a rotting grape shriveling into a raisin. 'No,' I said, the calmness of my voice surprising me. It was my teacher voice. 'There is obviously a mistake. Wren couldn't be dead. You must have looked at the wrong charts or something.' Isn't that what people on TV always said?

'No mistake, Mrs. Devon. I was at the scene that night.'

He cut himself off but I could tell he'd been about to relate convincing details to me about the size of the hole in her chest, the amount of blood, how he had closed her vacant eyes. He didn't understand. Those things didn't matter with Wren. She couldn't die.

'I need to ask you a few questions,' he said.

'Esther shot her cat,' I said. 'How's the cat?'

'Dead.'

I nodded. My sinuses filled with fluid and stung my nose and eyes. I wanted to cry but somehow I couldn't. Crying seemed too easy, a melodramatic cliché. Wren deserved better.

'Miss Kleinman is dead also,' Officer Simmons reported.

'Yes. Of course.' I sat up. My chest clenched in protest, but I ignored it. 'This is what happened. Wren and I went over to see BeeGee—'

'Who?' He stopped writing.

'Esther Kleinman. We ate, watched David Letterman in her refrigerator, Esther shot the cat, then me, then Wren, then herself. End story.'

'Why did she do it?'

'What do you mean?' I asked.

'Well, she was your friend. Why would she shoot you?' He tried to look innocent and boyish, but his eyes were tense and suspicious.

'I don't know. Maybe because she was a severe insomniac and had gone nuts from not being able to sleep. Maybe because she couldn't dream.'

'Drugs were found on the premises.'

'Shouldn't a detective be asking me these questions, Officer? Aren't you supposed to advise me of my rights?'

He looked hurt. 'We are a very small department, Mrs. Devon. As to your rights, I'm just asking a few questions. However, if you wish to have an attorney present, that is your right.'

'Listen, you found what, a couple joints?'

'I can't confirm or deny what we found, Mrs. Devon.'

'You find a couple joints and you think you've walked into the Colombian Connection? You think this was a drug deal gone bad, that BeeGee was running a crack house?'

'I'm just investigating all possibilities.'

'Then why'd she shoot the cat, Kojak?'

'Pardon?'

'If this was about drugs, why shoot the cat? He short changed her on a delivery of cocaine?'

'I can neither confirm nor deny anything to do with the investigation, Mrs. Devon.'

'Bullshit,' I said. 'Do you hear what I'm saying, Officer? Do you?'

He leaned backward, the way he had that night, and for an instant, in his startled face, Wren was still alive.

I closed my eyes and went back to sleep.

*   *   *   *   *

The doctor drew a picture of my left breast. She made it look larger than it was. I wondered if that was meant to cheer me up.

'This is your breast,' she said.

'Before or after the implant?' I said.

She smiled, but she didn't look up. She drew a small circle on the breast and scribbled it in with her pen. 'This is where you were shot.'

I wondered why we didn't just use my real breast, since it was already naked and I could see exactly where I'd been shot. A white gauze pad covered the hole, but I'd seen the hole too. Dark moist crater, like a tar pit hiding the tiny bones of extinct species.

She dotted the paper breast a few times. 'These are the powder burns.'

I looked at my breast, saw the tiny scabs on my skin where the powder had burned through my skin where my blouse had been unbuttoned. A V-shaped pattern. Ducks flying south toward my navel.

'Actually,' the doctor continued, 'it's good that you were so close. The bullet punched right through your chest and out your back. The police call it a "through and through". In one hole and out the back door. Less damage. The bullet doesn't have a chance to expand or fragment. If you were farther away, the same bullet might have killed you.'

'Like Wren.'

'Yes, like Ms. Caldwell.'

Dr. Jennifer Granger was at most twenty-seven. Naturally I hated her. Three years younger and she was diagramming my personal organs as if she'd known them all her life. I thought of snatching up her pen and drawing her face: short no-nonsense hair, brown as a melted candy bar, snub nose the size of a nipple; thin lips that if it weren't for lipstick you wouldn't even know were there. Here's the part I liked, she had a small rash of acne splashed across her chin. You could tell she'd tried to cover it with makeup, but clumsily, so she only managed to call more attention to it.

'This is your heart, Luna,' she said. She drew a heart under the breast. It looked very official. A real heart, like in cancer commercials. It looked like my father's knotted handkerchief swollen with my mother's loose pearls. 'This is where the bullet nicked you. The left ventricle.' She drew an arrow that pierced the heart Cupid-like. 'This is the bullet's trajectory. Shaved a little of the papillary muscle, but missed the arteries and valves. You were very lucky.'

'I keep hearing that.'

She clicked her ballpoint pen, retracting the ink cartridge. She looked up at me, an expression of concern wrinkling her features. That is how she would look fifteen years from now. 'Depression in these circumstances is to be expected, Luna. An act like this, so violent so—' she looked around the room as if searching for the right word —'random. So random. It shakes our sense of stability. Rattles primordial fears. That's to be expected.' She placed a hand on my bare shoulder. Her flesh was cool and soft. 'If you'd like, I can have a therapist talk with you. Your insurance will cover it, so don't worry about the cost.'

I didn't want to see a shrink or a wannabe shrink. I had papers to write and a class to teach. My thesis on the reclusive Thomas Pynchon still wasn't finished.

'When can I get out of here,' I asked.

'What about the therapist?' she asked.

'I'll think it over.'

She shook her head and rubbed the bridge of her nose the way people who wear glasses do, though she wore contacts. Old habits die hard. I rubbed my thumbnail along the seam of the hospital mattress.

'When can I get out?' I repeated.

She gathered up her clipboard and pen and started for the door. 'I'll see what I can do. No promises, though.' Like she was my lawyer negotiating a plea bargain. 'And think about the therapist. There's no stigma in asking for help.'

'Help me get out of here,' I said, pulling my gown back on. 'There, I asked.'

She chuckled and walked out of the room.

*　　*　　*　　*　　*

'Don't open your eyes,' he said.

I didn't.

'Hold out your hand.'

I did.

'Keep your eyes closed. Don't cheat now, keep them closed.'

'They're closed,' I said.

'Okay, don't move. Don't move. Do. Not. Move.'

My open palm filled with an unmistakable and familiar presence. My fingers curled around it.

'Can I open my eyes now?'

'Open, Sesame.'

I opened my eyes. I looked right at it and laughed. Laughing twanged the stitches in my chest. My left boob ached as if someone were tightening long brass screws through my nipple directly into my heart. But I kept laughing anyway. I couldn't help it.

Robby's penis was laying in my hand like a small flash-light. It was only semi-erect, but that was plenty large enough. On the head, he'd drawn eyes with a black mask around them, and red liner around the pee hole made it look like a mouth. He even had a tiny cowboy hat strapped to it with a rubber band. The entire shaft of the

34

penis was drawn with a web of fish scales all around it.
'Return with us now,' he intoned in his deep radio announcer's voice, 'to those exciting days of yesteryear and
the Lone Flounder.' He wagged his dick against my palm
as if it were swimming. 'Great idea for a TV series, huh?
The Lone Flounder swims up into the toilets of evildoers
and bites them on the ass. He'll have a girlfriend known
only as His Koi Mistress. What do you think? Am I a
fuckin' genius or what?'

'I think you'd better put it away before a nurse walks
in.'

'It'll give her a thrill. You wanna bet?' He skipped
around the room wagging his dick and humming the *1812
Overture*. 'Da dum da dum da dum dum dum. Hi Ho,
Scrotum.'

I laughed again. 'You're going to get Thumper thrown
out of here.'

His penis was Thumper. My vagina was Bambi. At first,
in those early lustful years, we'd called his penis Godzilla
because of that short film 'Godzilla Meets Bambi'. The
one where Bambi is playing sweetly in the woods and suddenly a huge prehistoric foot stomps her into a tortilla.
We saw that film on one of our first dates back in college,
so giving our sexual organs names seemed pretty funny at
the time. But I didn't like calling his dick Godzilla because
he'd sometimes call it God for short. At first, that was
funny too. 'Come and worship your God, Luna.' Or 'God
requires another sacrifice, Luna.' That kind of joking. It
cracked us up quite a bit. But after a while, it just made
me uncomfortable. Not that I'm religious, which I'm not.
It's just that I felt like we were ridiculing other people and
I didn't want every time we made love to be an act of
ridicule. So I changed its name to Thumper.

Robby removed the tiny cowboy hat and stuffed the
Lone Flounder back into his pants. He sat on the edge of
the bed and squeezed my thigh through the blanket. His
eyes turned watery and I thought he might cry. 'Jesus,
Loon. Jesus.'

'I know. Weird, huh?'

He just shook his head in wonderment.

'Wren's dead,' I said.

'I know. I can't believe it. I thought she was too tough to die.'

Did he ever think if I was too tough to die? Or was he surprised that I was alive instead of Wren? Was my being alive proof of a naturalistic world without moral order? Wren's death proof that the good die young? Robby had had a crush on Wren since I first brought her home. He couldn't take his eyes off her, stop talking to her. I never held that against him since it seemed that every guy felt that way about her. He never did anything about it, probably because he knew Wren would tell me.

'Robby likes you,' I'd told Wren once. We shared the same tiny office on the top floor of the English Department, where all teaching assistants were sentenced to serve their time. We were grading freshman compositions at our respective gray metal desks. The walls were a faded lime-green, which gave the whole building the drab air of an abandoned post office.

'You hear me?' I asked.

She looked up from the composition, her drugstore reading glasses resting on the tip of her nose. 'What?'

'My husband, Robby, who is my husband, likes you. Did I mention that he was my husband?' I expected her to say something like well, I like him too, pretending that she didn't know what I meant.

'Yes, I know,' she said, returning to her grading.

'How do you know?'

She slapped her pen down and frowned at me. 'Give me a break here, Loony.'

'I'm serious. How the hell do you know?'

'How the hell do *you* know?'

'I'm his goddamn wife. He talks about you in that way men have, you know, when they're so infatuated they need to talk about a woman, but they couch it in seemingly innocent observations. "Doesn't that Wren have an

interesting insight into Martin Heidegger's philosophy?"
When what they mean is "Doesn't Wren have an ass to
die for?"'

Wren laughed. 'Don't worry, he hasn't touched my ass.'

'And if he did?'

'Would you want to know?'

I hesitated. 'Yes.'

'Then I'd tell you.'

'Would you turn him down?'

She picked up her pen and tapped it absently against
the composition on her desk. I wondered how the student
would interpret those pock marks.

'I can't answer that,' she said. 'I don't know what I'd
do.'

That night I'd told Robby about my conversation with
Wren about him and he'd stormed around the apartment
waving his copy of Virginia Woolf's *To the Lighthouse*,
which he'd been reading in the bathtub. He had a towel
knotted around his waist but he was dripping all over the
carpet. He protested that he had no sexual interest in
Wren, merely intellectual appreciation. He did not want
to sleep with her. He was very disappointed in me for even
suggesting such a thing. Then he went on to list her faults,
punctuating each flaw with a slap to the cover of Virginia
Woolf's novel. Wren was self-centred. Wren was pushy.
Wren was a snob. Wren laughed too easily. Wren smoked
too much. Wren used too much biographical background
in interpreting literature. Wren's hair was too frizzy.

As the list went on, I realized I'd only instigated another disguised declaration of love. Standing there listening to him was like having your husband rehearse his
seduction speech for another woman. When I mentioned
this to him, his face grew red and he slammed his book on
the table and said, 'Women don't know shit about men!'

Now in the hospital, he seemed concerned about me
but somehow remote. A few months ago he would have
been camped out in my room, spending all his time with
me, grading his papers, doing his Ph.D. work, watching

television with me. He'd be talking about how he would take care of me once we got home. Make soup with oyster crackers, bring me *People* magazine. But now his back-pack was leaning against the wall, ready to be grabbed on the way out. This was just a visit, an obligation. Lending support to the soon-to-be-ex. Doing the Decent Thing.

'You made the television news,' he said. 'Local any-way.'

'I saw. They weren't very kind to Esther.'

He shrugged. 'She doesn't care anymore.'

'They all carried the same photo of Wren. That one she did as a joke, where she looks like she's posing for the cover of *Cosmo*.'

'I saw.'

'It's like no event is really a tragedy unless someone pretty dies.'

'This stuff is starting to itch.' Robby scratched his crotch.

'What?'

'This body paint on my dick. It's starting to itch.'

I gestured to the bathroom. 'Go wash it off.'

He went in and ran the water. While he was there he took a leak. He left the door open so he could keep talk-ing to me. I listened to the drumming of his urine against water.

'How's class?' I asked.

'We're finished with poetry. They're writing short stories now.'

'Are they any good?'

'One girl shows some potential. The others are all into the twist-ending syndrome. You know, someone wakes up at the end and it's all been a bad dream. Shit like that.'

'How's it going at the station?'

'Bunch of assholes. Nobody wants me to play jazz any-more. It's rock 'n' roll or nothing. Radio is dead.' He was scrubbing his penis with soap.

'How's the novel coming?'

'Novels are dead. I'm doing something different. A

non-novel. It's like a time-warp thing where all these yuppies are on this Love Boat cruise and the ship sinks. A small group of them wash up on this island where all these famous people from history keep appearing through this rip in time. Like Socrates and Shakespeare and Teddy Roosevelt. It's so cool, you get this tight-assed stockbroker type face-to-face with Mussolini and they end up discussing their daughters' braces. Fascism on Elm Street.'

Robby was in his last quarter of finishing his Ph.D. in English. When we were both undergraduates together ten years ago, he was one of the star writers in the department. His teachers expected great things from him. He'd published a few poems and stories in prestigious literary magazines. After graduation, he went right into graduate school for his master's and I went to work at an employment placement service, headhunting for executives. I had been an English major too, but I didn't write. My poems were sappy and my stories were about people who woke up at the end and the whole thing was a dream.

One of Robby's professors helped him get a New York agent and for about a year we were giddy with anticipation that Robby's first novel would be bought for big bucks, like those other young writers we kept hearing about. Then we would go to Hollywood so he could write the screenplay for even bigger bucks, only we wouldn't get corrupted like everyone else. But it never happened. Editors liked his style but lamented a lack of plot. Robby's second novel didn't fare much better.

After receiving his master's, Robby decided he didn't care about writing that much and preferred to have a family. He was very excited about this new direction we were going to take. He got a steady job at a radio station playing jazz records that I couldn't bear listening to. We worked at getting me pregnant, which was a peculiar feeling after the years of elaborate precautions and silent tension if my period was even a few days late. Finally I became pregnant and we celebrated as jubilantly as if he'd sold his novel. A month later I miscarried and the expression of relief on Robby's face was so plain that without even discussing it we returned to our cautious sex. Robby applied to return to graduate school for his doctorate.

I applied too, not out of any dedication to a new career, but mostly, I think, because I didn't want Robby to start looking at me with the same contempt he sometimes looked at his students. I didn't want to live through those after-movie sessions where he would patiently explain some literary allusion to me. It wasn't that he was snobby, it's just that he had a great mind and a true love of literature and couldn't understand why everyone else wasn't as obsessed as he.

Robby came out of the bathroom with a smoking joint between his lips. He inhaled deeply and offered it to me.

'This is a hospital,' I said brusquely. I don't know why I said that, I didn't care that he was smoking.

'Right, a hospital. You holding out for bigger and better drugs?'

'Robby, don't be an asshole.'

'You called me an asshole. That must mean you're feeling better.'

'I'm not feeling anything.'

He pinched out the tip of the joint and stuck it back in his pocket. He sat back on the edge of the bed. 'You don't mean physically, that you're paralyzed or anything.'

'No, Robby, I'm not paralyzed. I'm just . . . tired, I guess.'

Robby looked at me and for a moment it was the old look, the look of genuine love and concern. His long blond hair curled in a hundred directions at once. I wanted to reach out and touch his hair. Seeing his hair made me miss him more than holding his penis.

His eyes flickered, just a little, and I could tell he'd just remembered who we were now. He looked over at his backpack near the door. When he looked back at me I could see what was in his mind: his classes, his non-novel, his new woman. He was dating Dr. Helen Jaspers, the Dean of the English Department, eight years older but still trim and energetic. She was an expert on Milton.

'Tell me, Luna,' he said, his voice rich with sincerity, but his eyes blank as Milton's, 'tell me how you feel.'

He reached out and held my hand, his fingers in their natural grooves just like my thumbnail in my bra strap. There was a time, back in the Thumper and Bambi days, when that look, that hand wrapped around mine, that radio announcer's voice, would have made me pour out everything inside of me. But I wasn't sure if there was anything inside of me. I felt the bulky bandage on my back where the bullet had exited. It was as if that bullet hole had allowed whatever I felt about anything to leak out. Like there was no more of me left inside. Just the empty husk of Luna.

'Robby,' I said, squeezing his hand. 'I hate jazz.'

*   *   *   *   *

My father phoned the day I was being released. Nurse Glover had just handed me the plastic bag with my hospital toothbrush, shampoo, soap, and dental floss. You get to keep those.

'Hello?' I said into the phone.

'Luna, my God, I just heard. How are you, honey?'

'Fine, Dad. They're just releasing me today.'

'I'd been following the Tijamuchi River. I just heard.'

I'd called Dad the first day I was able to open my eyes. His phone machine in Houston had a recorded message informing the caller that Ben Masters was out of the country and wouldn't be back for four months, leave a message and maybe, if he had the time, he'd call you back.

'God, Luna, I just got back to a city with telephones. I called in for my messages. I couldn't believe it. Jesus, shot. How are you? What the hell happened?'

'I'm fine, Dad. Where are you?'

'Bolivia. La Paz. Incredible discoveries, sweetheart. I spent three months with a tribe that speaks nothing but original Altiplano. They've managed to avoid any contact with the mainstream population by moving up and down the river. They believe that the river itself is God. Women menstruate in the water. Pregnant women sit in the shallow bank to give birth. The elderly and the sick drown themselves so they may return the water in their bodies to God, who in turn returns it to the tribe. Incredible stuff.'

'Sounds fascinating.'

He cleared his throat uncomfortably, as if realizing this wasn't the time or circumstances to be going on about Bolivian women's placentas floating downstream. 'Well, you know me, sweetheart,' he said quietly. 'I get carried away sometimes.'

Dad had quit NASA the day after Neil Armstrong stepped onto the moon. I think he was disappointed by what they'd found there, which was pretty much what they'd expected to find. The predictable in people or in nature irritated him. NASA tried to keep him, offering him more money and a significant promotion. Alan Shepherd and John Glenn both called, asking him to reconsider. But he refused. Dad was looking for something special and he suddenly realized he wouldn't find it in outer space.

One day he gathered Mom and me into the kitchen. On the kitchen table was my old metal globe, the one with the dent in Spain where I threw my shoe when I got grounded back in third grade for beating up Kathy Hodges, the wimpy little bitch from next door. Dad reached over and spun the globe. It squeaked and wobbled and I remember wondering if the planet squeaked and wobbled that much when it turned. Maybe that's what thunder was. I got very excited thinking I may have discovered some new scientific theory, but then Dad started talking and I forgot my idea.

'This is my new job, ladies,' he said.

'Repairing globes?' Mom said with a smile.

Dad grinned back. He was in an exceptionally good mood and that made me happy too. Since I didn't really have a clue to what he did at NASA, the fact that he'd quit didn't really mean much to me. Mom didn't give any indication that she was worried either, so I looked at this whole thing as if Dad were just changing schools.

'This is the plan,' Dad said. 'I've decided to become an anthropologist.' He looked at me with a big smile. 'That means I study people, Luna. People from all over the world.'

'Not that again, Ben,' Mom said, not really annoyed.

'You know I've always been interested. The timing is perfect.'

Mom gave the globe a little spin. 'Anybody going to pay you to do this?'

Dad winked at me. 'As a matter of fact . . .'

Somehow Dad had gotten an assignment to go to some-place in Africa where a warrior tribe from the mountains was working on a crude pair of wings made from water buffalo hide stretched over elephant bones, hoping to use them to swoop down and kill their enemy across the river. Some magazine thought it would be ironic to have Dad go there and give his space-age perspective. He went and the article was successful. Other assignments followed. Dad studied on his own, reading Darwin to Thomas Henry, Huxley to Ashley Montagu, always with a book in his hand and an amazed expression on his face.

He became his own astronaut, launching himself into the remote corners of the planet, doing his own moonwalk along the Amazon. I think Mom played along because she thought he would burn himself out after a short while. Or maybe she really thought it was a good idea and was as excited as he was about changing our lives. I was only ten at the time and the only real difference to my life was that now Daddy went off to work in jungles and deserts instead of Houston. When he'd worked for NASA he'd taken a lot of trips, so it wasn't as if he was really gone any longer than before. But now when he returned he was tanned and his presents were something carved out of foul-smelling roots by barefoot natives instead of something with batteries bought in an airport gift shop.

That was twenty years ago. He'd been an anthropologist longer than he'd been a rocket scientist, but I still thought of him as the space physicist on a leave of absence, like a defrocked priest or something.

'What does the doctor say?' he asked.

'That I still have a heart.'

'Then you're going to be fine?'

'Yes, Dad. Good as new.'

'Robby knows what to do, right? How to take care of you?'

Nurse Glover steered a wheelchair through the door and parked it next to me. I made a face at it. She mouthed, *regulations*. I nodded.

'Dad,' I said, 'Robby and I are getting a divorce.'

'Because of this? That son of a bitch!'

'No, Dad, not because of this. We've been working out the details for a few months now.'

'Jesus, Luna.' He was silent for a while. 'You want me to come there, honey? I could be there by tonight or tomorrow morning.'

He would come if I asked. But I didn't want to have to ask. And, to be fair, I didn't know what I'd do with him if he did come. We were neither close nor distant, more like people who'd survived some great natural disaster who hold annual reunions.

'I'm okay, Dad. I just want to get back into the swing of things. Get back to teaching. Finish my degree.'

'How goes the hunt for the elusive job?' he asked.

'The job has gone from elusive to endangered. I'm sending out another fifty résumés before I declare it extinct.'

'Don't give up, honey. You can't give up.'

Sure, I can, I wanted to say. It's easy. Just ask the Bat-Faced Girl.

'Um, sweetheart,' he said, his voice hesitant. 'One thing.'

44

'What?'

'Uh, well, this isn't the best time, but it never is, we talk so seldom.'

'What, Dad?'

'I got married.'

'What?' Dad never talked about women, never seemed to be interested in them after Mom died. Widows and divorcees called for him incessantly. On occasion I'd even tried to arrange a date for him. But he always refused. This had to be one hell of a woman. 'Jesus, Dad, married.'

'Yeah, I know. I want you to meet her.'

'Sure. Is she in Houston?'

'No. She's down here with me.'

Great. another globe-spinning anthropologist putting a microscope to the natives. 'When are you two coming back so I can meet dear ole stepmum?'

'I'm not sure, honey.'

Pause.

'You see, I still have to teach her English.'

Throat clearing.

'I'm the first white man she's ever seen.'

'Jesus, Dad.'

'She has a very important job in her tribe. Very important.' His voice became animated again, the voice of Thomas Edison when the damn light bulb finally worked. Or Wren when she made me pull over that last night. 'The tribal elders believe that a little viper venom mixed with the semen of the tayra—that's a huge, extremely vicious weasel—produces a potion that keeps them forever virile. It's her job to milk the semen from the weasel and the venom from the viper. Extraordinary stuff, really.'

'Excuse me, Dad, you mean she jacks off weasels to make a sperm milkshake for these old farts so they can keep their withered peckers up?'

'In essence. Of course, it's easy to make fun from the comfort of the land where everyone thinks what the Nielsen families think. These people take this very seriously.

45

Hers is a very important position in the tribe. Very respected. She has three servants of her own.'

'Hey, I'm not making fun. At least she has a job, that's more than I have. I can't wait to see the home movies of stepmum hard at work.'

Nurse Glover tapped her watch in a friendly way and nodded at the wheelchair. I held up a finger to indicate one minute. I didn't really have anything more to say anyway. I was just goading him now and there wasn't really any satisfaction in it. Dad was being as predictable as the moon. Before Mom had died we'd been a fairly close family, even with Dad gone for months at a time. When he was home, we did everything together. Mom's exuberance held us together. When she died, he stayed with me for a year, but we hardly spoke. Finally he left me with his sister, Aunt Lydia. After that, he was gone for longer and longer periods of time. What did I expect from him now? To jet home to be by my side, watch TV with me at night while I graded freshman compositions on the pros and cons of the death penalty? Dad was looking for answers as far away as he could get from his own past.

'Actually,' Dad explained, 'I'm not permitted to photograph her until she goes through the Ceremony of the River next month. After that, it will be okay because her soul will be known by the river and can no longer be stolen by the camera.'

'Ceremony of the River? Sounds impressive. She becomes chief of the tribe or something?'

'No, it's the same ceremony all tribal men and women go through.' More throat clearing. 'When they turn fifteen.'

3

'Come in. Come in. Come in. Come in.'

I entered his office. 'Relax, Theo, I'm in already.'

'Sit, sit, sitsitsitsit.' Theo gestured grandly at the red leather wingback chair across from his desk. The brass studs lining the chair glinted in the fluorescent light like an airport runway at night. I shuffled toward the chair. Even after a week out of the hospital, a samba shuffle was the best I could manage.

'It's you,' he said with a boisterous tone. 'Really you.' He paced behind his desk until I had gingerly lowered myself into the chair. He watched me with barely concealed alarm, tugging at his gray, manicured beard. When I was finally seated, he dropped into his own chair. 'For God's sake, Luna, sit back and relax: Relax already.'

'Actually, Theo, I can't sit back. I have a bullet hole in my back.'

'My God, really?' He bounced forward in his chair, yanking on his beard so frantically I thought he might tear chunks out. 'I'd heard it was just the one wound.' He touched his own chest. 'How insensitive. I'm frightfully sorry. Sit any way you want, Luna. I'm serious. Relax however suits you.'

'You relax, Theo. I'm fine. Really. In fact, if I stand naked in a stiff breeze, the hole through my chest can whistle a perfect C sharp.'

Theo shook his head. 'How do you do it, Luna? How do you? How?'

'Just keep turning until the wind hits the opening like a Coke bottle.'

'You know what I mean. How do you keep your spirits up like this? You're so brave. Most women—hell, most men—would have curled up into a quivering ball of phlegm.'

'Phlegm, Theo?' I laughed.

'You know what I mean. I mean, I would have expected this kind of bravado from Wren, she was . . .' He gestured, indicating Wren was something unexplainable. 'But you, you're so . . . My God, how do you do it?'

'Drugs help.'

He forced a laugh. 'I know you're kidding, Luna. But around here, a university and all, we have to be careful about even joking about drugs. Even the offhand remark, the casual bon mot, can be misunderstood, misinterpreted.' He webbed his fingers together and wiggled them back and forth, I think to show how remarks get misinterpreted.

'I'm talking about prescription drugs, Theo.'

'Of course you are. I understand that. But someone passing by, a young student maybe, they overhear a fragment, they don't know the whole story. They tell their parents. Pretty soon I'm ass-deep in religious fundamentalists and undercover narcs.'

Theo wasn't just being paranoid. Three tenured members of the faculty had been arrested this year for drug possession. Two of them had been turned in by their own students. The third drove his car through his ex-wife's backyard Halloween party. The publicity had hurt campus enrollment.

'I'm sorry, Theo.'

He nodded relief. He stood up and paced around his office as if to measure what he had to lose in the event of a narcotics bust: hundreds of books about composition (one of which he wrote and we were required to use in all the composition courses), a facsimile edition of T. S.

Eliot's *The Wasteland* with notes by Ezra Pound, etchings by Balding Grien, a brass-studded red leather chair.

Dr. Theodore Bentley, fifty-eight, had been Dean of Instruction for the English Department Composition Program for eighteen years. He was a fussy little man who seemed to agonize over everything. He ran the thirty-three sections of freshman composition, all taught by graduate students, with efficiency if not imagination. To him, the teaching of composition was merely a matter of following routine, similar to filling in a crossword puzzle. Although he was born in Sioux City, Iowa, he had cultivated a sophisticated European look, dark suits and vests, cuff links, even affecting a slight British accent at times. When he got drunk or flustered, he quoted T. S. Eliot a lot. Thursday through Sunday evenings he moonlighted as a head waiter at a fancy French restaurant. He claimed it relaxed him and helped keep his ego in perspective. Plus, he made more money than as a full professor. His wife, Casey, was a boxy little woman with giant breasts who worked for campus security. She wore a snappy uniform and drove one of those golf carts, handing out parking tickets.

I watched Theo pace and tried to imagine him making love to his wife. I pictured him in his waiter's tuxedo, her in her starched blue uniform. That's as far as I could get without laughing.

He sat back down and looked at me. His gray eyes drifted to my breast. Beneath my sweater, I was wearing a regular bra with a hole scissored in as not to rub against the bandage. Still, everyone who knew about the shooting couldn't help but stare at my wounded breast the way people are compelled to pat a pregnant woman's belly. Perhaps they thought my breast should be smaller, as if part of it had been shot away. It made me self-conscious.

'They're still there, Theo,' I said.

'What?' He looked up. 'What? Of course they are. Of course.' He shuffled some papers on his desk, absently transferred a few file folders from basket to basket. 'Of course they are. I didn't mean anything. Was I staring? I didn't mean to stare.'

'I know you didn't, Theo.' I shifted in the chair. It was very uncomfortable to sit this straight. 'Look, I just dropped by to let you know I'm ready to pick up my class again.'

'So soon?'

'The sooner the better. I just want to get back to my class, finish the semester out. The doctor says I can start back on Monday.'

'Monday?' He frowned.

'Sure, what's wrong with Monday?'

'Monday.' He stood up and paced again, twisting a hunk of beard into a point.

'What's the problem, Theo? It is my class. I've only missed two weeks. Christ, my students miss more than that during ski season.'

'Monday,' he said, straightening an etching on the wall. 'I don't know. Monday.'

'Yes, Monday.'

He stopped pacing and sat back down in his chair. The walk seemed to have exhausted him. His face was gray and stern, like a head waiter's. 'Can't do it, Luna. I'm sorry.'

'What are you talking about? It's my class.'

'Well, technically, it's the university's class. You are assigned to teach it. Now we have someone else teaching it. I can't see that the students would benefit any to have their classroom dynamics disrupted again. We're almost at the end of the semester anyway.'

'What are you talking about?' My breathing became labored. Each inhaled breath felt as if the air were leaking out of my bullet holes before it had a chance to reach my heart. I tried to breathe deeper.

'Are you all right, Luna?' Theo asked.

'Yes, I'm fine. Just tell me what the hell is going on?'

'Of course, you will be encouraged to complete your

degree. If you need an extension of time to complete your thesis, I've been assured there will be no problem in getting one. And don't worry about the money. You will remain on the payroll as a teaching assistant until the end of the semester. So money is no problem.'

'I want to teach, Theo. That's what I do. That's what I'm applying to do after I leave here. It's why I came here.' The last part wasn't strictly true, but I didn't care about truth anymore.

'And you'll make a wonderful teacher, Luna. Wonderful.' He leaned back in his chair with a sigh. His face lapsed. His head waiter's expression was gone. Now he looked like an old man with financial worries. 'Luna, the circumstances of your accident are such that the university has to weather a whole new storm of controversy. A university employee shoots two university students, who are also employees. You can imagine the public-relations nightmare. If you were a parent, would you risk sending your child here?'

'I'm the victim here, Theo, not the criminal.'

'I know, I know. But just your appearance in the classroom is unnerving to some. And we know that drugs were found on the premises.'

'A couple joints, Theo. And I wasn't smoking any. Ask the cops, they did tests.'

'I know you weren't. But you were there. We're talking about appearances. The university has to appear as if they are taking things under control. Bottom line, we think it's better if you stay away from the classroom, except as a student.'

I wondered how Wren would have handled this. Because I knew that by the time Wren left this office she would not only have gotten her class back, she would have Theo apologizing. She would have used logic, she would have used emotion, she would have used threats. I could do that. But it wasn't just what she would have said, it was how. It was how she did things. That's what made her Wren.

'Relax, Luna. Go home and rest. Concentrate on completing your degree.'

I slowly stood. My lower back hurt from sitting so upright. My butt was numb. My breast ached as if I were nursing a sharp-toothed ferret. I probably looked like an old lady walking stiffly toward the door. I could see the pity on Theo's face and that made me even sadder.

'T.S. said something once,' Theo said. 'T.S. said: "Teach us to care and not to care/Teach us to sit still." Remember that, Luna.'

Now I was angry. I wished I could make my head spin like the little girl in *The Exorcist* and say what she said: 'Your mother sucks cocks in hell.' But I merely straightened myself into an erect pose of indignant pride and marched out of his office. I hoped I looked impressive, because inside, inside where Esther's bullet had tunneled through my organs, somewhere inside there I was curling up into a quivering ball of phlegm.

4

I poured a second helping of Cheerios and my wedding ring tumbled out of the box along with the toasted Os and clanked into the bowl. I poured milk over the cereal and the ring was lifted afloat by the Cheerios like tiny brown inner tubes. The ring was just a band of gold. No inscription. No family heirloom. The only distinguishing mark was a deep scratch from the time Robby had tried to teach me to skateboard on a steep hill and I fell, scraping all the skin off my palms and gouging the ring.

I ate around the ring.

I was standing at the ironing board, eating cereal for lunch while scissoring another bra. I'd had cereal for breakfast too, and it looked like I had just enough to get through dinner if I didn't get sloppy with the milk. I'd outlined the prospective hole in the bra cup with a black pen, then started cutting. The bra I'd been wearing for the past few days had bloodstains around the edges of the cutout. All the frayed threads were red and it looked like somebody's bleeding scalp hanging from my boob. There was nothing medically wrong, my doctor assured me, spot bleeding was perfectly normal. But it unnerved me to see blood on my bra.

The television was on and I listened to *Green Acres*. Occasionally, when the laugh track swelled, I'd look up from my surgical procedure to see what was so funny, but by then I'd missed it and all I'd see was Eddie Arnold looking perplexed at Eva Gabor in a nightgown.

I was wearing neon-green shorts but nothing else. My

bare breasts had enormous goose bumps from the fan on the table and the way they were all bunched together in a circle around my nipple kind of reminded me of the Bolivian natives my father was studying. I imagined them all gathered around to worship at the sacred altar of the Great River Nipple. I searched through the crowd of goose bumps for Dad's wife, but I couldn't find one that looked like a fourteen-year-old girl jerking off a weasel.

I did find one that looked a little like Eva Gabor, though.

The bandage on my breast was smaller now, the size of four postage stamps, but there was a yellowish crust on the gauze that the doctor explained meant it was healing. Perfectly normal. The wound on my back itched like crazy. At times I would back up to the refrigerator door and scratch it on the handle like a dog.

The doorbell chimed.

I spooned up another glob of cereal, careful not to touch the wedding ring. The Cheerios were starting to get soggy.

Robby had given me the ring ten years ago. We'd been living together off campus then. I'd come home late one night from my waitressing job at the Haus of Pies. We'd been pushing rhubarb all night because Mr. Braun, the owner, had gotten a good deal on rhubarb and made three times as many pies as usual. He and Mrs. Braun snapped at each other all evening in German because no one wanted rhubarb. Finally Mr. Braun blasted his wife with a tirade of German gargling and stormed out, leaving us shorthanded to clean up. Mrs. Braun, in tears, gave Tina and me each a rhubarb pie to take home.

Robby met me at the door, naked except for his father's white apron. He'd had a scraggly little beard then that made him look like a failed poet with Marxist sympathies. We hugged and my hand slid down the small of his back to that crevice at the top of his buttocks, which, as always, was a little moist from sweat. With a courtly flourish, he'd guided me to the kitchen where he announced, 'Dinner is served.' I expected another one of his gourmet feasts, delicate sauces over tender slices of exotically spiced fowl. Certainly our tiny table was set for something special: white tablecloth that used to be one of our bedsheets, fancy silverware he'd borrowed from a neighbour, candles stuck in beer bottles.

He seated me, snapped open a cloth napkin (once our pillowcase), and fluttered it onto my lap.

He handed me the box of Trix.

'What's this?' I said.

'Dinner, madam. Enjoy.'

I laughed, playing along. As long as it wasn't rhubarb. The box was new, so I tore open the top flap and poured the cereal. The colored balls clattered festively into the bowl. Then the clunk of the ring. The gold winked candlelight.

Robby proposed a toast: 'Let's get married and fuck until we can't walk and then get good jobs that make money but show a social conscience and then have children and raise them to be perfect and then buy a house that will become a gathering place for all the best and brightest of our generation who will sit in our living room and discuss theories of art while we're in the kitchen doing some gourmet fucking on the countertop making the world safe for democracy and prose poetry.'

'Why not?' I said, slipping on the ring.

So for the past two months, every time I opened a new box of cereal I tossed my wedding ring back inside, shook the box, and waited to discover it again and again. Like the precious prize it had been that first time. Back when I'd thought of the ring as a round key to a thick hand-carved door behind which was our bright and shining future.

Sometimes I'd thought of it as a homing device, if I ever got lost somewhere or even felt a little lost inside, I could show my ring and say, 'Look, this is where I belong. Take me there. I'm expected there.'

Not now. Now I belonged in front of a wobbly ironing

board, wolfing Cheerios and cutting up bras. I hoped the repetition of this ring-in-the-box ritual would eventually de-romanticize Robby's gesture and help me miss him less. So far it hadn't worked.

My friends all gave me mathematical formulas for when I'd feel better. Wren had said it took one month per each year that you were together. Esther had put it at one year for every six years you were together. Others had more elaborate equations, factoring in causes for the split up or averaging the age of the couple, how much stuff you had accumulated, were there pets, venereal diseases, pension funds. *Cosmo* said falling in love again immediately reduced 'down time' significantly. *Self* said to take up low-impact aerobics or dog breeding. The physicists of heartbreak. I imagined the experts in their white lab coats, scribbling twenty-digit numbers on a blackboard, trying to figure out why my stomach always felt as if I'd swallowed a cocktail of Drāno and thumbtacks. And tell me, Professor, why do I still smell Robby on my skin?

The doorbell chimed again, followed by heavy knocking.

I chewed another mouthful of soggy cereal and continued cutting the perfect hole in my bra. I hadn't noticed before, but I was making scalloped edges. I wondered if this was how Fredrick's of Hollywood got started.

Wren had discovered my wedding-ring ceremony once when she'd come over after an all-night paper-writing session and ate the whole damn box of cereal, nearly chipping a tooth on my ring. I'd expected some sort of big-sister speech, some condemning look. A lecture about sisterhood or womanhood or wimphood. About standing on our own feet, codependent no more. Instead she'd just shuffleboarded the ring across the kitchen table to me and sighed, 'With love, dear Luna, whatever works.'

I ate the cereal around the ring until the Cheerios were all gone. The ring lay at the bottom of the bowl in a shallow puddle of milk. I spooned the ring up and put it in my mouth. I had never done that before. It had no flavor.

That surprised me. I'd expected some metallic taste, like blood or pennies. I thought about swallowing it, letting it travel through my colon for a couple days to see the sights and pop out the other end. That should de-romanticize the little fucker forever.

The doorbell rang in an impatient code. 'Ms. Devon? Hey, Ms. Devon.'

I plucked the ring from my mouth and tossed it back into the Cheerios box. I shook the box and stashed it in the cupboard next to the potato chips. My movements were slow and deliberate, as if I had all day to do the simplest task. I wasn't in shock or any physical pain, it was just that my life had been reduced to only one goal now: to finish my Thomas Pynchon paper thereby securing my master's degree. I had plenty of free time now. I had no composition class to teach, so I had no papers to grade, no office to go to. I'd returned my petitions to Amnesty International with only two signatures, mine and Nurse Glover's. There were no more teaching jobs to apply for, all I could do now was sit back and wait to see where my life would go, like shooting down churning rapids holding onto a sponge.

The two people I knew best were Wren and Esther, so I wasn't burdened with a lot of friends coming by trying to cheer me up. Robby and I had been pretty much a self-contained unit. We'd spent most of our free time alone. Occasionally we would double date with another couple, but that would be the last I'd see of them until the next time Robby arranged another outing. I didn't mind this lack of socializing; I didn't really want people to know how much harder than everyone else I had to work just to keep up. My thesis on Thomas Pynchon was taking longer than it should, most of the other students were almost finished. Why had I picked a reclusive cult writer who never appeared in public and who some thought didn't even really exist? Still, there were over ninety doctoral dissertations and thirty books about the guy. *They* did exist, so did the novels, so did my deadline. Standing there now, I couldn't remember one literary thing about the man. What were his themes, his world vision? All I could remember was a rumor about the day Norman Mailer had somehow bullied Pynchon's secret address from someone and gone over to visit the hermit writer. The story has it that Pynchon saw Mailer coming down the street and leapt out of a two-story window and ran away rather than meet his fellow author.

'Come on, Ms. Devon,' the voice outside my door called. 'I know you're in there. It's me. It's Mark, Ms. Devon.'

Since the shooting, I'd followed the strict regimen of a novitiate. I attended my three graduate classes, took notes, and read thick novels no one but students read anymore. My classmates kept a cheerful remoteness, as if they feared my bad luck might rub off on them, maybe affect their grades. Robby called sometimes, but usually our words were out of sync with our feelings, like badly dubbed kung fu movies. Once he brought by a bag of groceries. We smoked a joint and discussed Emily Brontë. He kissed me on the cheek and left. All the air in the room seemed to leave with him.

'I'm not going away, Ms. Devon,' the voice outside my door continued.

Having no second-story window to leap from, I slipped into my customized bra and pulled on a baggy gray sweatshirt. There was no witty saying or clever drawing on my sweatshirt. All my sweatshirts and T-shirts were blank.

More thumping on the door. 'I'm totally serious. I'm not leaving till you see me, Ms. Devon.'

I opened the door. 'I see you, Mark. Happy?'

Mark smiled and leaned his bicycle against the building. He looked down at my bare legs. 'I've never seen you in shorts before.'

'I don't usually wear them to teach.'

'You should. It would motivate us more. The guys, anyway.'

He edged past me into my apartment. I stayed in the

doorway, holding the door open. He was wearing some kind of pine-scented cologne that stung my eyes. As he passed, I sniffed the sweet scent of breath mints too. His curly black hair was damp from biking. 'I've been knocking here for twenty minutes. Did that shooting affect your hearing or something?'

'What'd you say?'

He snorted. 'Very funny.'

I didn't mind seeing Mark. He was the smartest student in my comp class. Smart enough not to need me and cocky enough to know it. I had a feeling most teachers would feel that way about Mark. College was a formality for someone like him, a place to pick up a diploma for what he already knew or would learn on his own. He reminded me of Wren. Also, I think a part of me was glad he was here. I wanted him to do a Good-bye, Ms. Chips routine that would bring me back some of my lost enthusiasm. If anyone could, it would be a perfect student like Mark.

'This is nice,' he said, looking around. He walked about the living room, touching things briefly. He had a worn leather backpack slung over one shoulder. A silver bicycle clip pinned the right cuff of his jeans. 'It's not how I pictured your place, though. I figured you more for, I don't know, a cactus in every corner and Navaho blankets on the walls. That whole Southwest thing.'

'Why are you here, Mark?'

'To bring you your mail.' He reached into his backpack and handed me three envelopes. One was another bill from the Modern Language Association that I'd only joined to get their job list, two were from schools I had applied to for a teaching position. 'I saw them in your mailbox at school and thought I'd save you a trip.'

'Thanks,' I said. I put the envelopes behind my back. I didn't want him here when I opened them.

'Go ahead, open them,' he said, smoothing down a cowlick at the crown of his head.

'It can wait,' I said.

He picked up the glass unicorn Robby gave me when

I'd acted in *The Glass Menagerie* in our junior year. Robby had stolen it from the set after the last performance. Mark pointed the unicorn's horn at my letters. 'Open them. I know you're dying to.'

'Fine,' I said. I went through my usual ritual, hefting the envelopes, trying to figure out if an acceptance weighed more than a rejection. As if they used more words, more ink, thicker paper. While Mark wandered about stroking my furniture, I tore open the envelopes.

Dear Ms. Devon . . . Thank you . . . impressive application . . . sorry to say . . . keep on file . . . sincerely.

They read very much like my divorce letter.

'I could've told you,' Mark said, plopping down on the sofa. 'They don't write when they're interested. They call.'

'I know that,' I said. I did, too, but I figured that maybe they tried to call but somehow couldn't reach me, so they sent a letter. That could happen.

'My dad's a dean,' Mark said. 'Chemistry Department back in Ohio. He sends out a lot of those letters.'

I looked over at Mark. He was staring at my legs again.

'What do you want, Mark? I have to get ready for class soon.'

'No, you don't,' he said with annoying confidence. 'Your Brit Lit class isn't until three. And your Conrad class and the Fiction Workshop meet tomorrow.'

'Quite the little spy, aren't you?'

'You got anything to drink? I'm dying.'

I went into the kitchen and brought back a can of Diet Dr Pepper. I handed it to him and he smiled up at me. He was a charming kid, eighteen going on forty. His body was as lanky and hard as knotted rope. His face was angular, reminding me of home plate in a baseball diamond. In about ten years, when he had grown into his features, he would be quite handsome. Women would talk about him longingly.

I ignored his flirting. I didn't have the energy to deal with the moral and physical complexities of hopping into bed with him. He had a hard-on bulging at the crotch of his jeans, which he tried to cover by tugging his leather jacket down. Back when I was still living with Robby, I'd had an erotic dream about Mark, I can't remember what. I'd awakened slick with sweat and discovered I'd been rubbing myself against Robby's leg. I'd looked up at him and was embarrassed to see he was awake, watching. He rolled me onto my back and we made love. That was the last time we did it. Since the split-up, I'd stopped having erotic dreams the same way I stopped having periods when I went on the pill. Now I could hardly remember why I'd liked sex so much before.

'You think my bike's okay out there?' Mark asked.

'No,' I said.

He laughed. 'You're funny, Ms. Devon.'

'I crack me up. Now, what can I do for you?'

He wedged the Dr Pepper can between his thighs. He leaned forward, screwing his face into a serious expression. 'When you coming back, Ms. Devon?'

'I'm not, Mark. I'm convalescing. Didn't your new teacher tell you that?'

He shrugged, as if nothing the new teacher said could be trusted. 'How's your wound?'

'Better.'

He stared at my breasts as if he could see through my sweatshirt and bandage and was staring at the crusted hole itself. 'Can I see it? I've never seen a gunshot wound.'

I laughed. 'I don't think so, Mark. You'll just have to wait until you're old enough for a gunshot wound of your own.'

He nodded and sat back, pressing into the sofa. 'I've seen knife wounds,' he said. 'They don't look like much. Some guy at AA had one. Right here, across the gut.'

'You're in AA, Mark?'

'Sure. Me, my dad, my stepmom. It's a family affair. Even my little sister. She's fifteen. At least she's smart enough to get drunk on the cheap stuff. I guess we all got that boozer's gene.'

'I didn't know about that. About your family.'

'You don't know shit, Ms. Devon.' This was the first time Mark had ever said anything harsh to me. He hunched over a little and looked away from me.

I didn't know what to say, so I didn't say anything. My back wound was itching. I rubbed it against the back of the chair.

Mark picked up the heavy glass stein from the end table. My name was engraved across the glass. I had won the stein in a twelfth grade tri-state track meet. For three years my fiercest rivalry had been with Stephanie Cutter. She'd beat me in the long jump at every meet. She always took first place, I always took second place. Finally, at the last meet of our final season, she got sick fifteen minutes before the jump. We watched her on hands and knees in the middle of the field puking some foul goop. Turned out she had food poisoning. I won easily. I didn't keep the trophy around as a reminder of my triumph, but rather to remember that the only time I ever took first place in anything was because someone else forfeited. These life lessons help you keep a healthy perspective.

After a minute Mark put the engraved stein back and looked at me with a sly smile. 'I'm writing this paper,' he said, 'for Mr. Conner's Shakespeare class. He's such a fucking weasel, this paper's gonna blow his weasel brain away.'

Jack Conner was a fucking weasel. He was up for tenure this year and had begun a shameless campaign of glad-handing, party-throwing, and all around ass-kissing. He also spied on members of the tenure committee. Once I saw him in the faculty mail room, sneaking peeks at Dr. Loeb's mail. Sitting here now in my cutaway bra, the taste of Cheerios and sour milk in my mouth, it was hard to imagine that I'd been part of that department. It seemed as remote as my old summer camp days. I tried to remember what my shabby office looked like, the view through the grimy window. I couldn't.

'Listen, Ms. Devon,' Mark said with his usual enthusiasm. 'Listen to this. This is what I'm doing my paper on, you'll flip out. You know Guam, right? The island.'

'I've heard of it.'

He swigged his Dr Pepper. 'Well, just a few years ago there were six endemic species of bird in Guam. Endemic means these birds are found only on Guam.'

'I know what endemic means, Mark.'

'Right, sorry. Anyway, now the bridled white-eye and the Guam broadbill are extinct. Probably so is the rufous-fronted fantail. That leaves only three species left.'

'This all has something to do with Shakespeare?'

'Yeah, we're doing *King Lear*.'

'The rufous-fronted fantail plays Lear?'

'Trust me, this will all make sense. Meanwhile, back on Guam: these other three species are hanging on to existence by the tip of their beaks. Everyone's walking around scratching their heads, but nobody could figure out why this sudden decline in the bird population. Then in 1982, this graduate student named Julie Savidge goes there and finds the answer.' He clapped his hands together, startling me. '*Boiga irregularis*.'

'Sounds like jungle constipation.'

'It's a snake. She cut a bunch of them open and kept finding birds and birds' eggs. Thing is, this snake is not native to Guam. They figure it arrived on the island during World War II, probably imported to eat rodents. For a long time they called it the "Philippine rat snake", which made people think it was benevolent. But it's not a rat snake, it's a bird-eating tree snake and it's practically wiped out the whole fucking bird population.'

I was losing concentration, still trying to conjure the view from my office window. Was it the student bookstore that I stared at every day or the infirmary? How many mountains sliced the western horizon of Oregon? Didn't Wren and I used to feed sunflower seeds to pigeons on that sooty window ledge?

'Ms. Devon?'

I refocused on Mark. 'What do birds and snakes have to do with *King Lear*?'

'I'm getting to it.' Mark finished the rest of his Dr Pepper and balanced the can on the sofa arm. 'This snake was introduced into an environment where it had no natural predators and in which its prey had never learned to defend itself against it. I mean, the livin' was easy, man. Birds were jumpin' and the cotton was high. Fat City for the *boiga irregularis*.'

'God, you can be annoying, Mark. Did you know that? Are you aware of this irritating trait?'

'Yeah.' He smiled and I had to smile too. I suppose it was kind of flattering that of all the truly brilliant people around the department he could be telling this stuff to, he chose me instead. It was working, I was starting to feel something again, a positive attitude toward my career. Sure, why not me.

'I'm listening,' I said.

'They got something like three million of these snakes on this tiny island. They get in the electrical wiring and cause outages all the time. Anyway, they started this program to airlift the birds somewhere else, raise them, then bring them back when they've lowered the snake population.'

'Sounds like a lot of trouble,' I said. But I was encouraged to know that people somewhere were willing to bother. I probably wouldn't have.

'Thing is, Ms. Devon. Even if they succeed, they still lose. Islands are where species become extinct. That's why all those evolutionary biologist guys like Darwin and Wallace and Dammerman all go to these dinky islands to study life. Listen to this, I got this great quote.' He dug into his leather backpack, rifling the papers and notebooks, finally pulling out a book called *The Flight of the Iguana*. He opened it to a marked page and began reading: '"Small islands especially are the black holes to oblivion. Speciation proceeds more rapidly . . . The luckiest of the pioneers adapt to their new habitats. They colonize.

They specialize. They succeed. They become more sedentary than they were when they arrived—because the most restless individuals among them are constantly taking their genes elsewhere, flying off to escape or else to die trying. The others stay and stay."' He closed the book with a thump and whacked it against his thigh. 'Get it?'

I didn't get it. What's more, I suddenly realized I didn't care. I didn't care about Mark's paper, about King Lear or the fair Cordelia. Worst of all, I didn't care about teaching. I'd been moping around for days because of my lost class, but right now it was clear to me that I didn't really care if I ever went back into another classroom again. I tried to remember the faces of the students in my class, picture them all staring up at me as I explained how to write a footnote. Nothing came. I closed my eyes. I tried to picture Mark's face. I couldn't.

My chest started to ache and churn, as if there were something foreign inside. I knew the bullet had passed through me, but for that moment I swore I could feel it inside, feel its smooth head twisting toward the surface. There was thick scab beneath the bandage, but it seemed to be disintegrating now. It felt as if it would erupt and spew out the bullet. I tried to imagine the look on Mark's face when the bloody bullet spit through my sweatshirt and plopped onto the carpet. Work that into your next paper, buddy boy, I'd say with a wink.

'You okay, Ms. Devon?' Mark asked, leaning forward with a look of concern. 'You need some medicine or something?'

'I'm fine, Mark,' I said. 'Go on, go on. Tell me how Sheriff Lear cleans up Guam City.'

'It's that whole tragedy thing. The tragic hero striving to become godlike by avoiding his fate. That's King Lear's arrogance. But it's the same with us and those birds. We try to save them, only to return them to an island. It's the island that dooms them to extinction, just as we are all living on this planet, an island in space. And just as we are all doomed to extinction. But we strive to fight it anyway, despite knowing it is futile. Those birds will become extinct eventually, why not now? That's what I'm getting at. You see?'

I stood up. The activity in my chest seemed to have calmed down. I didn't feel the phantom bullet anymore. I walked toward the front door and opened it. 'Thanks for dropping by to cheer me up.'

'I know it's still a little rough,' he said, also standing. 'But what do you think of the thesis, the general concept?'

'It's good. Write it. I'm sure you'll get an A.'

He shook his head impatiently. 'I *know* I'll get an A. That's not what I'm asking.'

I looked over at the TV. *People's Court* was on. An old woman stood at the defendant's table gripping a walker. She had a green and red parrot perched on the walker. Judge Wopner asked her peevishly why she brought the bird to court. She snapped right back at him that the lady who called her to be on the show told her to bring the bird, that's why. I turned back to Mark. 'I don't know what you want to hear, Mark. Just do it. It sounds good to me. Very insightful.'

'Yeah.' He made a face and I could see he was disappointed. 'Hey, you see my new tattoo yet?'

'Jesus, Mark, not a tattoo.'

He took off his leather jacket and pushed up his T-shirt sleeve. He flexed his arm muscle. High up near his shoulder was a blue outline of a little girl, barefoot, peeking into a dark window. She had an old-fashioned dress on and a flower in her hair. The flower was colored with red ink. Above this picture are the words, in red ink. VIOLENT FEMMES, arched over the girl like a rainbow. Beneath the picture are the words, in quotes: 'Words all fail the magic prize . . .'

'Very nice,' I said. 'I can see why you'd want that permanently carved into your body.'

'You don't get it, Ms. Devon. You ever listen to the Violent Femmes? "Let me go on like I blister in the sun . . ." You know that song?'

66

Suddenly I knew how Esther must have felt, people coming by, spilling their lives on her kitchen table, then taking off again. Leaving the residue of their plans and hopes and triumphs and defeats to hang in the air, cling to dust particles there. And Esther sitting there, waiting for sleep, her valuables hidden in the appliances, camouflaged against burglars. Yet, she was being invaded hourly by people who stole her sleep. Well, she was sleeping now. Slice open the belly of the *Boiga irregularis* and you'd find Esther there, softly snoring, dreaming.

'I don't know the group, Mark.'

'See? That's the point. You probably thought you were cool once, back when you were my age. Smoking dope and listening to the Rolling Stones. You probably thought you had it all figured out. I guess young people always think that. But then something happens, right? Somewhere along the line they slip into comas or something. Not me. I got this tattoo of their CD jacket so I'd never forget my values, what's really important. If I ever start to dweeb out, I just look at this . . .' He held up his arm closer to me. 'Then I remember what it's all about. Who I am.'

'Gee, Mark, you're right. If only I'd gotten that tattoo of Glenn Campbell's *Rhinestone Cowboy* album jacket when I had the chance.'

Mark's face tightened into anger. I had seen him tense and frustrated in class before, but never this angry countenance. He stepped toward me and I felt a twinge of fear. 'I read something else in this book, Ms. Devon. Something very interesting about rape.'

I took a step backward. 'You'd better go now, Mark. I'm tired.'

'Not yet,' he said. 'I want to tell you about bedbugs. How they fuck. It's very interesting.'

I looked around the room for a convenient weapon. Something, if need be, to bludgeon my best student's head into a bloody pulp. Funny how different your possessions look when you're judging them for their value as a weapon. Beauty loses its impact, everything is heft. Pynchon's thick novel, *V.*, was lying on the coffee table. A couple sharp raps across the temple with that might be enough to curb his sexual appetite. I took a step toward it, he cut me off.

'Here's how it works,' Mark said. 'This particular type of bedbug has a penis shaped like a dagger. He doesn't insert it into any vaginal opening. Instead, he just stabs her in the abdomen with it. I mean that literally. He punctures her with his dick. That's how they have sex. In fact, sometimes when one male is fucking another female like that, his dick stuck in her gut, another male will come up and stab the male doing the humping. Then his sperm replaces the first guy's and he can impregnate the female. Interesting, huh?'

'You should go, Mark.'

'They call it traumatic insemination. Neat phrase. Traumatic insemination. It's like the weirdest fucking thing I've ever heard of. I'm trying to work it into my Lear paper, but I don't know. They think the whole thing came about because the males used to secrete some kind of glue from their dicks after sex. They'd use this glue to seal up the female's vagina so no other guys could screw her after him. Like one of those, you know, chastity belts. Ground squirrels still do that, glue their females' twats shut. Anyway, that's why they figure the bedbugs evolved their dagger dicks.'

I didn't say anything. He stared at my face, looking for something. I guess he found it, because he smiled and backed away from me, satisfied.

He slipped into his jacket and backpack as he walked out the front door. I followed him. He straddled his bike and looked at me. I realized then that I would probably never see him again, that this might be the last time I ever saw someone who was my student.

'I'm glad you came by, Mark,' I said. 'Take care with—'

'Did you believe me?' he interrupted. He looked at me with a morose expression.

'What?'

'Did you believe me? Before.'

'When? About the bedbugs?'

'About being in AA. That stuff I told you about my family. My little sister and stuff.'

'Yes, I believed you. Of course I believed you.'

He shook his head sadly. 'You really don't know shit, Ms. Devon. From now on you'd better be real careful.'

He swung his bike around and pedaled off. He turned as he jumped the curb and waved, a big smile on his face. Like we were best friends.

I closed the door and walked to the bathroom for some Tylenol. I wrestled the cap off and swallowed three little tablets, washing them down with warm water from the faucet. I was still bent over drinking from the faucet when another knock at the door startled me. I jerked a little, banging my lip against the faucet. I tasted blood.

The doorbell rang this time.

'Fuck you, Mark,' I growled. 'Fuck you and fuck King Lear and fuck dagger-dicked bedbugs.' The mirror over the sink revealed a little nick out of my lip, a tiny flap of skin bent upward. I pressed the washcloth against it and the bleeding stopped immediately.

I marched back to the front door, the washcloth still pressed to my lip. It tasted faintly of soap and mildew. I yanked open the door ready to blast Mark. But, of course, it wasn't Mark.

'Ms. Devon?' the elegant woman asked. Her manners were as impeccable as her makeup. Her clothes were expensive but not exclusive. Her white gold bracelet would have supported me for six months. The only crack in this perfect picture was the redness of her eyes and the faint smell of brandy on her breath.

'Yes—' I nodded—'I'm Ms. Devon.'

She smiled with such relief in her eyes, as if admitting who I was had been a great act of human kindness. She held out her small pale hand. 'I'm Kate Lansing. Wren's mother. Have I come at a bad time?'

5

'You two are goddamn lucky. I'm serious. You don't know, you were this close to being arrested!' The manager shook her finger at us, wheezing as she entered the front door of Wren's apartment. She was a short woman with a thin face and skinny swizzle-stick legs, but carrying about 200 steel-belted pounds around her chest, stomach, and hips. A big brass ring of keys jangled in her hand.

'Hi, Mrs. Naughton,' I said. 'We're just cleaning up a little.'

Wren's mother and I were standing at the sink of the kitchenette in Wren's apartment washing the dishes from Wren's last meal so we could pack them. I was washing, Wren's mother was drying. Even though there were only a few dishes, Wren's mother had a dish towel tucked into her skirt as an apron. It made her look somehow scientific, like an archaeologist or a coroner.

From the crusted remains on the pot, the single blue ceramic bowl, the small salad plate, and the soup spoon, fork, and knife, I guessed Wren's final meal at home had been her favorite: tomato soup, grilled-cheese-with-tomatoes sandwich, and barbecue potato chips. For a moment, I felt like a clever detective having this knowledge, being able to piece together this information from the few crumbs that were left behind. Then I realized these were useless clues, they told us nothing valuable. Nothing we really needed to know.

'I'm telling you, I was about to call the goddamn cops,' Mrs. Naughton continued. 'I hear something up here, I

71

know nobody's home, I figure, Sally, don't be an idiot, call the goddamn cops, that's what you pay taxes for. I had the phone in my hand and I was actually dialing.' She cupped her left hand as if it held a phone. 'I'd punched nine and then one before I hung up and decided to come up here first, have a look-see. Lucky for you two I did. I mean, who knows what a nervous cop with a loaded gun might do. Jesus.' She held her hand to her ample bosom as if stilling a wildly thwacking heart. 'Of course, what would I have done if you'd really been burglars? I shoulda called the goddamn cops, not taken any chances. That's what they're paid for, right? Sometimes I'm so goddamn stupid.' She laughed and the sound caught me by surprise. It was so young and delicate coming out of that hefty middle-aged body.

'I should have told you we were coming, Mrs. Naughton,' I said, rinsing the last dish, a chipped soup bowl. 'I should've called. I'm sorry.'

Mrs. Naughton walked deeper into the apartment and looked around, shaking her head sadly. 'Best unit in the whole complex. Lots of sunlight. You could grow a goddamn jungle in here.' She yanked open the drapes and sunlight flashbulbed into the room to prove her point. 'I wish I had a hundred like her. My life would be perfect then.'

I wasn't sure if she was talking about Wren or the unit.

'Mrs. Naughton, this is Wren's mother, Mrs. Lansing.' I didn't know whether Kate wanted to be called Mrs. or Ms., but this didn't seem like the right time to wave any flags.

'Kate,' Wren's mom said, putting down the dish towel to shake Mrs. Naughton's hand.

'Kate? That's my name too. Well, my second middle name. Sally Mary Kate Naughton. Not Katherine, mind you, just Kate. My mother insisted on it. You a Katherine?'

'Caitlin, actually,' Kate said. 'Somewhere along the line it just became Kate.'

72

'I like Caitlin,' I said, mostly to be saying something. We were standing in Wren's apartment chattering away like scared kids in a graveyard. The more mundane the conversation, the better we should feel.

Wren's apartment. I had been here a couple hundred times. I'd slept over on occasion, chopped vegetables, scoured the toilet, studied Chaucer, listened to Wren play Paul Simon's *Graceland* over and over and over while she took elaborate notes on the lyrics for her thesis. I'd fed her grilled cheese and soup last month for two days when she had the flu. I had my own key, just as Wren had one to my place. I looked over at the white sofa and winced, remembering that bizarre night last month. I felt a flush spreading across my face just thinking about it and I turned away so Kate and Mrs. Naughton couldn't see my embarrassment.

I'd been separated from Robby for six weeks then, still in a near comatose depression, bitching about how I'd probably never have sex again, how I didn't even remember how to have sex, what sex felt like. Wren comforted me without babying me. We played gin rummy, listened to more Paul Simon (until Wren threw an M&M at the CD player and said: 'For Christ's sake, Paul, go to fucking Graceland already'), ate frozen pizza and chunky applesauce. She made me stay the night. I slept in her bed, she'd insisted on taking the sofa. In the middle of the night, something woke me. Faint sounds. Like Saran Wrap being unrolled. I looked at the clock, almost three in the morning. I zombied out to the living room to check on Wren, thinking maybe she'd fallen asleep with the TV on.

And there she was. Naked.

She was standing, bent over at the waist, her hands gripping the arm of the white sofa like the handlebars of a motorcycle. Behind her was some guy, his face a scribbled blotch of black hair and dark shadow. I couldn't see his face and I didn't recognize his body. His hands were folded around her hips, pulling and pushing, the two of them hammering into each other like it was bull wrestling at the rodeo. I watched his buttocks flex and lapse, flex and lapse, as he pummeled her. At one point, he jerked back and forth so frantically that his penis slipped out of her. They both groaned with disappointment. He quickly readjusted his condom, pulling it tighter the way a woman tugs her panty hose, then worked his semi-erect penis back into Wren. She reached down between her legs and cupped his balls in her hand. Oh yeah, he said, oh yeah oh yeah. He attacked her with renewed vigor. Watching their bodies grind, listening to the slap of his hips against her buttocks, smelling their thick aroma all made me a little weak. I felt like saying something rude to them, something like 'Is that sofa Scotchguarded?' But the way they were going they wouldn't have stopped for me or anything, then I would be there watching and they would know it and it would all be too perverse. Right now it was just an accident, an erotic accident. I shouldn't have kept watching, I guess, but I did, rubbing my grooved thumb-nails against the hem of my T-shirt. Wren came first, Oh God, God, God yes. Then he came, Jesus, please, please, fuck yes.

When he pulled out of Wren, I saw his oily sweat dripping down her buttocks and the backs of her legs. Dozens of droplets sparkled up and down her legs and I thought of Paul Simon's 'Diamonds on the Soles of Her Shoes'. The man dropped to his knees and started licking the sweat from the backs of her thighs, moving higher. She laughed and wiggled her butt playfully.

I ducked back into the bedroom and quietly climbed into bed, trying not to disturb a single bed spring. I wanted very much to masturbate then, even slipping my fingers inside my panties and touching my clitoris tentatively. But I was afraid of making the bed squeak, then they would know what I was doing. I pulled my hand out of my panties and tucked it under my pillow. After a few minutes I heard the front door close and my bedroom door open. Wren walked into the bedroom. I pretended to be asleep, my eyes pressed closed. She ignored my pretence and sat on the edge of the bed. I could smell the scent of sweat and semen and vaginal juices. This is how I imagined the Amazon jungle to smell after a tropical storm has uprooted a few trees.

'You said you forgot how to do it, forgot how it feels,' she said. 'Well, that's how to do it. And' —she paused and I knew she was smiling—'it feels *good*.' She stood up and walked out.

We never spoke about it. The next morning we had breakfast and talked more about her plans to start her own magazine. She slurped coffee and ate two English muffins smeared with jam.

But a few days later when Aaron Franzen asked me again to go to the poetry reading put on by the English Department every Wednesday at noon, I accepted. Nothing much came of it, a couple movies, some sloppy kissing, a little massaging of my breasts under my blouse but over my bra, and long talks afterwards about his thesis on Philip Roth's use of Israel as a symbol for the eros part of the libido. Still, it was a step in the right direction, thanks to Wren's unorthodox teaching methods. Hell, now she was even a better teacher than I.

'This place is so clean,' Mrs. Naughton marveled, clapping her hands together. 'If my daughter were half this clean I'd consider God's work on earth done.'

Kate smiled and nodded. That's pretty much all she'd been doing since she'd arrived at my apartment. Smiling and nodding. It was getting on my nerves. I kept waiting for some burst of emotion, accusation even. None came. She'd flown in this morning from Omaha to claim the body. She didn't like to fly, she'd told me. Her husband loved to fly, so had Wren. She'd already been by the morgue to identify Wren for the record. The body was being shipped back to Omaha. Now she wanted to pack up her daughter's belongings and ship them back too.

'Where's your husband?' I asked on the drive over.

'Oh, Jim couldn't come.'

'He couldn't come?'

'No. Something came up.'

Wren had rarely spoken of her parents, but when she had it had been with affection. Unlike the other students in the department, Wren scorned what she referred to as 'trips down Evil Parent Lane'. In the Fiction Workshop we both attended (I was only in it because it was required), the stories were mostly about an alienated son or daughter fighting against the awful life they have because of a parent's incompetent or malevolent style of parenting. The ending was usually some melodramatic confrontation in which said child faces up to said parent and verbally rakes them over the coals. Something symbolic always happens after the big cathartic scene, like the cat leaps off the garage roof and breaks a leg or the kid walks off into the blinding snow, dropping a mitten that is quickly buried by the falling snow. To which Wren would shake her head and say, 'Another "Fuck You, Daddy" story.' Professor O'Keefe always laughed at that.

Mrs. Naughton shoved her hands into the jacket of her sweatsuit. Her keys jangled. She looked at Kate with sad eyes. 'It's a tragedy, Kate. No other way to look at it. The worst kind of tragedy.'

'Thank you,' Kate said, folding Wren's fisherman's sweater. I'd given it to Wren for her birthday. It had been hanging over the dining-room chair, waiting for Wren to grab it on her way out the door, late to meet somebody smart, somewhere nice, about something important.

'Tragedy, tragedy, all is tragedy,' Mrs. Naughton mumbled to herself, her eyes staring at nothing now, as if she were thinking about her own daugther, the possibilities for tragedy that awaited her.

I couldn't decide whether she'd deliberately misquoted the Bible or she was just being clever. Either way, the word tragedy struck me as funny, maybe because of Mark's recent lecture on *King Lear*. I thought of Lear now, seeing his dead daughter brought on stage. I thought of the birds of Guam being gobbled up by those intruder snakes. Bedbug erections. Esther the Bat-Faced Girl hiding her television set in the refrigerator. Tragedy. What's that?

On the way here, Kate and I had stopped by a discount office supply warehouse and bought a bunch of cardboard boxes you have to assemble yourself. Somehow driving behind supermarkets and pirating their old orange boxes seemed disrespectful to Wren. Kate would have unpacked those clothes later in Omaha and Wren's memory would smell of sweetly rotten oranges. *That's* tragedy.

'Well, hell,' Mrs. Naughton said, eyeing the pile of unassembled boxes, 'if it's packing you want, I can pack with the best of 'em. I've moved so often that I can pack a three-bedroom house faster than a box boy bags a cart of groceries.' She pushed up her sleeves and grabbed the top hunk of cardboard and had the thing folded and tucked and looking like a serious box in about ten seconds.

I picked up a couple of Mrs. Naughton's folded boxes and went into Wren's bathroom to pack. I thought maybe this room would be especially painful for Kate. The things we keep in the bathroom are morbidly intimate. This is where we watch the toilet for signs of blood in our stool, examine the darkening moles, the falling hair, the receding gums, the hidden lumps. Tylenol, toothpaste, and tampons, all the things we use to shore up our mortality while we cozy up to the idea of death. It's also a pretty good place to take a pee, which I did as quickly as possible. Somehow it seemed impolite to come over and whiz in Wren's bathroom, so I tried to flush the toilet quietly.

Although Wren was meticulously neat in every other room, in the bathroom she was a slob. Clumps of blue toothpaste sculpture pocked the sink. The mirror was spotted and smeared. Fingernail clippings crouched in the corners of the countertop. Strands of dental floss draped the edge of the wastebasket and curled on the carpet where Wren had carelessly tossed them after use. They looked like long white hairs, as if Edgar Winter had spent a few bad nights on the floor here.

I picked up Wren's wire hairbrush and started pulling out the hairs that were packed into it. I imagined Kate unpacking the brush in her Omaha kitchen, seeing Wren's hairs and starting to sob, collapsing against the immaculate countertop. As I plucked the clumps of hair from between the bristles of the brush, I thought of Robby, how when we kissed a few wild strands of my long hair would always somehow end up in our mouths. We'd still be kissing as I pulled them out and we could feel each hair slicing across out lips and tongues like thin wires and we'd go right on mashing our faces together as if nothing could be more important to our lives, our continued existence, than the endless kiss.

'How's it going?' Kate asked, startling me.

'Fine.' I tossed the hairbrush into the box and started stacking the Kleenex box and tissue roll.

'I could really use some aspirin,' Kate said.

I opened the medicine cabinet and handed her Wren's Tylenol. She tapped a couple out and swallowed them dry.

I stooped down and opened the cupboard under the sink. I'd never looked there before. An ancient curling iron I'd never seen Wren use was wrapped in its cord. The rest of the stuff was scattered about: an empty box with a disposable douche, spilled Q-Tips, three bars of strawberry-scented glycerin soap. A silver chain bracelet. A pewter earring shaped like a panda bear. And way in the back corner past the pipes and the Comet and the petrified sponge, a box of some kind of denture adhesive. I pulled it out and read the label. I must have been staring at it for a while, because Kate finally touched me on the shoulder.

'She didn't tell you?'

'What? Tell me what?'

Kate sat on the toilet lid. 'That girl, she loved to have secrets.'

'What secrets?'

'Wren wore dentures. Up here.' Kate curled back her upper lip and tapped her front teeth. 'Just a partial. Four teeth.'

I stared at the package. DenturKleen. 'Wren never told me.'

'I'm not surprised,' Kate said. 'She never told anyone anything important.'

'I don't understand,' I said slowly, stupidly. 'Her teeth came out? All the way out of her mouth?'

'Just those four. Had them knocked right out of her mouth. She almost choked on one of them. Lodged down her throat.' She picked up a stiff washcloth from the floor and began neatly folding it.

'How'd it happen?' I asked. 'A car accident?'

'That husband of hers.' Kate shook her head. 'The things he got her into.'

I expected her to say more, but she didn't. She just shook her head again, as if remembering Wren's mysterious husband, the questionable things he got her into. Oddly, she didn't seem angry at him. I was about to ask for details, when Mrs. Naughton appeared, an empty box in each hand and one under each arm.

'We move the party in here?' she asked.

'I was looking for aspirin,' Kate explained. 'I'm afraid I had one too many drinks on the airplane. I hope you don't mind, but I feel a little drunk.'

'Damn right I mind,' Mrs. Naughton said, dropping her load of boxes right there in the hallway. 'A little drunk is no good. You need to feel a lot drunk. Now that's something I do even better than folding boxes.' And she took off, kicking aside the boxes on her way out of the apartment.

I picked up two of the boxes and Kate grabbed the other two. We went into Wren's bedroom. This room was more like an office with a bed. Most of the room was dominated by the desk, four-drawer filing cabinet, the Apple computer, the bookshelves crammed with thick volumes. Wherever there was floor space against a wall, a stack of books grew three feet high like a well-tended garden.

On top of Wren's desk was a large open book. It was one of Wren's many art books and the page was open to a photograph of a bronze sculpture. Small yellow Post-It notes were stuck to the page all around the photo, almost obscuring it. Each note was crammed with Wren's tiny erratic handwriting that if you squinted looked like barbed wire. I peeled a few sticky notes away to better see the photo. The sculpture was of a nude seated woman, she looked old, with saggy breasts and a thick waist. Her head was bent down at an awkward angle, as if she were ashamed, yet her one arm is behind her back as if she weren't ashamed at all. It was hard to tell because of the angle of the photo, but it looked as if she might even be smiling. The sculpture was by Auguste Rodin and was en-titled, 'She Who Was the Helmet-Maker's Beautiful Wife.' The sticky yellow note beside her breast said 'see The Gates of Hell.' I closed the book and tossed it on the bed.

I pulled open the top drawer of the file cabinet, grabbed a handful of hanging files, and laid them into one of the boxes. Each file folder was neatly labeled. She had one for each course she had ever taken, all the handouts for the course, her papers, her notes.

'You know,' Kate said, opening Wren's underwear drawer, 'I didn't plan on roping you into this. I thought I could do it myself. Come here, pack everything.'

'Don't be silly, Kate. I'm glad to help.'

'Wren had spoken of you often.'

'You too,' I lied. When Wren did speak of her parents, it was in positive terms, but now that I thought of it, she rarely spoke of them as individuals, always as 'my par-ents', never as 'my mom' or 'my dad'.

'Jim would have been here,' Kate said. 'If he could have.'

'Of course he would,' I said. But I couldn't help but

wonder what kind of creep would let his wife do this heart-wrenching duty alone. I emptied another file drawer. This one contained bills to be paid, receipts, bank statements. The last two drawers were filled with essays and articles Wren had written about anything that popped into her head. Some had been published and there were copies of the magazines or tearsheets with the printed article. But most of the articles were in red folders with tabs that designated them as being for her magazine, the one she planned to start in a couple of years. She'd been stockpiling articles the way enemy nations hoard weapons. I packed them neatly into the cardboard box, thinking what a shame it was no one would ever read them. They were to be entombed in a dark attic in Omaha. Maybe in a few months or a year I'd write to Kate and suggest she send the articles out. Maybe knowing her daughter's words and thoughts still lived would comfort her. Maybe it would sadden her more. I probably wouldn't write anyway.

Kate made a noise, like a stifled whimper.

'Kate?' I asked, turning toward her. 'You okay?'

She was staring at the bedstand that held the alarm clock/radio, the reading lamp, a glass of water with air bubbles in it from sitting there for a few days, and the combination telephone/answering machine. The red light on the answering machine was blinking.

'Should I play it?' she asked. I was the only other person in the room, but she didn't seem to be talking to me. So I didn't say anything.

She sat on the edge of the bed, absently pushing the Rodin book aside. She stabbed one of the buttons. A faint whir sounded as the tape rewound. I'd heard Wren play her messages often enough to know that this machine didn't play the prerecorded message, so I was grateful we weren't going to hear Wren's chipper voice announcing, 'If you don't know what this is or what to do, I don't want to talk to you anyway. Bye.'

The first voice caught me by surprise. It was mine.

'Wren, it's Luna. I got your message about being in jail. I hope this is a joke because I'm too damn tired to fuck around tonight. Wren? Pick up, damn it.' Then I heard myself sigh. 'Okay, I'm going over to the police station. You'd better be there.'

I was embarrassed. I shrugged at Kate, 'I don't know if you heard about that, I mean, it was all a misunderstanding—'

Beep.

Kate waved me to silence.

The next voice was an unfamiliar woman with a very business-like but friendly tone: 'Ms. Caldwell, this is Linda Marley at *Orange County Today*. I just want to confirm your interview appointment with the magazine for next week. We have all read your sample articles and are most impressed. Please call me back at area code 714-555-4200, extension 356. Airline reservations have already been made in your name. I look forward to hearing from you and especially to meeting you. Good-bye.'

'She had a job offer?' Kate asked.

'Well, an interview.'

'It sounded like they'd already made up their minds.' Kate stood up with renewed energy, as if she expected Wren to come walking into the room and we would all go out for lunch and celebrate the new job. She picked up a pair of Wren's butt-floss panties and folded them twice like a doily.

I kept emptying the file drawers, packing folders against folders. There was more output in these folders than I imagined possible for one person. Wren had already accomplished more than I ever would in my whole life. She had a family and friends and a job interview. Even dead her future looked brighter than mine.

I realized my jealousy was irrational, so I tried to focus on some other aspect of Wren. I visualized her without her front teeth. When she spoke, her tongue would flap helplessly against her gum making her sound like Elmer Fudd. This visualization was a technique I'd learned from one of those self-help books. Okay, I know that they're ridiculous and that people who read them are pathetic and deserve both our pity and contempt and maybe a sharp rap against the skull with a brick. Yet, for a while after Robby and I broke up, I couldn't read enough of them. They're addictive. As long as you're reading one, you have this overwhelming sense of power, as if you really can overcome billions of years of cosmic determinism and change your life. They made you feel powerful, like you could crush a lump of coal into a diamond. My first book was, of course, on breaking up. It had the sensitive title of *Splitsville: A Bad Place to Visit, How Not to Live There*. Some of the advice was pretty standard, like don't listen to sad songs about people being dumped on. Until my divorce I never realized how many songs there were about splitting up. It's weird how lyrics that used to sound so unbearably cornball suddenly seem keenly insightful. Here's another helpful hint from the book: change the color of your toilet paper, the brand of your toothpaste, even the flavor of ice cream you buy. These are emotional time bombs constructed from shrapnel of selective memories of good times that will explode and shred you into weeping, writhing depression. After I finished all the breaking-up books I could find, I started in on self-esteem. Eventually I was reading books on problems I didn't have, male menopause, manic-depression, personal hygiene disorders, fear of the number 3. They were all filled with such hope that they made me hopeful too.

I stuffed another batch of folders into the box. Kate was folding skimpy panties, one at a time. I wondered if anyone was over at Esther's place, washing her dishes, folding her underwear.

'Kate,' I said, 'what happened with Wren's husband?'

'What do you mean?'

'You know, him being in jail and all. Did it have something to do with Wren losing her teeth? Is that what happened?'

'Now that's a story.'

'It is?' I encouraged her.

'Byron.' She shook her head again. 'That Byron.'

I leaned forward anxiously. 'What about Byron?'

'Okay, ladies,' Mrs. Naughton shouted as she huffed down the hallway. 'Prepare for some serious guzzling.' She held up two bottles of white wine by their necks, one in each hand like a proud hunter who'd just bagged an especially elusive prey. 'As my daughter says, let's party till we puke. Follow me. I got a nose for this kind of thing.'

I was more interested in hearing about Wren's mysterious husband and her missing teeth. But Kate closed the dresser drawer with a polite smile and followed Mrs. Naughton down the hall. I sat on the edge of Wren's bed, just where she'd sat that night she'd put on the sex show for me. Where did she ever come up with ideas like that? Where did she get the guts to do them?

Compared to Wren what had I done with my life? I'd married a man I'd loved, then spent the next ten years imitating his life. He'd gone to graduate school, so I went. He studied English, so did I. He taught, so would I. Sometimes I'd take a class that Robby had already taken and the professor would ask about Robby. I'd feel like I was a little sister following her big brother through high school. Robby had never pushed me into any of these decisions, I'd made them freely. It's just that I'd never been as self-motivated as Robby. When I'd see how excited he was about what he did, I figured maybe if I did it too I'd get excited about doing something. Maybe it had worked too, it was hard to judge sitting here with a bullet tunnel through my chest, on the bed of my dead best friend, her mother and her landlady getting smashed in the next room.

*   *   *   *   *

84

Mrs. Naughton was mixing Black Russians when I entered the living room. She wasn't using any kind of measuring glass. 'Here you go, Kate,' she said, pouring vodka with one hand and Kahlúa with the other. She swirled the mixture with her finger and handed it to Kate. 'Pardon the ham hocks.'

We each had four of those Black Russians. Kate didn't seem any the worse for them, though she spoke a little more slowly. Mrs. Naughton kept up a never-ending stream of chatter about the tenants from the various buildings she'd managed, their sexual perversions, the criminal activities. She'd been writing a book, an autobiography about all these places. 'I talked to Wren once about it, shot some ideas past her. I tried to get her to help me write it but, hell, she had so much work to do. She did give me some pointers though, you know, on how to structure the story and stuff.' She gulped down the rest of her drink. 'I'm calling the book, *Roomers Flying*. Get it? Like that old saying about rumors flying, only I have the rumors spelled like a room in a house, you know, roomers. What do you think? Catchy or what?'

'I'd buy it,' Kate said.

'Me too,' I said. My tongue tingled as if it were asleep and it hurt to talk, to have my tongue touch my teeth. A practical reason to be able to take out your front teeth. I curled my lip over my top teeth to simulate having no teeth.

'You lushes could use some music,' Mrs. Naughton said. 'Luna, why don't you do the honors.'

'Sure.' I walked over to Wren's CD player and pressed the Play button. Wren always had something on the player. I expected Paul Simon's music to start, but that's not what she had on. A woman's voice twanged out 'Walkin' After Midnight'.

'Oh, I know her,' Kate said. 'I can't remember her name.'

'Patsy Cline,' Mrs. Naughton said.

'Yes. Yes. I saw that movie about her.'

'*Sweet Dreams*,' I said.

'That's right,' Kate said. 'With that girl, that blond girl from *King Kong*. What's her name?'

Now, I knew the actress's name as well as I knew my own, I'd seen every movie she'd ever been in. But for some reason I couldn't remember it either. I pictured her face on the screen, trying to see the credits.

'Damn it,' Mrs. Naughton said, tearing the seal from a fresh bottle of vodka. 'I know her name. She was in *Tootsie*, remember?'

'And *Francis*,' I said. 'It's Jessica. Jessica something.'

'That's it,' Kate said. 'Jessica.'

'Jessica what?'

'Goddamn it,' Mrs. Naughton spat. 'Not remembering is driving me crazy. I mean, I probably know more about her than I do my own daughter. She's the one married to that Shepherd guy.'

'The playwright,' I added.

'The hunk,' Mrs. Naughton said. 'You see him in *The Right Stuff*. Jesus, I rent that movie every so often, then just fast forward to the parts he's in. Even those crooked teeth get me going.'

'Jessica. Jessica.' Kate sipped her drink and concentrated. 'Jessica something.'

'Hahn?' Mrs. Naughton said.

'No,' I said. 'That's the girl Jim Bakker seduced. The one who got her breasts enlarged and stayed at the Playboy mansion.'

'Jessica Savage?' Kate said.

I shook my head. 'Anchor woman who took cocaine and drowned in a car accident.'

'I can't think of any more Jessicas,' Kate said.

'Jessica Walters,' Mrs. Naughton said, but immediately dismissed it. 'Nah, she's the one who comes after Clint Eastwood in *Play Misty for Me*.' Mrs. Naughton slapped herself briskly. 'Goddamn it, she was also in that Nazi thing, *The Music Box*.'

I went over to the CD player and picked up the empty plastic case. It wasn't the soundtrack. The cover photo was of Patsy Cline, a round-faced woman with short permed hair wearing a blue scarf tied around her neck cowgirl style. She wore a cowgirl outfit, black with long yellow fringes and what seemed like embroidered roses on either lapel. She looked like somebody's mother all dressed up for the weekly square dance.

'Doesn't say anything about the movie,' I said.

'Let me see that,' Mrs. Naughton said.

I carried the case over to her. She stared at it awhile. 'The thing about the movie, the thing that got me,' she said. She stopped, just staring at the photo of Patsy Cline. I thought she would wither, slap herself again, or start crying.

'What about the movie?' I asked. 'What got you?'

Mrs. Naughton looked up. 'Well, just look at this photo, I mean the way Patsy Cline really looked. Now listen to her songs.' She paused so we could listen to a few lines from 'I Fall to Pieces'. 'I mean, these are all songs about getting dumped, right? And you look at this photo and you know this woman knows a lot about getting dumped. She's pleasant enough, but that hair alone, Jesus. But in the movie, that woman who played Patsy, that Jessica something. Can you imagine any guy leaving her. I mean, she's the one you'd leave Patsy Cline *for*. You see my point? I'm watching this movie thinking, give me a fucking break here. She was a good actress and all, this Jessica woman, but I don't buy this little twerpy Ed Harris guy leaving her. I think he'd kiss her ass every night, happy to have her. See what I'm saying?'

'Lange,' Kate said. 'Her name's Jessica Lange.'

'Yes!' I said, feeling a sudden relief. 'Jessica Lange.'

'Bless you, woman.' Mrs. Naughton took Kate's glass. 'You just won yourself another Black Russian.'

'I think I've had enough. I still have a flight to catch this afternoon. We have so much to do yet.'

Mrs. Naughton ignored Kate's protest and handed her the drink. 'First thing we need to do is kick Patsy's sad ass out of this room.' She stood up and marched to the CD player, fingered through the CDs, found one, ejected Patsy, and injected her selection. She cranked up the volume knob. The speakers boomed with a chorus of women's voices. Mrs. Naughton threw her hands up into the air and did a dance-shuffle across the carpet that looked like Topol singing 'If I Were a Rich Man' in *Fiddler on the Roof*. 'It's Melanie,' she said. 'You remember Melanie, don't you?'

I recognized the song. Something about 'candles in the rain'. Melanie was one of those folk-rock singers with a trembling urgency in her voice as if she had to get this song out with her last ounce of life, after which she would throw herself off a cliff. This song was very upbeat, though, about people coming together to love each other and fight the darkness. I asked, 'Is this about the Kent State shootings or the Chicago Democratic Convention?'

'Woodstock,' Mrs. Naughton said.

'You sure?'

'I was there.' She smiled. 'Yeah, I know it's hard to believe. I wasn't always me, you know.'

That struck me as a funny thing to say. *I wasn't always me, you know*. I looked at her, trying to imagine her at Woodstock. Maybe she was one of those naked women with painted peace symbols on her breasts and buttocks. Maybe she looked like that Rodin statue.

Suddenly Mrs. Naughton started to sing along with the song and do her *Fiddler* dance again. She made us sing along too. When the song was over she played it again and she stood in front of us like a conductor and we sang along again.

If this had been a movie or something, this part would come at the end, the part where we all bonded together, one of those Women Across Generations things, Sisters Under the Skin. But that's not how it really felt. There was no real camaraderie here, no sisterhood. It was just three lonely women getting drunk, singing off-key, each locked in a bubble with their own desperate thoughts.

When we were done singing, we heard a knock at the open front door. A skinny boy about twenty slouched nervously in the doorway. 'Excuse me, Mrs. Naughton,' he said. 'I need to sign out the vacuum cleaner. They said you had the key.'

She tossed him the big brass ring of keys. He stuck his hand out to catch them, but when he saw how many there were and how fast they were flying at him, he pulled his hand away and let the keys fall at his feet. He stooped over and picked them up. 'Thanks, Mrs. Naughton.' He looked at each of us as if he'd just interrupted a witch's coven, then left.

'Good kid,' Mrs. Naughton said. 'Wish I had a hundred just like him.'

Kate stood up and brushed the lap of her skirt. 'I think I'd better be going now,' she said. 'I don't want to miss my flight. What's the address here so I can call a taxi?'

'What about . . .' I didn't know what to call it. Wren's stuff? Wren's belongings? Wren's life? 'What do you want to do about all this?' I gestured around the room.

She smiled. 'You were such good friends, Luna. You should keep it. I know that's what Wren would have liked.'

'No, I couldn't. I mean it, Kate.' I did mean it too. I didn't want these mementoes of my own failure. The thought of her leaving it with me made me physically ill.

Kate walked over to me and cupped my hands between hers. The sweet scent of Black Russians cloyed the air between us. I felt somehow imprisoned and wanted to pull away from her.

'Luna,' Kate said. 'The reason my husband didn't come with me is because he's in the hospital. Nothing too serious, not a heart attack. Something with his nerves. It happened the day we heard about Wren. We were just getting out of bed when the police called. I was in the shower so Jim took the call. When I got out of the shower he was sitting on the bed weeping. He told me about Wren. We both cried together. Then I stopped crying. Jim didn't. He cried all day. He couldn't stop. I don't mean he couldn't stop feeling the pain or even having tears, I'm talking about huge chest-wrenching sobs. *He could not stop crying.*' She took a deep breath and calmed herself. 'He cracked three ribs just from crying. I had to admit him into the hospital.'

Mrs. Naughton shook her head. 'Poor man. Tragedy.'

'Yes,' Kate said, looking at Mrs. Naughton, then back at me again, her face leaning even closer. 'So you see, despite my devastation at Wren's death, I still have Jim to take care of. I have to think about him now. Looking around this apartment, I see Wren everywhere and it's breaking my heart. Right now, I don't think that's what Jim needs to see. I didn't realize that until now, until standing in these rooms myself.' She released my hands. My knuckles, all the joints hurt. She hadn't held me that tight, yet still each joint ached, as if she'd transferred some bad karma or something. 'That's why I want you to keep everything that's here. I've made arrangements with her bank and insurance company, but other than that everything here has nothing to do with the Wren that Jim and I shared.'

I didn't know what to say to that. What point was there in arguing? 'If that's what you want, Kate,' I said. 'I appreciate the gesture.'

She turned away as if she hadn't heard me and picked up her purse. 'I need to call a taxi.'

'No, of course you won't,' I said. 'I'll drive you to the airport. It's not that far.'

Mrs. Naughton rose from her chair and elbowed me aside. 'Don't be stupid, girl. You're too damn drunk to drive. I'm not.'

She was right about me being drunk. I felt hot and

wobbly, my mouth seemed sticky, like I'd been licking stamps for a few hours. Mrs. Naughton looked as fresh as if she'd been drinking nothing but Kool-Aid for the past two hours.

'One quick piss and we're outta here,' she said, trotting off to the bathroom.

Kate and I hardly spoke while we waited for Mrs. Naughton's return. I felt too drunk, too burdened by the legacy of Wren's possessions. I tried to think of some gracious way to give it all back. But I couldn't.

When Kate and Mrs. Naughton left I went into the bedroom and laid down on the bed. I crossed my hands across my chest in the pose of a corpse ready for viewing. This was a very relaxing position, wasted on the dead. I looked around the room and saw all of the things I'd just inherited, clothes, computer, furniture. A lot of loot. I watched the front door for about twenty minutes, half expecting Wren to walk in, explain how she pulled this hoax off.

When she didn't come in, I opened the Rodin book and looked at the same photograph of 'She Who Was the Helmet-Maker's Beautiful Wife'. I wasn't good at interpreting art, that was Wren's specialty. To me it just looked like a somewhat grotesque woman, maybe something they'd find in the attic of a beautiful dead woman, her personal version of *The Picture of Dorian Gray*.

I closed the book and closed my eyes. I thought about the birds of Guam being airlifted away from home so they could avoid extinction. I must have nodded off because when I opened my eyes, an hour had passed. But my mind was remarkably clear. Without thinking, I reached over, punched the button on the answering machine, and listened to Wren's two messages again. When they were over, I dialed the phone.

'Extension 356,' I said to the receptionist. I listened to the recording of Tracy Chapman's 'Fast Car' while waiting. When Linda Marley announced herself, I said, 'Ms.

Marley, this is Wren Caldwell. I'm so looking forward to interviewing with you. When exactly is my airline reservation?'

6

I was on my first date since taking over Wren's name and so far it wasn't going too well. We were standing in the All-Nite Mini-Mart and my date, Ethan, was arguing with the Asian kid behind the counter.

'Just check in the back, man,' Ethan said.

'There is no need to check in the back, sir.' The kid was straining to be polite. He had dark skin and a slight accent, but I couldn't decide what it was, Korean or Vietnamese, something exotic like that. At the first sound of conflict, I'd drifted to the back of the store, behind the metal greeting-card rack, positioned like an accomplice in a robbery. A fat teenage girl all in denim stood behind me, smoking a cigarette and playing a video game.

'Just check, okay?' Ethan insisted. He showed the kid his little pocket camera. 'I need the two-hundred-speed film. It's dark out, the flash on these cheapies isn't worth shit.'

'Sir, we are out. Look, the hook is empty.'

The boy pointed at the silver hook sticking out of the blue pegboard behind him. All around that empty hook were other hooks that had little yellow boxes of film. But not the kind Ethan wanted. He wanted special film so he could take snapshots of our date, though he hadn't told me yet where we were going.

I immersed myself in the dusty greeting cards, pretending I was here on important business, a last-minute card for a terminally sick friend. Slowly I turned the

93

wobbly rack, studying each colorful drawing, each sentiment or joke. Anything to isolate myself from the turmoil up front. Perhaps I could find a nice card for my new step-mom, though Hallmark seemed woefully lacking anything that started, 'On the occasion of your becoming tribal weasel whacker . . .'

'Look, man, just check for me, okay?' Ethan slid a five-dollar bill across the counter. 'Okay?'

The boy frowned at the bill with contempt. His thin face tightened, somehow got thinner. 'Sir, there is no film in the back. Please try another store.'

'That's bullshit, man. Okay? I used to work in one of these stores. We kept lots of stuff in the back. All kinds of shit. You're just too fucking lazy, man.' Ethan crumpled his five dollars in his fist and I flashed on Wren's blue panties in her fist. The fat girl behind me looked around from her video game at the fuss, lighting a fresh cigarette, sizing the situation up like a veteran street cop. 'Asshole,' she muttered and returned to the game.

The Asian boy kept a stiff but serene stare. He said nothing. I admired his composure in the face of Ethan's older, much larger presence. Ethan had to be at least twenty-eight, six feet two inches, and 190 pounds. The kid was six inches shorter and half the weight. Maybe his serenity came from generations of zen devotees. Maybe he had his hand on a shotgun under the counter. Double-barreled zen.

Ethan wouldn't accept the kid's attitude. 'So, what're you saying, man?' You're not even going to look, to fucking look, for chrissake?'

'No, sir, there is nothing to look for.'

'You dumb fuck. You lazy dumb fuck.'

'Fuck you too, sir,' the kid said.

*   *   *   *   *

In the car, Ethan was in a good mood. He seemed to admire the kid too, held no grudge. 'Kid had a mouth on him, didn't he?'

'Yours wasn't exactly idle.'

He chuckled. 'Yeah, well, that's my job. Occupational hazard.'

Ethan was a comedian, a stand-up comic who worked the local clubs, sometimes traveled to Los Angeles or San Francisco to do his act. I found all this out the first half hour I met him, which was two days ago when I'd moved into my new apartment. He lived in the apartment above me and had offered to help me unload the U-Haul trailer that contained all of Wren's stuff. Since then he'd dropped by a few times to help me arrange furniture, hang prints, draw maps to grocery stores. He talked a lot and didn't seem to mind that I didn't, which made him pretty good company at times.

'Wren,' he said. 'Hey, Wren.'

I looked over at him and he snapped my picture. The tiny flash made me blink. I rubbed my eyes. He wedged the wallet-sized camera next to the handbrake between us. 'Something to show our grandkids,' he chuckled.

It's much easier than you think becoming someone else. First of all, you get used to the name right away. It's not like in the movies or on TV when someone is undercover or pretending to be someone else and a guy calls them by their pretend name and they don't answer at first because they forgot that's who they now are. Someone calls me Wren, I respond immediately. Maybe even faster than I did when people used to call me Luna.

The mundane details of life swapping were pretty simple. I found Wren's birth certificate when I was packing up her files. I took it down to the DMV, told them I'd lost my driver's license, and had them reissue a new one, this one with Wren's name and my photo. After that I was able to get a passport, credit cards, and anything else I needed. Once I saw how easy it was, I was surprised more people, when their lives got too complex or disappointing, didn't just up and become someone else.

In the movies when someone wants to disappear, they fake their deaths in a flaming car crash or something. I didn't have to go that far. As far as I could tell, I'd disappeared the day Robby and I split up. Now all I had to do was fake my life.

A couple weeks ago, I'd flown down to Orange County for the job interview. Wren's mother was right, it was just a formality. They'd already made up their minds they wanted to hire Wren. They took me to lunch and dinner and put me up at the fancy Ritz-Carlton Hotel. They told me the magazine had a rich new owner and he had great plans for *Orange Coast Today*. He wanted a whole new look, a whole new tone. He'd fired half of the old staff the day after he bought it. Apparently I was the first personnel step in achieving this new image, though what the new look and image were to be was never explained to me. The day I interviewed, the new owner, Jonathan Krieg, still hadn't moved from New York, so I never did meet him. Everyone spoke about him with a certain fearful reverence, as if they weren't sure what he was up to, how to please him. No one there had actually met him yet, though we'd all read about him before in newspapers and magazines. I tried to look interested, though I didn't much care about any of that. I cared that my starting salary was $35,000, eight grand more than I would have made as a teacher, even if I'd been able to be hired as one.

'Did I embarrass you back there?' Ethan asked.

'I don't know. A little.' My palms were still sweating. I had the inky tattoo of a cartoon Snoopy across my fingers where I'd clutched a birthday card too tightly.

'Sorry. That's one of my pet peeves. No one seems to want to do their jobs anymore. The whole world has turned into one big self-service pump. There's no pride. That's why we're getting fucked by the Japanese. It's not just the lower wages, it's pride in what they do. They just make better quality stuff. Everybody over there, no matter how shitty the job, does it like his life depended on it. I saw this thing on *60 Minutes* about how expensive everything was in Japan. You ever been to Japan?'

'No.'

'Me neither, but coffee costs like five bucks a cup. Anyway, they interview this one guy who owns a little sushi bar or something on some prime real estate in Tokyo. The place is like as big as my kitchen, seats maybe eight people if two of them are amputees. The guy barely scrapes by. They offer the poor schlub a couple million bucks to sell his location. What do you think happens? The guy turns them down. He's like the seventh generation of sushi makers in his family and he likes what he does. He'd rather slice squid than ride around in a limo yakking on his cellular phone. That's what I'm talking about. Pride.'

Ethan was a very handsome man. He was trim and his face was both boyish and rugged. He had a gunslinger's mustache, which didn't go with his face. It made him look as if he were playing grown-up. The blond hairs hung over his upper lip and I felt an overpowering urge to trim them back. Even though he acted like a jerk with that kid, I liked that he didn't stay mad. His cheerfulness made me feel optimistic. I couldn't decide whether or not I was attracted to him.

'So, Wren,' he said, 'what exactly do you do at the magazine?'

'I haven't started yet,' I told him. 'I start tomorrow.'

'Are you nervous?'

'No. I figure there's plenty of time for a breakdown once they tell me what my duties are.' I really wasn't nervous. I had dozens of articles already written by Wren. I figured I could feed some of them to the magazine until I learned how to do the job properly.

'I always wanted to write,' he confessed. 'I mean, I write now, all my own material, my act. But I'd like to write, you know, something bigger.'

'A novel?'

He shrugged. 'Yeah. Or a screenplay.'

'With you as the star, right?'

He looked over at me and grinned. 'Sure. Why the hell not? Who else?'

I didn't say anything. I watched the traffic slow for the red light. The driver of the car in front of us tossed a cigarette out his window. It bounced off the fender of the car beside him. The other driver honked angrily, but the guy who'd thrown the cigarette just rolled up his window and ignored him.

Ethan began fidgeting during the silence. Quiet seemed to upset him. 'What will you be doing when you aren't working at the magazine?'

'You mean like hobbies?'

'Hobbies, sports, extra-curricular activities. Saving the whales, preventing fluoridation, assassinating a major political figure, stuff like that.'

I had to think for a moment. Should I tell him my interests or Wren's? Just how far in-character should I go? Wren liked to ski, I'd never been skiing in my life. Wren knew how to make pottery, work a loom, had parachuted from an airplane. I knew how to shop for bargains, how to love Robby.

'Jeez, I didn't mean to ask such a toughie. Would the contestant like another minute to think over her answer.' He started humming the theme to the *Jeopardy* game show.

'I'm sorry. I'm still a little disoriented from moving.'

'Believe me, whatever you enjoyed doing up in Oregon, you'll enjoy it even more down here. This is a great place.'

'I like it so far.'

'You'll like it even more after tonight.'

He didn't say it in a suggestive way, but suddenly I realized that he thought we might have sex tonight. Not that he expected it, but he hoped. That meant at some point tonight he would make his move. Except for one brief infidelity five years ago, I hadn't had sex with anyone but Robby in ten years. My dating sensors were weak, but now they started kicking in, beeping at certain phrases, looks. Later, he

98

would try to kiss me, then he would want to go from there. I had no idea yet what I would say or do.

He pulled into a parking lot and I saw the place we were going: The Laff Stop. A comedy nightclub.

'I thought you might enjoy some laughs. They have three comics each show. I've played here a few times.'

The parking lot was full so we parked on the street. The nearby residences were a little run-down, the yards brown and patchy, the windows protected by black bars. This looked like a high-crime area.

We stood in line at the ticket booth outside. I expected to hear large dogs barking in the distance, but all I heard was traffic whooshing by and some kind of bird half crying, half whistling. Its call was very regular, like a heartbeat.

'I did a gig with one of the guys we're seeing tonight. He's funny.' He said this in a grudging way that suggested he was so-so funny, not as funny as Ethan.

I was trying to figure out what kind of bird would make that kind of sound when Ethan spun around and flashed another photo. My eyes bled white and I blinked furiously.

'Just one more, Zsa Zsa, please,' Ethan joked. The people in line behind us laughed.

My blinking slowed down until I was now blinking in rhythm with that bird's cries. I tried to break the rhythm but it was hard to do. I got the feeling that the bird was mimicking me now, purposely crying out whenever I blinked. Ethan said something but I was still concentrating on stopping myself from blinking in time with the bird's piercing shrieks. Finally the bird stopped and I felt an enormous relief.

I clutched Ethan's arm. 'You promise not to take any more photos and I promise not to chew your face off. Deal?'

'Deal, Monty.' He grinned and pocketed his camera. 'I'm out of film anyway.'

So this is dating, I thought.

*   *   *   *   *

'You want to come in?' I asked after unlocking my apartment door.

'Sure,' he said, following me inside.

The apartment was larger than I needed. It had two master bedrooms, one of which I would have to rent out within the month if I was going to be able to keep paying the rent. I'd looked for a one-bedroom place, but the rents in Orange County were so high that I would have had to live someplace where everyone parked their cars on the lawn and the street lamps were always shot out. Linda Marley, the associate editor at the magazine, suggested I find a roommate, that's what a lot of young divorced women did. There were roommate services or I could just advertise in the paper, she'd said. After calculating my monthly budget, I saw the wisdom of her advice. But the idea bothered me, to be thirty years old and still living with a nonromantic roommate. It seemed too much like I was backsliding into adolescence rather than evolving into adulthood where one was supposed to be in charge of one's life.

'What do you do, Ethan?' I called from the kitchen while I poured a couple glasses of wine.

He followed me into the kitchen. 'You mean hobbies?'

'No, I mean occupation. Job security, dental insurance, that sort of thing.'

He gave me a hurt look. 'Oh, you mean what do I do in *real* life.'

I hadn't meant to insult him, but I couldn't imagine him making enough money doing his comedy act to support himself. 'Look, I don't know much about the comedy business. I didn't mean anything.'

'I buy textbooks.'

I handed him a glass of white wine. 'Sounds interesting.'

'Does it? Does it sound interesting to travel around to all the colleges and universities and buy back all the textbooks from snooty teachers who got the books free from the publisher anyway. A lot of them order every free copy they can so they can sell them to me at the end of the semester. Does it really sound all that fucking interesting?'

'You do make it sound pretty glamorous.'

He laughed. 'Hey, it pays the rent. That's what a job's supposed to do, right? Plus, I make some pretty good change from doing my act. That's where my future is, the real money. That's my career.'

He had performed some of his act for me that first night. His specialty was impressions of famous rock stars. He'd go up on stage with his guitar and sing their songs, only he'd substitute his own verses. Like, he did the Rolling Stones' 'Sympathy for the Devil', only his version was 'Sympathy for the Yentl'. He had a nice voice and he was moderately funny.

'I'm obsessed,' he said, finishing his wine quickly. 'I'm obsessed with Johnny Carson.'

I poured more wine into his glass. He didn't seem drunk, although along with the cover charge at the Laff Stop, they enforced a two-drink minimum. I was feeling a little light-headed myself. 'Obsessed with Johnny Carson,' I said. 'Sounds like a headline in the *National Enquirer*.'

'My whole life sounds like a headline in the *National Enquirer*. "One-Headed Boy Graduates College, With C Average! Gets Lousy Job! Parents Say: 'We Told Him So.'" But Johnny Carson, man. I watch his show every night, even the reruns. I tape them and watch them again. I'm determined to get on his show. That's all I need, all it would take. One shot. You know how frustrating it is to see guys who aren't nearly as funny get all that exposure. I mean, Johnny Carson is the ticket. He's the end of the rainbow.'

I didn't know how to respond. I said, 'There's always David Letterman.'

'No, no, no.' He shook his head vigorously, like a dog just out of water. 'David Letterman dominates his show too much. Even if you are funny people think it's because of Dave. He steps on your lines, then gets all the credit for any laughs. With Johnny, you're out there on your own. If you're funny there, man, he gives you that okay sign, then you know you're on your way.' He circled his thumb and finger into an okay sign.

'Do you have an agent or something? Can't you get an audition?'

'You don't audition for Johnny Carson. His scouts find you. They go out to all the clubs and look for talent to book. They're like talent ninjas, man. That's why I keep playing all the local joints. I figure one day they'll be there on the same night I am.'

I didn't ask the obvious: what if they already had been?

'I've changed my act so many times. I used to do the straight kind, you know, where you go up and talk about your crummy childhood and what well-meaning jerks your folks were. I mean, Jay Leno made a fortune doing that kinda crap. But then it seemed like all the hot acts were doing some crazy persona, screaming at the audience and shit like Sam Kennison, so I switched and did that for a while. I must've scrapped my act a dozen times. I mean, I follow the trends and when something is hot, I do it. And I'm just as funny as the other guys. I just don't understand what I'm doing wrong.'

A fragile silence enveloped us. The intimacy of his frustration made me uncomfortable. I had no answers.

'Just be yourself,' I advised.

*　　*　　*　　*　　*

We were naked. I'm not sure how it happened. The usual way, I guess, a button here, a kiss, another button. All along I was thinking that this wasn't such a wise decision.

I tasted the wine on his lips. He licked my teeth.

Where had this started? That first kiss, the one in the kitchen. I'd gone back for another bottle of wine but there wasn't one. He said he had some in his apartment. That's when I remembered that the wine we'd just finished had been his too. He'd brought it up that first day after we'd moved everything in. I guess I felt guilty for forgetting, so when he leaned across the counter to kiss me, I let him.

'Excuse me,' I'd said after the kiss.

'Too much tongue?' he joked.

I smiled. 'No, it was fine. I just have to go to the bathroom.'

'My kisses often have that effect on women.'

'I'll be right back.' I hurried off into my bedroom and closed the door. I grabbed the phone and carried it into the bathroom. Seeing the toilet, I realized I really did have to go after all, so I pulled up my skirt and pulled down my panties and peed while I dialed.

'Hello?' A woman's voice, throaty with a hint of Louisiana bayou still clinging to the vowels.

'Hi, Dr. Jaspers, this is Luna.' This was the first time I'd actually talked to her since Robby moved in with her. I wasn't sure what to call her. The last time I'd seen her she had been my professor, and unlike some of the other faculty, she preferred her full title. Still, it seemed ludicrous to call a woman who shared your husband's penis Dr. Jaspers.

'Hello, Luna, how are you?' She sounded honestly concerned.

'Fine.'

'Your health back to normal?'

'Just a couple scars. I've had to postpone swimming the English Channel this year, but otherwise I'm fine.'

'Good.' She said it in a solid, final way, like she meant to say 'Good for you, Luna, we're all proud of you.' I could see her small face pinched with concentration. She was barely five feet tall with thick kinky black hair that hung past her shoulders and made her look more like an Israeli freedom fighter than a professor.

'Is Robby there?' I sounded like I was in high school

talking to someone's mother. Can Robby come out and play?

'Hang on,' she said, 'I'll get him.'

Why was I calling him? What would I say? I wanted to hang up, but it was too late. I had to try to save as much face as possible. At least he didn't know where I was. I'd turned in forwarding address cards to the post office for both Wren's mail and mine. Then I'd phoned Robby and given him my dad's address in Dallas so he could send me the final divorce papers. I never did finish my Thomas Pynchon thesis, never did collect my master's degree. That was okay, because now I had Wren's three master's degrees.

The last thing I did as Luna Devon was to visit Esther's grave. I'd heard that her mother had been too ill with cancer to travel, so one of her brothers, an architect from Phoenix, had flown in, buried her, and put the house up for sale. Her headstone was small but somehow loving. Her name was at the top, under which was the date of her birth and the date of her death. Then there was a long passage in Hebrew, which I couldn't read. I kneeled down and touched the elaborate grooved letters, ran my fingertips along the rough crevices. I liked the way they felt.

'Hey, Luna, where are you?' Robby asked. He sounded sleepy, as if he'd just woken up. I looked at my watch. 11:37 P.M. Not that late for a Saturday night.

'Did I wake you?'

'No, I was just reading Tom Robbins's new novel.'

'I thought the novel was dead.'

'This one's driving the final nail in the coffin.'

I blew a loud raspberry into the phone. That's what I always did when he made those superior pronouncements about things.

He laughed. 'I've always appreciated your articulateness.'

I didn't know what else to say. I didn't want to tell him what I was up to, how I'd taken over Wren's life. I didn't want to tell him there was a man in the next room waiting to jam his tongue into my mouth. I didn't want advice or absolution, I was listening for something in his tone, the way I imagined a medicine man would look to the wind for signs. I too was looking for some sign. I just didn't know what it was. If this were junior high school, I'd have played a sentimental song over the phone for him, something like the Eagles' 'I Can't Tell You Why'. Then, when the song was over, I'd hang up and wait for him to call me back and say sweet things.

'You in Dallas?' he asked.

'Yes. Visiting Dad.'

'How's he doing?'

I told him about stepmom.

'Jesus,' he said, laughing. 'And to think I've been doing it all these years for free.'

I heard Dr. Jasper's husky voice in the background. 'She sounded worried, Robby. Ask her if she's okay.'

'You okay, Luna?' Robby asked.

I realized there was more concern in Dr. Jasper's whispered voice than in Robby's. It was too humiliating to have your ex-husband's new lover be so caring.

'Gotta go,' I said quickly, choking up.

'No, wait, Luna. Wait.'

'Gotta go . . .' I hung up.

There was no fucking sign. Just me being pathetic. I swallowed whatever emotion had bubbled up, washed my face with cold water, and returned to the living room and Ethan.

Which led to more kissing, unbuttoning, the lights off, and the two of us naked in my bed.

'Ow!' I hollered.

'Jesus!' he hollered back.

He lunged over and snapped on the lamp.

Until now he'd been doing all his foreplay on my right breast, the usual massaging and nipple pinching. Then when we were naked he'd started to suck on my left breast and his nose hit my bullet wound. I don't know how, but I'd forgotten about it. Until his nose probe.

'What happened here?' he asked, looking at my wounded breast, trying not to look too shocked. 'What the hell happened?'

'Hunting accident.'

'You hunt?'

'It was my first time.'

Now that he knew it was a bullet wound, he seemed less repulsed and more fascinated. He leaned closer, touched the edges. 'Does that hurt?'

'No.' It didn't. Actually, it hadn't hurt that much when he'd nosed it, I was more surprised than anything. I'd forgotten about it and now I was naked with some man who would see it. For the first time it occurred to me that every man I ever slept with would see this and ask what happened.

The wound didn't look too bad, just a small crater in the skin and some shiny scar tissue like a glob of melted plastic. Ethan switched off the lamp and lowered his lips to my wound. He kissed the skin all around it, then he kissed the scar. I suppose he was trying to be nice but his actions seemed so studied, like this was something he saw in a movie. Hero slobbers on poor girl's scar.

'Wren,' he whispered. 'Wren.'

'What?' I said.

'Nothing. I just like saying your name. It's poetic.'

That's the kind of guy he was. And maybe he was being sincere. I probably wasn't in a moral position to be judging anyone's honesty.

He kissed a trail down across my ribs and stomach into my thicket of pubic hairs. He nudged my thighs apart. Suddenly he stopped and looked up at me.

'When's the last time you had sex, Wren?'

'Jesus,' I said. 'What kind of question is that?'

He nodded sagely. 'That long, huh?'

I clamped my legs shut. 'Well, if I've waited this long I can wait a little longer.'

He laughed. 'I didn't mean anything by that. It's just that you're so preoccupied, like your head is somewhere else, doing your taxes, cleaning the hair out of your drains. You act like I'm a cop who picked you up for questioning. Relax.' He straightened his back. Looming over me in the dark this way I couldn't see his face clearly. I thought of that man I'd seen with Wren, the two of them hunched over the sofa, his hands clasped to her hips, pushing and pulling. Ethan's hand touched my cheek. 'I mean, if you want me to stop, I'll stop.'

Now I wasn't so sure I wanted to go through with this. He lived in the apartment above me. No matter how things went tonight, location would force us to see a lot of each other. I didn't want to have to start peeking out of my curtain every day to make sure he wasn't around before making a crazy dash for my car.

He leaned over and kissed my lips. His hand slid across my thigh. He whispered, 'Just tell me what you want. Tell me.'

*　　*　　*　　*　　*

The next morning I peeked through the curtains, didn't see Ethan. I made a crazy dash for my car.

7

I'd had my eye on the rearview mirror, looking for the car that had been following me all morning. That's how I thumped into the truck in front of me.

'I just hope you've got insurance, lady,' the man barked, climbing out of his pickup truck and slamming the door.

'I don't think there's any damage,' I said.

Six lanes of cars whooshed by us less than three feet away.

The man tugged his Dodgers cap low on his forehead as if he thought I might try to snatch it. He wore his hat backward, with the bill shading his neck and the little plastic adjustment strip puckering a swatch of skin on his forehead. He walked toward me muttering, 'I need this shit' under his breath. His red hair was long and his bushy beard completely hid his mouth, except for the cigarette that bobbed when he spoke. He wore heavy work boots with rawhide laces and mud caked around the soles. His jeans were faded at the knees, thighs, and crotch. His white T-shirt looked new, though the sleeves had been torn off. Underneath the shrubbery of facial hair, he looked to be about twenty-seven, but there was a rigidness and hostility in his walk that announced to the world that this was how he would be for the rest of his life, take it or leave it.

He ran his hand along the metal rim of the side of the truck bed as he walked toward me. The blue truck was a dented, rusting heap, but that's how it had been long before I'd bumped into it.

'Could be all kinds of damage you can't see,' he said. 'Tension damage to the axle, the frame might be bent. Could be anything.'

This was my first day of work and I was already twenty minutes late. I'd turned the wrong way on Harbor Blvd. and passed a mile's worth of No U-turn signs before being able to swing around again in the right direction. That's when I got distracted by the car in my rearview mirror, the one that had been following me all morning. It had also U-turned. Right now, I couldn't see it anywhere.

'I don't think it could be that serious,' I said. 'it was just a tap.'

'Do you have insurance or not, lady?'

I reached into my purse and pulled out my wallet. I removed the insurance card, which was in Wren's name. 'Right here.'

He reached for it but I stepped back. 'I showed you mine, now you show me yours.'

He gave me a sharp look. I held out my hand palm up, waiting. He plucked his cigarette from his mouth and for a moment I thought he was going to stub it out in my hand. Instead he threw it hard against the pavement. Red sparks bounced up. He didn't step on the butt, just left it lying there, bitter smoke curling up between us.

'You rear-ended *me* lady. That makes the accident your fault. I don't have to show you squat.' He pointed at my Oregon plates. 'In California, the person who caused the accident has to have insurance.'

'Actually, that's not true. Both parties must have insurance and must show their cards. Now, we can exchange this information on our own, or we can call the police and get a legal ruling.' I looked at his muddy plates. 'Your choice, Mr. 2HJY761.'

He gave me a slow-crawl look, his eyes starting at my ankles and slithering up my thighs to my chest and finally my face. This ritual seemed to relax him. He'd checked me out, figured me for just another tight-assed, sexless bitch in a suit who, even if he did somehow get into bed, wouldn't do what he wanted anyway. Now that he could dismiss me as a possible sexual partner, he got down to business. He kneeled down and studied the rear bumper of his car. The only visible mark was a three-inch line where I'd scraped off a little rust. Right next to the scratch was a partially shredded bumper sticker that said: SSDD (Same Shit. Different Day). He straightened up and used his baseball cap to swat the road dust off the knees of his jeans. 'Doesn't look like anything too serious. Guess I could fix it myself.'

I smiled. I never won these kind of arguments with men in pickup trucks or tool belts, so I felt a little cocky. I remembered those two university boys who'd tossed their beer cans at Wren and me, called us lesbos. How nervous I'd been. Now I was standing here with a man who, as a fashion statement, had deliberately torn the sleeves off his T-shirt. And I wasn't nervous at all. Was this how Wren had always felt?

Two young men on bicycles pedaled toward us. Our cars were hugging the right curb, blocking their paths. They were clean-cut, with short hair, white shirts, skinny black ties, dark trousers, and dark shoes. They passed us single file. One of them said, 'Good morning' as they coasted by.

The bearded man shook his head in disgust. 'Fucking Mormons.'

'Jehovah's Witnesses,' I said.

He shot me a dirty look. 'Same difference.' He re-adjusted his baseball cap and climbed back into his truck. He slammed the door and drove away.

I got in my Rabbit and started the engine. I took out some lipstick and pretended to be applying it while I checked my rearview mirror for any signs of the car that had been following me. So far I'd seen it three times this morning, a white Subaru with a bent radio antenna. The first time, it had pulled out of the apartment complex behind me and I only noticed it because it was clean and reminded me I should get my car washed soon. The second time I saw the car was when it exited off the freeway with me. Coincidence, I'd thought. But then, following me down Harbor Blvd. and making the same U-turn, that couldn't be coincidence.

Could it?

In my rearview mirror I watched a red Accord U-turn at the same intersection. A black Nissan did the same. Were they following me too? I looked all around, but still no sign of the white Subaru.

I shook my head. 'Duhhhh,' I said to myself and drove off.

Okay, maybe becoming Wren had made me a little skittish. No one around here knew who I really was, and if they did, they would just bust me, not follow me around. There was no international intrigue here, no mystery. As Wren had often said, I watched too much television.

Could be I was still a little shaken after last night's sexual interlude with Ethan. I even thought that it might be him in the white Subaru, so intoxicated with passion for me that even following me from several car lengths was better than not seeing me at all. Not that I wanted that. Mostly I wanted to forget last night.

'Candles,' Ethan had asked. 'Got any candles?'

'Why?'

'Candlelight would be neat.' He'd sat up in bed, grinning. 'Candles and maybe some music. Very romantic. You got something against romance?'

'My stereo isn't hooked up yet,' I told him.

He frowned. I was frustrating his timing. The stage wasn't properly set for sex.

'You got cable?'

'Cable?'

'Cable TV. You've got cable, right?'

I gestured at the decoder box on top of the TV on my dresser.

'Great!' He leapt out of bed and padded to the TV. His

butt was muscular, fuller than Robby's. Hairier too. He turned on the TV, flipped through the stations. 'MTV,' he said, looking smug. 'A little music for me lady.'

The video was old and grainy, Jim Morrison singing 'Don't You Love Her Madly'. Jim's eyes were squinting but expressionless; as if he were thinking about lunch, not love.

'This guy is so cool,' Ethan said, then started singing, '"don't you love her as she's walking out the door . . ."' Suddenly he jumped onto the bed catapulting me a few inches into the air. The covers fell away revealing me in my naked splendor. He shook his head and grinned. 'And me without my camera.'

By now I'd pretty much lost interest in Ethan but still was intent on the sex part. Somehow it seemed like a good initiation into my new life. Not that I wanted a new life of serial meaningless casual affairs. But it was nice to know that I could if I wanted. That my memories of sex wouldn't always be limited to picturing Robby. Besides, I hadn't had sex in so long, I'd invested too much importance in the act. I didn't want to be one of these bruised women who hoards her sexuality like a precious prize, a jewel to offer up to Mr. Right. When I did meet a guy I really liked, I didn't want to ruin it by putting too much expectation into the sex. I folded my glasses and placed them on Wren's clock/radio.

Ethan was a good lover. He did a variety of things and he did them well. But it all felt too rehearsed, like he was going down a checklist: let's see, we nibbled on the nipple, now let's give her a little finger action. As if this were his comedy act and he had to remember the right order of actions the way he'd remember the order of jokes. The goal for him wasn't to have sex with me, but for me to admire his sexual technique. I was less an object of desire than an audience with a convenient vagina. To him, my moans were applause, my orgasm a standing ovation.

I was surprised by his body. All evening I'd imagined us being the same physical size, even though I knew he

112

was bigger But in bed, I felt his shoulders, his hips, his legs. They made me feel smaller. He was gentle, but the thought kept coming back to me, He could hurt me. If he wanted to, he could hurt me. I'd never had that thought with Robby.

After Ethan ejaculated, he pushed himself up and grinned at me. 'That was soooo good. I thought I was going to pass out.' Then he laughed. 'Something else to tell our grandkids.'

I closed my eyes and pulled the pillow against my face.

'Wren?'

'Hmmm.'

'What're you thinking?'

'I don't know. Nothing.'

'Me too.'

I opened my eyes and lifted my head from the pillow. He was staring at me with doe eyes. I could tell he was about to say something mushy.

I excused myself and went to the bathroom again.

He called after me, 'Some guys make women weak in the knees, I make them weak in the bladder.'

I sat on the edge of the tub and laid my head on my knees.

I am not a mushy person. Declarations of love or friendship usually come from me couched in a joke or said in such ambiguous terms that I might be referring to something else entirely, the bean dip or a cold front from Canada. I know all the psychobabble buzzwords about such behavior, the unconscious fears of rejection and all that crap that college guys who want to go to bed with you use. And it isn't as if I didn't like hearing a little gushing directed towards me, I'd sop it up like most people. It's just that I don't think people know what they're saying sometimes. They think of words as disposable diapers, once used better not to be examined again. As if words were ethereal, airborne spores that can't be seen and therefore demand no allegiance. They don't understand how mere words can embed themselves so deeply. I mean, how was it possible for Robby to assure he loved me every day for ten years, to have said things like 'I want to live my whole life with you' or 'I'd die without you' or 'I'm happy only when I'm with you' and then dump me for a midget Milton scholar who tawks lawk thayat? One day he's gallantly telling me how if we were shipwrecked with a limited supply of food and water, he'd gladly drown himself to save my life, the next day he's waving farewell from someone else's bed. On Monday he'd have sacrificed his life for mine. On Tuesday, it's Hey, babe, you're on your own. Good luck.

What had changed? How had the atoms of our lives come to realign themselves?

This was Robby's explanation: 'It's not that I love her more than you, Luna, it's just different. It's like . . . it's like those fish, those anglerfish. In one species the male is about an inch and a half long, the female is ten inches. The male attaches himself to the female's body and hangs on until eventually his internal organs disintegrate and her system replaces his. He literally can't live without her. He never swims away because his body and hers are one, the tissue is fused. She can even cause him to discharge sperm when she wants. I'm not saying that's what happened with us. Sometimes I think I'm attached to you, sometimes you're attached to me. But I don't think we should be "attached" at all.' Here he wiggled his hands in front of him like two fish swimming parallel. 'Two people should be separate, swimming side by side perhaps. But not attached.'

8

When I pulled into the parking lot there was no sign of a white Subaru with a bent antenna. But I was still a nervous wreck. I hated being late for anything and I was thirty-five minutes late on the very first day of my new job. My stomach churned noisily as I ran into the building, heels popping against the floor like a cap gun. Apparently my Wren-like calm states were only temporary.

'Hi,' I puffed to the receptionist. 'I'm late.'

'Oh, hi.' She stood up and shook my hand. We'd met when I'd interviewed but I couldn't remember her name. 'I guess I'm your official welcoming party.'

'I'm sorry, I don't remember your name.'

'Billie. Billie Meyers.' Her hair was short and combed straight down, like the early Beatles. Her skin was pale, her lipstick radioactively bright. She wore black jersey pants and a white pirate blouse with ornate silver buttons, none of which were the same size or pattern. She also wore red suspenders, but backward, so the part where they usually cross at the back now crossed across her chest, separating her breasts. She was twenty-one, tops.

'Hi, Billie, I'm Wren.' I looked around the office. All the cubicles were empty. A couple Styrofoam cups of coffee sat half-full at desks. Suit jackets were draped around desk chairs. It looked spooky, like a science fiction movie where the population is wiped out and the survivors get to go through the shopping mall and take anything they want for free. 'Where is everybody?'

'Meeting Mr. Krieg.'

'He's here?'

'Just arrived this morning. Caught everyone by surprise. You should have seen their faces.' She laughed.

'Of all the days to be late.'

'Don't worry. People from out of town are always late the first few times. They can't figure out our weird traffic.'

I felt a little relieved. 'I couldn't make a U-turn on Harbor Blvd.'

The phone rang and Billie snatched it up. '*Orange Coast Today*. May I help you?'

She sounded like a cheery waitress: Welcome to Arby's, may I take your order. I liked that about her. When she hung up, she turned back to me with a big smile. 'I'm so glad you're working here. I read some of those articles you submitted. You're so smart. I'm totally jealous.'

I looked away, embarrassed. 'Thanks. Did they want me to join them in the meeting or what?'

'Linda said you should go see Debra in personnel, get the paperwork out of the way.'

'Where's that?'

'Down the hall. Suite 308.'

A sudden rumble of muffled laughter sounded. It came from the conference room at the back of the office. The door to the room was closed.

'Sounds like they're having a good time,' I said.

The phone rang again and Billie answered it. '*Orange Coast Today*. May I help you?' She winked at me for no reason I could think of. 'She's in a meeting. May I take a message?'

I started down the hall.

*   *   *   *   *

'You skipped one,' she said.

'Where?' I leaned closer to her desk.

'Here. Married or single.' Debra slid the form back across the desk and handed me her pen. 'Most people

116

skip weight. I remember one time, not here but the last place I worked, this woman argued and ranted, saying how this whole form was unconstitutional, an invasion of privacy. Like I really gave a flying fudge how much she weighed. I told her, hey, it's just for insurance purposes, but she was livid. Finally she scribbled in 120 pounds: I'm talking about a broad who tipped in at 185 after a two-week fast.'

My pen hovered over the two tiny boxes. Married. Single. Which should I check? How much had Wren told them about her past when she'd applied. Linda Marley hadn't asked about my husband, or maybe Wren hadn't mentioned Byron.

I checked single.

Debra looked at my checkmark and sighed. 'Good luck,' she said without enthusiasm. She looked to be a few years older than I and wore no wedding ring. She also had a heavy hand with the blush. Her cheeks were an unusual shade; if it were a shoe polish it would be called ox blood. She dressed a little young, as if she were trying to look like Billie the receptionist, despite their fifteen-year and twenty-pound difference.

'What happened there?' Debra asked, pointing a paper clip at my grooved thumbnail.

'Nothing. Nervous habit.'

She nodded. 'Me, I gnaw the cuticles. Look.' She held out her hands. They were perfectly manicured, but the skin around the nails looked raw and sore. I could see the various layers of skin peeled back. 'We all have our little flaws, I guess. I went out with this psychologist for a while, his office is up on twenty-eight.' She pointed toward the ceiling. 'He said chewing nails is a sign of self-loathing, that I wanted to consume myself.' She shrugged. 'I almost married him. Talk about self-loathing.'

I signed the bottom of the form and slid it back to her.

'Welcome, welcome,' Debra said, smiling as she handed me a large manila envelope. 'These are your benefits. Medical, dental, et cetera. We have an excellent plan here. You bust it, we cover it.'

'I'll try not to bust anything.'

'That's good too.'

The door behind me opened and Linda Marley, my new boss, stuck her head in. 'There you are. Hurry, we've got something for you.' To Debra. 'She can finish up here later. Okay, Deb?'

'She's done now,' Debra said.

'Great.' Linda opened the door for me and I went out into the hall with her. She set a brisk pace down the hall back toward the editorial offices. Our heels chattered chaotically, then mine seem to fall into rhythm with hers with no effort from me. It was like that bird last night, the one cawing in time with my blinking. 'Not much time to explain, Wren. Something happened this morning, Mr. Krieg wants you on it right away.'

'Me? I don't even know where the bathrooms are yet.'

'He thinks you're the only one who can handle it.' The coolness in her voice indicated she disagreed with Mr. Krieg.

'Look, Linda, I'm still a virgin around here. I don't want to get caught in any crossfire on my first day. What's going on?'

She stopped our forced march and looked at me. The frustration that had hardened her face eased a little and she smiled slightly. 'It's nothing, Wren. Really. Mr. Krieg has some new ideas, new directions he wants this magazine to go in. I have to get used to it, that's all. He's the one worth a few hundred million dollars; I'm the one with $438.45 in her checking account. He must know something, right?'

I opened the glass door for her. She entered, I followed. Linda Marley was about forty, I guessed from the fine lines around her eyes and mouth. She didn't bother covering them with makeup, which I admired. She wore a blue pin-striped pantsuit with wide lapels. A bronze woman swimmer frozen in midcrawl was pinned to her lapel. Her hair was blonder than mine and pulled tight into a Swedish braid that made her look businesslike but not manly. I suspected that when her hair was down, she looked like Faye Dunaway.

'What's Jonathan Krieg like?' I asked. 'Anything like the newspapers say?'

'He's just a man.'

I recoiled in mock horror. 'Not one of *those*.' Linda smiled and I said, 'What kind of man?'

'The worst kind. Rich. Powerful. A man who demands to get what he wants, even when he doesn't know what he wants.'

I screwed up my face. 'I don't follow, but it sounds damn profound.'

Linda laughed. 'I don't know what I mean either. It's easier to be profound that way.' She stopped at a wooden door with no name on it, knocked. 'Hello?' she said to the closed door.

'Yez, comb in, pleez,' the accented voice inside said.

I knew from television and *People* magazine that Jonathan Krieg was New York City born and raised, friends with movie stars and rock musicians, snappy dresser and dashing playboy who once dated Maria Shriver and Caroline Kennedy. He did not speak with an accent.

'Comb in, comb in,' the voice insisted.

I gave a puzzled look at Linda.

She smiled. 'Beware the Jabberwock, my son.'

She pushed open the door.

The man behind the desk was dressed in a rumpled black suit and plain black hat. His craggy face was consumed by a long black beard with two gray stripes. His sideburns were long springy curls. He smiled at us like Santa Claus. 'Shalom,' he said, waving us into the room. 'Shalom, ladeez.'

'Shalom,' Linda said.

'Sit, pleez,' he said. He gestured at the leather chairs across from the desk.

'Thanks, but I've got to run,' Linda said. She nudged me forward and said to the bearded man, 'You take care of my girl, okay. She's gonna be a star around here.'

He nodded enthusiastically. 'Of courz.'

'Uh, Linda,' I said.

'You'll be fine,' she said. She left, closing the door behind her.

The office was huge, the size of an airline lobby. The desk was an unpolished slab of dark gray stone the size of a door balanced on two stone pillars. The only things on the slab were a black telephone, some typed pages clipped together, and a worn blue book with gold Hebrew lettering on the cover. The Hebrew lettering reminded me of Esther's gravestone. I recognized the typed pages as one of Wren's articles. They seemed to glow unnaturally white against the cold gray stone. Suddenly the whole desk reminded me of a gravestone, as if the stone had been unearthed at some archaeological site, the lid of some dead pharaoh's sarcophagus.

'Hello,' I said to the elderly man, 'I'm Wren Caldwell.'

'Ya,' he said. 'Nize meeting you.'

'That's Rabbi Weiss,' the voice behind me said.

I turned. The Jonathan Krieg from *People* magazine came out of the bathroom drying his hands on a towel. He dried each hand separately, like wineglasses. His black hair was slicked back. He wore a black shirt buttoned to the throat and a thick white cable-knit cardigan sweater with pockets, which made him look natty and much younger than the fiftyish that I'd read he was. He was trim, his gaunt face making him look like he was leaning toward you all the time, ready to pounce. He reminded me of a corporate Dennis Hopper. He held out his hand to me. 'Hi, Wren, I'm Jonathan.'

'Hello,' I said, shaking his hand. The skin was warm despite the recent washing. 'I understand I have you to thank for my job.'

'Yes, you do.'

'Well then . . . thanks.'

He didn't seem to hear me. He crossed the room and stood behind the old rabbi, resting his hands on the older man's shoulders. 'Rabbi Weiss is from Israel. He lives on a kibbutz outside Tel Aviv. He walks with a limp because a terrorist grenade shattered his right knee. Show her your tattoo, Rabbi.'

Rabbi Weiss held up his hands in protest. 'Jonathan, pleez.'

'It's okay, Rabbi. She is an educated woman. This is also part of her education. She's a journalist now.'

Rabbi Weiss sighed as if indulging a favorite grandson, though the rabbi was probably only ten years older than Jonathan. He pushed up his sleeve and revealed a faded tattooed number on his forearm. The seven had a line through it in European fashion.

'Dachau,' Jonathan said. 'He was just a boy.'

'That was a long time ago,' Rabbi Weiss said, tugging his sleeve back down.

'His father was killed in the camps, not by Nazis, but by a fellow Jew who tried to rape his mother. The other man choked his father to death and then raped his mother anyway. How does that make you feel, Wren?'

My mouth was dry. The way he was looking at me I thought he was about to present evidence that it was one of my relatives who'd done it. I remembered something about being told my father's mother was half Jewish, though she'd never practiced the faith that I know of.

'How does it make you feel?' he repeated firmly.

'I don't know. Guilty, mostly. Also outraged.'

'Exactly!' He clapped his hands together and chuckled. 'That's exactly what we're looking for in the new *Orange Coast Today*. A new tone of outrage tempered with a hopeful sense of renewed purpose. We make our readers feel a little guilty, then tell them how to feel better. See what I'm getting at?'

'Not exactly.'

'Okay.' He thrust his hands into the pockets of his cardigan sweater and paced behind the rabbi. 'Rabbi, tell Wren why I flew you here from Israel. Why I am putting you up at the Four Seasons for the next three months. Why we are meeting every afternoon.'

Rabbi Weiss smiled. 'Bar mitzvah.'

'Oh, how nice,' I said. 'Whose?'

'Mine,' Jonathan Krieg said.

'I thought that happened when you were thirteen.'

'Traditionally, yes. But I was too busy when I was thirteen, too busy hustling a buck. I worked in a newsroom for a guy, a reporter name of Mannheim. Taught me a lot. He went on to Hollywood, burned out after three mediocre screenplays. Ended up doing celebrity interviews for one of the tabloids. Meantime, I bought the newspaper, sold it, bought a computer software company, sold it, bought a few more companies, sold them. I made my fortune, just like in the movies, just like the insipid movies Mannheim used to write. Sit, Wren, sit.'

I sat in the leather chair across from his desk. I had no idea what he was talking about. Rabbi Weiss didn't seem to follow either, or at least wasn't interested, because he opened the book in front of him and began to read. His lips moved, though he made no sound, and his body rocked slightly in a rhythm with his reading.

'Maybe this will help,' Jonathan Krieg said, coming around the desk and standing next to me. 'Feel this.' He crooked his arm to make a muscle.

I looked over at the rabbi, but he was lost in his silent chanting.

'Go ahead,' Jonathan urged. 'Don't be shy. Squeeze it.'

I squeezed it. It didn't feel too solid, not like Robby's.

'Well?' he asked.

'I'm not very good at this,' I hedged. 'I'm not much of a bodybuilder.'

'Honestly, tell me what you think. Is that one hell of a muscle or what?'

I thought of saying something half-hearted like, For your age . . . But that seemed an even worse insult. Wren would know what to say. I tried to imagine her here, answering. She'd make some joke, something like, That's not the muscle that counts, and everyone would laugh and forget the original point because she'd be on to something else, something she read about a recent study concerning muscle memory and a group of track and field athletes at some midwestern college.

'I don't know, Jonathan,' I said. 'Feels a little soft to me.'

'Exactly!' he said triumphantly. 'I'm in my fifties and I'm way out of shape. I look fit, but I'm not. That's why I hired personal fitness trainers. A husband-and-wife team, they moonlight as stunt people in the movies. Starting tomorrow, they will come over every day and beat me into shape. You know what else? I never finished college. Took two semesters and that's it. Hell, you want to know the truth, I didn't even finish high school. So I enrolled in Pacific West University, to whom I donated a medical wing last year. They're letting me finish my degree by doing independent studies. I hired a couple tutors to help me through my first semester. See what I'm getting at here?'

'Jonathan,' the rabbi said, tapping his watch crystal. '*Mach schnell.*'

'Yes, Rabbi.' Jonathan Krieg sat on the edge of the stone desk, facing me. 'It's never too late, Wren. That's my point. I can still go through my bar mitzvah. I can still get into good physical shape. I can still earn my degree. Human potential is limitless. It's never too late for people to become who they want to be. But a lot of people don't know what they want to be. That's where we come in. What we're going to be doing here at the magazine is helping them see what kind of people they want to become.'

I exhaled a deep breath that I didn't even know I'd inhaled. 'That's a tall order for a little regional magazine.'

'That's why I bought it. I could have purchased a more popular magazine, or even a daily newspaper. I could have gone to Los Angeles, Miami, stayed in New York. But this place'—he spread his arms out and turned slowly, like Julie Andrews in *The Sound of Music*—'this place is perfect. Orange County is one of the most expensive places in the country to live. Median house prices are over $200,000. You have desperately poor areas, openly gay communities, conspicuous wealth, Robert Schuller's Crystal Cathedral, one of the largest concentrations of Vietnamese refugees. We're going to double our circulation in less than a year. I guarantee it.'

'That's great,' I said. The force of his personality was so overwhelming, instead of being nervous, I felt good to be in his presence. He seemed so sure of himself, so clear about the nature of the world and his ability to make it do what he wanted, I was suddenly very relaxed.

I crossed my legs and my skirt slid up a few inches above my knee. The rabbi looked up from his reading and glanced at my legs. He smiled appreciatively and returned to his reading. I tugged my hem down over my knees.

Jonathan looked at his watch. 'We don't have much time. I have an assignment for you, part of the new direction of the magazine.'

'Yes?'

'You ever hear of Season Dougherty?'

'The name's familiar.'

'She accused her ex-husband of sexually molesting their daughter during his custody, so she sent the kid into hiding with her sister.'

'Right, I remember. The judge ordered her to produce the child but she wouldn't, so he jailed her. She's been in prison for the past few months.'

'Eight months,' Jonathan corrected. 'She got out yesterday after the state legislature passed that special bill limiting jail time in these cases. Same as that Washington, D.C. case.'

'That's good.'

'Except that I just got a call from a friend of mine at City Hall that she's been arrested again. Half an hour ago they found her ex-husband dead of a shotgun blast.'

The rabbi looked up and shook his head. 'Terrible thing.' Then he glanced at my legs and returned to his book.

'Are they sure she did it?' I asked.

'She confessed.'

I no longer felt that warm basking feeling. My stomach started to tighten. I had to pin my hand under my thigh to keep it from rubbing my bra strap. 'I don't see where I fit in here.'

'We have a window of opportunity here. I've arranged for you to visit the crime scene and then to have access to interview Season. You'll have a goddamn exclusive.'

'Me?'

'Yes.'

'I don't have any experience with this kind of thing. This is crime. You want a reporter. I do think pieces.' I opened my purse and pulled out a sheaf of papers. I'd come prepared with one of Wren's recent articles I'd printed out from her floppy disk. I thrust the papers toward him. 'This is what I write.'

Jonathan held up his hands and retreated behind his desk, behind the rabbi. 'I understand this is a little different for you. But so what? I hired you because I could see something special in your writing, a certain tone, an eye for just the right detail. Let's face it, our readership is eighty-seven per cent women. You have the voice of the contemporary woman. You are the nineties woman. You see the right slant on things, the slant that our readers want to see.'

'I just write about issues, Mr. Krieg.'

He shook his head dismissively. 'It's not about issues anymore, Wren. There is no more Women's Lib. Now it's just Women's Glib, the same issues but with a snappy, more ironic attitude. Right now we have a reputation as a glossy rag for pampered housewives. Our articles are puff pieces mostly designed to keep the ads apart. I want to change all that. Make this *the* magazine for the contemporary woman in Orange County. To do that I need to have someone who can talk to them, knows what they are thinking. Knows their language, the language of their hearts and souls.' He tapped his own chest over his heart. 'That's you, Wren.'

I squirmed in my chair. That's Wren, not me.

'You know what a sob sister is, Wren?'

'It's a newspaper term. Used to have something to do with women reporters or something.' I couldn't think. My chest was constricting around my bullet hole.

'In the old days, it referred to a reporter, usually a woman, who wrote sentimental feature stories, you know, children orphaned by train wreck, that sort of thing. Well, we're going to be doing a variation of that. You're going to be a New Age sob sister.'

I stood up, anxious to leave. 'I appreciate your confidence in me, but I don't see how this murder ties in to that whole improve-their-lives attitude you just told me about. This just sounds like old-fashioned sensationalism.'

'It's part of the harsh reality of the way things work. Remember, we're striving for impact here.' He slammed his hand on the slab desk. The rabbi didn't even look up. 'Outrage! Guilt! Outrage at what was done to this poor woman and her child, that we as a community let it come to this. Guilt that we didn't help her.' He softened his voice. 'Then healing as we explain how things got this bad, how to prevent them in your own homes and families. See?'

'No, sir, I don't see.' I waved my papers at him. 'Just read this. Did you know it's the Year of the Horse in Korea?' He started to say something but I kept talking. 'When the Buddha knew he was about to die, he invited all the animals to attend. Only a few showed up and out of gratitude he named a year after each animal. Many people think that a person receives some of the characteristics of the animal into whose year he or she is born.'

The rabbi lifted his head, his finger marking where he'd stopped reading. He watched me with interest.

'The problem in Korea this year is that women who are born during the year of the horse are considered skittish, a little wild. They are not considered good marriage material, therefore they are often shunned by the men. And now, with modern medical techniques, the parents can know what the child's sex is within a few months. The thing is, because it's the Year of the Horse, many Korean women, if they find out they are pregnant with a girl, are having their babies aborted. Can you imagine the implications? This policy has caused a severe shortage of women. There are half a million men within a certain age group who have no hope of marrying. That's what this article is all about. This has everything you wanted: Outrage! Guilt! Healing!' My cheeks were hot with passion. For a moment, I felt as if I actually had written this article myself. 'This is the same kind of New Age sob sister stuff that you want. The voice of the nineties woman.'

'Perfect,' Jonathan said, applauding. 'I love it. Really. It's great.'

'So sad,' the rabbi said, shaking his head.

I sat back down, exhausted.

'Trouble is, Wren,' Jonathan said, 'that's in Korea, half a world away. Season Dougherty is right here in Orange County in the Irvine jail. Her husband's body is in a Turtle Rock house right here in Orange County. And the name of our magazine is *Orange Coast Today*. You see a pattern?' He pushed up the sleeves of his sweater. 'I've managed to use a little leverage with an old friend to make sure you're the first journalist on the scene of the crime and the first with access to Mrs. Dougherty.' He tapped his watch the same way the rabbi had earlier. 'And our window of opportunity is slowly closing on our collective fingers.'

'*Ein ziemliches Mädchen*,' the rabbi said to Jonathan.

'He says you're a pretty woman.'

'Very pretty,' the rabbi nodded.

I stood up. 'Thank you.'

'Linda has the background information you need. But you'd better hurry.'

'What about this article?' I said, brandishing the pages.

'Maybe you can work it into the Dougherty piece. Better yet, use it when we do something about the violence at abortion clinics in Orange County. That'll work.'

I held my hand out to the rabbi. He shook it and said, 'Shalom.'

'Shalom,' I said.

'Good luck, Wren,' Jonathan said. 'This is the start of great things for both of us. It's great to be back in the swing of publishing again. Makes me feel like a kid still running around that newsroom.'

Was that what all this was about? I was hired so Jonathan Krieg could relive his youth. I was just part of the package, the team of human time machines gathered to help him recapture the youth he squandered amassing his fortune. The rabbi, the tutors, the husband-wife stunt team. And now me.

I closed the door behind me and stood, gathering my thoughts. What did I have to be angry about? I had a good job, the respect of my coworkers, even of my boss. Maybe it wasn't anger at all. Just fear. I didn't know how to interview a murderer. The only crime scene I'd been at was the one where I was the victim. I didn't want to get that close to other people's problems, didn't want to become intimate with their despair.

Through the door I heard the rabbi begin to sing in Hebrew. He stopped and Jonathan Krieg sang the same refrain, but haltingly, stumbling over the words. Then the rabbi sang again, even more beautifully than before. It was somehow mournful and cheerful at the same time. Jonathan tried again, his voice a monotone of determination.

'Wren?' Billie the receptionist called. 'Telephone. Line three.'

I walked to my desk, passing a few of my fellow journalists. Each stopped what they were doing to look up and say hello or welcome. I remembered a couple names but not most. Everyone was extremely friendly, but there was something in their voices, a tone they all shared, of grudging good humor and nagging jealousy. It's not my fault, I wanted to shout, I didn't ask Jonathan Krieg to make me the New Age sob sister.

My office was in a cubicle surrounded by those low temporary partitions that are covered with mauve cloth. The desk itself was a standard gray metal, not unlike the one in my office at school. Except this one had rubber bumpers trimming the edges. Also, the desktop was some sort of phony wood veneer. A flat ivory telephone with a row of clear plastic buttons sat next to a cluster of tape dispenser, stapler, and electric pencil sharpener. The button marked #3 was flashing.

In the middle of the desk was a blue file folder with a typed label on the tab: DOUGHERTY, SEASON. A typed note was clipped to the front with two addresses, Lester Dougherty's and the Irvine Police Department's. Detailed directions to each location were included. At the bottom, in florid handwriting: *Happy motoring, Billie.*

I sat down and pushed the folder aside.

Attached to the desk was a floating platform on which was bolted a Macintosh SE computer. I could see my face in the dark screen. My hair was down, which I had hoped would make me look a little more glamorous, like Rosalind Russell in *His Girl Friday*. My glasses reflected pinpoints of light. I took them off and placed them on the file folder. The right earpiece was still chewed off.

I picked up the phone and pushed #3. 'Hello, this is Wren Caldwell.'

'Thank God, thank God,' the man said. 'We've been looking for you everywhere.'

'Who is this?'

'Phil Sanchez over at Valley College. I've been trying to reach you for a week. Why didn't you tell us you'd moved here already?'

I felt panicky. Who was this guy? He seemed to know Wren, but how much did he know? An old friend/lover/colleague whom she'd contacted when she applied for this job? Would he come rushing over now and expose me to everyone?

'Uh, I'm sorry'—Phil or Mr. Sanchez? How close were

they?—'everything was so hectic with the move and everything.'

'I understand,' he said, but his voice was stern, a little put out. What had Wren done to him? 'However, you made a commitment to teach that course and classes start Monday. I called your old number up in Oregon but it had been disconnected. Information says your local number is unlisted.'

That was deliberate. I didn't want any of Wren's old friends leafing through the phone book to accidentally come across her name.

'I'd have replaced you, but the other person who teaches art history got a grant from the NEA and she took off for Mazatlan to paint. We really need you to live up to your commitment, Ms. Caldwell.'

Wren had applied to teach art history?

'You got the section you asked for, Monday nights six to ten P.M. Your class meets in Art 110. The textbook is in the bookstore, they'll give you a free copy. Your section is packed, so don't take any petitioners. Drop by the administration building and fill out the paperwork. You'll have a mailbox there in the Adjunct Faculty section.' There was a pause. 'You sound funny.'

Damn, he'd spoken to her before. 'Funny?'

'Different. I don't know, it's been a month. It's just, I don't know, I remembered your voice as being very . . . Hell, stop me before I make a complete ass of myself.' He laughed.

I laughed as best I could. I watched myself laugh in the computer screen. I looked like someone choking.

'Any questions?' he asked.

'Nope. Monday sounds good.'

'Okay then, if you have any problems, give me a call or drop in my office. Drop in anyway, I'd like to meet you. Your résumé impressed the hell out of all of us.'

'Thanks.'

'Well, good luck.' He hung up.

I hung up too. My hand was trembling. I picked up my

file folder on Season Dougherty, put my glasses back on, strapped my purse on, and wandered toward the exit. I had to go to a crime scene to view a corpse, then to jail to interview a murderer, then home to prepare to teach an art history course, about which I knew nothing. I could have backed out of the teaching, but Phil Sanchez seemed angry enough that he'd call the university in Oregon to complain about Wren Caldwell. I didn't want that.

'Good luck,' Billie said cheerfully as I left.

Around the corner was the floor's elevator foyer. I pressed the button and waited. I looked out the window at the parking lot below. There was my Rabbit, still needing a wash.

And there, parked next to my car, was a white Subaru with a bent antenna.

I jabbed the elevator button repeatedly. This time I was going to catch the son of a bitch. The elevator doors yawned open and I jumped in and punched my floor button. I watched the lighted floor numbers above the door flicker by like a countdown at NASA. My stomach was tight with excitement. Was this how my father felt waiting for his rockets to blast off. When we hit the ground floor, I ran out before the doors had completely opened, bumping my shoulder hard on the door. I pushed ahead of an elderly man to beat him through the glass door leading to the parking lot. I ran along the rows of parked cars until I found my Rabbit.

The white Subaru was gone.

'It ain't like the movies,' Detective Diesel said, snapping on a pair of surgical gloves. 'First of all, we don't stand around over the body and trade wisecracks.'

He squatted next to the body and stared at it for a couple of minutes. The body was dressed in gray jogging pants and a T-shirt that said Nike, Just Do It. It was sitting on the dining-room floor, back slumped against the wall, legs splayed apart like a wishbone. Someone had draped a red-checkered dish towel over the head. Dark blood had soaked through the cloth forming some strange Rorschach pattern that reminded me of sumo wrestlers colliding. Detective Diesel looked over the entire body head to toe without touching anything, as if he were about to give an estimate for the cost of hauling the corpse to the dump. He stopped to stare at the man's crotch. The shotgun blast had shredded the cloth and skin and muscle, leaving the lap nothing more than a chunky stew. The left leg's thigh bone was exposed, sticking straight up like a pink and white twig. The detective shook his head and looked up at me. My pen was poised for his insight into this kind of violence. 'If anything,' he said, 'television has ruined more cops. Especially the young ones. They all think they have to act like *Miami Vice*.'

I wrote that down in my notebook.

Detective Diesel reached for the dish towel covering the head. 'You sure you want to see this? I can always give you a peek at the police photographs later.'

'I'm fine,' I said. Actually, I really was fine. Maybe it

was morbid, but I felt somehow comfortable, more at ease right then than I'd felt since my own shooting. From the moment I'd regained consciousness in the hospital, way before I'd decided to slip into Wren's life, nothing around me seemed familiar. Everywhere I went, whoever I spoke to, I felt like an imposter, someone masquerading as a living person. I didn't even belong in Luna's body. Her skin didn't fit me, like I was walking around in a pair of too-big shoes. Every step further blistered me. Maybe that's what made it so easy to become Wren.

But here, walking around this fresh dead body, amid the sour smell of sweat and urine and faeces, I could relax. Be myself. I felt like a mini support group for the poor guy: Don't worry, pal, being dead's not so bad. I could tell him.

'Okay then,' Detective Diesel said. 'Let's see what we got here . . .' He pinched the two bottom corners of the dish towel and hesitated, like a magician about to snap a tablecloth out from under a fancy dinner setting. Then he delicately peeled back the dish towel. As Detective Diesel exposed more and more of the head, his own craggy, middle-aged face began to smooth out, the deep lines disappear. His jaw tightened, causing his small ears to flatten against his skull. He tossed the sticky towel aside.

The corpse had no face. It looked like lumpy chili or boiling tomato soup. A fat black fly landed on the face, about where a nose used to be. Detective Diesel brushed it away with the back of his hand.

The youngest uniformed cop walked up and wagged a finger at the corpse. 'See, I told you not to pick your zits.' He chuckled and winked at me.

'Donaldson!' Detective Diesel snapped.

'Yes, sir,' the officer said with some fear.

'Get me the fingerprinting gear. And keep your asinine comments to yourself. You understand me, son?'

'Yes, sir.' Officer Donaldson looked sheepishly at me, then back at Detective Diesel.

'Then move, goddamn it!'

'Yes, sir.' He ran off.

Detective Diesel shrugged at me. 'What can you do?'

'*Miami Vice*,' I nodded.

'Exactly.'

I took a couple steps closer to the body, stared at the damage. All that had happened here was that a load of pellets had collided with flesh and bone. On a molecular level it was just particles bumping into other particles, jostled electrons, atoms spinning into new orbits. Nothing had been destroyed. Only the configuration was altered, little more than a subatomic rearrangement of furniture. In the cosmic picture, what then had really changed?

'Have you done this a lot?' Detective Diesel asked.

'First time.'

He arched an eyebrow. 'You handle it well.'

'Thank you.' I was in a surprisingly good mood. The closer I got to the body, the happier I felt. I almost started humming. It was like coming out of a freezing snowstorm and huddling up to a warm fire. When I leaned over the corpse's face, my own bullet scar twinged. Maybe it was some sort of sympathetic vibration, I don't know, but my heart seemed suddenly closer to the surface now. If I scratched away the scar-tissue plug, I'd look straight down that dark tunnel and see my slippery heart fussing and squirming like a new baby. I rubbed the scar on my breast and one of the uniformed cops going through the hall closet nudged his partner and grinned at me.

Officer Donaldson returned with the fingerprinting equipment. Detective Diesel took the corpse's right index finger, rolled it across the ink pad, then rolled the inky fingertip onto a piece of cardboard.

'Is this necessary?' I asked. 'You already know who it is.'

'We *think* we know.' He held up the middle finger of the dead hand, offering it to me. 'You wanna try?'

'Sure.' I tucked my notebook and pen into my purse and knelt down next to him. 'What do I do?'

'Grasp it firmly. It's starting to stiffen up.'

One of the officers snickered and mumbled to another cop. They laughed. Detective Diesel's face flushed a deep red. 'I mean, you know, rigor mortis.'

'I know.' I prised the middle finger apart from the rest of his hand and dipped it against the pad that Detective Diesel held for me.

'Roll it from side to side. We want the whole print.'

I rolled the dead finger from side to side. Detective Diesel put down the pad and pushed the cardboard across the carpet close to my knees.

'Now do the same thing you did on the pad, roll it from one side to the other side. Firmly, but not too hard.'

I did so. The fingerprint appeared like a stenciled design. It was kind of pretty. Not unlike the art my friends with children have hanging on their refrigerators.

'Good job, Ms. Caldwell. You're a natural.'

'Thanks.' I stood up. A small smudge of ink marked the back of my hand. 'Is there really any reason to doubt that this is Philip Dougherty?'

'He fits the same physical description. We found his wallet with ID in his pocket. This is his house. We have a confession from the murderer who says this is Philip Dougherty. But with no face, it could be anybody.'

'You mean like on TV, whenever they find a body with no face, it's never who the cops think it is?'

'Exactly. As soon as they say, "The body's been burned beyond recognition," you know it's someone else.'

'But they always find a convenient watch or a necklace or something that indicates who they think it is.'

'Exactly,' he nodded, inking the thumb. 'Only this isn't television. Fingerprints don't lie. There are no two sets alike. Just like snowflakes.'

'Actually,' I said, 'I read recently where scientists discovered that all snowflakes aren't different. That the patterns are repeated.'

'Yeah?' He slipped a plastic bag over the corpse's hand and snapped a rubber band around the wrist to keep it in place. 'I hadn't heard that.'

'That's kind of interesting, though, isn't it? Imagine, there could be somebody out there with your fingerprints and he could be doing all kinds of nasty things that you could get blamed for.'

'It wouldn't surprise me.' Detective Diesel stood up, walked off a stiffness in his right leg. 'I guess that's why we now have DNA fingerprinting. Believe me, Ms. Caldwell, we're always one step ahead of the bad guys.'

'Just like *Miami Vice*?'

He smiled beautifully. 'Just like *Miami Vice*.'

*   *   *   *   *

'She's waiting to see Season Dougherty,' Detective Diesel said to the woman cop behind the desk. 'The chief said it was okay.'

'I gotta check with Dougherty's P.D. first, Bob,' she said.

Detective Diesel turned to me. 'P.D., that's public defender.'

'Thanks,' I said. I wrote that down in my notebook to make him feel good.

'I mean, you're getting the jump on the story, but the lady still has rights.' He seemed a little annoyed that strings had been pulled by Jonathan Krieg. 'She doesn't have to see you if she doesn't want to.'

'I understand.'

He nodded, turned back to the desk sergeant.

She hung up the phone. 'The P.D.'s in the building. We're still trying to find her.'

'Who is it?' Detective Diesel asked.

'Rebba Mallard.'

Detective Diesel nodded appreciatively. 'She's good.'

The desk sergeant shrugged. 'We're all good.' She looked him in the eye for some reaction, but Detective Diesel just nodded and turned toward me.

He guided me over to an orange molded plastic bench.

136

'You can wait here until they clear it. Meantime, I've got a living to earn. Nice working with you, Ms. Caldwell.'

'Now that we've fingerprinted a corpse together, you can call me Wren.'

'Okay, Wren. See ya around the scene of the crime sometime.' He started to walk away.

'Can I ask you a quick question?'

He smiled. 'That's what you have been doing, isn't it?'

'This has nothing to do with the murder. It's hypothetical.'

'Oh,' he nodded knowingly. 'You have a friend.'

'What?'

'That's how hypothetical questions to cops always begin. "I have this friend who . . ."'

'Okay, I have this friend who hacked up her in-laws and is going to ship parts of the bodies to Johnny Carson and Joan Rivers in an effort to make them friends again. She wants to know if she should turn herself in.'

He laughed. 'Okay, I deserved that. What's the problem?'

'What do you do if you think someone's following you?'

'Do you know him?'

'No. I don't know. I haven't seen his face. I don't even know if it is a him. Just the same car.'

'There are a lot of cars in southern California, you're bound to see some repeats.'

'This is definitely the same car.'

'You want to file a report, be on the safe side?'

I shook my head. I couldn't afford any kind of investigation into my past. 'It's probably nothing.'

'Get the license number, give me a call. I'll run a check.'

'Thank you.'

'Meantime, stay out of dark parking garages.'

'I will,' I said, shaking his hand. 'Thanks for all your help.'

He seemed embarrassed by my gratitude, lowering his

head as he walked away through the doors marked AUTH-
ORIZED PERSONNEL ONLY.

I sat on the hard orange bench and reviewed my notes.
They were neat notes, numbered and lettered the same as
if I were in a literature class. I hadn't lost the knack. Still,
I had no idea how to turn them into an actual article that
anybody but a paid professor would want to read. I could
whip up a theme paper maybe, with footnotes and a bibli-
ography. I closed my notebook and tried to think of an
opening line, one that would grab the reader. Nothing
came. Maybe I could call Robby, have him help me without telling him what it was about. I began concocting elaborate stories to convince him. That made me even more
depressed. Why, at every moment of crisis, did I still think
of Robby? Before, when Robby and I were together and
happy, some couple we knew would be splitting up and
they would weep and look desperate. I would be sympathetic. Months later I'd see one of them and he or she would
still be unhappy and ragged-looking and I'd think, Snap
out of it, get on with your life. I wanted to go back in time
and take the old, smug me and shake her by the shoulders,
tell her to have some *compassion*, damn it. Now it seemed
to me that breaking up was less an event and more like a
nasty virus that lodges in your spine and reappears at
every moment of weakness and doubt.

I noticed the ink smudge on my hand again. I licked my
fingertips and rubbed the spot off.

I tried to imagine what Season Dougherty was doing
right now. What did a woman do all day in prison? Was
it like those women-behind-bars movies that guys like so
much; did she have to fend off lesbian advances from
thick-necked women carrying broom handles? Was she in
there right now sharpening the edges of a spoon she
smuggled out of the cafeteria to fight off raging dikes? Or
was she at this moment poring over dusty law books, rubbing her weary eyes, adjusting her reading glasses in the
dim light, as she searched in vain for some legal precedent
that would win her freedom and reunite her with her

daughter? Was she a monster, a crazed bitch with a shot-gun, who coldly smiled as she blasted her ex-husband's genitals into oatmeal? Or was she the self-sacrificing Ulti-mate Mother, willing to give up her own life to protect her innocent daughter? I tried to adopt an attitude toward her, but it was difficult. I wasn't in any position to take the moral high road here.

The glass door banged open and a little girl about seven ran into the lobby from the parking lot. She wore a denim skirt bleached almost white, white socks, sneakers, and a lime-green T-shirt. She was carrying a man's wallet in both hands and laughing giddily.

A man about thirty-five followed her into the building, holding the hand of a little boy, about eight or nine. 'Whoa, there, Judy,' he called to the little girl. 'Can I have my wallet back?'

She giggled, held up his wallet, then put it behind her back.

'Jud-ee, Jud-ee, Jud-ee,' the man said, imitating Cary Grant.

'Judy, Judy, Judy,' she repeated, imitating him.

'Okay, Nurse Judy. This is important surgery. We must save the patient. The fate of the free world rests in the balance. Scalpel.' He held out his hand, palm up.

'Scalpel,' she said, placing an imaginary instrument in his palm.

'You have to slap it in. Smack, like this.' He slapped his own palm. 'Again. Scalpel.'

'Scalpel.' She slapped his hand hard.

'Screwdriver,' he said.

'Screwdriver.' She slapped his hand again.

'Let me,' the little boy begged, twisting out of the man's grip.

The man turned to the boy with his palm open. 'Chain-saw.'

'Chainsaw,' the boy said gleefully, and slapped the hand as hard as he could.

'Wallet,' the man said to the girl.

'Wallet?' she asked.

'Sure. The patient's wallet to pay our bill.'

She laughed and slapped the wallet into his palm. He put the wallet into his back pocket.

'Good job, guys. Looks like the operation was a success. The patient has two heads so now he has someone to laugh at his knock-knock jokes. Now, wait for Daddy over there.' He pointed to the blue bench next to my orange one. They ran over and sat down. The man talked to the desk sergeant in a low voice I couldn't hear. She looked directly at me, then whispered something to him. He whispered something back. She laughed, then the man laughed too.

'Hang on,' the desk sergeant said in a friendly tone. 'I'll see what I can do.' She picked up the phone.

The man thanked her and sat down with his children. He wasn't very tall, I noticed, only a couple inches taller than I. And he was a few pounds overweight, giving his face a smooth, slightly puffy look. His blond hair was short and neat. His clothes were casual and baggy, but expensive.

The little girl took out a flat plastic case the size of a deck of cards. The case was filled with water and had a plastic frog inside. A bunch of colored little balls floated around the water. Apparently when you pressed a button, air shot into the water and swirled the balls around. The object was to have the floating balls go into the frog's mouth. After Judy played with it a minute, the little boy started to grab for it.

'You can't do it,' he said.

'Yes, I can,' she screamed. 'I can too.'

The man snatched the case from both their hands and said, 'Let's see how fast Daddy can do it. If I can get them all in Kermit in under three minutes, I'll take you guys out to lunch at Bullwinkle's.'

'That's not Kermit,' the boy said.

'Ready, set, go,' the man said and started working the game. The kids cheered and hollered, shoved at him to

140

make him go faster. For no particular reason, I checked my watch when he started.

When he manoeuvred the final colored ball into the frog's mouth, he held up his hands and shouted, 'Time.' He looked at his watch, which was thin and gold.

'How long, Daddy,' Judy asked. 'Did you make it?'

I looked at my watch. Five and a half minutes.

'A hundred and seventy-three seconds,' he said.

'How many minutes is that?' the boy asked.

'Less than three!' he said.

'Yea!' the kids yelled. 'All right! We're going to Bull-winkle's.'

The desk sergeant put her hand over the receiver and said to the man, 'Still checking, Mr. Richard.'

'Thanks,' he smiled. His little boy whispered to him. They both stood up and walked over to me. 'I've gotta make a pit stop with Mark. You mind keeping an eye on Judy for me?'

'Well, I . . .' I guestured toward the desk sergeant to indicate I had business.

'Should be just a minute or two. We won't even wash our hands.'

I laughed. 'Please, wash your hands.'

'Thanks.' He turned back to Judy. 'Judy, come sit over here with the nice FBI lady.'

'I'm not FBI.'

'Really? You look sort of undercover sitting here.' I must have looked startled because he quickly added, 'I'm kidding. Actually, you look like a girl I used to date in high school. She broke my heart and kept my letter sweater. That wasn't you, was it?'

'Could be. Was the letter for band?'

'Ouch,' he said, wincing and clutching his heart.

I couldn't help smiling. 'Don't you have some hands to wash?'

'Right.'

Judy sat next to me on the bench. She didn't look at me, though, just kept playing with her frog game.

'Be right back, sweetheart,' he told her and led Mark down the hall to the rest rooms.

Judy and I sat on the orange bench, neither of us speaking. The silence seemed somehow heavy with accusation. I should speak to the child, but I didn't know what to say. To me, children were like the primitive natives my father studied, mysterious creatures with rituals and customs I couldn't begin to understand.

'Hi, Judy,' I said.

'Hi,' she said, without looking up. Colored balls swirling around a plastic frog mouth riveted her more than I could.

'My name is Wren.'

'Huh?'

'Wren. Like the bird.'

'What kind of bird?'

'The wren. Haven't you ever heard of a wren?'

She shrugged.

I opened my purse. Maybe I had something in there that would be of interest to a little girl. Some makeup, wallet, checkbook with temporary checks, keys. Grownup stuff that didn't even interest me.

Then I found the earring. It was hooked through my keyring. A long gold dragonfly with one red ruby for an eyeball. I'd found it while cleaning out Wren's nightstand, sitting at the bottom of the drawer. There was no other jewelry in that drawer, just this lone earring, so I figured it might be special to her. I'd searched everywhere for the matching companion, but never found it. There was something about it, I don't know, like a talisman or something. I don't know. I decided to keep it in my purse as a goodluck charm. I'd stolen Wren's life, maybe I could have her luck too. I'd carried it with me ever since.

I held it up to Judy. 'See? A dragonfly. Neat, huh?'

She looked up, unimpressed. 'It's just a bug. Mark eats bigger bugs than that.'

'Oh.' I put the earring away.

My stomach started to cramp. I rubbed my thumb

142

against my bra strap. I should know what to say, I was a woman, a potential mother. I owned a womb, for chrissake. It was like an empty garage inside me, waiting to house a new car. What kind of mother would I be if I couldn't even talk to this child? Even if I didn't want to become a mother, it should be because I chose not to, not because I was unqualified for the job.

I realized that I hadn't much thought about that option since breaking up with Robby. I'd thought about how I would bluff my way through my job. I'd thought about meeting men, maybe even one man I could love. But those thoughts about my future usually ended with that big passionate kiss after which he tells me for the first time, I love you. Waves might be crashing in the background, I'm not sure. But after that, what?

Motherhood?

*   *   *   *   *

This is what I remember about my mother.

'The first time I had sex,' Mom is saying, 'was very unusual.'

I am twelve. Mom is sitting on the sofa amid a group of men and women. Dad is sipping a cognac and standing by the fireplace. He is smiling. As always, Mom is the life of the party and he looks proud of that fact. I am drinking ginger ale and picking out all the cashews from the bowl of mixed nuts.

'How did we get on this subject?' Mom laughs. 'Why don't we dance instead?'

'Come on, Barbara,' people urge. Someone has turned down the stereo, which is playing 'Me and Mrs. Jones' by Billy Paul.

'Let's just say it was different.'

'And probably illegal in most states,' Dad says.

Everyone laughs. I laugh too, happy to have a mother who is so popular.

Everyone thought my mother was the most fun person in the world. She was exactly the kind of woman Korean men feared were born during the Year of the Horse. Coltish, wild, able to leap corral fences and keep running.

'His name was Buddy. Wasn't it Buddy, Roger?'

My dad nods. 'Buddy Hirsch. Remember, he said that was the Jewish version of Buddy Holly.'

Dad wasn't actually there, but he knows my mother's stories better than she does. He never seems to tire of hearing them. This is the first time I've heard this one, though. I pop a few more cashews and hope they don't notice I've finished washing the glasses they needed.

'Anyway, you remember that terrible science fiction movie *Night of the Scorpions*?' Mom curls her index fingers into scorpion tails. 'You know, radioactive waste contaminates these scorpions in the desert and they mutate.'

'Oh, yeah,' Dr. Lester says. 'They grow as big as houses and attack this little town.'

'That's the one,' Mom says. She touches her finger to her nose and points to him. He grins and looks around as if he's just won something. 'They shot that whole thing near Palm Springs, where I was staying for the summer with my aunt. Good God, Aunt Lena, I just remembered she had no left earlobe. Her little wiener dog went nuts on her one summer and bit it off.'

'Skip the violence and cut to the sex,' Marsha, Dad's secretary, says.

'Goodness you're a randy bunch. Okay, okay. Well, the film company needed extras, so my cousin Lisa and I went down and got bit parts. We played high school cheerleaders at this keg party. We're still in our little skirts, making out with the football team, when this giant scorpion crashes through the wall and stings the quarterback right in the balls.'

'Jesus,' someone says and everyone laughs again.

'So the quarterback obviously wasn't this Buddy person,' Phyllis Ryerson, our neighbor, says. 'Not in his condition.'

'No, Buddy wasn't actually in the movie. He was the writer.'

I was sitting cross-legged on the floor. From my vantage point I noticed all the debris on the floor, napkins, nuts, pretzels, chips, crackers, half a Swedish meatball. Tomorrow morning I would have to clean up all this before Mom got out of bed. Not that she expected me to. She would scold me for not waiting until she could help, then hug me for my thoughtfulness, kiss my hair, and call me Loony Tunes, like the cartoons. In truth, I only did it because any housework done with Mom's help took twice as long and was only half as clean. She was a lousy housewife, I guess, not because she didn't do all the things expected of a woman then. She cleaned and cooked and seemed to actually enjoy doing it. She just did a crummy job. Dad and I were always rewashing the dishes, recleaning the sinks and toilets, reironing clothes. We never let her know; Dad always made it a kind of secret agent game between the two of us to do these things when Mom wasn't around. She never noticed the improvement, either, which only made the game more fun.

'Poor Buddy,' Mom says, chuckling. 'He hadn't written the original movie, some old hack had. But the hack was in Italy working on a spaghetti western when the actress starring in our little epic got smacked with a giant mechanical scorpion tail and broke her leg. She was out of the film and they'd already shot half of it. They needed to change the script. So the producer brought in his nephew, Buddy, who'd wowed his family by getting a couple of his short stories published in literary magazines. Buddy was only twenty that summer. He'd never written a script, he'd never even read one. He was so nervous he couldn't keep a meal down.'

'You relaxed him, eh, Barbara?' Marsha says.

'I was still a virgin, remember. Anyway, Buddy and I met on the set. He came over to the house a couple times for dinner. I think he was homesick and even a one-eared aunt was better than that alcoholic cast and crew. Well, one night we drove over to the warehouse where all the equipment was stored. He had a little writing office there where he worked on the pages. We started acting out his new pages. I played the leader of the mutant scorpions.'

'Type casting,' Dr. Lester says.

Mom did have one household speciality. She knew every home remedy and trick there was. She studied those household tip books the way some people study law or medicine. It was almost spooky the way she pored over those books, like a witch or something dabbling in the blackest of magics. If I came home with bubble gum stuck to my jeans, she immediately rubbed peanut butter on it and, abracadabra, the gum was gone. Cut a turnip in half and rub it under your arm as a deodorant. Anything that had a dual purpose fascinated her. She was an alchemist by nature, I think.

'I was killing him,' Mom says. Here her voice gets wistful and she touches her thin bangs in a girlish way. 'I'd picked up one of the small scorpion tails they used for the models and was stinging him to death while he crawled across the floor to save a little child. This was the part for the actress who'd broken her leg. Since she had to be killed off, she'd insisted she die a heroine. Plus, she could crawl with the cast on and they could just shoot the top half of her body.

'So I was chasing him across the floor, stinging him with this fake tail while he read his lines. Somehow he turned over onto his back just as I was whacking him and I caught him right in the'—Mom laughs but with a pained expression—'the balls.'

'Life imitates art,' Dad says.

'I dropped to the floor, and I don't know what I was thinking, I just rubbed him there the same as if it had been his shoulder or something. One thing led to another.' She shrugged, not interested in the details.

'So that's when you saw your first real scorpion tail,' Dr.

146

Lester says. Other people say stuff like that too. Everyone laughs after each remark.

Mom sips her drink. She tilts her glass and looks out over the rim and sees me. I think she's going to get mad and send me away, but she just winks. Suddenly I want to tell them a better story about Mom. The one she told me last week. Listen, I want to say, this is even better, much better.

I had come home from school almost crying because there had been talk at school about eliminating sex education classes and my friend Julia said that those classes taught girls how to have periods. Suddenly I was terrified we wouldn't get the class and I wouldn't know how to get my period. When I asked Mom about it, she smiled and said I didn't have to worry, it would come without me doing anything. I was skeptical, after all, Julia had known about French kissing causing pregnancy. Mom stubbed out her cigarette and grabbed a tangerine from the refrigerator. Using one of our many dull knives, she slit the skin about two inches. She squeezed. Thick syrupy juice beaded along the slit. 'Taste it,' she said. I was afraid; this wasn't how you were supposed to eat a tangerine. 'Go on,' she said, making it sound like a dare, an adventure. I ran my finger along the cut and licked my finger. 'Good?' she asked. I nodded. 'Sweet.' That's what happens to us, she explained, to women. We ripen and turn sweet, just like fruit. And when we are at our sweetest, we overflow a little. We're luckier than this fruit, though. We ripen every single month. She grinned as if we were sharing the most delicious secret. 'Don't boys ripen?' I asked. 'Sure,' she said, 'but then they just rot.' She laughed and poked my ribs and called me Loony Tunes.

That's the story I want them all to hear, not the stupid one about scorpion tails and stupid Buddy Hirsch.

But then there is music, the Rolling Stones' 'Tumbling Dice', and everyone is dancing. Mom drags Dad away from the mantel and they are dancing the Mashed Potato.

I return to the kitchen to wash more glasses.

Whenever I hear that Joni Mitchell song, the one with the lines, 'I want to get up and jive/Wanna wreck my stockings in some jukebox dive . . .' I think of Mom. That's how she was. For many years I'd wished I were more like her. When people were planning a party, I wanted to be the first person they thought of to invite.

But my stockings weren't meant to be wrecked in passionate abandon, they were meant to be washed out in cold water at night and draped over the shower door to dry by morning.

* * * * *

'Who's punishing whom?' he said.

'Pardon?' I said.

'Well, I'm gone two minutes and you two look like one of you stole the other's boyfriend. Judy, did this lady steal Jimmy Dolenz from you?'

Judy giggled and shook her head. 'Jimmy Dolenz is dumb.'

'You love him,' Mark taunted. 'You told me so.'

'I did not. I hate Jimmy Dolenz.'

'Whew, another week in which I don't have to worry about boys.' He wiped his forehead with the back of his hand. The gesture reminded me of Detective Diesel brushing the fly from the corpse's stewed face. 'Hey, thanks for watching her for me.'

'That's okay. No trouble.'

'Look.' He held out his hands, turned them over. 'We washed them. Show her, Mark.' Mark thrust his hands at me and flipped them back and forth.

'Very good, boys,' I said, which made me feel like a mother. Not the good kind who slits open tangerines and explains the world, but the other kind, the spoilsport who spot-checks for washed hands.

I looked over to the desk sergeant, hoping for some

word about Season Dougherty's public defender. But the desk sergeant was still on the phone.

'My name's Davis Richard,' the man said.

'He has two first names,' Mark said, as if this were a regular routine.

'We all do,' Judy added.

'Congratulations,' I told her.

'She's named after a bird, Daddy,' Judy said. 'Robin, I think.'

'Wren,' I said. I held out my hand to him. 'Wren Caldwell.'

He shook my hand. All the men I was meeting today either washed their hands before shaking mine, or put on surgical gloves shortly afterward.

'People are always getting my name confused,' he said, sitting next to me on my now crowded orange bench. 'Sometimes they call me Davis, sometimes Richard. Sometimes Dick. I'm hoping the latter is just because of the Richard.'

I looked at the children, wondering if that last comment wasn't a bit risqué for them. They just sat there playing with the water frog, not really listening to us.

'What are you doing here?' he asked. 'Bailing out your mother for too many speeding tickets?'

'My mother's dead,' I said flatly. I don't know why I did it. Yes, I do. I resented how comfortable he was with me, how funny and glib he could be, how spontaneous. I didn't like the fact that I liked him. I didn't like that the desk sergeant liked him. And I was jealous that he could speak to kids better than I could.

If I expected my news to embarrass him, it didn't work.

'So's theirs,' he said, nodding at the children. 'Died in labor with Judy. You wouldn't think that would be possible in this day and age, would you?'

My throat tightened. 'I—I'm sorry,' I said.

He shrugged. 'That's okay. I lied. We're divorced, she lives in Encino with her new husband, an orthodontist.'

I started to say something like 'You bastard' or worse,

149

but I swallowed it back for the kids' sake. I stood up. 'Nice to meet you, Mark and Judy.' Then to him, cold and steely, 'I have some notes to take. I need to be alone.' I started for the blue bench.

He got up and followed me. 'I know you think it was a terrible thing to say, but you deserved it. I wasn't hitting on you or anything, just talking. You tried to zap me, right?'

I turned to face him. 'Look, I'm just here doing a job. You took your son to the rest room, I watched your daughter. That concludes our business.' I sat on the bench trying to look cold as Barbara Stanwyck.

He sat next to me. 'We're going to do some fancy dining at Bullwinkle's when we're done here. Care to join us? The place is loud but at least the food's lousy.'

'I don't think so, thanks.'

'Mr. Richard?' A woman appeared from behind the AUTHORIZED PERSONNEL ONLY door. She was a homely woman with a hatchet face and a severe suit that might have fit her once when she was fifteen pounds lighter. Now the seams stretched into sutures, like long sloppy scars over her hips.

'Yes.' He quickly ushered her across the lobby, talking animatedly to her as they walked. He pulled out some papers from his jacket and handed them to her. She put on reading glasses and read them. They spoke a little more, shook hands, then split up. She came over to the desk sergeant, spoke briefly, then hurried out the glass doors into the parking lot. She was practically running.

Davis returned to the bench and took each child by the hand.

'I'm sorry, Ms. Caldwell,' the desk sergeant said. 'But Ms. Mallard left specific instructions on behalf of her client. Mrs. Dougherty will not be speaking to any reporters.'

I bolted up. 'When? When did she say this?'

'Just now. That was Rebba Mallard.' She pointed to the parking lot. I ran over to the glass doors and looked out.

The hatchet-faced woman was driving away in a black Isuzu.

'What the hell's going on?' I said to the desk sergeant.

'I told her who you were,' she said. 'She chose not to speak to you.'

I spun around to face Davis Richard. My anger was great, all the more so because I was afraid I'd blown my first assignment and would lose the job I'd done so much to get. 'What did you say to her?'

His children cowered a little, holding his hand tighter and snuggling up to his legs. Jesus, now I was frightening little kids.

'It's a long story,' Davis said with a smile. 'I can explain it all at dinner tonight. I promise it won't be at Bullwinkle's. Deal?'

10

I spoke softly into the phone so no one could overhear me:

'Here's the thing with breaking up. Forget whatever I said before. This is the real scoop, what it all comes down to. What you must never forget. When you're with someone for a long time, your bodies change. I've read studies about women friends who, just because they spend time together, start to menstruate at the same time. Their cycles become sympathetic. That's what I'm talking about here. Only with a man, it's something else, something even stranger. You develop this special vision. As if that other person causes you to mutate, boosts you up another step on the evolutionary ladder. You get this third eye or something. With this eye you can actually glimpse the future. It's like the door to your future has been left open, just a crack, and you can peek through. In that sliver of light you can see the two of you sitting there years from now, a little grayer, a little crankier, but there's still two of you sitting on that ratty sofa watching TV sitcoms and reading movie reviews in *Newsweek*. He tosses you a pretzel from a bowl without looking, you sip from his beer without asking, you both still laugh when your cat licks her butt. God, that's a comforting glimpse. You think, I can live with that. But when you break up or divorce, whatever, it's as if that door has suddenly been slammed in your face. You can no longer even imagine what your future will be like. Wait, I take that back, you can imagine, you start imagining, and what you imagine is horrible, like being on the Sahara set of *Lawrence of Arabia* and no one else is around, just windy desert stretching to the ends of the universe, and you close your eyes against the peppering sand and start walking in no particular direction, your footprints dusted clean as soon as you make them.'

'Wren,' Linda Marley called from across the room, 'can I see you in my office.'

I hung up the phone. 'Sure, Linda.'

I turned, saw Linda march into her office. She left the door open for me and I saw my future through the crack: You're fired, imposter!

I pushed the phone across the desk so everything was in its place. You couldn't even tell that anyone had ever actually sat at this desk. Which was true, I guess. I hadn't done any real work here, just this last phone call to my own answering machine. I thought about what I had just done: called my own machine and discussed the meaning of breaking up. Tonight I would go home and play back my messages and I'd have to hear it. If my life were a self-help book, how would what I'd just done be interpreted? Either it was an example of a proactive healing step one could take to come to grips with the addictions of one's life, or it was a pathetic symptom of a deeper neurosis. Some choice.

'So, how's the story coming?' Linda asked as I entered her office. A little thought-for-a-day calendar stood next to her phone. Today's thought was IN A FIGHT BETWEEN YOU AND THE WORLD BACK THE WORLD. KAFKA.

'I've hit a snag,' I said.

She leaned back in her chair, her expression one of concern, not gloating, which I appreciated. 'What kind of snag?'

'One named Davis Richard.'

'Christ. what's he up to now?'

'You know him?'

'Sure. One-time video whiz kid, started in the waterbed business, ended up producing some of those early celebrity exercise videos. Made a fortune by the time he was twenty-five. What's he got to do with a murder case?'

I told her what had happened at the police station. She didn't look at me while I spoke. Instead, she glanced around her office, studying the Victorian motif-flowered wallpaper, wainscoting, antique desk—as if she were contemplating a new decor. When I finished my story, she looked at me and shook her head. 'What's your next step?'

'I was hoping you would tell me.'

'It's your story, Wren. Jonathan gave it to you.'

'Yes, I understand that. But if Season Dougherty's lawyer won't let me speak to her, then what can I do? I guess I could interview everyone else involved with the case, piece a story together that way.'

'Yes, you could do that,' she said without enthusiasm.

'But that's what everybody else is doing, right?'

'Probably.'

I sighed. I felt frantic, like I was in the middle of a quiz I hadn't studied for. 'I could speak to Mr. Krieg, see if he has any other connections he might rattle.'

'Jonathan is out of town.'

'What? He can't be.'

'I drove him to John Wayne Airport myself.'

'But a couple hours ago he was outlining his daily schedule of rabbis, fitness freaks, and tutors. He came here to fulfill his dream of running a magazine. Christ, he was so evangelical about it all.'

Linda laughed. 'Yes, well, real business intruded. He has an empire to run. He got wind of a hotel up for sale and he's on his way to Miami. He took the rabbi with him, though, if that makes you feel any better.'

'He could still make a few calls, From Miami.'

Linda yanked a long strip of tape from her dispenser and wrapped it around her two fingers, sticky side out. She leaned across the desk and brushed the sleeve of my jacket. The tape clogged with lint. 'Wren, what have you got that no one else has?'

I shrugged. 'Stringy hair?'

'Concerning this story. What lead do you have?'

I thought. 'A dinner invitation.'

She pulled the tape from her fingers, wadded it up, and tossed it into her waste can. 'Well then?'

*   *   *   *   *

I climbed out of the car and stared at the sign above the door.

'I'm not going in there,' I announced.

Davis pressed a button and the door locks in his car thudded closed. It reminded me of those movies in which kidnapped heiresses are always being locked into the backs of their limousines while knockout gas seeps in through the ventilators. Except I was no heiress and this was a Ford Taurus station wagon. Although it did have a car phone, it also had coloring books and broken crayons on the floor.

'Be brave,' Davis said, taking my hand.

'I didn't much like the experience the first time around. Why would I want to do it again?'

'That's the point. This time it's just for fun. Now we don't have to be so geeky.'

I looked him over. The easy smile, the same casual clothes as earlier, only with the addition of a sports jacket with patches on the elbows. 'I can't imagine you ever felt geeky anywhere. You were born a lifetime member of every club.'

He laughed. 'That's the nicest thing you've said to me since we met. I'm encouraged.'

'Let's go in.'

The restaurant was called Prom Nite. They stamped the backs of our hands as we went in, a little red pineapple. It had been a lot of years since I'd had my hand stamped. I stared at it, flashing back on some of the places Robby and I used to go back in college that did this. Robby had always balked at the process, I'd enjoyed it, as if it were some form of validation. You're Okay, move on in here with the others who are Okay. We'd formed a community of The Okay.

'Relax,' Davis said, misinterpreting my stare. 'It's just part of the ambiance. It's just food dye.' He licked the back of my hand and the pineapple was gone. 'See?'

The back of my hand tingled coolly as his saliva evaporated. A light shiver giggled up my spine. I brushed my hand against my wrist but it was already dry.

Davis held the door open for me and I entered.

The interior of the restaurant was a replica of a school gymnasium that had been decorated tackily for a prom. There were even basketball hoops strewn with twisted crepe paper and balloons. The wood floors were glossy with various painted lines for basketball and volleyball. Bleachers lined both sides of the room. A mirrored ball hung in the middle of the room, rotating slowly as red and green and yellow lights bounced off and sprayed the room with colored-light shrapnel. The waitresses wandered about dressed in sixties-style prom queen outfits, complete with crinoline slips and plastic tiaras. Music from the fifties and sixties played over a scratchy loudspeaker system for authenticity. When the Everly Brothers' 'Cathy's Clown' was over, a man's voice came over the PA system. 'Attention, students,' he said, 'there will be no meeting of the chess club next week because club president Herman Glimpshir will be in Baltimore at the science fair. Thank you.'

'What do you think?' Davis asked.

'Reminds me of *Carrie*. Minus the blood.'

A balding man in a white suit and red bow tie cut through the crowds and headed straight for us. His close-cropped beard and heavy eyebrows reminded me of John Ehrlichman, after Watergate when he was a writer. 'Davis, good to see you again.' The bald guy used both his hands to shake Davis's hand.

'Don, business looks good.'

Don looked around the bustling room as if noticing the people for the first time. 'Making a living, man. You know.'

They both nodded as if there were some deeper meaning. I'm not a male basher, but I hate when guys do that. One of them says something inane and they both pay respect to it with a moment of thoughtful silence accompanied by world-weary head nodding. Maybe Mom was right. Boys just rot.

'Don, this is Wren Caldwell. She's a writer with *Orange Coast Today*. Wren, this is Don Hamilton. He owns the joint.'

Don shook my hand. 'Now I'll be sure to renew my subscription.'

'Thank you,' I said.

'So, what's it like to work for Jonathan Krieg? Is he as strange as the *Wall Street Journal* says?'

'What does the *Wall Street Journal* say?'

Don looked surprised. 'You know, that he's very . . . well, strange. You know.'

'I guess I'll have to read that article,' I said.

Don looked disappointed that I hadn't revealed any juicy Jonathan Krieg anecdotes.

'What're our chances of getting a table?' Davis asked.

'Just leave it to Principal Hamilton, kids.' He escorted us to a table, whispered something to a passing waitress, and seated us. 'Enjoy, enjoy. No making out behind the bleachers and no smoking in the lavatories.'

'Thanks, Don,' Davis waved.

'Nice meeting you,' I said.

'Same here,' he said and walked away.

When Don Hamilton had disappeared, I asked, 'Have you known him long?'

'Since high school.'

'Band practice together?'

He smiled. 'Football.'

'Seems like a nice guy,' I said. 'And successful.'

'Couldn't get a date at his own prom. That's probably what gave him the idea for this place.'

There was something about his tone that surprised me. He wasn't saying it in a harsh or bitter way, rather in a dismissing way, as if Don's whole existence could be summed up by that one statement. It was what a popular kid might say about an unpopular kid.

'Fortunately for most of us,' I said, 'there is life after the prom.'

'I don't know about that. High school is where your potential is measured, catalogued, and put on display. After graduation it's just a matter of living up to that potential, coloring the numbers. Alfred Hitchcock used to plan out his movies, figure out every single shot before he ever got near a camera. He once said that after he'd planned it, the actual making of the film was boring. See what I mean?'

'The fun part of our lives is high school? That's a bit depressing, don't you think? Christ, if that's true I'd have nothing to look forward to but hemline checks and bad cramps.'

'Didn't you like high school? I bet you hung with the popular crowd. You have that look.'

What look? I wanted to ask. I remember mostly driving a carload of girlfriends between places. I could see me behind the wheel of my dad's Fairlane trying to collect gas money, though I hardly remembered where it was we were always going. But I didn't want to go in that direction with Davis. 'Can we talk about Season Dougherty? She hung with a pretty popular crowd too. Until this morning.'

A waitress arrived at our table. Her blonde hair was clamped down with one of those plastic tiaras, but a couple of the fake diamonds had fallen out leaving black eyeless holes. She wore a fresh corsage on her wrist. The smell of lilacs choked off my appetite. 'Mr. Hamilton says to take special care of you two,' she said. 'Can I start you off with some drinks?'

We both ordered beers. She left, her crinoline crackling like radio static.

Davis took a deep breath and laid his hands flat on the tablecloth. 'Okay, Wren, let me explain what happened today. I've been in the home video business for about eight years. I'm very good at producing videos so I've managed to make a few bucks at it.'

I pulled out my steno pad from my purse, flipped open the cover, and read from my notes. 'You've made over five million dollars so far and counting.'

'You've done your homework.'

'You're good at videos, I'm very good at homework.'

He looked across the table at me with a troubled expression. He avoided my eyes. 'What you don't know is I've been having serious tax problems.'

'How serious?'

'Well, whatever bread and butter we don't eat tonight, I'm taking home.' He smiled. 'Okay, maybe not that bad, but bad enough. When I got into this business, there was no competition to speak of. Now every kid with a Minicam is producing videos. You can't make a killing anymore, not like when I started. Also, I've never been a very good businessman, not when it comes to squeezing figures into those narrow columns.'

The waitress returned with our beers and a complimentary basket of french fries smothered in chili. Davis ordered shrimp and I ordered chicken.

'Anyway, for the past few years I've been trying to get into the legitimate end of the movie-producing business. You know, made-for-TV movies, theatrical releases, that sort of thing. Because of who I am, the fact that I've made some money in this end of the business, people in Hollywood will see me, take me to lunch, listen to my ideas, tell some jokes, and then brush me off like a poor second cousin. If I want to invest money in one of their films, then they're interested. If I want them to invest, they're not. Hollywood mathematics. So, I decided I needed some hot properties that would force them to deal with me.'

'That's what this is about?' I must have spoken loudly because several nearby diners looked over at me. I lowered my voice. 'You made a *movie* deal with Season Dougherty? Jesus, she just killed her husband and you were already thinking about a goddamn movie?'

He shook his head. 'It wasn't like that. I'd signed the papers with her a month ago, while she was still in prison. I saw a good TV movie in it, something starring Bonnie Franklin maybe or Elizabeth Montgomery. For the past month I've been trying to cut a deal with the networks on her story. One of those heroic-woman-triumphs-over-the-system kind of movies, with a last scene of her and her daughter walking off together hand in hand, freeze frame on their smiling faces. No one knew she was going to go after the poor bastard with a shotgun.'

I watched his finger bat a crumb across the tablecloth as if he were playing hockey. 'Now that she has shot-gunned the poor bastard, where does that put your project?'

'I closed a deal late this afternoon. The studios were bidding against each other for the project all day.' He couldn't help but smile.

'So now you're a movie mogul.'

'Well, I'm making a movie.'

'Then why not let me interview Season Dougherty. The publicity is only going to help your movie project.'

He shook his head. 'No can do, Wren. We're still hoping to get her acquitted. We don't want your magazine screwing with the outcome of this story.' His finger chased the crumb across the tablecloth to within inches of my hand. He stopped and for a moment I thought he was going to touch me. He didn't, but my skin still heated up fast as if he had. I didn't move my hand away.

'So where does that leave us?' I asked.

'Having dinner. Enjoying each other's company.'

'You could have told me all this at the police station. Or over the phone when I called you back.'

'Do you want to be here? If not, I'll take you home right now.'

I looked at him. His blue eyes glistened a little, his jaw was clenched tight. Maybe that's what sincerity looked like, maybe that was his negotiating face. I couldn't tell. 'Pass me the fries,' I said. 'I still have one unclogged artery somewhere.'

He smiled. 'So, tell me about yourself, Wren. Tell me everything that you wouldn't want the *National Enquirer* to find out.'

'I sometimes sleep in flannel pyjamas with feet on them. I guess that's my darkest secret. That and the clump of hair clogging my bathroom sink.'

This time he did reach over and touch my hand. Just briefly, a little squeeze of my knuckles and then gone. 'Really,' he said, his voice soft and low. 'I'm interested.'

Me too, I thought. But what do I tell him, Wren's life story or mine? Last night with Ethan it was easy, he wasn't all that interested in my past. And the few times he did ask about me for the sake of keeping the conversation going, I didn't mind feeding him chunks of Wren's life. After all, the entire evening was more like being in a stage play anyway.

This was different. Not that I had any genuine feelings for Davis Richard. Too early for anything like that. But something was going on. Atoms were smashing into each other, colliding all over the place like a slam dance. That produced heat. Yet, who was he attracted to, me or Wren? At that moment I didn't want to be Wren anymore, trouble was, I didn't want to be Luna either. Luna had such bad luck.

So I told him about my degrees in art and philosophy and English. I told him about my writing, my plans for a magazine. I sounded enthusiastic, the way Wren always did, the way she'd always known what she wanted.

161

'I've read some of your stuff,' he said. 'Very impress-ive.'

'My stuff? Where?'

'You submitted some articles when you applied over at the magazine. A friend made copies for me and messengered them over to me this afternoon, after we met.'

'A friend? You have a spy at the magazine?'

'Spy might be too romantic a word. I have a friend who keeps an eye open for anything interesting that might make a good movie.'

'A paid friend.'

'Those are the best kind.'

'How did you get to be such an expert in cynicism?'

'Divorce.'

'So you're one of those guys for whom divorce is an excuse to be a bastard.'

'I didn't need an excuse.'

'Oh, really? What's next, you mash a grapefruit half in my face?'

He held up his hands in surrender. 'Let's stop right here. I enjoy this bantering with you, but this isn't who I am. Maybe I'm trying too hard with you, I don't know. But I'm not really that cynical, unless you consider someone cynical who suspects professional wrestling may not be all on the up and up. And that politicians aren't all altruistic. Other than that, I coach my kids' t-ball and soccer teams. Believe me, you can't do that with a cynical attitude.'

We ate our meals, talked about the world in general. Davis was witty without making a point of proving it. He was surprisingly informed about world politics, knew which South American country was doing what and how to pronounce all those tricky names of the leaders who were always shaking their fists when they made speeches.

After dinner he drove me back to the office where I had left my car.

'I'll follow you home,' he said.

'No need. I can find it.'

'Just to be safe.'

I thought about the white Subaru, but it was nowhere in sight. Just my Rabbit in the parking lot and his Taurus station wagon with the Teenage Ninja Mutant Turtle coloring book in the back seat and a broken burnt umber crayon. 'Okay,' I said. 'Sure.'

I drove onto the freeway and he stayed close behind me. I decided to change lanes for no particular reason, to see what he would do. He changed too. I changed lanes again. So did he. I slid into the center lane and cradled my car between two huge diesel trucks. He dropped behind the second truck. I darted into the left lane and sped up, passing half a dozen cars. He sped up and passed them too. I drifted into the far right lane behind two Asian women in an old Corvette. We crawled along. He crawled behind us. I was encouraged, almost happy.

When I pulled into my assigned parking space, Davis kept circling the lot until he found a place to park. I hadn't really counted on that. I had expected him to just pull up, say good night, and keep going.

Now he was walking toward me, hitching his pants, looking like nothing in the world bothered him, a man you couldn't insult or intimidate. He even kicked a stone across the lot and stopped to see how far it went.

'You're the weirdest driver I've ever seen,' he said, smiling.

'Thanks for seeing me home.'

'I'll walk you to the door. I'm a full-service date.'

'This isn't a date.'

He looked over his shoulder at a black Jeep that was pulling into a space across the lot. When he looked back at me some of that former confidence was strained. 'What do you want to call it?'

He leaned forward then and took both my arms in his hands. I knew he was going to kiss me and I wanted him to. For the first time since breaking up with Robby, I wanted a man to kiss me for some reason other than breaking the monotony of not being kissed.

We leaned into each other, I guess, because I was suddenly off-balance, kept from falling to the pavement by the weight of his body against mine. I could feel his body heat through his clothes. My skin went tropical. His hands slid to the small of my back and dug into the skin, two fingers pressing my buttocks.

His chin had a little afternoon stubble and I could feel the skin on my chin and cheek being scraped raw. It burned a little, but I didn't mind.

We broke apart and started walking up the walkway toward my front door. A few plump snails spotted the sidewalk like raisins in white bread. I looked up at Ethan's apartment above mine and saw the curtain move as if someone had just ducked back. I didn't know what I would do when we reached my door. Should I invite Davis inside? What would that lead to? I couldn't sleep with him tonight, not after having slept with Ethan last night. It didn't matter that this was different, that I really wanted this man who made celebrity exercise videotapes and who could speak to children. If I slept with him so soon after Ethan, I would feel too much like a prom-night slut. Okay, maybe that was a little outdated, but that was me. Me, not Wren.

We stopped in front of my apartment door and kissed again. He pulled me tighter to him, until I could smell the faint tang of his morning after-shave, something musky. His hand slid farther down my back and grabbed a fistful of buttock. His thigh bumped up against my pubic mound like a tree stump. I opened my legs a little and pressed closer.

Music from someone's apartment filtered out around us. *Sha la la, do be wa, dum dum dum, yup yup dum. Oh, blue angel* . . . Roy Orbison's mournful voice was perfect for this. I felt completely engulfed by Davis, the music, his cologne, the cool night.

'This is the kind of movie you should make,' I whispered. As I spoke, my lips moved against his. He nodded and kissed me harder. I ground myself against his thigh and he rubbed his crotch against my hip. We gyrated to the music. Perhaps I would ask him to stay after all.

'*Oh, blue angel, don't you cry Just because he said good-bye . . .*'

I had that same record. It used to be Robby's but he'd overlooked it when he'd taken his half of our collection. I think he'd left it because of that scratch toward the end—

'*Oh, blue ang—blue ang—blue ang—*'

I pulled my lips away from Davis just as the door to my apartment opened. Now the music blared loudly, the needle finally hopping the scratch as usual.

'Hey, Wren, you're finally home,' the strange man in the doorway said cheerfully.

Davis's hands fell away from my back, his thigh retreated from between my legs.

'You don't think that's too loud, do you?' the strange man asked, nodding at the record player.

I looked at him, my face frozen in shock. He was in his early thirties and tall, a couple inches over six feet. He was wearing only a pair of beach shorts, so I could see he was lean and muscled. His long brown hair was pulled back and tied into a ponytail with a white athletic sock. His bushy mustache hung over his upper lip like a grass awning. In his right earlobe was an earring: a gold dragonfly with a red ruby eye. The same as the one I carried in my purse.

He was smiling in a bright happy way, leaning against the doorjamb. My 1st Place Long Jump stein filled with beer was gripped in one hand a half-eaten chocolate donut in the other. 'We're a little low on groceries, hon. But we'll fix that, now that your beloved Byron is back in town.' He kissed me on the cheek and looked at Davis with a friendly grin. 'So, who's your friend?'

11

. . . and then the stranger was kissing me.

His hand, cold from my trophy glass, cupped the back of my neck and pulled me forward as he leaned over. I strained my head against his hand and crowbarred my elbow against his chest. But his lips swooped down and brushed against mine quick as a raindrop.

'Ow!' he hollered as if stung. His scream vibrated against my lips. I smelled the beer on his breath. He jerked away. 'Owowow, Jesus, ow!' He hopped around on one foot, accidentally splashing beer onto his shorts and down the front of my skirt. 'Damn, that hurts! Damn!'

'What hurts?' I said. My elbow is pretty bony so I guess I could've, if not bruised a rib, maybe pinched a nerve or something. Or maybe I'd bit him without knowing it. I licked my lips for blood. I tasted shrimp dinner, leftovers from Davis's kiss.

'Cramp,' Byron gasped. He took long limping strides, marching in choppy circles around Davis and me. The sidewalk was polka-dotted with brown snails that despite his apparent agony he hopscotched around. Every other step he hammered his first hard against his right thigh, as if driving in a stubborn nail. After a couple orbits around us he slowed down to steady hobbling gait. 'Jesus, that smarts. Wow.' His eyes shone with tears. He was knuckling them when he stepped blindly forward and we heard a loud crunching sound that at first I thought might be his toe cracking against the sidewalk. He lifted his bare foot.

The gooey remains of a crushed snail clung to his sole like a flattened potato chip. He put his foot back down without scraping off the snail, as if it weren't there. If it had been me, I'd have been under a steaming shower by now, wire scrub brush in one hand and pumice stone in the other. But Byron just stood there gulping beer with one hand and rubbing his tenderized thigh with the other. 'B-12,' he said. 'I've got this intestinal thing so I don't absorb vitamin B-12 right and I get these god-awful cramps.' He leaned up against the doorjamb, out of breath. He moved his glass of beer back and forth between Davis and me as if he were toasting each of us. 'So,' he said, 'you guys fucking each other or what?'

'What?' I asked, shocked.

'Hey, Wren, nature is nature, right? I've got nothing to bitch about. I've been away and you've got needs.' He winked at me. 'Boy, have you got needs.'

I started to protest, but all that came out was 'Oh, shut up' in a peevish little girlish voice I didn't even have when I was a little girl.

He sat down in the open doorway and stuck his feet straight out. With one hand he unknotted the white athletic sock that bound his ponytail. He shook his head from side to side. The ponytail disappeared in a flurry of whipping hair that now hung down to his shoulders in thick corkscrew curls. He mopped the crushed snail remains from his foot with his sock, then snapped the sock like a whip. Snail fragments flung off and scattered across the sidewalk like bits of a soft-boiled egg. The sock had a wet snail-guts stain on the sole. He pulled the sock onto his foot anyway. He dug into his pocket for the matching sock and crossed his leg to put that one on too. As he lifted his leg, I could look straight down his pant leg and see he wasn't wearing anything under his shorts. His bald penis lay curled in a nest of dark pubic hair like a baby condor they'd recently hatched at the zoo. I looked away.

'Like I said, I've been away. Whatever happened, happened. None of my business. You two could have humped and pumped your way across this entire state, it don't bother me. The past is past.' He dug his fingers into his thigh muscle, massaging until the skin turned bright red. He looked up at Davis and smiled. 'Thing is, guys, now I'm back.'

The sprinklers suddenly came on, hissing water onto the thick green foliage that the Pine Stream Apartments prided itself on. The air smelled wet and tropical. The sidewalks were quickly crowded with more snails. Brown clumps like inflated mushrooms dragged themselves across the concrete leaving shiny fluorescent trails dotted behind them. Oddly, the snails didn't move in a straight line, the trails were winding like Arabic writing, even though they seemed to be merely crossing the sidewalk. For some reason, that bothered me. Even a snail must know what a straight line is. I was angry with the snails for their inefficiency. Half a dozen of them were swarming the remains of the snail Byron had crushed, munching silently on the body parts.

Byron stood up, wiggled his toes inside the socks. He lassoed the three of us with a circular finger motion. 'I guess we've got some figuring to do here, mathematically speaking. The way I see it, two into three just won't go. At the very least, it wouldn't be sanitary. One of us will always be stuck with sloppy seconds.'

What had Wren seen in this guy? I admit, he had a certain manic energy and dreamy bad-boy look. But there was a dangerous aura about him. It was like standing too close to a performance artist who has soaked himself in gasoline and is now jumping back and forth over a lighted candle.

'Did you know there were no bricks in your toilets? Don't you know there's a water shortage down here? I filled up a couple of your Baggies with flour and wedged them into the tanks until we can pick up a few bricks.'

I wanted to say something, take control right here and now. Tell him to take his snail-slimed socks and clear out, or else.

But I had secrets now. People with secrets must step carefully. I composed myself, softened my voice. 'Listen, Byron, I think we—'

'Ssshh, ssshh . . .' He turned around and lightly kicked the door open the rest of the way. The doorknob banged into the foyer wall. 'I love this song. This guy is so clever. Listen . . .'

I listened. Sometime in the past few minutes, Roy Orbison had been replaced by some guy with a low morose voice. He sang slowly, like a man with a sink full of dirty dishes and last week's *TV Guide*:

> 'I saw a stranger with your hair
> Tried to make her give it back
> So I could send it off to you
> Maybe Federal Express . . .'

Byron snorted laughter. 'Those lines always crack me up. Kid sitting next to me on the Greyhound ride down here, econ major at USC, played that on his portable CD player. Kept playing it over and over. He had his headphones on but he kept singing along with it in this horrendous voice that sounded like a lawn mower stuck in a clump of foot-high weeds. People kept giving him the evil eye, but he just read his textbook, made notes in the margins, and kept right on singing. Turns out he's just gone all the way up to Oregon to visit his high-school girlfriend, the former Miss Pine Cone Festival, and she dumped him the day he arrived. She'd fallen in love with the manager of the toy department of the local K mart. Who would guess the Pine Cone Queen could be so cruel?'

'And you stole his disk,' I said.

He looked surprised. 'Stole it? Why would I do that?'

'You mean he just gave it to you? A perfect stranger just gave you a CD because you liked a song you hadn't even heard properly?'

'He didn't give it to me, sweetcakes. I won it.'

'You won it? How did you win it?'

'A bet.' He didn't say anything more.

I imagined him shuffling a deck of cards he'd marked in prison, the backs a sleazy pornographic photograph, probably two women, both a little too fleshy, long flat tongues exposed like thirsty spaniels.

'I don't get it,' I said. 'Why didn't you "win" the CD player too?'

'I didn't want it. I'm not greedy, Wren. You of all people know that. Remember New Orleans?'

I moved closer to Davis, was comforted by his cologne.

Byron grinned and reached up and pinched his dragonfly earring as if he were activating some hidden switch, secretly photographing Davis and I with our stunned and dopey expressions. I noticed for the first time that the tip of his left little finger was missing down to the first knuckle. The top of the stump was white and waxy like cake icing. The sight of it made my stomach clench. I started to reach for my bra strap for some serious nail rubbing but caught myself and clutched my purse instead. I slid my thumbnail up and down against the shoulder strap. Byron smiled at me as if I'd just done something he'd physically made me do. Even though I knew he hadn't, my face flushed with hot blood. I dropped my hand to my side.

'Hey, hey, hey, guys!' Byron clapped his hands festively. 'This isn't going to be much of a homecoming party if I'm the one doing all the talking. I've been starving for conversation with non felons. Tell Uncle Byron everything.' He nudged Davis with his elbow. 'She still do that water spout trick in the bathtub?'

Davis ignored him and stared straight at me. 'You're married, Wren?'

Byron slipped a bare arm around my shoulder, his hand with the glass of beer resting heavily on my collarbone. 'For almost two years now. Didn't she tell you?'

'Your paperwork at the magazine said you were single.'

I ducked and twisted away from Byron's arm. 'We've been separated.'

'Two years,' Byron nodded. 'But I'm out of prison now and we can start over. Make up for lost time.' He grinned at me lewdly.

'Prison?' Davis looked at Byron, acknowledging his presence for the first time. 'That sounds interesting.'

'Yeah? In what way?'

'I don't know. I guess the challenge. See if you can take it. Guys always wonder, I think.'

'Yeah, well, the challenge. There is that, I suppose. You don't look for any big meaning in the experience. You just want to do your time and get out.'

'I guess it's only interesting if you're watching it in the movies.'

'Oh, you want interesting? Prison lore. Inside information. How's this: You know what the most popular book in prison is? Guess.'

Davis looked at me, then back at Byron. 'A law book?'

'The Bible.'

'Oh, right. Everyone turns to Jesus because it looks good to the parole board. Is that it?'

Byron laughed. 'Some, sure. But that's not the reason. It's the paper, man. They use a high quality paper that's opaque and very, very thin.' Byron pinched his finger against his thumb and pretended to take a long drag on a cigarette. 'Very uplifting, very spiritual.'

Davis shook his head in amazement. 'You mean they tear out the pages and use them to roll cigarettes?'

'That interesting enough for you?'

Davis laughed, so did Byron. They seemed like old buddies.

'What were you in for?' Davis asked. 'If you don't mind my asking.'

Byron's grin cinched tighter. Gone was any sign of being buddies. Just that fast. 'I do mind, yes.'

'Sorry, I didn't mean to pry.'

'If you want to know if I got cornholed, fucked in the asshole, just ask. We're practically family here. You wanna inspect the evidence? C'mon, don't be shy. Here,

171

take a peek.' Byron dug his thumb into his waistband as if to yank down his shorts.

Davis looked at me. So did Byron. As if they expected me to say something or do something, change the course of events that suddenly seemed to be rushing toward violence.

'I have to go to the bathroom,' I said. I had no idea what to say to either of them. I didn't want Davis to think I'd been leading him on, but I couldn't afford to have Byron tell who I really was. I went inside the doorway. I needed to settle this thing with Byron, alone. 'Davis, thank you for dinner. I'll talk to you later.'

'You going to be all right?'

I looked at Byron. I searched for some sign that would answer Davis's question. But Byron was merely staring up into the night sky, his face now childlike with concentration. Would I be all right with a guy who smoked the Bible?

'Where's Orion?' Byron suddenly asked. 'I can never find Orion. I know about the belt thing, the three little stars, but I keep seeing those three stars everywhere.'

'There,' Davis said, pointing. 'That's Orion.'

The three of us looked up.

'That's the belt, there's the sword.' Davis wagged his finger as if sketching in the details, connecting the dots.

'Yeah,' Byron said. 'That's it all right. Amazing. Makes you think, doesn't it?'

'About what?' I asked, an edge to my voice.

'What do you mean?'

'What exactly does it make you think about? The vastness of the universe? The insignificance of man? The origins of superstitions? What?'

Byron nodded. 'No wonder I can never find it, I don't know what it means.'

Okay, I knew I was being a born-again bitch, but what other weapon did I have at that point? With a man like Byron, there was only so much bluffing a woman could get away with. It's like arguing with a cop, you can only

172

push so far before your eye starts dropping to the gun on his hip. Men always have the unspoken threat of physical violence. Even if the last time they threw a punch was on the playground in third grade, they still have that knowledge that they could throw another one if they had to. They possess the logic of knuckles. And Byron, with his long ragged hair and missing finger and dragonfly earring, was particularly threatening. Was I in any danger from him? I knew he'd had something to do with Wren's missing teeth. He'd just been in prison. How had he lost that knuckle? I imagined a prison fight over cigarettes in the machine shop while the paid-off guards looked the other way. Certainly keeping Wren's identity wasn't worth my life, or my teeth. I had options: I could leave. I could always go back to being Luna.

Jobless.

Homeless.

Loverless.

That Luna.

I made a face at the prospect.

Davis looked over and caught me screwing up my face. 'Are you going to be all right?' he asked again. He enunciated each word slowly, like someone from a crisis hotline. I loved his soothing voice. Byron's scratchy voice sounded like a plastic shovel repeatedly stabbed into a dune of coarse sand.

'I'll be fine,' I said.

He touched my arm briefly, just grazed the hairs of my forearm. Byron was still staring up at the stars, so I didn't think he noticed.

Suddenly Byron, without looking, reached back and took my hand. He pulled me to his side. His hand felt moist and slippery. I sniffed. His skin smelled like my obscenely expensive skin lotion, the French stuff Robby had given me last year for our anniversary and that I had doled out drop by precious drop like a youth elixir. He reeked of its herbal scent. First my trophy glass, now my lotion. I pulled my hand free. He didn't seem to notice.

Byron pointed heavenward again. 'You guys remember when they used to pronounce Uranus, Your Anus?'

'What?' Davis said.

'Who do you think decided we should change pronunciation? I don't think it was the scientists. I think they probably got a kick out of it the old way. Can't you just picture a bunch of them sitting around in white lab coats surrounded by billions of dollars of sophisticated equipment, and one of them saying, "I think we should send a probe up to Your Anus, Doctor." And all of them cracking up, doing variations. "Can we find boosters big enough to get all the way up to Your Anus?" "We have to see if there's intelligent life on Your Anus." And they're all laughing and spitting up their coffee and donuts at this. What do you guys think?'

Davis and I stared at him.

'I'll call you tomorrow,' I said to Davis.

Davis nodded, hesitated a moment, then shoved his hands into his pockets and ambled casually away as if he'd just spent an evening playing miniature golf.

Once we were inside, Byron closed the front door and locked it. 'Boy, did you think that guy would ever leave?'

'I was about to say the same thing about you.'

'Me? I'm the last person you want to be throwing out of here. I give your whole masquerade veracity.'

'Veracity? Where'd that word come from? Prison course in power vocabulary?'

He smiled. '*Chacun à son goût*. It means, "each to his own taste".'

'You speak French?'

'I wasn't born in prison.'

'Just to serve time in one.'

He sighed. '*Homo lupus homini*.'

'Stop showing off. Hitler spoke French too.' I didn't know if that was true.

'That was Latin, not French. It means, "man is a wolf to man". Get it?' He gulped down the last of the beer. 'Remember that line from *The Adventures of Robin*

Hood? Errol Flynn says something insulting to the evil prince and one of the prince's toadies bellows, "You speak treason!" And Flynn grins and says, "Fluently." That was the coolest.'

I thought of Wren's missing teeth. 'You're no Robin Hood.'

'And you're no Wren Caldwell. So fucking what?' The anger in his voice startled me; it was as if he'd just yanked barbed wire through my closed fists.

'Do you drive a white Subaru?' I demanded.

'If I had a car, why would I have taken a Greyhound down from Oregon? You ever use the rest room in one of those things?'

That surprised me. I had assumed that the person following me today had been Byron. I'd even been relieved to have that mystery finally solved. Jesus. Who else was poking around in my life? I needed to think, to get away from Byron and figure out what I would do now.

'I'm going to the bathroom,' I said, taking off down the hallway. In the bathroom I could think things through. Maybe I could sneak the phone in and call someone for advice, even Robby if I had to. This was an emergency. Robby would help.

'Careful,' Byron hollered after me. 'I've left a few of my things out.'

I didn't stop. 'You can repack them when I get back.'

As I walked into the bathroom, I reached over to flip on the light switch. But before my fingers found it, my foot stepped into gravel and started to skate out from under me. I fell backward, blindly catching myself on the sink with my elbow before hitting the floor. 'What the hell . . . ?' I stood up and groped the light on.

I was standing with one foot in a litter box.

Byron stood in the doorway. 'That's Hector's.' He walked into the bathroom and swept aside the shower curtain. A long-haired gray cat was lying in the tub, his head resting on a small sample bottle of shampoo. He opened one eye, then closed it. Byron pointed. 'That's Hector.'

175

'You're just out of prison, for God's sake. When did you have time to get a cat?'

'I won him.'

'You win a lot, don't you?'

'I'm very lucky.'

I shook green cat litter from my shoe. 'I don't care how you got him, get him out of my bathroom.'

'Well, the other bathroom didn't have a window, just that little overhead fan. Let me tell you, no matter what they advertise on TV, soiled cat litter stinks. So I switched bathrooms with you. Believe me, you're better off.'

I looked around the bathroom. My hair dryer was gone, so was my jewelry box and my soap dish in the shape of a porcelain hand. Everything was gone except the sample bottle of Prell shampoo under Hector's furry head.

'And,' Byron continued, 'since this bathroom goes with this bedroom, I switched them too.' He hooked a thumb over his shoulder. 'You're down the hall now.'

I ran into my bedroom. My covers and sheets were gone. The mattress was bare. A pair of men's torn jeans and white underpants were strewn next to the Sealy Posturepedic label. I slid open the mirrored closet door. My shoes and dresses were gone. His three white shirts and two black pants hungs pathetically in the huge double closet. On the floor was a pair of battered running shoes and a pair of new black loafers polished to a scaly gloss. I stomped over to the dresser and yanked open the top drawer. My underpants, bras, garter belt, stockings, and panty hose were gone.

'I already moved your stuff for you. Figured it's the least I could do.' He smiled at me as if waiting for thanks.

'This is my room, my dresser, my clothes, you bastard. How dare you touch my stuff!'

'Well, actually this dresser was Wren's. I know because we bought it the week after we were married. It's only fair I get some use of it now.'

'You don't really think I'm going to let you stay here, do you?'

He threw himself on the bare mattress, hands webbed behind his head. 'I don't see what choice you have.'

'I can throw you out, that's what choice I have.'

'You mean physically? You mean you're going to come over here and physically throw me out?' He smiled, but not in a threatening way. More like he was curious how I'd do it.

'Not me personally,' I said. 'That's what police are for.'

He sat up, crossing his legs Buddha style. 'I suppose so. Of course, when they ask who's making the complaint, what name will you give them?'

I thought for a moment, leaning against the empty dresser. 'Whatever name I give them, they'll still kick your ass out of here. And if you're on parole, they'll toss you right back into jail. Are you on parole?'

'Nope. I'm free and clear. More than I can say for you.'

'What's that supposed to mean?'

He shook his head. 'Never mind. I'm not your therapist. Aren't you going to call the cops?'

I sat on the opposite edge of the bed. I was exhausted, drained. 'You can't just bust into my home and blackmail me into letting you stay.'

'Who's blackmailing anybody? I'm just looking for a place to stay while I get my life in order. Isn't that what you're doing?'

'You have no right to talk about what I'm doing. You don't know anything about me. You don't have a clue to what I'm doing.'

'And I don't much care. I'll just be here long enough to take care of some business.'

'What kind of business?'

'Being lucky.'

'What about Wren?'

He gave me a cold stare, like we were passing on the cell block. 'Wren's dead.'

'Yeah. You don't act too broken up.'

'You aren't exactly anointing the room with tears,

177

babe.' He gestured to include the contents of the apartment. 'You made out okay.'

I stood up, walked to the window. I looked out and saw Ethan walking across the dark parking lot in his bathing suit. He had a Spuds McKenzie towel slung over his shoulder and two cans of beer he was holding by their plastic cuffs. He was heading in the direction of the Jacuzzi.

I had not cried since Wren's death. I hadn't shed a single tear. I had felt awful, devastated, wrung out, all those things people say they feel at a great personal loss. Yet, I had not cried once. What awful things did they say about me? More than anything else I'd ever done or not done in my life, I felt most guilty about that.

I changed the subject. 'How did you find me?'

'I talked to Kate. She told me about giving you Wren's things.'

I thought of Kate. She had cried. 'How is Kate?'

'Tough. One of the last of that breed. Pioneer stock.'

I nodded.

'Anyway, I wanted some of Wren's papers, letters mostly, and some photo albums. So I started tracking you down. It wasn't hard. The tricky part was figuring out why you'd purposely tried to disappear with that dead-end address in Texas. That got me curious. A few phone calls placed after Wren's death from her phone were down to this area. I checked that against where her transcripts were sent. The rest was easy.'

'For a criminal maybe. What were you in prison for?'

'Trespassing.'

'I don't want jokes, I want some straight answers.'

'Relax, you're safe. I'm not after your money or your body.'

'What happened to Wren? How did she lose her teeth?'

He smiled. 'Wren told you about her teeth? I'm surprised. She didn't want people to know.'

'What happened?'

'An accident.' He held up his left hand and wiggled the stump of his little finger. 'Accidents happen.'

The phone next to the bed rang and I jumped.

He reached for it. 'I'm expecting a call. Do you mind?'

'Yes, I mind,' I said. I marched to the phone and snatched it up. 'Hello?'

'Are you okay?' Davis asked.

'Yes, fine. How'd you get to a phone so fast?'

'Car phone.'

'Oh, right.' I looked over at Byron, who kept grinning at me, like he was my big brother about to tease me about some boy calling to ask me to the dance. I picked up the phone set and walked as far away from him as the cord would allow. I turned my back.

'Can you talk?' Davis asked.

'Sure.'

'You're not in any danger, are you?'

'No. I'm fine.'

There was a long silence and I thought we got cut off, maybe he was passing under some electrical wires or something.

'I don't know what to say,' he said. 'I like you, Wren. I just want to know what's going on.'

'It's complicated.'

'Just tell me this. Am I out of the picture?'

I hesitated. Things were complex enough right now without adding a romance. But then I remembered that kiss, how I'd wanted to drag him inside.

'Are you sure you're okay? There's something about that guy. I don't know. He's your husband, you know him better than I do. There's something about him, though.'

'Let me call you back tomorrow, Davis, okay?'

'You didn't answer my question. Am I out of the picture? What was going on between us tonight?'

I sighed. He wanted an answer. He deserved an answer. God knows, I didn't want him out of the picture. I wanted him very much in the picture. I turned around and looked Byron straight in the eyes as I spoke into the phone.

'You're not out of the picture, Davis. Things may be a little out of focus right now, but I can make you out just fine.'

'Good. That's good.' He sounded very happy.

The Call Waiting tone sounded.

'Hold on a second, Davis, I have another call.' I pressed the button and said hello. As always, for the first second I expected to hear Robby's voice.

'Where is he?' the brusque voice demanded.

'What?'

'You deaf or just stupid? Where the fuck is he?'

'Who do you want? Byron?'

'Yes, I want Byron. Put Byron on the line. I would very much appreciate talking to Byron.'

'I'm on the other line, he'll have to call you back.'

'I don't give a fuck about your other fucking line. Put him the fuck on or I'll wrap the other fucking line around your fucking throat, you fucking moron. One phone call and I can have you fucking killed within the hour.'

I pressed the button. 'Davis, I'll call you tomorrow. Good-bye.'

I handed the phone to Byron. 'Your father, I think.'

'Did he threaten to have you killed?'

'Yes.'

Byron took the phone. 'Hey, Grudge, what's up? . . . Right . . . How much? . . . Okay, an hour.' He hung up the phone. 'I've got to go.'

'I'll help you pack.'

'Just for a while. I'll be back.'

'Nice friends you've got. He threatened to make a phone call and have me killed within the hour. Like he was ordering a goddamn Domino's pizza or something. Can he do that?'

Byron stooped down beside the bed and pulled out a black leather attaché case. He opened it with the lid facing me so I couldn't see inside. He reached in, checked the contents, closed the lid. 'I'll be back later.'

'You can't stay here,' I said. 'I've got to rent the other

room out. I don't make enough to pay for this apartment.'

Byron turned his back, pulled his shorts down, and kicked them off. Naked, he grabbed his underpants from the bed and stepped into them. Then he pulled on his jeans. 'How much?'

'What?' I said.

'How much rent will you need to charge?'

'I don't know. Four hundred, I guess.'

He dug into his jeans and pulled out a thick roll of bills. He peeled off five $100 bills and handed them to me. 'First month plus utilities.'

I fanned out the bills. A large red stain blotted the corner of the top bill and got progressively smaller with each subsequent bill until the bottom hundred, which was spotless. 'What's this?' I asked. 'It looks like blood.'

He pulled on a blue Nike sweatshirt and came over and examined the bills. 'Yeah, that's blood all right.'

'What's blood doing on your money?'

'Don't worry,' he said, slipping into his loafers, grabbing his case, and running for the door. 'It's only dog blood.'

12

Two days later Byron still had not returned.

Four of the five $100 bills were sealed in a plastic Baggie and taped to the underside of my desk drawer at the office. The fifth bill I gave to Detective Diesel and asked him to do me a personal favor and have the bill tested.

He raised an eyebrow, thick as a root. 'Tested for what?'

'This.' I showed him the reddish-brown blotch.

'Looks like blood.'

'Probably animal blood,' I said. 'Dog.'

'What would dog's blood be doing on a hundred-dollar bill?'

I shrugged. 'Might be somebody mugged a blind person who had a seeing-eye dog.'

'Might be or already happened?'

'I don't know, I'm just guessing.' That was the only explanation I could come up with. That is, if it really was dog's blood. 'Believe me, as soon as I know anything definite, I'll let you know.'

'You don't strike me as the kind of irresponsible reporter who would risk letting a violent criminal go free just for a byline.'

'I'm not. I'm not even a reporter, I'm just a writer. A magazine writer.'

'I'd hate to be wrong about you. I don't like being wrong about people. Makes me nervous. You start misjudging people in this business, you'd better retire fast.'

I patted Detective Diesel's arm assuredly. 'You're not wrong. I'm no Lois Lane. This is only a personal matter.'

'This have anything to do with that car that's been following you?'

'I don't know yet.' I hadn't seen the white Subaru all day.

He waved the bill between us. 'This turns out to be human blood, you and me are gonna have a sit-down. A long one.'

'Absolutely.'

He gave me a stern look, like a man in pyjama pants and sports jacket picking up his teenage daughter from the police station after midnight. 'Do you know what you're doing, Wren?'

'Don't worry, Detective, everything's under control.' I slapped on a confident smile and held that pose for a few seconds until he nodded and walked off down the corridor toward the forensics lab. He held the $100 bill pinched between thumb and forefinger, away from his body, as if it were a poisonous multilegged insect. When he turned the corridor, I deflated my smile and walked on wobbly legs back to my car.

*　　*　　*　　*　　*

The first day after Byron left, a bunch of people at the office took me out for a welcoming lunch. I'd just arrived at the office, twenty minutes late because of my visit with Detective Diesel. I'd covered by saying that I'd made another attempt to visit Season Dougherty, but no one seemed to care that I was late anyway. Billie Meyers, the young receptionist, had organized the whole lunch, including reservations at an Indian restaurant called Sitar by the Sea.

'Don't get your hopes up,' Billie explained. 'There's no sea.' Apparently there was an original Sitar by the Sea in

Redondo Beach that did in fact have an ocean view. That was too far away. The one we were going to was in Anaheim, near Disneyland.

Linda Marley, my boss, begged out at the last minute after she got a phone call. With the receiver wedged between neck and shoulder, she peeled off her cardigan sweater and waved us on, mouthing, 'I'll catch up to you later.' I saw her slip her American Express card to Billie.

In the elevator Billie said, 'I like your hair.'

'Me?' I said. People rarely complimented me on my hair. I have that look, I don't know what you'd call it, but whenever I'm shopping in a bookstore, other customers think I work there and ask me where Jean Auel's new novel is. That look.

Billie touched my hair. Her nail polish was French style, robin's-egg blue around the base, tipped with white half moons. She stroked my hair once. 'It's so natural, like you don't have to do anything to it.'

'I've done everything to it but set it on fire.'

She nodded seriously. 'Now that you mention it, it is a little dry.'

*   *   *   *   *

When I returned from lunch there were three yellow While You Were Out messages from Davis. They all said, 'Call me!' The last one, which came in just ten minutes earlier, said: 'Don't make me stomp your snails.' Kirstie, who took the messages, wrinkled her nose and frowned when she gave them to me. 'What's that mean? Is that sexual?'

I was sitting at my desk reaching for the phone to call Davis when Linda Marley tapped me on the shoulder. I turned. 'Hey, boss.'

'Sorry I couldn't make lunch,' she said.

'That's okay. Thanks for picking up the tab.'

'Any progress on the Season Dougherty interview?'

'Some. I had dinner last night with Davis Richard.' I fanned out his three yellow messages.

She made an approving face. 'Very impressive. Did you sleep with him?'

'Is that everybody's favorite question?' I asked. If she would have asked me that yesterday I'd have been shocked and stuttered out some lame answer. But after half an hour exposure to Byron, I was battle hardened. 'No, I didn't sleep with him. I'm working a story, not a street corner.'

She touched my shoulder. 'Take it easy, Wren. I have to ask these questions.'

'Because you're worried about the ethical position of the magazine?'

'No, because I'm nosy.' She laughed so hard she started coughing.

'Yuckety yuckety yuck,' I said, deadpan.

She kept laughing. Just when she'd slow down and seem about to stop, she'd start up again, laughing louder than ever. It was like a child playing with the volume control on a radio. When she laughed, the skin around her eyes accordioned into a dozen folds. This was the first time I was conscious of her age, which someone at lunch had placed at forty-four.

Finally she stopped laughing, dabbed her eyes dry, and tugged on the back of my chair. 'Let's go,' she said.

'Go? Where?'

'Meeting. Jonathan Krieg is back in town and waiting to see you for an update on the Season Dougherty interview.'

'He's back already? He just left yesterday.'

'He finished his business. Today he's ten million dollars smarter. Now he's back, checking his list to see who's been naughty or nice.'

'Which list am I on?'

'Let's find out.' She gestured toward Jonathan's office and I followed. I had the feeling that she knew something

185

but wasn't telling me. Linda was a friendly woman, but she could be very mysterious. At lunch Clive Remick, the magazine's restaurant critic, had toasted her with: 'She's the best managing editor we've ever had. Unfortunately, we're the best fuck she's ever had.' Everyone had laughed. I didn't ask what he meant because I didn't want to get involved in any office politics. I just wanted to get by. Besides, she seemed to like me, though we weren't exactly chummy.

We walked to Jonathan Krieg's office door. Yesterday the door was bare, today his name was painted on in plain black lettering. Under his name, the single word: PUBLISHER. I popped in a Breathsaver to kill the tandoori lamb taste in my mouth. Linda rapped on the door like a cop. 'Jonathan?'

'Uunnnnh . . .' came the muffled grunt.

Linda opened the door.

Jonathan was bent over, his hands grasping the seat of a straight-back chair. Straddling his hips was a muscular blonde woman in a two-piece workout outfit. Her black bottoms were cut high over her hips, cinched at the waist with a wide yellow belt. Thick ropy veins stemmed out from under the cloth covering her vagina. The strip of cloth was so narrow she had to have shaved her entire pubic area. Her midriff was bare, exposing square muscle platelets up and down her abdomen that reminded me of a turtle shell.

'Uuuunnnh . . .' Jonathan said. He was wearing shorts, a T-shirt, and new Reeboks. He had a starburst varicose vein at the back of one of his knees.

Standing next to the chair was the male counterpart to the woman riding Jonathan's back. He was equally blond and equally muscular, though his skin was chalk pale. A small Band-Aid covered his left nostril where it looked as if he'd had a skin cancer removed. Her muscles were crowded like a city skyline; his were great slabs like rocky mesas. His were so large the rest of the room suddenly seemed small and airless.

' . . . six . . .' he counted.

'Uuuunnnh . . .' Jonathan said, lowering his hips and raising them again. His face was slick with sweat. His varicose vein looked bloated with blood. His mouth hung open as he gulped air.

' . . . seven . . .'

The muscular woman smiled at me. 'These are called donkey raises. Want to climb on with me? What are you, a hundred and fifteen?'

'Hundred and eighteen,' I said.

'Uuuunnnnh . . .' Jonathan huffed. He looked over at me with panic in his eyes.

'I think he can take it,' she encouraged.

I shook my head. 'I'm not sure I could. I just ate.'

' . . . nine . . .'

Jonathan's last effort was shaky. He lowered himself okay, but he couldn't seem to push himself up again. His arms wobbled, his legs started to buckle. Three drops of sweat slid off his nose into the carpet. He was stuck at half mast.

The muscular woman surreptitiously angled her toes downward to touch the ground, taking some of her weight off Jonathan's back. With a mighty grunt, he hoisted her the rest of the way up. She quickly dismounted, slapping his butt playfully. 'Not bad, masked man. Same time tomorrow?'

Jonathan nodded, too out of breath to speak. He collapsed into the chair.

'Remember, only the tough get buff. Maybe that should be boffed.' She laughed.

Her blond companion laughed too.

'Hi, I'm Vicky,' the muscular woman said to me, offering her hand.

Reluctantly, I extended mine. I expected a bone-crunching grip to send me to my knees. But she shook with only a moderate firmness.

'Vicky, this is Wren Caldwell,' Linda said.

'Hi, Wren. This is my husband, Karl.'

187

Karl waved as he packed their gear into a duffel bag. 'Hey,' he said.

'Hi.'

Vicky reached into the side of her shoe and pulled out a card. She handed it to me. It said: Vicky and Karl Mueller. Executive Fitness. Your Place. Your Convenience. (213) 555-4328.

I backed up a couple steps. For some reason, I felt nervous having such a muscular woman standing so close to me. I wasn't homophobic, it just made me feel inadequate, like watching Davis with his kids. 'I didn't know I looked that bad,' I joked.

'Looks are nothing,' Karl said mysteriously. I had the feeling Karl wanted to be someone's guru.

'Karl means, a person can look good on the outside, but still be weak. Everyone worries about their weight, but they should worry about their muscle tone, the fat content, that sort of thing. We do a lot of work in this building, no problem to fit you in.'

'Thanks,' I said. 'I'll think about it.'

She shrugged, looked disappointed. 'That's okay. This intensity isn't for everyone.'

I hadn't really intended to think about it, but now I felt bad, as if I'd not only hurt her feelings but proven myself to be a wimp. 'I just started here,' I explained. 'I have to wait until my schedule settles down.'

'Sure,' she said.

Jonathan Krieg came to life. 'Great idea, Vicky. A kind of corporate fitness program. I'm sure we'd get a break on rates from the insurance company, plus it would be a business write-off. What do you think, Wren?'

I nodded, forcing enthusiasm. 'Great idea.'

'Whatever,' Vicky said. She hoisted one of the duffel bags. Metal clanged against metal at the motion. The muscles across her chest wrenched. Her top was cut low enough that I could see her breasts were just nipples on the end of another slab of muscle. I was impressed.

When they left, Jonathan motioned for Linda and me

to sit. He pulled a small white towel over his face and inhaled, the towel conforming to his face like plastic wrap. I thought of Season Dougherty's husband, the dish towel over his chowdery face to keep the flies off. Jonathan sat with the towel over his face without moving for so long I feared maybe he'd passed out or had a heart attack or something. I looked at Linda but she kept her gaze on Jonathan, her expression cool and professional.

After a couple minutes had passed, Jonathan exhaled loudly and the towel billowed like a sail and fell from his face. When he spoke, it wasn't to either of us, but to an imaginary audience in general, as if he thought documentary cameras were always waiting in the wings. Recording.

'I've been around,' he said. 'I've done some things. I've learned from my mistakes. Guy gets to be my age, has had my successes, he might get a bit cocky, think he's'— here he made finger quotes—"arrived", But I have found there is no such thing as arrival.'

Linda said, 'Life is not a problem to be solved but a reality to be experienced.'

He pointed at her excitedly. 'Exactly. That's exactly what I meant.'

'Kierkegaard said it.'

He looked uncertain. 'Of course. The point is, I've never stopped experiencing. I'm the type of guy—'

I cringed. Wren and I once made up a list of the Ten Commandments of Dating. Commandment number six was 'Never shall ye date anyone who starts a sentence, "I'm the type of guy . . ."' (unless he is Dion singing 'The Wanderer': *'I'm the type of guy who never settles down . . .'*).

'—who lives for the climb, not the actual getting there. I don't care about sticking my flag at the top of the mountain, I care about the next ridge to climb. See what I mean?'

Neither Linda nor I said anything.

'The point is, I don't do anything half-assed. I've decided to do this magazine. I've set some goals for the kind of circulation I want and the kinds of stories I think will get me that circulation.' He looked at me with a frown. 'This Season Dougherty thing. Linda tells me you haven't interviewed her as planned.'

'No, sir. I went to the jail but she wouldn't see me. She'd already signed away the rights to her story to Davis Richard.'

'Who's he?'

Linda said, 'Local entrepreneur. Did celebrity exercise videos.'

'He's looking to break into feature films with this deal,' I said.

Jonathan twirled his towel and snapped it at a nearby potted plant. A chunk of leaf flew off in shreds. 'I've already negotiated with a studio for the rights to our exclusive articles on this case. But none of that will work without an interview. That's the key.'

'I'll probably be seeing Davis later today. I'll talk to him about it.'

Jonathan twirled his towel forward, then backward, then forward again. The whole time he was twirling, he stared at me, directly at me without flinching. This continued for a full minute, maybe longer. Linda stared at him, he stared at me. I rubbed my thumbnail against the edge of the chair leg behind me.

'Wren,' he finally said, 'Linda and I have been discussing the situation. Perhaps we were overzealous in sending you out on such a complex assignment right out of the dugout, so to speak. Maybe you need some seasoning first. You need to get to know your way around town first. See who's who, what's what.'

'I can get the interview,' I said. 'I just need a little more time.'

'That's what I'm saying. Take your time. I'm blaming me here, not you. I rushed you into something without giving you enough time.'

Linda said, '"Time is the longest distance between two places,"'

'I hadn't heard that before,' he said.

'Tennessee Williams.'

'Oh. I like it.'

Linda didn't smile, didn't look at me. She stared straight ahead. Whose side was she on?

'Anyway, the point I'm making here is that we'll be assigning someone else to the story for now, maybe have them do the legwork and bring you in for a rewrite. Maybe you were right when you said this isn't your kind of story.'

And I'd meant it too. Then. But now something else was involved. Luna would have expected this, would have even welcomed the relief from pressure. But I was Wren now. Wren's life had gotten me the job, but after one day Luna's personality had me close to getting fired. I had a job I would have never otherwise gotten, I'd met a man like Davis, who I would otherwise never have met. Thanks to Wren's life, I had a chance to change mine. Biology is not destiny. If I failed here, midnight would strike and Cinderella would be back to her old ragged self. I had to get that interview.

I stood up. 'I can get the interview. Trust me.'

Linda turned toward me. 'Actually, Wren, Jonathan and I have been talking about another new area for the magazine to explore. Something we've never done before. I think you'd be especially suited for it. It's challenging.'

'What about the interview?'

'I'll be taking care of that personally.' She looked at Jonathan.

He rocked back in the chair and folded his towel into triangles like a small flag. He smiled at me. 'You'll thank us, Wren. Wait and see. You'll love this new assignment. It has everything the public wants. I've already set up a meeting. You have twenty minutes to get there.'

191

13

Twenty-five minutes later.

'Hello,' I said, offering my hand. 'I'm Wren Caldwell.'

'First things first,' he said to me. 'Did you bring the money?'

'Yes,' I said.

'Cash? This is a cash kind of business. They told you that, didn't they?'

'Yes, they told me. I brought cash.'

'When I say cash, I'm talking about, you know, the actual green stuff. Real money. Not a voucher, not a purchase order, not a check. Not like in department stores when they ask if you're paying cash or charge, you say check, they say that's the same as cash. It's not. Nothing's the same as cash. Cash is cash.'

'I understand what cash is,' I said. 'Can I sit down now?'

'Okay, sit.' He gestured to the chair across the table. I sat. The chair was ladder-backed and black, lacquered to a high gloss with a pink pillow on the seat. The table was the same black, except for the middle, which was thick turquoise tile. The luncheon menu was written with pink and turquoise chalk on a small chalkboard in front of me. There were five items, four of them fish. The place was called Sante Fe Depot and the cuisine was supposed to be southwestern, though I didn't think fish was a big southwestern specialty. 'I already ordered,' he said. 'I don't have much time.'

He was smoking a smelly cigarette, something French I think, that was black and twisted like licorice. There was no ashtray on the table so he flicked the ashes into the vase with the fresh-cut pink carnation. A few of the patrons from nearby tables were giving him hostile looks. Since he ignored them, a lot of those looks were then directed at me. I squirmed under their glares.

'Isn't this a nonsmoking section?' I asked.

He shrugged. 'I'm not smoking.'

He spread the pink linen napkin out on the table in front of him. He smoothed it, ironing it flat with the heel of his hand, then with the edge of the chalkboard menu. Slowly he lowered the burning tip of the black cigarette to the napkin, just enough to make a charred brown circle, but not enough to burn a hole or catch the napkin on fire. His concentration was intense, he never looked up at me. I could tell this was not just a pyromaniac episode, he seemed to be making some sort of pattern. But it was one I couldn't yet recognize. He spoke without looking up: 'I don't know you, you don't know me, we don't know each other. You're new at this, I know that and you know that I know. So maybe you think: "Well, the little bastard is going to try to take advantage of me." Right? You thinking that, Wren?'

'Yes,' I said. 'I'm thinking that.'

'Okay, good. Very good. I'm glad you said that. That means you're sensible. I can do business with someone sensible.' He glanced up at me and smiled, then returned to touching his cigarette to the napkin. The burn marks were beginning to cluster like brown pearls. 'The fact is, I *will* try to take advantage of you. Every single chance I get. I'm here for the money, strictly the money. As long as we both know that going in, then we can do business.'

'Then let's do business.'

He nodded, but didn't look up. He leaned closer to the napkin, his face only inches away from the tabletop. He lowered his cigarette tip so slowly it was excruciating to watch. He looked so damn intense, like he was defusing a terrorist's bomb. My stomach began to knot up with anticipation. He eased the glowing tip a molecule lower, until it didn't exactly touch the napkin, but the heat singed a few of the pink threads. The result was an unusual shade of rust-brown. Whatever he was making, it began to take on a certain beauty.

'What's your last name again?' he asked.

'Caldwell. Wren Caldwell.'

He stuck the brown cigarette between his lips and offered me his hand. 'James Smith. And that's my real name. Spelled just the way you think, no y instead of i, no e at the end.'

I shook his hand. 'Nice to meet you, James.'

James was about twenty. His face was smooth, still a few years from shaving daily. Three small blemishes clustered on his neck under his left ear.

'James,' I said, 'why doesn't one of the waiters come over and make you stop smoking? Isn't there a fire law or something?'

'Is there?' He dabbed the burning end rapidly against the napkin like a sewing machine needle. I could see now he was creating a face, a woman's profile. The rapid spotting was the hair. The effect was startlingly real, the hair seemed to thicken with texture. He cocked his head and studied his work, frowned, and shook his head with displeasure. He took a deep drag that brought the tip of the cigarette into a bright flare, and once again began dabbing the napkin. An elderly couple two tables away scowled at us. I gave them back a weak smile but that didn't seem to carry much weight with them. The man threw his credit card down on the check and waved at a waiter.

'I thought this was supposed to be a sort of clandestine meeting, James. We shouldn't draw any attention to ourselves.'

'Why? We're not doing anything wrong.'

'For starters, smoking in a nonsmoking section is illegal.'

'Illegal, but not wrong. Big difference, Wren. Besides, I'm not really smoking. I'm creating.'

I looked around at the waiters as they glided swiftly

around the tables. They all wore black pants, white shirts, and those corny square-dance string ties with a hunk of turquoise embedded in the silver slide. None of them even looked our way. 'I don't understand why someone doesn't come over here and tell you to stop. My God, you're burning a napkin. *Their* napkin.'

'They know me.'

'You eat here a lot?'

He shook his head. 'First time.'

'First time? And they know you?'

He looked up. 'You're not from around here, are you?'

'You mean Orange County? No, I'm from up north.'

'San Francisco?'

'Oregon.'

'Oh, you mean *really* up north.' He studied me a second, actually looking at me for the first time. His eyes were pale blue, almost white. The rest of his face was an odd mixture of nonmatching parts. None of his features went with the rest of his face, as if the nose, the lips, the ears, everything had been borrowed from various other bodies and slapped together to make his face. The resulting effect made him seem sickly. 'My dad's a producer. He makes TV movies.'

'Anything I've heard of?'

'How would I know what you've heard of?' He grinned. 'Sorry, that's my dad's line. He always says that when people ask him that question. He picked it up from some novelist buddy of his who, I think, got it from William Faulkner or Raymond Chandler, which gives you a perspective on the amount of originality around here.' He flicked an ash into the vase. 'My dad's movies all have the word confession in it or diary, as in "Confessions of a Mistress" or "Diary of a Groupie". You know.'

'And he eats here a lot. That's how they know you.'

'They know me because they know me.' He shook his head. 'Let me show you.' He gestured at a waiter, a young man in his early twenties with tinted glasses.

'Yes, sir,' the waiter said.

'Hey, man, how's your screenplay coming along?' James asked.

The waiter looked startled a moment. 'Pardon?'

'How's the script going? I heard you were almost done.'

The waiter's formal demeanor thawed slightly, his face sagging into artistic turmoil. 'Yeah, well, I'm having a little trouble with the third act. The third act is a bitch.'

'You'll crack it,' James said. 'Could we get some wine for the lady? Wine, Wren?'

'Diet Coke will be fine.'

The waiter, dazed, a little confused, nodded and left.

'See what I mean,' he said. 'I never saw that guy before in my life. In Los Angeles everyone you meet is a wannabee actor or director. But in Orange County everyone's a fucking scriptwriter. Cuts down on the commuting into the city. There aren't many producers living down here yet, so my dad is pretty well known. I can't tell you how many places I go, someone manages to slip me their script to give to my dad.'

'And do you?'

'Depends. Like I said, I'm in business to make money. They pay me a few bucks, I'll see Dad gets it.'

'What's a few bucks?'

'You have to gauge the person, figure what they can afford. No less than fifty, that's for sure. I've gotten as much as five hundred though.'

I couldn't help smiling at his wise-guy routine. 'If everyone else is an aspiring writer, what are you? An entrepreneur?'

'An artist.' He smiled and returned to barbecuing his napkin.

The waiter brought me a Diet Coke. He hesitated, staring at James, waiting for him to look up. I got the feeling that now that he'd thought about it, he was ready to pitch his script much better than before. Only James refused to look up. Finally the waiter drifted away.

'Okay, here's the thing,' James said, looking up now. 'Here's how we work it. I call you whenever I've got something, we meet, I give you what I've got. You pay me. Simple enough?'

'Depends. What have you got today?'

He reached inside his sport jacket and pulled out a folded piece of paper. I read it.

'Jesus,' I said.

'You can keep it. It's a photocopy.'

I read it again. Legal stationery, with a design that incorporated the lawyers' initials. Much more impressive than Robby's lawyers' stationery. The letter was addressed to a famous TV actor who played a surgeon-turned-private-detective who specializes in locating missing children. The attorney who wrote the letter was not one of the partners mentioned in the firm's logo. Nevertheless, he made it clear that his client was only twenty and pregnant with the actor's child. Naturally, if some financial settlement could be reached, none of this need go public.

I folded the letter and looked at James. 'How old are you?'

'Eighteen. But I seem older, right?'

'Yes, you do.'

He nodded, returned to torching the napkin. This was my new assignment. Gossip gathering in Orange County. I would be given my own column, though I would use a pseudonym, Missy Carver. Jonathan told me that was to protect the integrity of my real name, which they still had great hopes for on more legitimate articles. Afterwards, in the hallway outside Jonathan's office, Linda confided that the pseudonym was to protect the magazine: once I'd established Missy Carver as a valuable name, I couldn't hold up the magazine for more money by threatening to walk. 'The name is copyrighted,' she'd said.

'What went on in there?' I'd asked. 'With Jonathan.'

'What do you mean?'

197

'You could have backed me. You saw the messages from Davis Richard. That's a solid lead.'

Linda had looked off then, not at anything in particular unless it was the Sparklets water cooler. She looked as if she were trying to remember my name. 'My backing you would have done no good for you, he'd already made up his mind. But it would have hurt me because he would have had to overrule my suggestion, which would have given him more a sense that he would be better off running this magazine without me. He already has his doubts about you.'

'Why? There wasn't anything I could do.'

'That's not the point. He set up an exclusive interview and it didn't happen. That makes Jonathan look bad, weak. But not if he has someone to blame.'

'Me.'

'Exactly.' She turned and looked me in the eyes, smiling slightly. 'You don't trust me now, do you? You can't be sure whether what I just told you is the truth or a cover for some secret agenda of my own. Right?'

'Right.'

'Welcome to the Hotel California,' she'd said and walked off.

I laid the attorney's letter on the table between James and I. The famous actor in question had a hilltop home in Laguna and could be seen walking his wife and Doberman along the beach on weekends. Definitely Orange County gossip, the kind guaranteed to be picked up by the wire services. Missy Carver would hit the scene in a big way.

'How do you do it, James?'

'Concentration,' he said, burning an eyebrow on the portrait.

'Not your art. This stuff. The gossip.'

'Oh, that.' He leaned closer to the napkin, executing a tricky arch to the eyebrow. Satisfied, he looked up. 'Friends in low places. I operate a baby-sitting service made up of high school and junior high school kids. Be-

198

cause of my dad's contacts, I get a lot of the wealthy clientele. Once you're inside somebody's home, you're bound to find something incriminating. Hell, if I showed you some of the photographs and videotapes alone. Man, the stuff people like to tape themselves doing. I mean, why bother. It's not like you need a record, like you'd forget how or anything.'

'Why don't you sell those? The tapes and photos, I mean.'

He gave me an angry grimace. 'That wouldn't be right.'

I didn't bother arguing. I didn't want the photos or tapes anyway. I didn't even want this letter. I wanted that damn interview with Season Dougherty.

'So your baby-sitting brigade rummages through these famous people's houses until they find something juicy? Then you sell the goods to some tabloid?'

'That about covers it. Except now I'm selling it to you.'

'How did Mr. Krieg get in touch with you?'

James laughed. 'He didn't do squat, man. One of my girls baby-sat for the guy who used to own this magazine. She found out about the sale. I figured new broom and all that, this would be a good time to approach Mr. Krieg about my services. I practically doubled my price with that move.'

'Why do you do this, James? It can't just be the money, not if your father is as well off as you say.'

He grinned. 'God bless the child who's got his own, you know what I mean?'

'But don't you find this kind of sleazy?'

'Man, people who want to be famous deserve everything they get. They did it out of greed and ego in the first place. Now, are you gonna pay me or lecture me on morality? I mean, you don't have to buy my goodies if you think it's so wrong.'

I looked around, made sure no one was looking, then quickly slid an envelope with $800 across the table. I whispered, 'That's the amount Mr. Krieg agreed upon.'

He blew on the tip of the cigarette just as he dabbed it to the napkin. An eye seared into the napkin below the eyebrow. He clamped the cigarette between his teeth, took the money out of the envelope, and counted the bills.

'Isn't this supposed to be a little more secretive?' I asked.

'What for? Cash changes hands all the time around here. They'll think I'm either your dealer or your love slave.' He grinned. 'All here. The letter's yours. I'll have more for you over the weekend. That's our busiest time.' He stood up, held up the napkin like a matador cape. It was magnificent. Each feature was finely shaded, the eyes slightly frightened but steady. The lips puffy yet tense. Hair oddly permed, the owner desperate to give it some life, the way paramedics try to shock heart attack victims back to life. The profile was of a woman struggling to hold still, not to bolt for the nearest exit. The profile was of me.

'That's very good,' I said. 'Can I have it?'

'No.' He smiled. 'You can buy it.'

'Sure.' I opened my purse for a twenty.

'A hundred.'

I tossed the twenty down and took the napkin. He let me.

'Unusual medium,' I said. 'Cigarette and linen.'

'I like fire. Usually I do blowtorch and copper. Or firecrackers and papier-mâché. I'm thinking about something now, a new piece using glass and a shotgun. I like to use things that destroy to create. Nothing is ever destroyed, it just changes shape. You know what I mean?'

'Any work that means all that is worth more than twenty dollars.' I handed him another ten-dollar bill.

He looked confused a moment, then stuffed the bill in his shirt pocket.

'What happens when you become a rich and famous artist?'

'Then you can start going through my underwear

drawer and selling *my* secrets.' He smiled and handed me the restaurant bill. 'Meanwhile . . .'

I paid the bill.

14

I was crawling beneath the telephone tree. That's what it looked like, a stainless-steel cactus tree with three telephones branching off a metal post. Each station was separated for privacy by small squares of clear plastic the size of cafeteria trays. The phone tree was planted in concrete between the student bookstore and the snack stand among the aluminum picnic tables and benches, also sunk into the cement. Students still registering for summer school were walking back and forth, laughing and talking. Some just sat on the benches or lawn with heads tilted toward the hot sun. Some smoked cigarettes in that careless and confident manner that made me wish I still smoked too.

Instead, I was on my knees hunting for the quarter I'd just dropped.

While I was down there among the cigarette butts and nuggets of chewing gum, a barefoot boy skateboarded up to one of the other phones and made a call. All I could see were his skinny legs, clothed in baggy shorts that hung past his knees with a Vision Street Wear patch at the hem of one knee. Both shins had scabs where it looked like he'd skidded across pavement. He stood on the skateboard and rocked side to side while he talked to someone named Durango about last night's date with Brook.

' . . . of course I went down on her, dude. I mowed box till my fucking lips went numb.' He listened. 'No way, man, never again. It was awful. Her pussy should have a

202

warning label like on those medicine bottles: Danger! If swallowed, induce vomiting.' He laughed.

I found my quarter and stood up, angling a little so the boy on the phone could see me through his plastic tray. Maybe I thought I could embarrass him or something. I don't know why I bothered. I guess because it was something Wren would have done and I was still in character. In high school when I played Laura in *The Glass Menagerie*, I'd limped around school for a week after the play was over.

The boy was bare-chested, his T-shirt tucked into his waistband and draping down over his butt. At most, sixteen. The receiver was clamped between his head and shoulder, freeing his hands to scratch at the phone with his keys. He looked over at me. Then he smiled in a flirtatious way and winked.

Suddenly I was angry. The tips of my ears were burning. I wanted to tear off the plastic tray between us and smash his face like some avenging Bionic Woman, watch him slo-mo backward over a few steel picnic tables. I didn't know why. I wasn't a raging feminist slapping on THIS EXPLOITS WOMEN stickers everywhere. And he was just a kid; he'd either grow out of his stupidity or he wouldn't. My world didn't hang in the balance. What did it matter to me? Except . . .

Except he hadn't even been embarrassed. He'd seen me glaring at him and it hadn't mattered. He'd felt no shame. If he had seen Wren, the real Wren, he'd have blushed, looked down, hung up, and skated away. I knew that. I wasn't mad because he'd insulted women, I was mad because he had insulted me. I was still a ghost of a person, as hollow as a dried bone. Children and animals could see through my charade the way they could recognize a vampire.

I removed my glasses and a strand of hair that had been pinched in the hinge was yanked out of my head. I winced and cursed my glasses for the thousandth time. They always did this. By the time I was forty, I'd be plucked bald. The pain drowned my anger and I returned to the phone, thumbing my quarter into the slot. Ghost or not, I still had mortal pressures: a job killing me, a possible new boyfriend calling me, an ex-convict living with me, a white Subaru following me, an interview with a murderess eluding me, a teaching job haunting me.

I called the magazine. Billie answered.

'You got a message from a Detective Diesel, Irvine PD,' she reported.

'What'd he say.' I braced myself.

'He says: "Arf, arf."'

'"Arf, arf."'

'Yup. That's all. That make any sense to you?'

'Some.'

'It's not sexual, is it?'

'Photos will follow,' I said.

She laughed.

So, the blood on the money was dog blood after all. Byron had told the truth. I should have felt better, but I didn't. What was dog blood doing on the money in the first place? I started imagining some satanic ritual, pentagrams, ancient ornate daggers, scratchy wool robes. Puppies whimpering in iron cages.

'Any other messages?' I asked.

'Another one from Davis Richard. And I quote: "I took you to the prom, now it's your turn to put out. Call me." *That's* got to be sexual.'

I laughed. 'If it is, you can read about it in my column.'

'Oh, yeah, I heard you're doing a gossip column now. Congratulations. That is so neat.'

'It's something I always wanted to do. That and cure cancer.'

'I think it's a great idea.' She sounded genuinely excited. She paused, lowering her voice to a whisper. 'We've been a little too stuffy around here. Most of our articles are just puff pieces, booster crap meant not to offend any potential advertisers. But I figure, advertisers don't care what you say as long as you deliver the subscribers. Right?'

'Mr. Krieg would certainly agree.'

'He's wonderful, isn't he. Guess what he's doing this morning?'

'Skydiving from the top of the building?'

'He's putting chalkboards in all the toilet stalls. Men's and women's. He said having a bowel movement is subconsciously destructive and puts people in a destructive mood. That's why they scratch graffiti in the stalls. This way they can still do their graffiti and not destroy the stalls. Good for morale, good for maintenance costs. It's like, no detail is too small for this guy. Cool, huh? Maybe you could write an article about the chalkboards for the mag?'

'Actually, Freud said that defecating was a creative act, not destructive.'

'Well, the idea's the same, right? Keep the stalls from getting all marked up. We could have this cool photo layout of various stalls and their graffiti. That would be the "before" picture. Then we'd show how neat and clean the stalls are after the chalkboards are installed. Show how the graffiti changes, from limericks to poetry. Something like that. Think I should pitch the idea to Linda?'

'With you writing it?'

'You bet. It's my idea.' Her voice was loud now, with a bitter edge. 'I started working here so I could learn the business. I've got my degree in English, you know.'

'I didn't know.'

'Two years at a JC and two at Cal State Long Beach. I worked on the school newspaper.'

The boy next to me hung up his phone, checked the coin return for change, then skated away. His T-shirt flapped like a cape behind his butt. By tonight he'd probably be back in Brook's arms. Where would I be?

On the phone, Billie explained how she would pitch her idea to Linda. She told me about her term papers in her English classes. She got all As and Bs. All things considered, Billie was probably more qualified to be writing for the magazine than I was. She had more practical experience than I just by answering phones at the magazine. I had a little more education, but none that really was applicable here. I'd worked on the high school yearbook writing snappy captions to go with our candid photos. Like, we'd have this photo of Tom Novinger coming out of the boy's bathroom, the smoke still evident over his shoulder, and I'd add the caption: *Tommy continues to conduct private experiments to verify the Surgeon General's warning against cigarette smoking.* That was the extent of my journalistic experience. But now I wore the blessed Coat of Wren, magically transforming me into a valuable commodity.

I felt doubly guilty now for failing to get the interview. First, for damaging Wren's perfect reputation and second, for having a job Billie was working hard for but which I'd basically stolen. I had to try harder, justify my good fortune. Maybe if I could persuade Linda to give me another crack at Season Dougherty, she'd back me with Jonathan.

'Billie, transfer me to Linda's phone.'

'No can do, Wren. Linda's down at the Irvine Police Department.'

My hand tightened around the phone. 'She got the interview?'

'Not with Season Dougherty. Your prom pal Davis Richard has a stranglehold on that. Even Mr. Krieg hasn't been able to budge him yet. But she did manage to get an interview with Season's cell neighbour.'

Damn, that was a good idea. One I should have thought of. Wren would have.

I told Billie I'd be back in the office in an hour. I hung up.

'Do you have change for the phone?' a hefty girl with volleyball kneepads loose around her ankles asked me. She held out a dollar bill.

'Sorry,' I said. I dug in my change purse and found another quarter, which I offered to her.

'No, thanks. I'll just get a Coke from the snack stand. They'll give me change.'

I watched her walk away. Her legs were stocky with muscle already losing ground to fat. For some unknown reason I felt my sinuses flood as if I might cry. There was nothing significant about my exchange with the girl, no parallels with my life. I never played volleyball. A stranger never offered me a quarter. I'd never been hefty. But somehow everything on this campus seemed so familiar, like I was back in college again waiting at the student union building for Robby to get out of Bible as Literature so we could go up to his dorm room and screw before his roommate got back from water polo practice. If I checked my purse would I find my old diaphragm?

I quickly sat on the closest aluminum bench. Across the table a young boy wearing Walkman headphones looked over at me and nodded. 'Smog,' he said. 'Stage two alert.' Then he closed his eyes and turned his face back toward the sun.

I just sat there, concentrating on breathing. I was shivering, my mouth dry, the part of my throat that never sees light, scratchy. It's what druggies call 'thirsty'. When would this kind of thing end? You go along in your life, you're not thinking about the past, then Whack! you get nailed on the back of the head with a two-by-four of lethal memory. It's like a wormhole opens up beneath your feet and you're sucked down, like those people in the old *Invaders from Mars*. And as you fall, your chest and stomach are turned into a clothes dryer and all your organs are tumbling against each other, rearranging themselves inside you. Suddenly there's Robby. The two of you are naked on his narrow dorm bed. Cat Stevens's voice is muffled from the room next door. Robby suctions his mouth around your breasts and blows, making a wet farting sound. You both laugh hysterically, partially for the joke, but mostly because you can see how happy your lives together will always be.

I pressed my hands to my eyes. They were dry. No

tears. That was important. I could live without Robby, I'd already established that. I mean, hell, I was doing it. Then where did these flashes of profound heartbreak come from? A girl asks for change and I go to pieces. Where was the safety in that?

I stood up and walked into the Valley College bookstore. I needed the textbook my art history class would be using. On Monday, six short days from today, I would be teaching a subject I never even took.

*　　　*　　　*　　　*　　　*

The back room had all the textbooks arranged alphabetically by subject. Art 110 was easy to find, bottom shelf between Art 105: Art for Teachers and Art 112: Application of Color Theory. Each course had a card taped to the shelf telling who the instructor was and when and where the class met. Under Instructor's Name for my class they had neatly typed Staff. That's me.

I knelt down and examined the textbook. It was the same book that I'd found on Wren's desk the day I went to clean her apartment with her mother. The one with all the notations in the margins around that strange Rodin sculpture, 'She Who Was the Helmet-Maker's Beautiful Wife.' I was relieved. At least now I'd have Wren's notes to work from. Maybe, like everything else I'd been doing, I'd be able to fake my way through.

'Can you tell me where the diaries are?' a woman asked.

I looked up. She was asking me, that bookstore curse I have. She held a dull-eyed bowling ball of a baby straddling her hip. Her T-shirt barely contained her huge breasts. The legs that stuck out of her shorts were pale and bruised. A rash of pimples reddened her cheek. She was about twenty-three with a very enthusiastic expression.

'I'm sorry,' I said. 'I don't work here.'

'Oh.' She looked confused and a little hurt, as if I'd just tried to dampen her enthusiasm. 'I'm looking for diaries.'

I looked around the room. 'These are all textbooks. I would think the diaries would be in the front room.'

She nodded but didn't leave. She hiked her sliding baby higher on her hip. 'I want to get one of those nice diaries, you know, the kind that have padded covers and stuff. I'm going to write in it every day to tell my baby what it's like to be a mother. That way she'll know when she's grown up. I think that will make us closer.'

I looked at the baby. She was cramming her fist into her mouth. I thought about those diaries, stacks of padded covers with cute ducks or bunnies on them. Inside the chronicle of her mother's daily joys and sacrifices. Every diaper changed cheerfully, every burp translated into a first word, every gaseous squint tortured into a sign of profound thought. Each page of the diary would be crammed with the unbearable burden of hope. Those volumes will surely drive her daughter out of the house, with only an occasional phone call on holidays while her naked lover made obscene faces at her from the bed.

'I'd check the other room,' I pointed. 'By the cash registers.'

'Thanks,' she said and walked off humming.

15

That night Davis and I cruised Harbor Boulevard in search of a suitable motel to have sex. He took the occasion to explain how he got divorced.

'Beirut,' he said. 'That's what caused it.'

'Beirut?'

'That whole terrorist thing.'

'Terrorists caused your divorce?'

He nodded. He drove the Taurus station wagon without changing lanes. Cars sped up behind him, their headlights brightening the inside of the car like a flare. Impatient, they'd whip around him and rumble off. Usually we'd catch up to them at the light and they'd avoid looking over at us. I felt uncomfortable having all these irate emotions fired in our direction.

'Am I driving too slowly?' he asked.

'No, why?'

'You're fidgeting with your purse strap.'

'Nasty habit. It's a substitute for my old heroin habit.'

He laughed. I liked that he laughed at my jokes, especially the stupid ones. It made me want to say something nice to him. 'You drive like a man who is happy.'

'Huh?'

'Cautious, like you have something to lose.'

He smiled. 'I drive like a father.'

The radio was on, but the volume was so low I couldn't actually recognize any of the songs. Occasionally I'd make out 'baby' or 'love' or something easy. It made all the songs seem the same, interchangeable.

'Meanwhile, back in Beirut . . .' I prompted.

He sighed. 'You know how something across the world, an event that has nothing to do with you can snowball until it finally comes crashing into your life? Like Rube Goldberg contraptions.'

'Those drawings of machines where a bird pecks at a feeder and that causes a chain reaction that eventually lights a match.'

'Exactly my point. He fills the whole page with these elaborate chain reactions that take all the ingenuity and intellect of millions of years of evolution and in the end it does something simple, like light a match. It's overkill. That's what I'm talking about. It's like all the forces of nature and world politics conspired to wreck my marriage.'

He was silent while we waited at a light. Since I didn't know what to say, I kept quiet too. I wanted to tell him I understood some of his pain, tell him about this afternoon at Valley College when a girl in volleyball kneepads almost caused me to cry. But that was Luna's life, not Wren's. He wouldn't be interested in Luna.

After leaving campus, I'd returned to the office. Linda was out, still interviewing Season Dougherty's cell neighbour. Jonathan Krieg, having solved the bathroom graffiti problem, left for a celebrity fund-raiser. I'd finally reached Davis by phone and we'd arranged for another dinner, someplace without any ambience. After my lunch with James Smith and his flambeau napkin art, I wanted someplace that served hamburgers and fries and paper napkins. He took me to Bob's Big Boy. Halfway through the meal we both knew we were going to end up in the sack that night. The only question was where to find a sack. He had kids and a baby-sitter at his place. I had the looming prospect of Byron returning. As we walked through the parking lot toward his car I said, 'Let's find a motel.'

Motels whizzed past us. Capri Motel, Surf Motel, Sandy Inn. I didn't point them out because I didn't want to interrupt his story. Not because I wanted to hear about his divorce right then. Apparently, he needed to talk this through, like a man dutifully informing you of a past sexually transmitted disease. So I listened. I didn't want to be rude before sex.

I turned off the radio to indicate my interest. He looked over at me gratefully, but he didn't speak. I tried to change the subject. 'What's all this?' I asked, pointing at the stacks of newspapers in the back seat. 'Recycling?'

'Nope, they're all today's papers.'

I angled around in my seat for a better look. There were at least a dozen newspapers, all from different cities: Akron, Ohio's *Beacon Journal*; The Atlantic City *Press*; Greensboro, North Carolina's *News & Record*. 'What are you, a news junkie?'

He laughed. 'Strictly business, believe me. I just scan them for some interesting human interest story, something local, that might make a good movie. Lots of producers do this. Helps them get a jump on the studios.'

'Like with Season Dougherty?'

'Yes, like with Season Dougherty. As a crusading mother, she was of minor interest to the guys with the big bucks. That's how I was able to get her rights so easily. If I'd waited until after she shot her husband, I wouldn't even be in the bidding.'

I let the subject drop. This would be bad timing.

'Do you have a particular motel in mind?' I asked. 'An old favorite?'

'Why?'

'We've passed half a dozen already.'

He pointed out the window at a seedy motel with a raunchy tropical motif next to a bowling alley. 'Patty Hearst stayed there when she was on the run with the SLA.'

'Perhaps we can get their Che Guevara suite.'

He chuckled. 'You're very funny, you know that?'

I started to say something about how easily amused he was, but for the first time that I could remember I just accepted the compliment. When you're cruising for a motel to have sex for the first time with a guy, pointing out your own flaws isn't a good idea. I smiled at my joke, laughed lightly.

He reached over and laid his hand on my thigh. High on my thigh, maybe six inches from ground zero. I liked the feel of his hand there, the weight of it on my skin.

'Those Lebanese.' He shook his head and squeezed my leg at the same time, like the two movements were related. 'Remember how Danny Thomas used to talk about being Lebanese on his old show? Let me tell you, Beirut is not filled with a bunch of Danny Thomases.'

'I never watched him. He's before my time.'

'I'm two years older than you. Remember, I read your application. I know all about you.' Davis looked over at me. 'Besides, with cable TV, nothing's before anyone's time anymore. There are 187 million televisions in this country. That's almost one television set per person. No show ever dies. Today when your old man says when I was your age we used to blah blah blah, his kids tune in and see what he's talking about.'

'Except they aren't watching what really happened, just what people idealized.'

'Isn't that what memory is anyway? Just what your subconscious has selected to remember, and even alter when it suits. There is no such thing as an accurate memory because any incident you see is corrupted by your senses, which aren't accurate recording devices. They interpret what they perceive.'

'I didn't realize you were such a philosopher.'

'I'm a producer, which makes me a media apologist.'

'Is that another phrase for bullshit artist?'

He started laughing hard, though not hard enough to take his hand from my thigh. If anything, it slid even higher up. 'Quit teasing me,' he said.

'What?'

'That whole speech I just made. I got it from you.'

'From me?'

'Come on. I had my secretary at UCLA all morning hunting down every article you ever published. Boy, you've been in some obscure publications. That whole television and memory deal I just babbled, I read it in *The Journal of Popular Culture*. Very high-brow title, Test-Pattern Babies: the New Immortality.' I'm quoting you almost directly.'

'Someone should have washed my mouth out with soap.'

He laughed. 'You're probably the smartest woman I've ever known. I couldn't understand half of what you wrote about.'

'So I'm smart because you couldn't understand it?'

'Oops.'

'And why would you think it's a compliment to say the smartest *woman*, which has a certain superior connotation, like saying I'm the tallest dwarf you've ever known.'

I don't know what prompted me to start saying all this, except that I was so unnerved by his catching me not knowing Wren's article that I decided to launch a counter-attack to keep him from wondering why I didn't remember my own opinions. Along with everything else, now I had to read the dozens of articles Wren had published. I doubted I would understand them any better than Davis.

'So, now that you've discovered my latent chauvinism, Doctor,' he said, 'can you recommend a cure?' The thing that most impressed me about him right at that moment was that despite what I'd said, he hadn't withdrawn his hand from my thigh.

'Yeah,' I said. 'Pull in there.' I pointed to a motel down the street. Quixote Inn. Two plaster Don Quixotes crossed lances over the entrance.

We waited at the light, again in silence. Only now his hand slid up against my crotch and two of his fingers began massaging my clitoris. I'm usually a slow builder but this time I felt the heat right away. My hips rocked against his fingers. By the time he pulled into the Quixote Inn, I'd come in a muffled moan. My panties were wet and my thighs sticky. I flopped back against the seat. I said in a chipper voice, 'Well, I guess we can go home now.'

'And miss the best part?'

'What's the best part?'

'When I get undressed and tell you all the reasons why I'm not in better shape.'

I laughed. 'Go, get us a room with a TV. We're making imperfect memories.'

He climbed out of the car and walked into the office. I watched him talk to the man at the desk, a large Chicano man in a Hawaiian shirt and smoking a pipe. Davis filled out the form and paid cash. I could see their lips moving during the entire transaction. The Chicano man laughed heartily. Davis smiled at him and said something else and the man laughed again. Then he returned to the car. I got out when I saw him coming because the inside of the car smelled extremely musky. I flapped my skirt to circulate some air before he came around the car.

'Ready?' he asked.

'The night man didn't say something like "Nice to see you again, Mr. Jones," did he?'

'Turns out his father used to live in the same Mexican village where my family used to go camping during the summers.'

'Did he recognize you?'

'No. It just came up in conversation.'

'How does something like that come up in conversation?'

He shrugged. 'I don't know. People like me, I guess.'

*   *   *   *   *

Getting naked is the hard part.

Remaining sexy while rolling panty hose down your legs requires a certain flair. There is no dignified position. Even Kim Bassinger must look like she's in a Lucille Ball

215

skit while trying to squirm out of them. There's something about the amount of effort it takes removing panty hose that, according to Robby, makes a woman look like she has something to hide. He said that the first time he'd watched a woman (not me) take them off was like seeing a lizard shed its skin, both wondrous and repulsive.

Davis removed his clothes quickly and efficiently and was standing naked just in time to see me fling the wadded nest of panty hose from my toes. I yanked off my panties and reached around between my shoulder blades to unfasten my bra. Most of my bras fasten in the front, but Robby once told me that, though that is more practical, men liked to see a woman reach around her back. Very erotic, he'd said. We both stood up and peeled back the blankets. The sheets were bright white and stiff as we crawled in. We pulled only the top sheet over us. He reached over and turned off the light. All of our actions seemed so practical, goal-oriented.

'What happened?' he said, touching my bullet wound.

'Appendix. I had a bad doctor.'

He let it drop.

We scooted together and hugged. Davis's penis poked me in the stomach, then slid flat between our stomachs like a folding blade in a pocketknife.

'I'm sorry,' I said suddenly, sitting up. The sheets fell to my waist. Even in the dark I could see my nipples. They seemed absurdly long. I pulled the sheet up over them.

'What's the matter?'

'I'm sorry, but I have to talk business first. I should have said something earlier. I don't know why I didn't.'

He laughed. 'Business? You really are funny.'

I looked over at him. 'Not that kind of business. Season Dougherty business.'

He sat up. His chest was matted with curly blond hair.

'I need to interview Season Dougherty. What we're doing here, being naked and all, has nothing to do with her. This is going to happen no matter what you decide. But if I wait until afterward to ask you, then I will feel

216

like a whore. If you say yes, I'll feel like you paid me, and if you say no, I'll feel somehow bad, I don't know, like the sex wasn't good enough or something. There's a chance I'm not being completely rational right now, but it's important I get all this out in the open.'

'Okay. Business first.'

'Well, that may have been an unfortunate choice of words on my part.'

He smiled. 'You got heat at work, right? Jonathan Krieg turning up the burners?'

'He's stuck me on a gossip column. Two days ago I'd have been grateful for that. But now I've got something to prove, I guess.'

'I can't make multi-million-dollar decisions in a bed at a place called the Quixote Inn. Despite what you've heard, Hollywood doesn't operate like that.'

'Oh.'

'Now, if we were in a Jacuzzi, that would be different.' He laughed.

I tried to laugh too, but it came out more like a sigh.

'This is awkward,' he said.

'I shouldn't have said anything. Jesus, I'm stupid. Forget it.' I put my arm around him and tried to pull him back down.

'No, I'm glad you brought it up. I was going to say something later because I didn't want you to think this was a ploy to get you into bed. Anyway, I need someone to write the book about Season Dougherty's case. The studio thinks a book will promote movie sales. Besides, there's every reason to believe this thing will become a bestseller on its own. I've already had a few informal chats today with some publishers. With the national publicity this case has been getting, we're talking about an advance of a hundred thousand. Of course, you split that in half with me and the studio. Still, fifty grand ain't bad.'

'What makes you think I can write such a book?'

'Hey, I read all your articles, remember? You think I

sent my secretary to the library all morning out of lust? Well, okay, partially lust.'

I ran my thumbnail along the seam of the sheet. Ten minutes ago I was a failure, demoted on my second day of work. Now I was being offered fifty thousand dollars to write a book. I guess even dead, Wren's charmed life continued.

'There would be a conflict of interest with the magazine,' I said, 'If I did the book, I'd either have to quit my job or allow them to excerpt the book.'

'Excerpts could be arranged. For a fee.'

'Even so, Jonathan wanted to make the movie deal himself. He may just fire me anyway.'

'Fifty thousand is good severance pay. Besides, I expect to have more books coming my way. This is only the start.'

I thought about it a few minutes. A television from some other room was cranked up pretty loud and some brassy theme music that was vaguely familiar as belonging to a cop show echoed around the room. I didn't know what to do. With fifty thousand I could disappear again. Of course, first I had to write a book, something I had no idea how to do unless Thomas Pynchon figured in it somehow. What should I do?

'Can we just fuck now,' I said.

'Sure.'

We started the usual way, I guess. Stroking each other. Touching lightly here and there, then darting to some other place like fugitive fingers. Basic Foreplay 101. A couple of nights ago Ethan had performed his foreplay as if it had been something he'd read out of a manual. Like doing the Heimlich Manoeuvre or something. Davis was different. He was gentle, slightly awkward, but confident. He knew where we were going and that, sooner or later, we'd get there. He was a lot like Robby. Though there was something reserved about Robby's sex, as if everything he did he had at the back of his mind might be documented later in some scholar's biography of him, therefore he'd better not screw up posterity now. I'd not ever thought of that until just then, but I knew instantly it was true.

Davis had his finger up inside me. I ground myself against his hand and he decided to slip another finger inside. That was nice too. I lay back with my eyes closed, smelling the antiseptic bleach of the dry sheets. I wished I'd had more experience so I could say that this was the best time or the second best time or something. But I'd only had sex with four men in my life, two of them during the past two days.

When Davis was ready to enter me, he was very considerate. He positioned the head of his penis against my vagina but didn't push it in. He kind of rubbed it around a little, like a drug-sniffing dog checking out a package at customs.

Dog. Blood. Money. Byron.

Could that be the explanation? Byron was involved in drugs and had killed some cop's dog eluding a dragnet. I opened my eyes. Davis smiled and thrust into me. My legs angled even farther apart to accommodate him. I reached around and grabbed his buttocks, urging him forward. He pumped harder, then stopped suddenly. I opened my eyes again and saw his eyes clenched, his teeth grit. He held perfectly still, trying not to come. I held still too. I felt like a teenager in my parents' living room hearing a noise from their bedroom.

A minute later Davis started to move again. He didn't talk. Neither did I. Robby liked to talk during sex. He said things like 'Beg me to fuck you' and 'Fuck me till my eyeballs pop.' And sometimes, in a more playful mood, he'd sing the music from Disneyland rides: 'Yo ho, yo ho, it's the pirate's life for me,' and I'd point to his penis and sing, 'It's a small world after all . . .'

Davis came before I did, but he politely continued thrusting until a few minutes later I came too.

'So,' I said, rolling over, 'now that you've had your way with me, you still want me to write the book about Season Dougherty?'

He kissed me. Then he lay back against the headboard and cupped his hands behind his head. 'This is the only time I wished I smoked. It gives you something to do with your hands while you talk.'

'Try origami.'

He laughed. 'God, that would make a funny scene in a movie, wouldn't it? This couple just finishes making love in some seedy dive with the neon sign sizzling outside their window.'

'Hot summer night. No air-conditioning.'

'Right. Just a fan blowing across a bowl of ice. She gets up, naked, takes one of the ice cubes and runs it along her neck and lips. Then she picks up a couple sheets of paper and hands him one and says, "Origami, Nick?"'

'And he says, "No, thanks, I'm trying to quit."'

He laughed again. When he laughed he made me feel somehow smarter and funnier than I really was.

'The American hostages in Beirut,' he said.

'What?'

'My divorce. It started when the Lebanese terrorists released one of the American hostages a couple years ago.'

'That professor.'

'Right. We're sitting at home watching the news. My wife and I. Actually she's in bed. I'd just come back from checking on Judy, who'd had a stomach-ache.' He looked at me again, his face serious. 'She had checked on her earlier, I'm not trying to make myself out as a better parent. Lila is a fine mother.'

'Lila's your wife?'

He nodded solemnly. 'Anyway, I'm climbing back into bed and Lila's watching the news. She's got the newspaper spread out in front of her and a bowl of double-fudge ice cream in her hands. She eats a bowl every night. Not that she's fat, she's thin as a broom handle. She just likes ice cream.'

'Just tell the damn story, Davis,' I said with a laugh. 'I'm not judging anyone.'

'You're right. I don't know why I do that. Apologize

for everything. Before the divorce I never did that. I think it's just that my divorce was my first failure at anything. I've always succeeded, always got what I wanted. Breaking up with Lila kind of shook my confidence.' He shook his head. 'Okay, so Lila's watching the TV all serious-looking, like there's going to be a quiz on it later. I ask her what's on the news. She shushes me and says, "Listen." I listen. One of the American hostages has just been released by the terrorists. He's been held captive for three years. He's walking toward a plane, waving at reporters, looking pale and frail, like he'd been locked up with Dracula for three years. When the segment about the hostage is done, Lila taps her spoon against an article she's reading in the newspaper. She's very animated. Ice cream drips onto the article. "You know what it says here? This expert on hostages says that they have to be retrained before they can enter society again. They have been isolated so long that they have to be taught how to speak. That's why they have to wait before letting them have a news conference. Also, they can't make decisions. They can't decide what clothes to wear, what food to eat." She's talking a mile a minute. I'm looking at her and she's got tears in her eyes and I'm thinking, What a compassionate woman to feel so much for these poor hostages. Then she says, "Davis, those are all the same symptoms I have. I have all the symptoms of a Beirut hostage." Next thing I know, we're divorced.'

Another TV show theme filters up through the motel courtyard. I laid perfectly still and didn't say anything. I was trying hard to come up with something comforting.

'Hell of a story, huh?' he said.

I opened my mouth, hoping something compassionate would spring out on its own. When it didn't, I pulled the sheet off his waist and lowered my mouth onto his penis.

16

'Shouldn't we talk?' he asked.

'About what?'

'About what just happened. Don't you watch TV? This is where we discuss, in muted voices and sensitive terms, how we feel about having had sex.'

I muted my voice. 'What would we say?'

He shrugged, looked around the Bob's Big Boy parking lot where we'd returned for my car. We were standing on a white line in the three-foot alley between his car and mine. My key was inserted in the car door, my fingers grasping it, ready to turn. He was leaning against his car, arms folded casually like he'd just stepped out of a crowded bar for a smoke and a look at the stars. He stepped up behind me and wrapped his arms around mine. My breasts squeezed together and looked bigger. I leaned back into him. He pressed his nose to my neck and breathed deeply. 'I thought I'd say something sensitive like: "You fill up my senses, like a night in the forest."'

'Ah, poetry.'

'Well, John Denver.'

I laughed, 'The classics, huh. What would I say in response?'

'Something equally sensitive. Like: "Life could be a dream . . ."'

'If you would take me up to paradise up above . . .'

'Sh-boom, sh-boom. See, men can open up just as well as women.'

I twisted around and faced him. We kissed. He smelled like Ivory soap from our motel shower.

'Baby-sitter,' I reminded him, tapping his watch crystal.

'Right.' He looked at his watch. 'Right.' He pecked me on the lips and ran around to the driver's side and jumped in. The passenger window hummed as it electronically lowered. He scrunched down so he could see me. I bent over. His face was soft and gentle, like a slept-on pillow. 'Call you tomorrow. Meantime, think about the book deal. I'm serious about it.'

'Sh-boom, sh-boom.'

'I mean it, Wren. This has nothing to do with that.' On 'that' he hooked his thumb over his shoulder in the general direction of the Quixote Inn. 'Just think about it.'

'I will.'

He drove off, waving at me into his rearview mirror. I waved back until his twin red tail-lights merged with the rest of the traffic. I was still waving after I was sure he couldn't see me. I looked at myself waving, observed the absurdity of the gesture. A hand flopping up and down. Or wiggling side to side. I tried both. A couple teenage boys honked and waved back as they drove by. I laughed and got in my car.

On the freeway drive home I remembered something important. After Davis and I had made love a second time, I'd dozed off for just a few minutes. Instantly, I'd started dreaming. I was black. I wore my hair in a modest afro like Angela Davis, the seventies radical professor. Sammy Davis, Jr, was trying to persuade me to teach Greek to Jewish kids in the ghetto for $10,000 a year. 'I can't do it for that little,' I told him. 'I'd starve.' He said, 'Do it for our people.' 'But I'm not Jewish,' I told him. 'And I don't know Greek.' He shook his head angrily, 'So? You're not black either.' When he said that I cried. He put his hand on my shoulder and said they'd throw in a condo along with the ten grand. Then I woke up. Tears were in my eyes but I'd wiped them on the pillow before Davis had noticed.

I arrived home a few minutes before ten o'clock. I couldn't believe it was so early, considering all that had happened today. A month ago my day would have consisted of two hours in class, two hours teaching, followed by ten hours at the library. The monotony of the days blurred them into a swampy sameness. Like the taste of oatmeal. I'd had to constantly consult a calendar to know what specific day it was. Before that, when I was with Robby, there was always something to distinguish the days, give them identity. Later, Wren did the same thing for me. This was the first time I experienced such variety of experience on my own.

But variety takes its toll. I was exhausted and dying for bed. The insides of my thighs were a little sore from where they'd gripped Davis's hips.

I followed the trail of snails up the sidewalk to my front door. For some reason, they reminded me of communism. I thought of them with those little fur hats. That made me laugh. A couple of snails were suctioned to my door. What could they hope to find on my door?

I noticed the lights weren't on inside, which I hoped meant Byron wasn't home yet. On the drive over I'd practiced my Farewell to Byron speech, in which I emphatically inform him that this living arrangement was not going to work out. He would have to find another place. I'd even help him pay for it if he was short on cash, maybe I could scrape up a couple hundred a month. Okay, that was like paying blackmail, but I was in the middle of a $50,000 deal and I couldn't afford to have him blabbering about Luna Devon.

As I unlocked my front door, I could hear Ethan upstairs strumming his guitar, working on a new gag song for his comedy routine. He kept playing the same three chords over and over from the Bee Gees' 'I Started a Joke'. Each time he'd sing a variation of the title. 'I started to poop . . .' Pause. 'I started the Pope . . .' Pause. 'I strangled the Pope . . .'

When I opened the door the stench from inside

thwacked me in the face like a thrown pie. 'Ohhh, Jeeeeesus,' I winced, cupping my hand over my nose.

I left the door open and quickly unlocked and slid open a couple of windows.

'Christ!' I pulled my blouse up over my nose like a surgical mask and began hunting for what I assumed was a dead and rotting body. 'Hector! Hector!'

As I neared the bathroom, the stench cranked up a couple notches. I flipped the light switch. The cat litter box looked as if it had been bombed by chunks of mud the size of ice cubes. Each little chunk was coated in green litter. They looked almost decorative.

A little yellow plastic shovel the same color as the litter box rested against the toilet. I grabbed it and began sifting. I flushed the bombs down the toilet. The window was barley open an inch; I flipped the lock and shoved it the rest of the way open. I stuck my head out and took a deep breath of fresh air.

Whatever satisfaction I had in disposing of the problem ended as I walked back toward the living room and was again hit by the foul smell, stronger than ever. And fresh. I heard a muffled noise. Rhythmic. I looked across the room and saw the top leaves of my fichus tree rustling. I circled the sofa, stepped over a small coffee table, and marched straight for the plant. Standing inside the sixteen-inch pot, Hector was digging the dirt, pawing it behind him to cover up several more moist nuggets.

I grabbed him by the scruff and hoisted him out of the plant. 'You little shit,' I scolded. He just hung limply, the skin at his neck pulling his eyes almost shut.

I carried him into the kitchen and dropped him on the floor. He landed on all fours, crouched defensively, looked around, then sat down and began licking his paws.

'I hate you,' I told him. 'I just wanted you to know.'

A stack of 9-Lives cat food cans sat on the counter. They had not been here this morning when I'd left. Also, next to the lidded trash pail stood a brown Lucky's grocery bag. Inside were a couple of open cat food cans and all the soda and fruit cocktail and soup cans from the trash. Byron had rooted through my trash and dumped all the cans in the bag. Written in thick black Magic Marker on the front of the bag was CANS (recycle!).

Next to the bag were two new porcelain bowls shaped like sleeping cats. One contained water, the other was empty except for a few pasty smears where the food had been.

Apparently Byron had been able to interrupt his mysterious travels long enough to pop home, feed the cat, and sort my garbage. How did he get in? I hadn't given him a key. But then again, he was an ex-con and he knew people named Grudge. So, anything was possible.

I opened a can of sliced veal and dumped it into Hector's bowl. He sauntered over, sniffed, licked at the sauce a little, then sat down and began licking his butt.

'Hey, *I* didn't buy it for you. Save the food reviews for your master.'

After I cleaned out my fichus, I started running the bathwater. I dumped in a packet of lilac bath salts hoping they would mask the heavier odor still apparent throughout the apartment. I undressed in my new bedroom, the smaller bedroom where Byron had stuck me. My panties were wet from leaking on the drive home. I tossed them into the laundry.

That's when I noticed the blinking light on my phone answering machine. I hadn't had a message on it since moving here, so I'd stopped checking it. Probably a wrong number, but I pressed the button anyway. The tape kept whirring and rewinding as if the entire tape had been used. I grabbed a pen and opened the *People* magazine to a page with a tampon ad that had a lot of white space for notes.

First message: 'Okay, man, I spoke to the rocket king like you asked. He says, and I'm reading directly from the paper he gave me, so there ain't no fuckin' screwups. Okay, he says: "7866." Got that? Seventy-eight sixty-six. He's waitin' to hear from you, man.'

Second message: 'Byron! You're out! Living proof that the judicial system doesn't work. Listen, I got this number from T-Bone. I hear you're still in the game. Anyway, if that's true, I know where there's some money if you want me to broker. I sure as shit am not leaving my name on this thing, so if you don't recognize my voice, well, then fuck you anyway. If you do, give my sister a call. She knows how to reach me.'

There were six more messages, all for Byron, all equally cryptic. No one left their name or number where they could be reached. There were a lot of hints about large sums of money, but no specifics as to how much or where this money would come from.

I sat naked on the edge of the bed. I hadn't written any of the messages down. What was I in the middle of here. The rocket king? Was this some kind of espionage thing? The Jet Propulsion Lab was nearby.

I pulled on some sweatpants and a T-shirt and cranked off the tub faucet. I popped the tape cassette out of Wren's machine, and took it to the stereo in the living room. Wren's stereo system included a high-speed tape-to-tape dubbing deck. I copied Byron's messages onto a blank tape. I needed a place to hide it until I'd decided which authorities I should send this to. FBI? CIA? Detective Diesel? There was no place in the apartment he considered private. He'd already gone through my belongings once. Hiding it at the office would be tricky. My job was already in jeopardy. I could show up one day with my desk drawers empty.

Hide in plain sight. Poe's purloined letter trick. All I needed was a tape he was sure not to listen to. I ran my finger across the plastic spines of the cassette cases trying to decide the extent of Byron's musical taste. Most of the cassettes Robby had bootlegged from friends' albums. When we'd split, he'd given them all to me, which I'd thought was a generous gesture until Wren informed me that the albums he'd been copying belonged to Dr. Helen Jaspers.

227

'Yes,' I said, tilting one case forward. The Carpenters. I labeled the copy of Byron's messages *Karen Carpenter Sings Songs of Love and Devotion* and tucked it into the case, back between Kate Bush and Tracy Chapman.

The original tape I tossed onto Byron's bed. After removing the label, I stuck the actual Carpenters tape back into the answering machine for future messages.

I closed and locked all the doors and windows, stripped, and climbed into my tub. The hot water burned the insides of my chafed thighs. I closed my eyes and sank down until the water touched my chin. I tried to think constructively, formulate some kind of plan of action. Take Davis's offer to write the book. Quit my job at the magazine. Kick Byron out. But every plan had holes. Could I trust Davis to deliver on the contract?

I looked down at my pubic hairs waving in the water like seaweed. Was that clump of skin, hair, and crevices the reason he was doing this. Or was it because he admired Wren's credentials? Which answer would be less insulting to me?

Now the questioning wouldn't stop. Would Jonathan Krieg be so mad that he tried to blackball me? He could probably do that if he wanted. And that might cause people to look into my past a little too closely. Was I even capable of writing such a book, did I have any of the skills necessary? Also, if I did write the book, I'd have to publish under a pseudonym. Wren's name couldn't suddenly appear nationwide without somebody figuring out the truth. Perhaps I could use Luna Devon as my pseudonym? I smiled at the thought and hot water crept up to my lips.

I sensed a presence in the room, staring at me. Thinking it was Byron, I quickly opened my eyes, ready to grab for a towel. Hector stood on the edge of the tub looking at the water. He lowered his paw tentatively until it touched the water, then he jerked it back.

'It's water,' I informed him. 'Cats hate water.'

He leaned farther over and dipped his head until he

could sniff the water. Then he stuck his tongue in and started drinking.

'That's hot water,' I said. 'You have fresh cold water in your bowl. God, you're stupid.'

He kept slurping away.

I watched him drink. His gray tail kept flipping back and forth, brushing my shoulder. It tickled and I had to keep scratching my shoulder. Finally, I grabbed his tail and held it a few seconds and he stopped swishing it. Instead, it drifted over the side of the tub and floated on top of the water.

'Hey, I want to wash my face in here.'

He sat back and started licking his butt again.

'You're disgusting,' I said. I kicked the drain lever with my foot and felt the water start to suck out of the tub. I laid there and let it. Hector didn't move. I thought of BeeGee's cat, Sphinx, a moment before she'd shoved the cocked gun against his chest. The blood, the clumps of wet fur stuck to my face. BeeGee had loved that cat. Once, she had taken a week of work without pay to stay home and care for him when he was sick. I remember making a joke about it at the time and Wren saying Bee-Gee was lucky because she was loving in the way people were genetically programmed to love, before romance fucked it all up. I was still with Robby at the time, so I told her she was full of shit and went back to grading compositions about why we have a drug problem in this country.

But this was the question Wren had asked: Do people have a greater need to give love or receive love? She'd said we needed more to give love. A child with his teddy bear. He makes that bear real, gives it personality, and kisses and hugs it and weeps hysterically if it rips along a seam. The bear gives no love back except that which the child imagines. 'People with pets are no different,' she'd said. 'People train the pet to respond in a way that they then interpret as love because it makes them feel all squishy inside. But it ain't really love, just the reflection of that

229

person's need.' 'What about people loving people?' I'd asked. She'd smiled. 'Same thing. And not just in romantic relationships. Look at mothers and daughters. Same ole same ole. We don't resent others not loving us as much as we hate them for taking away our opportunity to love them. It's loving that gives us identity, not being loved. Once we come to accept that about ourselves, we'll all be a lot happier.'

The last of the water swirled down the drain. Hector and I watched it go together. I looked at him. He lowered his head as if expecting me to scratch it. 'Forget it,' I said, getting up.

I stepped over him and out of the tub, dried off, and dressed back in my sweats and T-shirt. Dressing for bed was new for me, but with Byron lurking about somewhere, I wanted to be prepared for anything.

I went to the kitchen for a ginger ale. On my way back past the front door, I peeked out between the shades down the front walk. I didn't see Byron. Just more snails. A clump of about ten of them were knotted together atop something. I could go out there right now, I thought, and bring one back and give it a name and keep it in an aquarium and feed it and put little colored rocks in with it and talk to it at night and maybe grow to love it. Seeing it every day, talking to it, watching it slither—after a while, I probably would love it. Is that the best we can do after millions of years of evolution? Love a snail.

I started to turn from the window when something gleamed out of the corner of my eye. White.

Subaru.

Across the small parking lot, parked against the red curb. A bent clothes hanger for a radio antenna.

I flung open the front door and hit the pavement running. I don't know why I had this sudden burst of courage or outrage or something. I just knew that I was pissed. My bare feet smacked the sidewalk twice before I felt the fragile crunch of snail shell under my heel. That could have been the one, I thought, the one I brought in to love. Too late now, I kept running.

The driver saw me. A bearded man about forty-five. He'd been drinking coffee from a Styrofoam cup and reading the newspaper. He quickly crumpled the paper and batted it aside. He clamped the coffee cup between his teeth and started the car.

'Hey!' I hollered, racing toward him.

He shifted into first, but he must have bitten through the cup, because suddenly it dropped from his mouth except for a half moon of Styrofoam still between his teeth like a wafer. His window was up, but I could hear the muffled yowl of pain as the coffee spilled into his lap.

Behind me were heavier footsteps. I glanced over my shoulder. Ethan, barefoot and bare-chested, wearing only his Jockey shorts, ran full speed with a hammer in his hand. He reminded me of Thor. I didn't stop or say anything. I kept racing for the Subaru.

But the driver managed to screech out while I was still ten feet away. 'Hey!' I called after him. I slowed, feeling the gravel and ground snail shell digging into my foot.

Ethan kept running after the car. When it was clear he wouldn't catch it, he hurled his hammer. It somersaulted through the air and, surprising both of us, struck the Subaru's trunk before bouncing to the ground. Encouraged by his markmanship, he began shaking his fist and shouting. 'Get out of here, you fuck! You son of a bitch! I see you again, I'll rip you a new asshole! You hear me, motherfucker? I'll kill you!' When the Subaru had shot out of the apartment complex, Ethan bent over, his hands on his knees, catching his breath. Still panting, he turned and looked up at me. 'So, who the hell was that?'

17

'What's wrong with this?' Jonathan Krieg asked, smacking a folded copy of last month's *Orange Coast Today* on his desk and sliding it across to me.

Somewhere in the room an insect, a fly or mosquito or something desperate, was buzzing. It made that fussy sound, like when they batter their wings against glass, that sound like sizzling neon. I looked around the room anxiously.

'A quick scan's all you'll need,' he said.

I picked up the magazine and started reading the article circled in red ink.

'Just read the first paragraph,' he said. 'The first paragraph is plenty.'

I read. It was a book review of a novel I had never heard of let alone read. For somone holding a master's degree in English, I was surprisingly dumb about current writers. I knew some names—Ann Beattie, Yannick Murphy, Richard Ford, Frederick Barthelme—enough to fake intimacy if their names ever came up. At a party, I had once referred to Amy Hempel as a 'staggering talent', though I hadn't read a single word she'd written. My own studies, which had mostly consisted of catching up to what all my younger peers had already read, had kept me firmly rooted in pre-twentieth century writers. The only living author whose complete works I'd actually read was Thomas Pynchon. And he was a recluse; nobody knew who or where he was.

'I want your opinion,' Jonathan said, pacing behind his

desk. He had his corporate raider outfit on today: light gray double-breasted suit and red paisley power tie overlapping his belt like a crotch bib and pointing straight down at his penis as if it were a Red Tag Sale item. 'I want to know what you think of this piece of writing, Wren. Your expert opinion.' He held up a cautionary finger: 'This is important.'

The review was by our free-lance columnist, Judith Dwyer-Horowitz. She taught comparative literature at the University of California at Irvine and had once reviewed books for the prestigious *New York Review of Books*. I hadn't met her yet, but word around the office was that she had been fired from that job after a bit of a scandal. Apparently, she received free copies of books from publishers to review, but since she received many more than she could possibly read, she sold them to bookstores. This was some sort of ethical breach and and *New York Review of Books* printed an apology about her conduct when they announced they'd fired her. She rarely came to the office: her reviews arrived by fax. She had a better scam going than I.

'Just the first paragraph,' Jonathan prodded. He looked over his shoulder at the window. The buzzing was starting to get to him too.

While I read, I crossed my legs and scratched vigorously at my ankles. For some reason they itched like crazy.

Jonathan hit his intercom. 'Billie, come in here please.' He clicked it off without waiting for an answer from her.

I concentrated on the review. I could sense from Jonathan's agitation that something was up. This review thing was some kind of test. I wasn't sure what was being tested. My stomach was already being tag-team body-slammed by the rest of my internal organs because I'd made up my mind to tell Jonathan this morning all about Davis's book offer and be fired or quit. But before I'd had a chance, he'd called me in and shoved this review at me.

I had to tell him about Davis. I'd reached my personal best for sneaking around and wanted to at least have this one thing out in the open. Do one right thing today, Luna. Just one. The lines between right and wrong used to be as clear to me as black telephone wires against a blue sky; now ethics were cellular. Voices were somehow sent, somehow they arrived. There were no means, nothing to judge. Just results.

Billie entered the office looking like a rock singer posing as a nun. She was wearing a black knit skirt, matching black cardigan sweater, adobe-white blouse, and a black bow tie. Her thin legs were sheathed in textured black hose, capped with black patent leather shoes that came to a lethal point. Her expression was of nervous anticipation acid-washed by raw ambition. She'd never looked more beautiful.

'Yes, Mr. Krieg?' she said. He gestured at the chair next to mine. She sat on the edge of it, her narrow bottom perched like a gull on the railing of a boat.

'Tell Wren here what you told me this morning. About Judith's reviews. This one for example.'

Billie smiled guiltily at me. She needn't have. I admired her ambition, coming in early, ambushing Jonathan before the rabbi or bodybuilders got to him. I wanted her to succeed. I just didn't want to look like a fool in the process.

'Well, Wren,' she said, her voice deeper, more professional-sounding than she'd ever been as a receptionist. She reminded me of Robby's radio deejay voice. 'I was telling Mr. Krieg that I thought we've indulged Judith's peculiarities long enough. If the magazine is going to take a new direction, I think all aspects of it should also be redesigned.'

I nodded encouragement, having given up reading the first paragraph after a few sentences.

'Be specific,' Jonathan said. 'What's wrong with Judith? This review specifically.'

Billie shrugged as if it was all too obvious. 'Well, in the first place, her selection of books to review. She chooses novels that are too esoteric, too literary for the kind of

234

audience we're pursuing. This isn't New York City. We're a coastal community, more leisure oriented. Very few people will go out and buy this book and even fewer will actually read it, even if she gives it a rave.'

'I've read this book,' Jonathan Krieg said. 'I loved it.'

Billie wilted a little, but the tumblers in her brain clicked into place almost instantly, inflating her posture. 'But you're not our target audience, Mr. Krieg. I am. Me and my mother.'

He smiled, pleased. 'Go on.'

If it was the job of book reviewer she was after, I thought she'd just snagged it. She looked over at me and I smiled for her. I reached down and raked my ankles again.

'But what else is wrong with this review?' Jonathan continued, frowning now. 'Something else . . .'

'Well, the prose style is a little too dense, too many elaborate metaphors, too many references to other writers and books. On the whole, it's too academic. Mainly, our readers want to know what the book's about and whether or not to plunk down twenty bucks for it.'

'That makes sense.' He glanced back at the window. The buzzing had taken on a furious high pitch. He walked over to the window, searched it from top to bottom. Nothing. The buzzing stopped. 'Does that make sense to you, Wren?'

I looked down at the review again, rereading the first few sentences. I'd read Judith's reviews when I was studying the magazine before coming down here. I didn't like her reviews, though not for the same reasons Billie just mentioned. But I didn't want to torpedo Billie's chances by disagreeing. After all, she'd gone after her success; I'd merely stolen mine.

'Wren?' Jonathan repeated. His voice suggested he enjoyed watching these little gladiatorial confrontations.

'I haven't read this book,' I admitted. 'So maybe this isn't a fair assessment.'

'You've read Judith's other reviews. You're familiar with her style.'

'Yes.'

'Well, one needn't have read the book being reviewed to know whether or not one likes the reviewer. I mean, you don't have to see the movie to know Siskel and Ebert are dickheads. Right?'

I glanced at Billie. Her posture was erect and tense, as if expecting a spinal tap. Her hands were folded piously on her lap. She was absently picking at a cuticle on her thumb.

'I agree with Billie,' I said. 'I don't like Judith's reviews either.'

'For the same reasons as Billie?'

'Somewhat.'

'She's too academic, prose too dense? Her selections are too literary? Her attitude too New York City?'

I shrugged. 'Not exactly. I kind of like a dense prose style in the reviews. And I don't mind that she picks books that are more literary and less popular. I don't think the readers of our magazine who bother to read the reviews care about anyone's opinion about the new Danielle Steele or Robert Ludlum. They're going to read those books anyway. What they would like is a conversational knowledge of current literature so they can talk about these books without ever having to read them. Cultural literacy today is merely recognizing a name, not having any intimacy with it.'

Jonathan laughed. 'Keen insight. You sound like one of your own articles.'

This 'keen insight' came from my own experiences trying to keep up with the likes of Robby and Wren. I was the prototype of the cultural 'illidiot' (Wren's term), saved from being excluded from party conversations about post-structuralist semiotics by a quick scan of reviews in the library. I was barely able to pass for intelligent that way. I knew the names, I knew the buzz words. I guess long before I faked being Wren, I'd faked being Luna.

236

'Let me get this straight,' Jonathan said. 'Are you saying to keep Judith's reviews?'

Billie looked at me with a strangled expression, as if her black bow tie had suddenly tightened around her throat on its own. Cuticle flakes from all her fingers confettied her black skirt.

'No, Jonathan,' I said. 'I don't like Judith either. But for a different reason. Well, here's an example.' I stabbed my finger at one of the sentences and read aloud: '"This author has a rare intelligence and almost psychic ability to read people. How else can you explain her unerring insights into characters of every social class and age group. These characters are unflinchingly accurate."' I shook my head. 'How the hell does Judith know these are accurate portrayals? She should say that the characters are written so they are believable, that we care what happens to them. But what she says here is that because she herself is such a goddamned genius, with the ability to know what people of all ages and social statuses are thinking, she can recognize this same genius in others. That's what I don't like about her reviews. They're all about how smart Judith is.'

Jonathan's face was expressionless. He quietly sat down behind the desk. He opened a desk drawer and pulled out a white yarmulke and placed it on the back of his head. He dragged his Hebrew book across the desk and flipped it open. Then he started reading aloud in stuttering broken Hebrew, his finger running from right to left under each word.

Billie looked at me. She contorted her lips to signify her confusion. I shrugged. We sat there and waited for him to finish. I'd known Jonathan Krieg long enough now to know he never did anything without a lesson. Like a lot of successful people, he equated success with wisdom. It wasn't enough to be rich and famous, he wanted people to think he deserved it because of his higher plane of thinking. Every knucklehead with a car phone thinks he's Yoda.

The obnoxious insect must have changed locations,

because the timbre of its buzzing was different now, a faint sputtering, as if it were running out of gas.

When Jonathan finished a couple of minutes of tortured reading, he closed his book and looked at us with a huge smile. 'Not bad, huh? Two weeks ago I couldn't read any Hebrew.'

'That's amazing, Mr. Krieg,' Billie said.

He looked at me for a reaction.

'Two weeks?' I said. 'Only two weeks?'

He nodded modestly. 'What's amazing is that I still don't understand a word I'm reading. But to be bar mitzvahed, I don't have to. I've just got to read the words and give my speech.'

'Oh?' Billie said. She wasn't getting it. The Big Message. I wasn't getting it either, but at least I knew there was one to get. I also knew that, like most would-be teachers, he would tell us exactly what he meant, then he'd grin moronically at his own wisdom. Since, as a teacher, I never thought of myself as having any wisdom, I never fell into that trap.

'My point is, Billie,' he said, 'Wren is right. I don't have to understand what I'm saying. I'm performing a ritual to be accepted into the fold. That's all people ever do. They spend their lives performing elaborate rituals to be accepted by this group or that. Family, school, job, romance, it's all the same. From plucking your eyebrows to saving your soul. It's all ritual. Now, how does that apply here? We print book, movie, and theater reviews. Do you think we do that because our readers are hungry for the arts? No, they just want to be able to have an opinion, even if it's someone else's. Our subscribers read book reviews because they don't have the time or patience to read the book. But they still want to be accepted into the fold of the well-read, the intelligent, the best and brightest.'

'I see,' she said, uncertainly.

He took his yarmulke off and tossed it back in its drawer, probably next to his vitamins and exercise shorts. 'Billie, you are now this magazine's book reviewer.'

Billie's rump hopped in her chair. 'Thank you, Mr. Krieg.'

'I believe in rewarding ambition.' He held up a finger and wagged it like an old rabbi. 'People who only do what they're told have to be told what to do. But go-getters, they get on the go. See what I'm saying? You understand what I'm telling you here? You have the proper education and I've read a couple of your writing samples. I think you can do the job.'

'Thank you, Mr. Krieg. I really can.'

'However, until I'm sure you've got the right slant on what we're looking for, I want you to clear your book selections with Wren first. Also, Wren, you are responsible for editing Billie's work. This is going to be a team effort. Any questions?'

'No, sir,' Billie said and stood up. A few cuticles flaked to the floor. The rest stuck to her black skirt in a crazy mosaic pattern.

I stood up. This didn't seem like the best time to tell Jonathan about Davis's book contract offer. If I quit or was fired now, as part of his Samurai-art-of-war style of management, he might take back his offer to Billie. I couldn't bear to see that. Fifteen minutes ago, telling Jonathan the truth about the book contract would have been right, now doing so seemed hurtful, wrong. More cellular ethics.

Billie and I walked to the door. I wouldn't be able to hold off telling him long, maybe a day or two. If he found out about it on his own, it could be disastrous. Once my honesty was questioned, who knows what kinds of checking he might do on me.

As Billie opened the door for me I said quietly, 'Billie, I'm going to need your review by tomorrow morning.' I was about to offer some complicated explanation for such haste, but before I could she chirped in 'Okay!'

'Wren,' Jonathan called as I was exiting.

I turned. 'Yes?'

'When you get a chance, give that Judith what's-her-fuck a call and tell her she's fired.'

'You want *me* to tell her?'

'Yes, I do. You are now in charge of book reviews, so it follows you should weed out the old before planting the new.' He made a pulling motion, I guess representing pulling weeds though it resembled masturbation.

I knew enough about editing as a teacher to recognize the importance of the job. But I'd been hired for my writing, now I was baby-sitting someone else's. Jonathan wasn't testing me, he was punishing me for blowing the Season Dougherty interview. Ordering me to fire this woman was a way of letting me know how disposable *I* was. Sending me down to the minors to coach a young comer. But I had a secret, a fifty-grand-stick-it-up-your-ass-book-contract-offer secret.

'Yes, sir,' I said to him. 'I'll call her right away.'

He nodded.

I returned to my desk and called Davis's office. Before I got too cocky, I wanted to be sure that the book offer was still good, not just a postcoital expression of endearment, his way of saying 'that felt good'.

His secretary said he was out.

'When do you expect him back?' I asked.

'He's out of town, Ms. Caldwell.'

'What?'

'Hawaii. He flew to Maui this morning. However, he did leave a message for me to tell you that he would contact you as soon as he was able.'

'Anything else?'

'Uh'—I heard the sound of rustling paper—'no, that seems to be all.'

Suddenly I didn't feel so confident.

'And he didn't say when he'd be back? Give a time? A day?'

'No, ma'am, he didn't. This was an unexpected business trip. He called me from the airport an hour ago just as they were boarding.'

'What kind of unexpected business pops up in Maui?'

She laughed. 'This is crazy business, Ms. Caldwell. Mr. Richard can disappear for days at a time. But he gets things done.'

You know those commercials where some guy is sitting in a chair and suddenly a bunch of money (or tires or cereal boxes) erupts under him and lifts his chair straight up as high as a skyscraper. That's how I felt. Like I was teetering.

I decided to take advantage of my darkening mood. I called Judith Dwyer-Horowitz and, struggling to keep my voice from cracking, told her in the kindest terms possible that due to a change in the magazine's ownership and direction we would no longer be needing her book reviews.

'Oh,' she said, unconcerned. As if I'd just told her tomorrow would be balmy.

I wondered if maybe, in my efforts to spare her feelings, I hadn't made myself clear.

'You're fired,' I clarified.

I heard a chewing sound. 'Well, that's that then. Thanks for calling.' As she was hanging up I heard her say to someone, 'Not so much salt, you'll kill the ginger root taste.' To which a young man replied, 'I've got your root taste, right here' And they both laughed like lovers. Click.

I slowly lowered the receiver toward the cradle. My hand shook a little from the trauma of having just fired a woman. My throat was clogged with cement, my colon was spasming like poking a hot copper wire against an earthworm. As if I'd been the one fired. Meantime, Judith what's-her-fuck was cooking ginger roots and laughing seductively. I hated her.

I scooted my chair back past my partition. 'Gordon.'

Gordon Saunders, the magazine's most prolific article writer, was two-finger typing on his Macintosh. He would sometimes have two articles in the same issue, one on FBI manhunts in Orange County, the other in fingerpainting competitions among preschools.

241

'Gordon,' I repeated.

'Hmmm . . .' He didn't look over.

'Who runs UCI? The head enchilada.'

'Chancellor Cummings.'

'Thanks.' I scooted back to my desk. I stabbed Judith's number again.

'Hello?' she said pleasantly, still chewing something.

I pinched my voice into an officious whine. 'Ms. Dwyer-Horowitz?'

'Yes?'

'This is Chancellor Cummings's office. We've had a very serious complaint from a student about repeated acts of sexual harassment from you. The chancellor would like to see you in his office first thing in the morning. You may want to bring your attorney.'

'W-what?' she choked. 'What are you talking about?'

'The police will explain everything. Good day.' I hung up. After a minute or so she'd call the chancellor's office and discover my call was a prank. But for that minute she'd suffer some of the anguish I had when I'd first called her. There, I thought, staring at the phone, I'd done one good thing today after all.

The telephone rang and I jumped. Had they traced my call back to me already? 'Hello?'

'Hey, Wren. It's James.'

'James?'

'James Smith. Your pipeline to the stars.'

I refocused my thoughts. Gossip column. Oh, yeah, my job. 'What's up, James?'

'Time for more of that cash. Five hundred baby Cs.'

I laughed. 'For five hundred dollars, this gossip better be about me '

'Give me twenty-four hours and I could dig up something on you.'

I let that drop. 'What have you got?'

'The name of a certain famous muscular movie star who is on the cover of every major magazine because he has a hot summer release.'

'What's he done to merit our attention?'

'Actingwise, not much. But last night he had a secret emergency visit by a prominent physician, whose daughter happens to go with a guy who works for me. Seems our muscle-bound megastar got his dick caught in a Dustbuster. Suffered some lacerations around the head, and I'm not talking about the one on top of his thick neck.'

I wanted to laugh. It was funny. But I couldn't. I couldn't help but wonder how it was I brought Wren from writing about the nature of human relationships and art and philosophy to quick blurbs about some poor shlub humping his Dustbuster.

'I need to check on something first,' I said. 'Let me call you back.'

I saw Linda push through the glass doors, say hi to Billie, and march straight back to Jonathan's office. I absently scratched my ankles.

I called the business department to find out what my budget was on gathering gossip. Unlimited, I was told. Jonathan was serious about this column. I told them I'd be by later for five hundred in cash. They said the paperwork would be done in twenty minutes.

I sat at my desk and drew a series of circles. Some of them I gave eyes, some ears, some noses, but never any combination. One I gave hair and feet, but that didn't seem to give it any advantage over the others.

And I thought about Davis in Maui. Robby in Oregon. Dad in the Amazon. Byron, who knows where. And me at my desk, drawing circles with appendages. I drew a penis on one circle.

I couldn't be sure about Davis and the book contract. In fact, I couldn't be sure that even if it was a genuine offer, I could do it properly. What if he discovered I was incapable after a chapter or two? Then he'd fire me and I'd be out the money and my job. I needed to get focused here. I had a well-paying job. I needed to rededicate myself to it. Forget pie-in-the-sky schemes of big money.

Work hard and store your nuts, that's the lesson of the ant and the grasshopper. I drew a pair of walnuts beneath the penis.

I smiled. I was sorry I'd called poor Judith with that immature prank. I drew Judith's surprised eyes on a circle. I chuckled. I felt much better now. I knew what to do, how to act. Who to be.

I reached for the telephone to set up an appointment with James Smith. Just as my fingers touched the phone, it rang. I pulled away as if stung. Then answered it. 'Hello?'

'Wren, could you step into my office a moment, please?'

'Sure, Jonathan.'

I walked down the hallway, knocked, and entered. Jonathan was standing at the other window, looking up into the corners, as if searching for that same insect. Linda sat on the sofa. One low-heeled pump was off and she was rubbing her arch.

'Hi, Linda,' I said.

She smiled stiffly.

'Wren,' Jonathan said, turning toward me. He was frowning. 'When were you going to tell us about your book deal?'

My insides freeze-dried. I looked down. 'There is no deal.'

'Davis Richard didn't offer you $50,000 to write the Season Dougherty bio?'

'He offered. I didn't take it.'

Linda stopped rubbing her foot. 'Did you turn it down?'

'Not yet.'

Jonathan came around the front of his desk and stood less than two feet from me. 'And you didn't think you owed it to us to tell us about this offer?'

'I haven't taken it.'

'But you're considering it.'

'No, I'm not. I'd decided not to take it.'

He shook his head. 'Maybe. Maybe you weren't. You

know the bastard already made the film deal? *My* goddamn film deal.'

I nodded.

'He thinks he pulled something. But I'm not done with
him. Tell your boyfriend I'm not done with him.'

'He's not my boyfriend.'

Jonathan made an exasperated face. 'Whatever.' He
walked back to his desk. 'In the meantime, you're fired.
Clear out your desk and leave.'

He turned his attention back to the window and continued his hunt for the defiant bug.

PART TWO

How to Cope with Desire, Both Natural and Unnatural

18

'That is so *flattering*!'

I shook my head.

'Really,' she said, nodding enthusiastically. '*Very* flattering.'

'You think so?' I said.

'Absolutely.'

I turned to look in the three-sided mirror. I was thin as a paper cut, with no stomach, no butt, and fist-sized breasts. What was there to be flattered? I'd picked this bland one-piece suit because it was cut high enough over my chest to hide my bullet scar. Red lightning bolts zig-zagged down the shiny black material over my breasts and along my ribs until they stopped at the top of my crotch. It was like having two fingers pointing, saying, 'Look here, boys, hot snatch!'

When I gazed at my image doubtfully, the plump sales-girl pointed at a circular rack at the back of the store. 'We have some very lovely suits on sale back there. I just stocked them this morning. Thirty per cent off.'

'Thanks,' I said and retreated back into the dressing room.

I sat on the wooden stool. In the narrow dusty mirror of the tiny room I looked pale and bookish. Even my red lightning bolts didn't help. My white panties peeked out where I'd tried to tuck them up under the high French-cut hips of the swimsuit. Was anything more pathetic than cotton panties sticking out of the leg of a sexy swimsuit? I took off my round steel-rimmed glasses and knuckled

249

my eyes. If they ever remade the movie *Carrie*, I would play the simpleton lead.

Getting fired is like having your wisdom teeth pulled. You keep rubbing your tongue over the gum where the tooth used to be. Maybe you're fascinated with such a radical change in so familiar and intimate a place as your mouth. You can't keep yourself from prodding. Once this fleshy curbside had a hefty tooth parked there; now it's just a cavernous void. Once I had a loving husband; now I have someone else's ex-convict husband. Once I had a terrific job; now I had lightning bolts pointing at my vagina. As if my crotch needed to be jump-started or something.

A few pubic hairs poked out of the elastic leg like wires to a burglar alarm hastily snipped. I hadn't shaved the area in a while, avoiding the red chicken skin look that my irritated skin takes on for a week afterward. With my fingertips, I pushed the stray hairs under the legs of the swimming suit and panties. How had I come to this place in my life, sitting in a small room arranging my pubic hairs? When I was about five, my mother and I were taking a bath when I reached out and touched her thick tuft of pubic hair. 'Does it hurt to have hairs grow there?' I'd asked. Mom had laughed, climbed out of the tub, and returned a minute later with a can of Reddi Wip whipped cream. I still can picture her shaking that red and white can as she stepped back into the tub and made me stand up. She lifted my arms and whooshed a white foam mound in each armpit and a foam donut around my belly button. 'That's what it feels like,' she'd said. We'd laughed and washed off. I wished she were here now to answer my questions. But what would I ask: 'Mom, how come I screwed up my life so badly that I've got to pretend to be my dead friend?' What answer could she possibly give me, what playful demonstration using tangerines or whipped cream?

I took off the bathing suit. The crinkling of the plastic crotch protector made me feel even worse. It seemed so accusing. As if it had been put there especially for sleazy people like me, who used their dead friend's reputation to get a job, then dirtied that reputation by bungling the job. Just as I might dirty the crotch of this bathing suit if they hadn't anticipated sluts like me and taken these extreme precautions. I imagined myself in a police lineup with other women, all of us naked, lying back on gynecological examination tables, our legs up and apart, our feet strapped into the stirrups. *Number three, could you scoot forward please.*

I'd gone from Jonathan Krieg's office out the door and straight to the mall, wandering around South Coast Plaza as if I had a purpose. Trying to look like a busy executive with only twenty minutes to buy an expensive gift for the boss's dinner party that night. I'd stopped in the swimsuit store because they'd had a window display of bathing suits in a tropical setting that reminded me of Hawaii. Tanned mannequins, cardboard palm trees, gray sand, and a couple of rubber starfish. A hand-painted sign that read MAUI WOWIE SALE! It made me think of Davis. If his word was any good, I'd be writing the Season Dougherty book as soon as he returned from Maui. That book was all I had now as a career. I guess trying on swimsuits was some sort of good-faith gesture, as if I were showing Davis I trusted him. It allowed me to think of myself as hopeful rather than gullible.

In the meantime, I still had that part-time job teaching Wren's art history class. Maybe I could kill a few classes by lining up visits to museums and getting guest lecturers from local art galleries. With any luck, I'd never have to actually talk about art myself. Just to be safe, though, I needed to be getting home to make some lecture notes. Right now that class was my only sure source of income.

I lifted my foot up onto the wooden bench and scratched my itchy ankle. Tiny red bumps circled my ankle like a rash of measles. The skin was swollen and raw from my scratching all morning. A few bled. My other ankle was identically afflicted. I leaned closer to inspect.

Flea bites! Another gift from Hector. When I got home, Hector was going to adopt the identity of an outdoor cat.

But I didn't go straight home. I didn't feel up to confronting Hector or, worse, Byron and his bloodstained money. Instead, I went to a movie, a bargain matinee at the four-plex across the street from the mall. The elderly white-haired man who tore my ticket wore a faded black tuxedo and white gloves with snaps at the wrist. He called me young lady and made a grand sweeping gesture toward the theater door number four. The pimply kids who worked behind the concession stand snickered at him behind his back as they shoveled popcorn. That made me feel even sadder so I hurried into the dark theater. The film had already started. It was a comedy. The main character was a beautiful young prostitute. She'd been hired to corrupt a crusading lawyer who was running for governor. His wealthy ex-wife was running against him. The ex-wife had hired the prostitute, but the prostitute and lawyer fell in love. The prostitute wore garter belts a lot. The ex-wife carried a small poofy dog that yelped and tried to bite people. I was the only one in the theater, so I didn't feel bad about laughing a lot, even at the dumb parts. When the movie was over I bought a tub of popcorn and a Diet Coke and sat through it again.

During the second show a few more people joined me, scattered throughout the theater like spies not wanting to be recognized. A couple of giggly girls about sixteen sat two rows in front of me and started talking adoringly about a boy in their class named Todd. Then another one of their friends ran down the aisle with an excited expression. 'Kristy! Guess what?' she said, plopping down next to them. 'My cousin will take the rabbit.'

'She will!' Kristy squealed with delight. She and the new girl gave each other a high-five. 'That is so cool.'

'Yeah, she'll pick it up next week when they've finished building the cage.'

'That is so great! Oh, wow!' Kristy squirmed happily in her seat.

The theater darkened. As the previews for coming attractions ran, I couldn't get over how thrilled Kristy had been at this news. It was as if someone had told her she'd won a million dollars, or she would never die or feel pain or sadness again. But all that had happened was someone taking a rabbit off her hands.

I shook my head and stuffed my mouth with dry popcorn. What makes people happy? Can you experience the same level of joy from winning an Olympic gold medal as you can from winning a game of Monopoly? A person is starving, they find half a bag of soggy potato chips, aren't they as happy as the stockbroker who closes a big deal on his car phone on the drive home to his mansion? Perhaps the human body is just an organism that endures only so much unhappiness; it adjusts to the circumstances and must find its quota of pleasure the way it must demand a certain amount of food and sleep. If so, everybody in the world is really the same amount of happy. Mini-evolution, kind of like Emotional Darwinism. Like those South American bedbugs Mark had told me about, developing dagger penises because the vagina was plugged up. Same principle here. The organism *will be happy*, even if it means reassigning values to achieve it, even reversing values completely. I'd read in a self-help book that you could force yourself into being happy by clenching a pencil between your teeth for a few seconds, tricking the body into thinking you were smiling. But that was just first aid for the blues. This was very different, perhaps even profound. I perked up, thinking I could be on to something profound. I'd come in here depressed, but I'd laughed at the dumb movie and felt better. If the rest of my life had been better, would I have laughed at the movie? Was I just as happy now sitting jobless in a dark theater behind Kristy with rings of bleeding flea bites around my ankles as I had been married to Robby with a ring of gold around my finger?

I wriggled in my seat excitedly. This must be how Wren felt when she had one of her ideas, like when we were driving along that last night and she'd forced me to pull over. What if my idea was right? What if researchers somewhere discovered that the human organism is generally always the same amount of happy. They find some scientific way to measure it, like brain waves or cholesterol level. So, it doesn't matter what you do or buy or who you marry, your brain will adjust and find other things to fill its happiness quotient. If this were true, would they even reveal the results to us? What would happen to our economy? Our whole society is built on the concept that we can be happier if we buy this or that item. Or find someone new and improved to love. Suddenly we discover that it isn't so. What would happen then? We'd stop buying clothes and makeup and let our memberships to health clubs lapse. We'd stay married to the same people. My mind sizzled and crackled as if charged with electricity. Maybe I could write this idea up myself, just as Wren would have. Maybe sell it to some magazine.

But the more I sat there watching the young prostitute in a garter belt and the ex-wife with her snarling little dog, the less I felt the idea had any merit. After a while, the idea seemed to have leaked out of my body and run down the theater's sticky concrete floor along with the spilled Cokes and flattened popcorn.

When the movie was over for the second time, I left the theater and drove back to the office. It was almost dark now. I'd left work earlier without cleaning out my desk because I'd been too dazed, too upset. Not that there was much of importance, I'd only been there a few days. But I did leave Davis's unlisted home number on a paper in my desk. Not to mention Byron's bloodstained $400 taped to the bottom of my drawer. Right now, that money might come in handy. Which reminded me, I would have to swing by Detective Diesel's office sometime and pick up the other hundred-dollar bill. Without a job, I no longer cared about evidence against Byron or the mysterious dog blood. I cared about rent.

Everyone was supposed to be gone from the office by

now, but I knew Steve Hawkins, the layout designer, often stayed late to work on his freelance jobs illustrating children's books. He had a brood of eighteen-month-old triplet girls at home, so he found it difficult to do any work there. He would let me in.

But when I arrived at the offices, Steve was gone. However, the glass door was unlocked, so I walked in. Cautiously, I sneaked across the room toward my desk. I had no idea who was still here this late. By now everyone would have known about my being fired and I didn't want to run into anyone to explain.

My desk drawers were already empty. The pens and yellow legal pads were gone. The stapler, tape dispenser, ruler. So were the notes I had taken on the phone. James Smith's phone number. My doodles of the circle people with single appendages. Everything. I had ceased to exist. Again. Well, that was their stuff, they had a right to it. But the money and Davis's phone number were mine, damn it, and I wanted them. I reached under the desk drawer and peeled off the $400. I counted the four bills twice before stuffing them into my purse. But where was Davis's phone number?

I patrolled the desktops of my colleagues like a Coast Guard cruiser searching ship wreckage for survivors. Maybe someone thought Davis's unlisted number might come in handy someday, maybe some closet screenwriter here wanted to send his completed screenplay to him. Desktops were for the most part bare. Reporters locked their Rolodexes in their desks at night, some even took theirs home. Not that we could honestly be called reporters, but some here had been at one time or fancied themselves as ones now.

Finally I made my way to Linda Marley's office. The light was on, her open briefcase was next to the desk. I quickly looked over my shoulder. She was the last person I wanted to run into here. Still, I was here, she was nowhere in sight. She owed me. I ducked into her office and started searching her desk. I could feel my pulse like snapping fingers in my throat. Sweat slicked the backs of my knees. My left eye throbbed. I fingered through the While You Were Out slips, the galleys of upcoming articles, memos from Jonathan Krieg.

'Hello, Wren,' Linda said behind me.

I turned and smiled pleasantly. 'I left a phone number in my desk. It's gone.'

She nodded sympathetically. 'Right here.' She walked past me and rummaged through some papers I hadn't yet gotten to. I smelled a strong scent of booze as she breezed by. I noticed her movements seemed awkward as she sloppily groped papers aside. She wasn't wearing shoes. 'It's here somewhere.'

Suddenly I felt too uncomfortable to stay. As if I'd walked in and caught her masturbating or something. 'I'll call you tomorrow,' I said. 'I shouldn't have come back.'

'You shouldn't have gotten fired. You shouldn't have taken Davis's deal.'

I didn't want to get into all that with her, so I just kept walking. 'I'll call you tomorrow.'

She followed me, staying right up to my shoulder, though I noticed she was wobbling a bit. 'I was counting on you, Wren. I picked you out myself, brought you to Krieg's attention. I'm good at spotting talent and you've got it. God knows we could have used some of it around here.'

'I did my best.'

'Bullshit!' The word came out kind of wet and slurred. Her saliva misted my arm.

'I don't want to talk about this now,' I said.

'I don't care what you want. We're not talking about you here, we're talking about me. I was counting on you, goddamn it.'

'Then why didn't you talk Jonathan out of firing me?'

'Talk him out?' She laughed. 'Hell, I had to *convince* him to fire you.'

I stopped and faced her, not hiding the shock on my face. 'I don't get it.'

'You don't, really?' Now she seemed surprised. She licked her lips with an uncooperative tongue. 'This is my magazine, Wren. I've worked on it since it was started. From the first fucking issue eight years ago. We had Susan Anton on the cover. Remember her? She was famous for being tall and dating Dudley Moore. And tan, she had a helluva tan.' She paused, swallowed dryly, her tongue making loud smacking sounds. 'The previous owners didn't care about the contents of the magazine. They just wanted to build advertising revenues to a certain level, then sell. That was their plan from the beginning. To make that happen they wanted fluff. I gave them fluff. I can write 5,000 words about anything from shopping for jelly to Flag Day parades. Words are like ether, you know what I mean. Evaporate faster than a fart. Poof.' She gestured with her hands to show an explosion. 'You know what I mean?'

I nodded.

'Then along comes Jonathan Krieg, self-made asshole, and he wants to play Ben fucking Bradlee for a few months, maybe a year. Run around shouting "Stop the presses!" or some goddamn thing. Use the magazine as a legit springboard into movies. Oh, yes, he wants to make movies. Everybody wants to make movies. No matter how rich they are, how much money they've made at something else, they all eventually come to Hollywood. Why? Glitz and tits. They want to be high priests at the only real religion this country has. Movies.' She stopped, took a deep breath, adjusted her tongue, which flopped along her lower lip. 'Yeah, yeah, yeah. It's an old story. I should know, I wrote it a hundred times for this magazine. You know what Jonathan will do next year or the year after? He'll dump us on someone else. But you know what? You know what?' She grabbed my forearm tightly. I felt nervous, as if I were being accosted by a bag woman. I tried to pull away, but she held tight. Her eyes were red and the stale odour of alcohol she breathed into my face made my stomach clench. 'You know what?'

'No, what?'

'I'm still here. I was here when I got remarried. I was here when I got divorced. I was here when I had a lumpectomy. And I'll still be here no matter who owns this rag or what kind of crap they want to print in it.' Her fingernails were digging into my arm and I thought I might have to hit her hand to break free. I tried to twist away, but she hung on as if this were a rodeo. 'It's like every actress over thirty ever interviewed in *People* or on *Entertainment Tonight*. You know how they describe themselves? As survivors. "I'm a survivor" they like to say to the camera. "I'm no flavor of the month. I'm a survivor." You know what I say? Fuck you, bitches. You don't know what survival is. If you're still around when you're forty or, God forbid, nearing fifty, then talk to me about your goddamn survival. But most of them marry some other actor or director who's got a hit show or movie or music video and then they can afford to be goddamn survivors. You know? You know what I mean?'

The way she glared at me, her eyes fogged over with liquor, but with a dark pinpoint of rage lasering through —I don't know, I had the uncomfortable feeling she was talking about me, that she knew who I was, what I was doing. I almost expected her to call me Luna. Her fingernails, short and blunt, sliced through my skin. But I didn't feel like pulling away anymore. I pushed the arm toward her as if it were a life preserver. She deserved it. Dig in, I thought. You're a better man than I am, Gunga Din. I wanted to tell her I understood. But words snared on the clump of barbed wire lodged in my throat. My mouth was open, but nothing came out.

'Mom,' a female voice behind us said softly.

Linda and I turned to the glass door at the front of the office. A young girl, maybe seventeen, stood there, dressed in a hooded sweatshirt, long shorts, and suede hiking boots. She was thin, as thin as I, with straight red hair. She had a kind face, with full lips that curved into a smile even when she wasn't smiling. She looked like the kind of kid who always brought home damaged birds and shivering animals and nursed them back to health or gave them elaborate funerals, the kind of kid everyone assumed would grow up to be a veterinarian or a nun.

'Hi, honey,' Linda said cheerfully. 'What are you doing here?'

'You're late. I called, but the answering service picked up. They wouldn't ring me through.'

Linda released my arm to look at her watch. 'Late?'

Linda's daughter sighed and shook her head parentally. 'Jesus, Mom. Have a heart.'

I looked at my forearm. Four bluish half-moon bruises tattooed the skin. I rubbed them.

'Hi, I'm Sara Marley.' She walked toward me, limping slightly. I noticed a long white scar curving around her knee. She held out her hand and I shook it.

'Wren Caldwell.'

Sara's face brightened. 'Oh, yes. I've heard all about you. I read a couple of your articles Mom had lying around. They were great. I didn't understand some of it, but I could tell it was smart. Deep.'

'Thanks,' I said. I looked over at Linda. She stood swaying slightly, her eyes unfocused. She looked frail in her stocking feet.

'Could you give me a hand?' Sara asked me.

'Sure.' I lifted my hands as if to carry something, then let them drop. 'What do you want me to do?'

'Get her downstairs to the car. I'll drive her home.'

'I'm perfectly fit to drive,' Linda announced.

'Don't fuss, Mom.'

'I don't need this shit from you, Sara Couldn't-Walk-Until-You-Were-Two-And-A-Half-Wetted-Your-Bed-Until-You-Were-Eight-Sucked-Your-Thumb-Until-You-Were-Twelve Marley!' Linda jerked away from us with such violence that she stumbled forward a few steps and bumped into a desk. A six-inch run in her stocking splayed upward between two toes. 'Remember who the mother is around here, okay?'

'You're the mother, Mother.'

They both looked at each other and laughed a kind of giggly mother-daughter laugh.

Sara nodded at me and we both slid arms around Linda's waist and guided her toward the door.

'I'd better lock up first,' Sara said. She went back into Linda's office and grabbed her purse, shoes, and brief-case. After digging through the purse a few seconds, she came up with a crowded key chain with a silver rape whistle attached. She locked Linda's office, then followed Linda and me out the front door and locked that too.

In the elevator, Sara and I held Linda upright.

'This isn't necessary, guys,' Linda kept saying, but she made no move to pull away. In fact, she slumped a little in our arms, as if relieved of a great burden.

'Don't worry about her,' Sara said. 'This isn't chronic. She's not an alcoholic or anything.'

'No, no,' I rushed to agree. 'Of course not.'

'She only does this when she has a new date.'

'A new date?'

'A date with someone new. She's supposed to go over to the Performing Arts Center tonight for some opera thing. I haven't met him yet. A lawyer, I think. Real estate law.'

'Did you pick up my dress from the cleaner?' Linda asked in a moment of alertness that passed as quickly as a sneeze.

'Got it, Mom. Everything's set. All we gotta do is sober you up within the next hour and a half. I think a couple laps in the pool ought to do it, don't you?'

Linda nodded.

Date. It sounded so odd. Linda Marley was at least fif-teen years older than I. With a teenage daughter. Is it still called a date then? That word doesn't seem dignified enough somehow for her age. Was this what I would be doing fifteen years from now? Getting drunk because I had to face another new man, another evening of revealed backgrounds, old regrets, war wounds? Like legless veterans slapping our stumps and describing how we felt the moment we stepped on that buried mine that pulverized our limbs into a fireworks burst of hot blood and charred bone.

'Date,' Linda said, as if reading my mind. 'Date sounds like a swear word, doesn't it?' She didn't look at either of us so we didn't answer. She made a face and started talking with a kind of Brooklyn swagger in her voice. 'Don't date with me, pal. I'll date you up bad, motherdater. Oh, yeah, well date you, buddy . . .' The rest was mumbled.

Linda lifted her head in another flash of alertness. She turned her head toward me. 'I'm going to still be running this fucking magazine when Jonathan New-Age Krieg is serving time for insider trading or whatever they finally catch him for. Believe it, Wren.'

'I believe it.' I did.

'That's why I had him fire you. Season's cell neighbour told me about your deal with Davis. I knew Jonathan would blow his colon. If I didn't suggest he fire you, eventually he'd end up blaming me for everything. After all, I was the one who'd championed hiring you. See my problem?'

'I see,' I said. 'You were saving your ass.'

'Surviving.'

The elevator door opened at the lobby and Sara and I struggled to pull Linda out. Her last speech seemed to have drained her energy and she slumped against us with all her weight. I lurched under the sudden burden.

'I can take her from here,' Sara said, limping a few steps away from me with her mother.

'I don't mind.'

'That's okay.' She seemed protective now, I guess because she knew her mom had fired me. 'We're fine. It's just that she hates the opera as much as she hates first dates. She'll be fine, though. A few laps in the pool. That always works.'

'Good luck, then. Nice meeting you.' I started to walk away. I didn't hear any footsteps behind me so I knew they weren't moving. I stopped and looked back. Sara was staring at me.

'What?' I asked.

'You're smart, Wren. My mom's smart too. But she never answers my question.'

'What question?'

'If she hates the opera and hates first dates, why does she go?'

The fact that that question had never occurred to me struck me as more depressing than any answer I could give.

* * * * *

I stopped at the 7-Eleven market on the way home and bought a large bottle of Kahlúa and two of vodka. At home I placed the three bottles on the coffee table in front of me like small pets I was about to groom. I turned on ESPN and watched beach volleyball while I got drunk on Black Russians.

Being drunk felt good. For one thing, my lips tingled. As if a line of chorus girls in spiked heels were can-canning back and forth across them. My lips became extraordinarily sensitive. Bright lights or loud noises made them wince. All my other senses seemed dimmer. I could hardly hear the TV or smell Hector. Suddenly I could feel everything through the outer membranes of my lips. Changes in temperature or movement registered there first. I had the distinct impression that if I pressed some-one's fingertips against my lips, I'd be able to distinguish individual fingerprints. Feel the bunched swirls of skin like icing that distinguishes corpses and criminals. I picked up a *TV Guide* and closed my eyes. I opened it randomly, pressed the page against my lips: 11.00 PM *Cheers*. Sam proposes to Diane for the second time.

Amazing!

I imagined myself as some comic-book heroine. Lip

Woman! It made me more decisive. I jumped up from the sofa humming loudly what I thought might be Lip Woman's brassy theme song, which sounded a lot like the theme to *Bonanza*. I grabbed Hector's cat-litter box and food and water bowls and carried them into Byron's bedroom. I also deposited Hector in there, closing the door after him. Let him spread his fleas and stench in there for a while.

After that I didn't feel much like Lip Woman anymore so I went into the kitchen and poured vinegar on my flea bites and that helped the itching some.

Having left the world better than I found it, I sat at the kitchen table and drank more Black Russians. Once I stuck my tongue into the glass and started lapping it up the way I saw Hector drink. That was fun for a while. My chin was cool from the vodka and sticky from the syrupy Kahlúa. Then I decided I should stop drinking like Hector and take more advantage of my decisive mood. I started jotting down numbers, trying to figure out how much it might cost to start my own magazine. The more I thought about the idea, the more excited I got. I'd screwed up Wren's reputation, but it was possible to salvage it again. I'd name the magazine after her, like *Lear's* or *Mirabella*, and I'd print all her articles to get started.

I had no idea if the figures I was fooling around with were even close to accurate. Mostly I guessed. I started with the $50,000 I would earn from Davis, and created a budget from that. I wrote very neatly, which made it look even more official and possible. I liked the idea of someday telling a talk-show audience that I'd worked out the details of the magazine at my kitchen table while drunk on Black Russians and holding a cat hostage in a convict's room.

The phone rang while I was sketching possible magazine names over Arsenio Hall's face on the cover of *TV Guide*, but I didn't pick up. I listened as the answering machine informed the caller that no one could come to the phone. Then the beep. Then: 'Hey, Byron, pick up the fucking phone, man,' the familiar caller said. 'It's Grudge, man.' Pause. 'Okay, here it is. I'm just passing this one along, so I got no fucking stake in it whatsoever, okay? This is all I know: McIntire told me that Landry is looking for you. Landry's fucking crazy, man. I wouldn't fuck with him if I were you. Okay, I delivered the message. You make up your own fucking mind, okay?' Click.

I sighed, sipped my Black Russian. How had a man named Grudge become part of my life? Why was his voice with threats and veiled violence allowed to fill up my kitchen like the smell of burnt toast? Ever since Byron showed up it was as if some rip in another world, an alternate dimension, had opened into my world and now gruesome creatures were worming through the hole into my life.

I went to the living room and turned off the TV. I put a Rickie Lee Jones CD on. I turned it up louder than usual because I thought the musical notes could kill the harsh notes of Grudge's voice, like antibodies or enzymes or something. I wanted to purify even the sound integrity of the apartment. Sterilize the karma. It was, after all, *my* apartment. Only the sounds I invited in should live here.

I couldn't find the song I wanted. Maybe it was on a different album. I couldn't remember the title, just that it was a love song. Her love songs always sound like threats. Love me or else.

Finally I gave up and just pressed PLAY. Rickie Lee sang,

> 'So you keep talking in many languages
> Telling us the way you feel
> Don't stop confiding in the road you're on
> Don't quit, you're walking Satellites . . .'

I had no idea what that meant, so I hauled Wren's art book to the kitchen and started making notes on the art works she'd marked. My handwriting was less precise now, barely legible, but I figured it wasn't the fault of the writing, just that my eyes were bleary from drinking; it would be more readable in the morning when I was sober.

I turned to a page that showed a greenish statue of a half-woman, half-man figure. The caption said it was made of copper alloy with semiprecious stones. Crafted in Nepal about the year 1000, it was called 'Androgynous form of Siva and Uma'. The book said this was a representation of Ardhanarisvara, The Lord Whose Half Is Woman, devised by theologians to emphasize the non-duality of the divine principle uniting masculinity and femininity. I underlined that, figuring I'd try to understand it later. The figure had four arms, though one of the male arms was broken off as was one of the male legs.

Wren's bold printing crowded the margins: *Influence of Indian Gupta art: compare with Matisse's Indian period— his search for constant light: feminine principle of Hindus: the god Siva, consort Uma.* An arrow was drawn indicating the figure's garment with the word *dhoti* at the other end of the arrow. A crooked arrow pointed at the upraised arms with Wren's note, *cosmic unity.* And angled in the narrow left margin, her handwriting slanted in a hurried scrawl: *Religious art as objects, not of worship, but of focal points to review fundamental principles. Compare with Siva dancing figure. No lesson is ever learned but must be relearned. Function of art to reteach the same moral lesson by evoking passion.*

A circle was drawn around the figure's single female breast. A line led to the margin where, in larger, more ragged handwriting than Wren's, someone had written: *38C! Cosmic Implants!*

I laughed. Who had written that? Someone Wren had sat next to in art class? I wished he or she were here sitting next to me now. How else would I understand all I needed to by Monday? I didn't see all this stuff that she'd noted and I didn't know all about Hinduism the way she did. I needed a third eye that could view the world the way Wren had. That could see what lurked behind the foliage of the obvious. I picked up my pen and drew an eye on the page, right in the middle of the forehead of the copper figure. Then I drew one on his/her single female breast. That made me laugh.

I had a great idea. I pulled off my blouse over my head, popping a button in my clumsiness. The white button skittered across the kitchen floor and pinged against the cupboard, where I left it for Hector to ingest and perhaps choke on. I unclasped and shrugged off my bra. I picked up the pen and began drawing a large eye around the bullet scar on my breast. The pen against my skin tickled and I chuckled as I outlined the eye as if I were using eyeliner. Then I drew the eyeball, using the scar tissue as the actual retina. I colored it in with blue ink.

'Suddenly Lip Woman becomes . . . *Tit Woman!*' I announced with a flourish and a few bars from *Bonanza*. 'The all-seeing, all-dancing, all-talking eye of Modern Woman.' I walked around the kitchen holding my breast with both hands, pointing the inky eye like a camera at things, saying, 'Ahhh. Yup. Everything is so much clearer now. Symbolism, hidden meaning, we laugh at your puny disguises.'

I drank another Black Russian and decided that I would use my new super vision to look through Byron's stuff. He knew all about me. Now I would know all his secrets too. I wouldn't have to be afraid of him. I ran down the hallway, still cupping my left breast, as if I were steering my body with it.

Byron's room was neat as a monk's cell. Hector was sitting on the bed licking his tail with long strokes. I went around the room opening drawers and closets, pointing my breast like a Geiger counter. Hector ignored me, concentrating on his tail. His attitude seemed very professional and it occurred to me that perhaps I'd judged him too harshly. I petted him and a flea leapt onto my wrist and then onto my super breast. I trapped the flea between my two thumbnails and squeezed until the body popped, leaving a tiny drop of blood on my thumbnail. The blood, I realized, was Hector's.

I wiped my thumbnails with the blood and minicorpse on Byron's pillow and continued my search. I hauled his battered suitcase out from under the bed and noticed for the first time that the tartan design on the cloth was the same as on Wren's luggage that I'd used to move in here. This case was part of her set. I flipped it open. It was empty except for the old photo album I'd given him that first night. When I'd first found the album in Wren's apartment, I'd been surprised to see that many of the photographs had been removed. The only ones in it were of Wren or Wren's family and friends. A couple of me and Robby. Now as I paged through the album, I saw that the missing photos had been restored. They were all photos of Wren and Byron. One showed them each wearing a dragonfly earring. Byron still had all of his fingers. In every one they were both laughing. They looked like the happiest couple in the world. In Robby's and my albums, we're usually grinning. This was the first time I noticed how different grinning and laughing really were. In one photo, Byron was bare-chested, holding a bottle of beer in one hand and shooting a squirt gun with the other. Only he was shooting right at Wren's crotch. The front of her shorts was soaked but she was bent over laughing. Some-one had written *Hemingway Goes a-Courting* at the bot-tom of the photo. It was the same handwriting as *Cosmic Implant*. Another photo showed them in bed surrounded by open cartons of Chinese food. Wren is straddling him, wearing a T-shirt and panties. She's holding up a cross formed with two chopsticks to Byron's face and threaten-ing to plunge a third chopstick through his heart. Written across the bottom: *Sylvia Plath's Honeymoon*.

I put the album back in the suitcase. My breast was not impressed.

The bathroom wasn't any more rewarding. Byron used kid's formula Aim toothpaste, the shiny red stripe swirling through the toothpaste like a candy cane. He shaved with the same brand safety razor as I; then I realized it wasn't just the same brand, it was in fact my damn razor he was

267

shaving with. I removed the blade and scraped it along the edge of the wooden cabinet, nicking and warping the edge as much as I could. Then I replaced the razor and laid it neatly on the sink, waiting for his next shave. The rest of my search uncovered only one unusual item. Under the bathroom sink were ten rolls of Xtra-Soft toilet paper stacked so tightly that the cupboard door didn't close all the way. I started pulling each roll out, examining them for some clues. I held them up to my breast 'eye' as if consulting a Ouija board. Were these used to smuggle drugs, perhaps into or from prison? Was that what those mysterious phone calls were about? The guy named Landry who was after Byron? My breast was perplexed.

'Running low?' Byron said. 'Or just expecting the runs?'

19

I looked up from my place on the bathroom floor where I sat cross-legged, surrounded by scattered rolls of toilet paper, holding one such roll up to my naked breast like a silencer to a pistol. Byron was dressed in an expensive three-piece blue silk suit he hadn't had when he'd first moved in. His white shirt was starched and glowing like a TV screen in a dark room. The shirt was buttoned up to his throat; he wore no tie. His dark hair was slicked back and tied in a modest ponytail with a rubber band. His eyes were hidden behind sunglasses, which had a yellow Carl Jr.'s star on the fluorescent green temple frame, part of the fast-food restaurant's current promotion ($1.99 with a Western Burger and small fries).

I grabbed a damp bath towel from his shower door and draped it over my chest. I dropped the toilet paper roll on the floor with the others, not bothering to restack them. 'Close the door,' I said, looking his outfit over. 'An ill wind must be blowing.'

'That's something Wren might have said. You're getting better.'

'Help me up,' I said, holding out my hand.

'God helps those who help themselves,' he said. 'Look it up.' He leaned back against the doorjamb and crossed his arms.

'At least now I know who you think you are.'

'I yam what I yam.' He did a pretty good Popeye chuckle.

'Yeah, the God of Ass Wipes.' I threw a roll of toilet paper at him. He let it bounce off his chest.

He laughed and removed his sunglasses. His hand absently drifted up to his dragonfly earring, which he fondled while he stared at me. His half-size little finger looked fake in this light, like a rubber prop. Actually, except for his new clothing, he didn't look so hot right then. His face was sallow, with dark blue bibs under each eye. His eyes looked loose and watery, as if he'd been in a brisk unrelenting wind. Dark stubble peppered his jaw. He looked exhausted.

'You look like shit. Here, clean yourself up.' I tossed another roll of toilet paper at him. He didn't flinch this time either, like he was used to having things hurled at him. The roll grazed his shoulder and continued out into his bedroom. It bounced under his bed. Hector dove after it.

'What, you don't like my new duds?'

'So the emperor has new clothes.'

He just laughed again and offered me his hand. 'You crack me up.'

'I wish your skull could say the same thing.' I ignored his hand and grabbed the sink, pulling myself up to a sitting position on the toilet seat. From there it was fairly easy to get to my feet, though once I stood the carpet seemed to be rolling forward faster than I was walking, like one of those airport people movers. I knotted the towel around my chest and held on to the sink as I walked toward the door. Byron stepped aside for me to pass. He grabbed a roll of the toilet paper from the floor and followed me.

'Tough day at the Wren biz?' he asked, walking beside me. He kept tossing up a roll of toilet paper with one hand and catching it with the other, back and forth, like a juggler with one ball. 'By the way, who are you supposed to be now? Luna being drunk or Luna pretending to be Wren being drunk? 'Cause this isn't how Wren acted when she was drunk. Although the eyeball tattoo on your boob is a nice touch.'

'Fuck you.'

'That's more like it. More theatrical flair. That's my little Wren.' He applauded.

Slowly I navigated the hallway by keeping my hands firmly suctioned to the wall like a lizard. Byron juggled the toilet roll and kept pace beside me.

'What do you think the first thing a guy just out of prison would buy?' he asked.

'I don't know.'

'Guess.'

'A woman or two.'

'Yeah, some would. Or drugs. Booze. I've known some to blow it all on toys for their kids. Some on a gun, looking to get even with somebody or other they imagined did them wrong.' He hefted the toilet paper, bounced it off the wall and caught it. 'Me, I went straight to the grocery store and cleaned them out of toilet paper. The softest, sweetest smelling brand they had. I mean, I was squeezing and sniffing toilet paper for about an hour.' He shook his head and made a face. 'The kind they use in prison . . . man, they must make it out of ground glass and barbed wire.'

I kept walking, hand over hand along the wall. Easy does it. Avoid barfing in front of this man at all costs.

'Forget the electrified fences and snarling dogs. Just string that prison toilet paper around the place, and no one could break out.'

'Maybe it's a subtle form of rehabilitation,' I said. 'Negative stimulation. Every time you wipe your ass you'll remember why you don't want to go back to jail. Usually they work on the brain, but I guess they picked the part you guys use most to do your thinking.'

Byron didn't say anything for a minute, just followed along, not even tossing his roll now. Like he was chewing on a tough problem. Then, just as we entered the kitchen, he said, 'I think I'm starting to see why you don't like being you.'

I swung my hand at his face. He saw it coming and had

plenty of time, but he made no move to stop me or dodge the blow. He watched my hand smack his cheek and he kept walking as if nothing had happened. That made me angrier. I'd had my ineffectualness ground in my face all day. I wanted to hurt him, show him what Lip Woman and Tit Woman were capable of. Something had to get to him. Some blows had to be worth fending off. 'You get your phone message?' I asked, nodding toward the answering machine. 'Some guy Landry is hot for you in a bad way. Sounded pissed. Very pissed.'

I looked over at his face for a reaction. I was rewarded. Landry's name was like splashing onion juice in his eyes. He tried not to show any expression, let the name bounce off him like the toilet roll, like my slap, but fear squeezed his eyeballs. Fear and weariness. Now I was kind of sorry I'd sprung it on him like that. I walked into the kitchen.

'"*Stooop, in the naaame of looove . . ." Awkk.*' Standing in the middle of the kitchen was a black iron floor stand cage with a brightly colored bird over a foot tall walking erectly along a perch.

'Good God, now what?' I said.

'"*My world is empty . . . without you, babe . . .*"'

'He's an *Amazona* parrot,' Byron explained. 'His name's Motown.'

'His name's Dinner in about two minutes. That's how long it'll take me to reach the oven.'

Byron laughed, but when I started toward the oven, he stepped between me and the cage.

'I want him out,' I told him. 'I mean it.'

'"*You can't hurry love . . ." Awk.*'

'Jesus.' I shook my head. His voice sounded small and tinny, as if coming out of a cheap transistor radio. His tail was green but his chest was a brilliant red. He had a blue comb of spiked feathers on his head. These were colors unseen outside a Crayola box.

'The guy who used to own him is an ex-con named Berkshire. He has a hard-on for Diana Ross. He taught the bird all her song titles. He dances a little to "Baby

Love."' He turned to the bird. 'Mo, do "Baby Love."
C'mon, "Baby love, my baby love . . ."' Byron did a
dance shuffle by the way of encouragement.

'Give him back to the owner.'

'I said used to own. He's all mine now.' Pause. 'I won
him.'

'You won him? Just who the hell are you gambling with
that you always win such junk. Can't you at least win cash
and valuable prizes like every schmuck on a game show.
A goddamn Toyota maybe. On *Jeopardy* they win cash,
did you know that? You come home with a fucking bird
that thinks it's a Supreme.'

Byron stared at me with a hard expression, a prison-
yard expression. 'You don't get it, lady. You know how
long Berkshire had this bird, how many years it took him
to teach it to memorize all these stupid titles? You have
any idea how much he loved this clump of bird shit and
feathers? I didn't just win a bird. I won a man's most valuable possession. I took what he cared about most in this
whole fucking world, except maybe his pecker.'

'Congratulations. You make it sound so noble.'

'"*Touch me in the morning . . .*"'

I leaned my face against its cage. 'If you're still here
then, I'll touch you all right.' I opened the silverware
drawer and showed the bird a carving knife. He angled on
his perch with one black eye staring at me. I tilted the
steak knife so the overhead light glinted off the blade into
the bird's eye. He blinked once and turned his back to
me.

Byron took off his fancy blue jacket and draped it over
the cage. Motown immediately was quiet. Byron sat
wearily at the kitchen table and rubbed his eyes. 'Okay,
forget appealing to your nobler senses. Think about this:
These birds are brought up at great expense from Mexico
and South America. They don't breed well in captivity,
which makes them even more valuable. Vocabulary aside,
you're looking at over two thousand dollars' worth of
bird.'

'Two thousand dollars?' I whistled. 'He's growing on me.'

I opened the refrigerator and found a can of Byron's beer. I walked it over to the table and dropped it in front of him. It fell on its side and started rolling toward the edge of the table. I let it. I wondered if that meant the table was slanted or the whole apartment complex was. Byron didn't seem to notice and the can kept rolling until it plunged over the edge like a barrel shooting Niagara Falls. Barely looking, Byron reached out and lazily snagged the beer in mid-air. He pressed the cold can against his forehead and mumbled thanks to me.

'Baseball?' I asked.

'What?' He looked at me blankly.

'The way you snagged that beer can. I used to watch a lot of baseball on ESPN.'

He yawned loudly. 'I played some. College scholarship.'

I stared at him a long moment, still trying to figure him out. What had happened between him and Wren? What about the beatings? I sat in the chair across from him, determined to get some truth out of him. 'What happened to your finger?' I asked him.

'What finger?'

'C'mon.'

'She crossed her legs too fast.'

'Yeah, fine,' I said. I walked back to the refrigerator, grabbed a Diet Coke, and slammed the refrigerator door. The ketchup bottle rattled against the salad dressings.

'What? You toss me a beer and you think that's a front row ticket to five acts of my life?'

'You dumped your life on me the moment you came in here blackmailing me.'

'I'm not blackmailing you. I'm just renting a room. A stuffy, dusty room I might add.'

'And if I don't want to rent you this stuffy, dusty room?'

He shrugged. 'Life is full of choices. That would be one choice.'

'Then my choice is for you to take your flea-bag cat and Diana Ross here and find other accommodations.'

'And it would be my choice then to tell everyone you know that you're impersonating my dead wife and see which of them has you arrested for fraud first.'

'If that's not blackmail, what is it?'

He looked up through sleepy eyes and smiled. 'Negotiating. Getting to yes. Isn't that all life is? Everybody trying to get what they want, figuring out what they're willing to trade for it. Same thing in love or business. Like kids trading baseball cards. The only worthwhile question anymore is "how much?"'

'Gee, just what I wanted to hear right now, more prison philosophy. What were you, the jailhouse Buddha?'

'Am I wrong?'

I sat down and sipped my soda. 'What is it you want? What are you doing here?'

'That's not open for discussion.'

'Oh, right. I forgot. Big, tough mystery man. He has secrets. A Past. All you need now is a theme song and you can have your own TV series.' I hummed a little of my 'Bonanza/Lip Woman' theme for him.

Byron stood up, drawing himself upright like an athlete about to compete against his arch rival. I thought he was going to hit me. But I didn't duck or flinch. I just waited for the blow with grit teeth, just as he had done with my slap. But it didn't come. He just walked off into the living-room. When he returned he was carrying what was left of the Kahlúa and vodka. He poured some Kahlúa into my Diet Coke can.

'Any other astute observations about me you want to share?' he asked.

I shook my head. 'I think that pretty much covers it. Except you're probably the type of guy who begins sentences with "I'm the type of guy . . ." Am I right?'

He looked at the scrawled figures on the paper I'd written on earlier, then at the doodles on the *TV Guide*.

'*Wren's Nest. The Wren Report. Wren's-Eye View.* What the hell is all this?'

'Nothing!' I grabbed the *TV Guide* away, ripping Arsenio's face in half.

'Jesus,' Byron said, shaking his head. 'It's too pathetic. Now you want to start the magazine she always talked about. Jesus, lady, get a life.'

'I have a life.'

'Your *own* life.'

'Mind your own business, okay? You have no idea what I'm doing. Just butt out.'

'Right.' He slid the torn magazine across the table to me. He studied my figures for a moment before tossing them over at me too. 'Where are you going to get fifty grand?'

Like I was going to tell this ex-con compulsive gambler anything about my money. 'I dunno. Save it, I guess.'

'Save $50,000? How? You don't even have a job anymore.'

I spun around and glared at him.

'Relax,' he said. 'I wasn't spying. I just phoned you at work today to warn you about the bird and they said you weren't working there anymore. What happened? They finally ask you to write something?'

Here's the funny part: I wanted to tell him everything that had happened. There was something freeing about talking to him, I guess because he knew the truth about me. I could be me, not Wren. I didn't have to dazzle, be smart, be witty, be insightful. I could paint an eye on my boob and get drunk and it didn't matter. But then again, I had to be wary of him too. This could be part of his whole routine to get at the $50,000 he thought I had. Stay sharp, Luna, I prodded myself. Constant vigilance is the price of . . . something. Churchill said that. He smoked fat cigars. Sometimes a cigar is just a cigar. Freud said that.

What had I been thinking of again?

'Saving fifty grand,' Byron said.

'What?'

'You asked what you'd been thinking of.'

Jesus, I was speaking aloud without knowing it. I pushed the spiked Diet Coke away from me. 'Since I've lost my job, Byron, there's nothing left for you to threaten me about.'

'Sure there is. If there weren't you'd have tossed my stuff on the front lawn by now. That means the game is still afoot, as Sherlock Holmes would say. Let's see, who is left who would be interested in your little charade. Probably that bland-looking boyfriend of yours.'

'He's not my boyfriend. He's a business associate.'

'Oh? You guys were doing some fancy dry-humping business the other night.'

'Go ahead and tell him,' I bluffed. 'I don't care.'

'Okay, just as soon as he gets back from Maui.'

I slapped my palm onto the table. 'How?'

'That time I was spying.' He made a telephone sign with his outstretched thumb and little finger. 'One thing you learn in prison is how to get information by phone. Inside those walls, the telephone is a lethal weapon.'

'Is that why you're afraid of Landry? Tell me about Landry.'

He looked at me with sad eyes. 'You're not drunk enough.'

'We can fix that.'

*   *   *   *   *

Byron leaned his head back against the cement lip of the Jacuzzi and sang:

'It's the story of a dork named Brady
Who got tired of pounding his pud in the shower

277

So he married this hagged-out bitch with three
   nubile daughters
And sniffed their panties while doing the laundry.'

I made a face. 'Pounding his pud?'

'You prefer whipping his lizard? Stroking his dolphin?
Paddling his canoe?'

'None of the above.' I sipped more Kahlúa and Diet
Coke and shrugged. 'Why are guys so raunchy?'

He belched. 'Is that a rhetorical question?'

I tried to belch back, but nothing came out.

'Your turn,' he said.

'I never watched *The Brady Bunch*.'

'Bullshit. Everybody watched. It was like a satanic cult
or something. You watched, wondered if the brothers and
sisters ever tried to peek at each other naked.'

'God, you're gross.'

'I can get grosser. Unless you admit having watched the
show.'

'Okay, I watched a few times. In reruns. When I was
sick in bed and unable to change the channel. Between
news broadcasts and specials about the Middle East.'

'Yeah, right. Let's hear your verse.'

I shifted on the tile seat, letting the jet of warm water
thutta-thutta against my lower back. Thick bubbles boiled
up along my ribs tickling me a little. We'd been sitting in
the Jacuzzi for about half an hour, drinking and rearranging the words to some of our favorite TV shows. Byron
got the idea after I told him about Ethan's comedy act.
We'd already done the themes to *Gilligan's Island* and *All
in the Family*. I don't know why I was doing this with him.
I didn't even like him, and I certainly didn't trust him.
After all, he was blackmailing me and who knows what
violence he'd done to Wren to drive her away.

I looked down at my breast. A light bluish smudge
stained my skin where I had drawn my eye. 'My eye is
gone,' I said sadly. Words felt as thick and heavy as the
bubbles stumbling along my rib cage.

278

'Sing,' he said.

I looked at him. His face was still tired-looking, but he was smiling the way he had in those photos in Wren's album. His dragonfly earring dripped chlorinated water.

'Tell me about your earring. Wren saved the matching one, so it must have meant something to her. There's got to be a story behind them.'

'Sing.'

'What about Landry? Why are you afraid of him?'

He looked down in the lighted water and spread his fingers like a bride staring at her new wedding ring. Only he was looking at his stubby little finger. 'Sing,' he said softly without looking at me. 'Just sing.'

I tilted my head back and took a deep breath and sang:

'It's the story of a slutty lady
Whose husband died under suspicious circumstances
He was pretty young to have an insulin-induced heart
    attack
Especially since he wasn't even diabetic.
So she married a geek named Brady,
And spanked him with a wire brush almost every
    night,
And made him bark like a dog and beg for sex,
Which he was used to from his first wife
Before she ran off with a tattoo artist named
    Chowder Head.'

Byron splashed water across the Jacuzzi at me, laughing heartily. 'I feel like I just desecrated a church or something.'

'You started it.' I splashed water back at him.

I heard the sound of metal scraping against cement. Byron and I both turned and saw Ethan dragging a pool chair across the cement from the pool area to the Jacuzzi. He had a six-pack of beer dangling from one finger and a hammer gripped in his other hand. He eyed Byron with suspicion. 'What's going on?' he asked me.

'Hi, Ethan.' I tried to rub off the ink splotch from my breast by pretending to splash water around me. 'Ethan, this is Byron.'

Byron held out his hand to Ethan. But Ethan didn't move, he just stared grimly, tapping his hammer against his leg. Byron dropped his hand. 'What's the hammer for? Mosquitoes?'

'Wren here had some trouble the other night, some creep in the parking lot. Didn't she tell you?'

'No.' He looked at me. 'What happened, Wren?'

'Nothing. Some guy following me. Probably a mistake.'

'Yeah, well, we did some damage to his car with this baby, didn't we, Wren?'

I nodded.

Ethan hefted the hammer in his right hand as if he were just itching to use it again. 'The bastard took off like a Mormon at a wet T-shirt contest.'

Byron gestured at Ethan. 'Come on in and join us, Ethan. You can bring your hammer if you want.'

Ethan didn't move, he was still assessing the situation.

'Byron's renting the extra bedroom,' I explained. 'We're roommates.'

'Roomies.' Byron smiled.

'Roommates? I didn't know you were looking.'

'Sure you did. I told you I couldn't afford this place.'

'Yeah, but I thought you meant female roommate. I mean, if I'd known, I could've recommended someone.'

I could tell by the way he looked at me that he meant himself.

'My last roommate pissed in the sink,' Byron frowned. 'I hate that.'

'I'll try to cut down,' I said.

'I had a roommate that did that,' Ethan said. 'Got drunk, pissed in the kitchen sink. I pissed in his cologne bottle to get back at him.'

'Did he stop?'

'No. He just pissed in my Kool-Aid, then I pissed in his salad dressing, and he pissed in my car wax . . .'

'It's nice to know men can work out their disputes,' I said.

Byron and Ethan both looked at me, then at each other, then shrugged at the same instant. It was like watching synchronized swimming. That made them both laugh like old pals. Ethan tossed his hammer on the chair, stripped off his T-shirt, and hopped into the Jacuzzi. He offered Byron a beer, which Byron took.

'Beer, Wren?' Ethan asked.

I shook my head and showed him my Diet Coke. Another two unopened cans sat behind me, along with my bottle of Kahlúa hidden under my towel.

'What were you guys singing?' Ethan asked.

'You heard us?' I asked, embarrassed.

'Yeah, me and half the complex. The words were a little garbled, but it was definitely some species of singing.'

'You ever watch *The Brady Bunch*?' Byron asked.

'Sure. You see *A Very Brady Christmas* a couple years ago, where they brought them all back together for a re-union? That was so weird, I mean, the girls had actually had sex by then. Can you imagine them giving head? Jesus.'

With some encouragement from Ethan, Byron and I reprised our verses. Ethan joined in with a pretty funny verse or two of his own. We laughed and drank. I got a little overheated and stretched out along the edge of the Jacuzzi while Byron and Ethan had a contest who could stay underwater the longest. Ethan gave me his watch to time them because it had a stopwatch in it. They started breathing deeply, gulping air.

'Maybe we should make a little bet,' Byron said. 'Just to keep it interesting.'

'Sure,' Ethan said. 'How much.'

Byron smiled, looked at me as if to say, See how easy it is. I scowled at him, which made him laugh. 'A buck.'

'A buck? That's all? Shit.' Ethan signaled me. 'Tell us when to go.'

'Go,' I said unenthusiastically.

They both dunked their heads under the water. Ethan spread his arms and legs and did a dead man's float around the Jacuzzi. The jets pushed him around the small pool into walls, but he didn't react. Byron just sat on the underwater bench with his head tilted forward like a devout man lost in prayer.

One minute thirty seconds.

Ethan was leaking bubbles around his head, but otherwise was still floating.

Byron hadn't budged.

Two minutes twelve seconds.

Ethan was standing now, both hands clasped at the back of his neck as if he were shoving his own head underwater, drowning a stubborn puppy.

Byron hadn't budged.

Two minutes thirty-two seconds.

Ethan expelled all his air and whipped his head out of the water, gasping for air.

Byron hadn't budged.

'Shit,' Ethan said. He waded over to me and looked at his watch. 'I thought the bastard was already up. I couldn't see him underwater because of the bubbles. I thought he was already up. Shit.'

Three minutes.

Three minutes ten seconds.

'Maybe we should do something,' I said.

'Let's wait a little,' Ethan said, but I could hear the nervousness in his voice. He took a few steps toward Byron, his hands ready to yank him up.

'Three minutes thirty seconds!' I announced.

Ethan plunged his hands in and pulled Byron's head up. Byron opened his eyes. 'What?'

'That's three and a half fucking minutes, man.' Ethan couldn't hide the mixture of panic and admiration in his voice.

Byron's expression was oddly calm. I had the feeling that while he'd been under he hadn't really cared whether he came up for air again or not. If he did decide to come up, it would be because he was bored, not because he needed air.

Byron pointed at Ethan. 'You owe me a buck.'

'Absolutely. It's just that I couldn't see you. I thought you'd come up before me. I coulda stayed down longer. Next time I'll wear goggles or something.'

We drank some more, chatting on and off about nothing in particular. Once I nodded off for a few minutes. When I awoke, Ethan and Byron were discussing baseball batting averages. Ethan was very drunk but Byron didn't seem affected by his drinking.

I swatted at a fat mosquito that flicked around my leg. I noticed several red welts that hadn't been there before I'd fallen asleep. 'I'm going in. The mosquitoes are turning me into a buffet.'

'You gotta fight back,' Ethan said. He took some of my Diet Coke and poured it on the crook of his arm. 'Wait.'

We waited.

After a few minutes I said, 'What are we waiting for?'

'Be patient. This is neat.'

About five minutes later a mosquito landed on the sticky Diet Coke on his arm. It fussed there a moment until it settled in and started drinking blood. We watched it drink for a minute.

'Aren't you going to swat it away?' I asked.

'Ssshh . . .'

Suddenly Ethan flexed his arm and the mosquito exploded in a wet puff of blood and ragged body parts, like a small plane in a midair collision.

'Jesus!' I said, wincing.

Ethan looked over at Byron expectantly, like he was trying to make up for his underwater failure. 'Weird, huh?'

Byron stared without comment or expression.

'Thing is, you gotta wait until they're slurping your blood, then when you flex, you shoot so much blood into them they just pop. Like killing a vampire, right?'

I flashed on the photo in Wren's album, the one where

283

she's pretending to be Sylvia Plath driving a chopstick stake through Byron's heart. I looked at Byron, wondering if he was thinking the same thing. I couldn't tell, he had on his blank prison-yard look. 'Actually,' Byron said, 'you just killed an expectant mother.'

'Right,' Ethan chuckled. 'Like you could tell. What she have, swollen ankles and haemorrhoids?'

'What makes you think it was a she?' I asked, somehow feeling my role of defender of all female species was being usurped. As a woman, isn't this the kind of thing I should know?

'Only the females bite.'

'What do the males do?' I asked. 'Order take-out?'

'They sip nectar from flowers.'

'Jesus,' Ethan said with disgust. 'Faggots.'

Byron looked at Ethan with a cold stare. 'I don't like that word.'

Ethan froze, started to say something, thought better of it. He shrugged in some sort of apology.

Byron continued, his voice soft and professional. 'And the females only drink blood because they need protein for their eggs, which they lay in batches of about 200.'

'Great, then I just killed 201 mosquitoes with one flex.'

'More like 2,001, since they lay about ten separate batches in their lifetime.'

'What's the big deal?' Ethan said, squirming a little, as if Byron were judging him. 'They're just mosquitoes. They spread diseases and stuff. They kill hundreds of people a year.'

'Millions. That's why they're so valuable. They're responsible for the air you breathe.'

'Let me guess, they eat plants and fart oxygen.' Ethan was turning petulant, feeling picked on.

'You've heard of the rain forests, right? The ones in the Amazon, the Congo basin, Southeast Asia?' Byron looked at me.

'Make your point,' I said. 'I have another class in fifteen minutes and the prof hates it when I'm late.'

Byron laughed. 'Okay, here's the short of it: the rain forest accounts for half of the world's oxygen, yet we're cutting them down at a steady rate. Since we've been talking about it, another ten acres have been cleared. One of the main defenses against clearing them any faster are the 2,000 species of mosquitoes that attack the workers and settlers, spreading yellow fever, malaria, dengue, filariasis, and o'nyong-nyong fever. These little suckers are keeping the rest of the world alive.'

Our former mood of drunken good cheer now shattered, we sat there in mournful silence a few minutes. At least Ethan and I did. Byron cheerful as ever, hummed the theme to *Green Acres*, finally singing, ' "Darlin' I love you but give me Park Avenue." '

'I'm going in,' I announced again. I gathered my Diet Coke cans and empty bottle of Kahlúa.

'Come on, guys,' Ethan said. 'Let's make up something to go with *The Partridge Family* theme.'

'I don't remember how it goes,' I said.

Neither did Ethan or Byron. We each tried to hum some of it, but no one could remember enough to trigger anything. We did *The Addams Family* instead, snapping our fingers and getting grosser and grosser in our lyrics.

'That guy who played on that show,' Ethan said. 'Uh, John Astin, he was Mr. Addams—'

'Gomez Addams,' Byron offered.

'Right. Gomez. He was married to Patty Duke in real life. Remember her?'

' "*Patty loves to rock 'n' roll/A hot dog makes her lose control* . . ." ' Byron sang.

'Yeah!' Ethan laughed. 'She played identical cousins. Jesus, I had the hots for her.' Ethan shook his head at some wistful memory and popped open another beer can. He pointed his can at Byron. 'I like your earring. I had my ear pierced a few years ago, but I don't wear an earring 'cause of my job. The damn hole's grown shut now. But it looks good on you. What is it, a moth?'

'Dragonfly. It was a gift from my wife. Instead of rings,

during the wedding ceremony we exchanged earrings. She had one just like this.' He reached up and touched his.

'Earrings instead of wedding rings. That's very cool.' Ethan nodded enthusiastically. 'But why dragonflies? You some kind of bug expert or something? I mean, if it were my wedding, I'd of picked something more romantic, like moons or unicorns or something.'

Byron smiled. He hoisted himself up onto the lip of the Jacuzzi so only his feet and shins dangled in the water. He gestured with one hand like a magician about to cast a spell. 'Dragonflies, when they are about to mate, fly to some pond or river where the eggs will eventually be laid. The males arrive some time earlier than the females. Then they space themselves out along the banks, each holding and defending his territory while awaiting the females.'

'Shit, that sounds like a Club Med trip I took once. Every guy sitting along the pool waiting for chicks.'

'When a female dragonfly approaches the male, he sometimes does some courtship dancing and buzzing and she lets him know whether or not she likes it. Then they copulate.'

'I don't think fucking should be that complicated. I think you should just be able to walk up to someone and say, "Hey, let's fuck" and then the two of you go at it. That's what I think. And if more people were honest, they'd agree. That's what I think.'

Byron continued his story as if Ethan hadn't spoken. 'Sometimes the dragonflies start screwing while still flying, then they land and finish off. It can take a few seconds' —he looked at me—'or a couple hours. The female then goes off to lay her eggs, sometimes with the male still attached to her.'

Ethan laughed. 'Jesus. The La Bug Method of delivery. "Keep buzzing, dear, don't forget to buzz deeply now."' He laughed some more.

Byron smiled, his story apparently finished.

I stared at him. Why hadn't he told me that story when I'd asked him about his earring?

'I don't get it,' Ethan said. 'Which part inspired the dragonfly earring? The screwing for a couple hours?'

Byron shook his head. 'The flying together. When we were together, it was like we were flying. When we were apart, I felt like I was standing on the muddy bank of some swamp waiting for her.' He closed his eyes and the weariness I'd seen in his face earlier seemed to rush back all at once.

'Yeah, I know what you mean,' Ethan said. 'To me love is like handing someone else a sharp butcher knife and hoping they don't stab you with it. That's how I feel all the time when I'm in love. I don't think that's healthy, do you?'

'I'm not sure love is healthy.' Byron kicked some water at me. 'What do you think, *Wren*? What does love feel like?'

I guess I could've ignored the question, or made something up. Or used what Wren had once told me: 'When I'm in love,' she'd said, 'it's like one of those appliances that runs either on batteries or you can plug in. Like a portable cassette player. When I'm in love and away from that person, I feel like I'm running on batteries, like I can feel them draining, running lower with each movement. When I'm with that person, I'm plugged in, the current is constant, miraculous.' I could have said that. But for some reason I decided to answer straight. 'When I'm in love . . .' I rolled over onto my back and stared up into the sky. I couldn't see any stars, just a faint fingernail sliver of moon crowded out of the sky by black clouds. I thought of Robby and suddenly horses started stampeding across my stomach. Tears drowned my eyes the way Byron had submerged his head in the spa so long. 'When I'm in love I have the feeling that I'm suddenly a different person. That I can see more now, like I just took a giant leap up the evolutionary ladder. I start to think that I should go back and reread every book, resee every movie I've ever known, because I'm so different now, so much *more*, that I'd feel differently about everything I experienced before. What I loved I might now hate, what I hated, I might now love.' I shook my head and tears spilled out along both sides of my eyes. 'I don't know what I'm saying.'

'Me neither,' Ethan said. He turned back to Byron. 'I like your dragonfly story better. It's weird how everybody seems to know some bizarre *Wild Kingdom* story that they relate to their own lives. My mom used to always tell me and my sister about all the different species that are monogamous, you know, mate for life. Like crows, they mate for life. But I think that was more for my dad's benefit than ours. Me, I saw this documentary once about the three-toed sloth, you know, that big bear-like thing, lives in South America I think. Anyway, what I heard was, the sloth goes up into a tree and does nothing but eat and sleep for a whole month. Then at the end of the month, he climbs down the tree and takes a shit. It's got to be a world-class shit if he waited a month to do it. Anyway, as soon as he starts laying cable, hundreds of insects that have been living in his fur come running out to lay their eggs in his shit.' Ethan stopped and drank from his beer can. His face was serious and sad. 'I mean, that's how I feel sometimes. Like Johnny Carson is the sloth and I'm some insect waiting for him to take a shit so I can jump into it and lay my eggs.' He looked confused a moment. 'I guess the eggs must be my comedy routine. But when they hatch, man, then everything will be right. I'll be okay.'

There was a long minute of silence while Byron and I stared at Ethan. Ethan stared down at the bubbling water like a man perched on a bridge deciding whether or not to jump.

'You have any animal stories, Wren?' Byron asked me. 'Any that pertain to your life?'

I thought of the dagger-dick bedbug a moment. I shook my head. 'I guess I need to watch more documentaries.'

I stood up and picked up my towel. Byron stood up too, handing me my empty cans of Diet Coke and the empty

bottle of Kahlúa. 'Why didn't you tell me about your earring when I asked?' I said.

'You didn't ask for the right reasons.'

'Fuck you.' I wrapped the towel around my waist and
walked back to my apartment. As I strolled along the
bushes, I saw a white car pulling into the parking lot. 'Not
again!' I growled. 'Get out of my life!' I stopped and
hurled an empty Diet Coke can at it. The can dinked off
the rear fender. I expected this to send the car screeching
out of the lot as it had before; instead the car screeched
to a halt and I could see now that the car wasn't a Subaru,
it wasn't even white, more like a pale yellow. The driver,
a young man with a shaggy mustache, jumped out of the
car and started yelling at me. 'What the fuck's wrong with
you? You nuts, you stupid bitch!'

I ducked around the bushes and ran into my apartment.
I locked the door but kept my ear pressed against it. The
bushes kept him from seeing which apartment I'd entered,
but he was outside looking at all the doors. He knocked
on one of my neighbour's doors.

'It's three o'clock in the morning, asshole!' someone
yelled from one of the apartments.

'Fuck you,' the guy said.

'I'm calling the cops,' the voice responded.

'Good!' the guy from the yellow Jetta shouted back.
But a few seconds later he stomped off, got in his car,
parked it, and disappeared into his apartment.

I was shaken, my heart pounding, my legs wobbly. I
was vaguely ashamed of having gotten drunk. Now that
fear had sobered me up, I started to wonder about Byron,
about the shiny blue suit, the bird, his insect lore, his
interest in my money. I went to the kitchen and got the
serrated steak knife out of the drawer and carried it back
to my bedroom. I placed it under my pillow.

I went to bed. Faintly, mixing with the sound of the
apartment complex's running streams, I could hear Byron
and Ethan singing new lyrics to the theme from *The Facts
of Life*.

I woke up sometime later, out of a dream I couldn't remember but still felt. I was thick with melancholy. The doorknob jiggled. I thought of Byron, drunk, fingering his dragonfly earring.

'Go away,' I said.

No answer.

'I've got a knife.'

Giggling. Two people, one female.

'I've got a knife,' I said louder. My hand groped under the pillow for the knife, but I couldn't find it.

'She's got a knife,' the female whispered. I swore it sounded like Wren.

'A what?' Byron said.

'A knife, A fucking knife.'

They laughed.

'Wren?' I said. I tried to climb out of bed. But I couldn't find the knife and no way was I opening the door without a knife. I closed my eyes and waited until the voices disappeared.

20

When the doorbell rang, I lifted my head from the toilet seat where I'd fallen asleep. My left cheek was numb where the curved edge of the seat had pressed against my face. I remembered it being about 5:30 A.M. when I'd stumbled out of bed, fallen to my knees with nausea, and crawled into the bathroom. I started heaving for about forty minutes. At first it gushed out like in *The Exorcist*, then it settled down to sporadic spasms. Sweat slicked my skin and pasted my hair to my face. Exhausted, I'd just laid my head on the seat and finished off the night there.

The doorbell chimed again.

I didn't move, hoping Byron would answer it and send whoever it was away. Probably Grudge or one of his mysterious gambling buddies, ready for another day of scavenging. Bottom suckers, Wren would have called them.

The doorbell rang repeatedly, an insistent Morse code.

I hugged the toilet bowl, the porcelain cool against my naked chest. The small room smelled like vinegar and coffee. Slowly I pulled myself upright, knowing now how difficult it was for an ancestral missing link to first learn how to walk. I wobbled slightly, hands grabbing at the walls for balance. As I passed the bathroom mirror, I noticed a curving indentation along my cheekbone, a line deep as a saber cut from the edge of the toilet seat. Charming. Like a movie Nazi with a dueling scar from Heidelberg. I yanked open the medicine cabinet and dry swallowed four Advil.

I pulled on running shorts and T-shirt and sang softly, '"The Brady Bunch, the Brady Bunch . . ."'

I unlocked my bedroom door and moved the chair I'd wedged against the doorknob last night, I guess to keep Byron out. Then I remembered hearing Wren's voice, and Byron's, the doorknob jiggling, their laughter. An alcohol-induced dream, I decided. On the bed, the serrated blade of the steak knife was sticking out from under a thrown-back sheet. I was lucky not to have cut myself on it in my sleep.

The doorbell was still chiming intermittently. Why hadn't Byron answered it? Had he been killed in his sleep by one of his ex-con cronies over a gambling debt? His throat slit and his money stolen? I just hoped they took the damn cat and bird too.

I staggered my way to the front door and pulled it open, shielding my eyes against the bright morning sun. An impossibly cheerful Davis stood there holding a fresh pineapple.

'Good morning, sunshine,' he said, shoving the pineapple at me. 'Maui's finest. Brought back at great expense and inconvenience. Ever try to store one of these under your airplane seat?' He kissed me on the cheek, right on my toilet seat crease. He probably thought it was from a pillowcase seam.

He grabbed the pineapple back and marched straight for the kitchen. 'Pineapple is also great for hangovers. Follow me.'

I did, shuffling after him like a frail convalescent. 'How'd you know I wouldn't be at work?' My voice sounded coarse, like it was passing through a cheese grater.

'My spies are everywhere.'

'Then how'd you know about my hangover? You got any spies in here?'

He smiled, tapped his nose, and sniffed. 'Kahlúa. I had a little problem with booze once. Nothing a couple weeks in an expensive clinic and a few hundred AA meetings hasn't cured.'

We went into the kitchen. The iron bird cage was still in the middle of the room, Byron's jacket still covering it. 'What have we got here?' Davis asked, peeling back Byron's jacket. Again I flashed on the dead body of Philip Dougherty as Detective Diesel peeled back the kitchen towel from his butchered face. The hungry fly diving in . . .

'"*Stop in the name of love . . .*"'

Davis laughed. 'Now you're talking,' he said to the bird. The bird repeated the song title a few more times, shifting its head to keep an eye on us. Davis threw the jacket back over the cage.

'Some kind of South American parrot,' I said. 'Byron won him.'

'Raffle?'

I shrugged. 'Poker, I think.'

'I play a little poker,' Davis said. 'I wonder what the stakes are. Can't be too high if they're paying off in birds.'

'You don't want to play with him,' I warned.

'Does he cheat?'

'I don't know. I just know he wins.'

'So do I.' He went through a few drawers before he found the right knife. Then he started hacking off the outer skin of the pineapple.

'Byron . . .' I said. I glanced toward his bedroom.

'He's gone. Left about five minutes before I knocked. He walked down the street and caught a bus.'

'Coincidence?' Every word cost me great energy, so I used them sparingly.

'Not really. I've been waiting outside for an hour.'

'Really? An hour?' I smiled. *That* was romantic. I looked more fondly at the pineapple, whose inedible core Davis was now carving away.

'I take it,' Davis said, concentrating on his cutting, 'that since you didn't know he was gone, you were either passed out or you sleep in separate bedrooms.'

I considered my answer. Admitting separate bedrooms was risky. Why would husband and wife sleep in separate rooms, especially when the husband is just out of jail? I massaged the toilet seat crease in my face and shrugged. What the hell. The man waited outside my apartment for an hour, brought me pineapple from Maui. 'Separate bedrooms.'

'Good. I know it's childish and sexist and probably a sign of latent something or other, but the thought of him having sex with you rode me with spurs the whole time I was gone.' He looked at me with a tender expression. 'I missed you.'

'Me too.'

He turned, knife still in hand, the blade slick with pineapple juice. I thought of Ethan's definition of love last night, like handing someone else a sharp knife and hoping they don't plunge it into your heart. I thought of the knife under my pillow. Of my mother slicing a tangerine to teach me about periods.

'If this were a movie,' he said softly, 'I'd say something clever here.'

I stepped toward him and he dropped the knife on the counter. It spun on the countertop like a compass needle. Davis opened his arms and I stepped into them. His arms tightened and we kissed. I kept my lips pressed together because my mouth tasted like coffee sludge. But he drove his tongue between my lips, parted my teeth, and swabbed the inside of my mouth. I relaxed in his arms and let it happen. Let it all happen.

His hand slipped under my T-shirt and massaged my breast, the unscarred one. He tweaked my nipple a couple times and it popped up like a jack-in-the-box. His hips fastened against mine and began to grind. I could feel his stiff penis mashing against my pubic hair. I reached down to his waistband, wedging my fingers inside. Davis sucked in his stomach a little and my hand plunged inside his pants. I found his penis, hard but bent at an awkward angle. I pulled it free like a trapped animal and it straightened along his stomach. A few drops of sticky semen glazed my fingers.

We yanked each other's pants down to our ankles. I stepped out of mine since I didn't have any shoes or underpants. Davis's pants puddled around his ankles like shed skin, his polo shirt bibbed modestly over his crotch. He gestured at the kitchen table, which I didn't understand. He turned me around so I was facing away from him and placed his hands on my hips. He walked me to the table, his steps shuffling like a chain-gang prisoner in leg irons. When we reached the table, he bent me forward so my chest was across the tabletop. A couple of stale crumbs of cereal from breakfasts gone by knuckled into my skin. Davis stepped between my legs, his hips wedging apart my thighs. Then he was in me.

One leg of the table was slightly shorter, so it wobbled when he did, but that seemed to add to the whole naughty ambience. Davis gripped my hips, his fingers biting into my skin as he thrust forward, easing as he rocked backward. I was a little worried that he might notice some of the mottled cellulite at the backs of my thighs, spotlighted by the bright morning sunlight illuminating the kitchen. But when I looked back over my shoulder, his eyes were closed tight, his tongue wedged in the corner of his mouth like a little boy concentrating on hitting his first baseball. I felt a warm tingle of tenderness for him right then, though I wasn't in a good physical position to demonstrate it. So I just moved my hips with even more enthusiasm. His hips slammed into my buttocks with a wet slapping noise as his movements became more intense. His hands gripped the tops of my shoulders, pulling me down on him as he thrust forward. He was grunting softly.

He slipped one of his hands under my hips so his finger could press my clitoris. With each thrust I felt an extra sensation as I slid along his finger shaft. Just picturing him behind me, knowing he was staring down at me now, looking at my most intimate and private parts as he slid in and out of me, heated my skin all the way to my scalp. I came, arching my hips up, then slamming them down on the table, crushing his hand. If it hurt him, he didn't let on. Maybe this was how Bryon had lost his little finger, I thought, then forced the thought away as some sort of betrayal to Davis.

When Davis came, it lasted for a long time. His hips convulsed, he rested, then another spasm as he squeezed more semen into me. Finally, he collapsed on my back, hugging me and kissing me between the shoulder blades. His lips were cool on my spine.

'Aloha,' he said. 'Ready for a big surprise?'

21

The jail was pretty modern, I guess. Bright paint every-where and the smell of new carpet.

Season Dougherty, wearing an orange prison jumpsuit, sat on the other side of the Plexiglas partition speaking through a battered black telephone. There were deep gouges scarring the Plexiglas between us, as if someone had banged their receiver in frustration. I had my tape-recorder running, a suction cup microphone attached to my receiver. A young uniformed officer sat at a gray desk filling out a questionnaire for Scientology. We were other-wise alone.

The last and only time I'd been to a jail was when I'd picked up Wren the night we were shot. What would she think of me here, interviewing a murderer, having had sex on the kitchen table only an hour ago, sleeping with a knife under my pillow, getting drunk with her husband?

'Better get dressed,' Davis had suggested after our kitchen-table romp. 'We only have an hour until your appointment with Season.'

We'd showered together, lathering each other and laughing as our hands lingered here and there.

'Tell me about Maui,' I'd asked him while shampooing his hair.

'I ate a pig that had been buried in the ground all day.'

'Was it good?'

He made a face. 'I couldn't tell. I was too busy feeling like a grave robber.'

'Is that why you went, for the cuisine?'

'Ow, you got some in my eye.' He squinted his right eye.

I tilted my head under the shower and filled up my mouth with water. I spit the water in his right eye.

'Thank you, Florence Nightingale,' he said, rubbing his eye.

'Why'd you go so suddenly?' I left off the important part of the question, 'without calling me first.'

He got a serious expression on his face. 'Let me tell you a little something about the movie business. It's not like anything else you're familiar with. It doesn't run on logic. In other businesses, the product is the goal of the business. You make a product, you sell it, you make money.'

'Thank you, Karl Marx.'

He laughed. 'In Hollywood, movies are a by-product of business, like toxic waste. The goal is power, every individual trying to prove to others that they have power. Sometimes to prove that, you actually have to make a movie, which most people consider an annoyance. Think of it as a big pissing contest. Movies are merely the liquid you drink so you can piss. Pissing is the goal, not nourishment. And when you stop to drink, that means you're not pissing. Someone else is pissing in your place. But they stop to drink, that is make a movie, because once it's done, they can go about the real business again.'

'Pissing.'

'Right. Getting power.'

'To do what?'

He looked surprised. 'Nothing. It's the end in itself. Okay, here, this'll make it clear. It's like bodybuilding. These guys build up their muscles, pumping weights every day of their lives, hours at a time, dieting constantly, shaving the hair off their bodies, practicing posing routines in front of mirrors. What for? To look good. They don't do anything with their strength. In fact, strength isn't the issue, that's never measured. *Looking* strong is the point. Their muscles aren't used to do anything except make bigger muscles. It's all about flexing. Same in Hollywood.

298

Making a movie is how we pump up, but the muscle is basically useless, for show. See?'

'I don't think I care enough to see. Besides, what's this got to do with you going to Maui?'

'I heard about some woman over there, a lawyer, she'd just gotten a divorce and took her two young boys sailing in Maui. A whole unite-the-family recovery thing. Anyway, big storm comes up and sinks the boat. She rescues her boys who are trapped in the sinking ship. Very dramatic stuff, underwater diving, attacked by jellyfish or some such thing. I thought it might make a good MOW.'

'A what?'

'Movie of the Week. You know, true story family drama, woman in peril, lots of adventure, and a happy ending.'

'So the kids are all right?'

'They will be in the movie version. Remember, "based on a true incident" covers a multitude of sins.'

'What happened to the real kids?'

'One lost his leg, the other's in critical condition. The mother's in therapy. The ex-husband is suing to get the kids back claiming she was negligent.'

'But in your version one kid will just have a limp, the other a sunburn, and the mother will wisecrack as she walks bravely down the beach with her sons.'

Davis pointed a finger at me. 'Now you're thinking like a producer.' He shut off the shower and grabbed a towel. Quickly he began to pat me dry. 'I flew to Maui to wrap up the rights before anyone else got wind of the story. I'd like to get lucky again, like I was with Season, signing her up before she killed her husband. If I'd waited one more week, I wouldn't even have been in the top five bidders.'

'It's an ill wind that doesn't blow some good.'

He looked at me as if wondering if I was being sarcastic or not. 'You up to writing this book?'

I stepped out of the shower and stared at myself in the foggy mirror. Blurred by the mist, I looked like a ghost. Davis wiped the towel across the mirror and I could see myself more clearly. There was still a tiny spot of ink on the scar tissue on my breast. I thought about Season Dougherty, what had gone through her mind when she'd pulled the trigger and blasted her ex-husband in the crotch and face. Like some B-movie cliché of a rape victim getting revenge. I tried to see her action from a positive angle. Not as destruction, but creation. She hadn't torn a hole in the fabric of the universe by murdering a human being, she'd mended it by protecting her daughter. She had seen a need and filled it. Like an inventor. She had invented protection for her daughter.

Or maybe she was just a murderer.

*   *   *   *   *

'Where did you shoot him first? Face or genital area?'

'You get right to it, don't you?'

'I'm curious.'

'The autopsy report will tell you.'

'Yes, it will.'

She looked at me, studying my face. A faint smile curled her lips. 'You mean, did I want to punish him or kill him? If I shot him in the crotch first, then maybe I was out to punish him and killed him as some sort of afterthought. If I killed him first, the crotch shot was just a mother's sexual outrage. The former's murder, the latter is diminished capacity. Right?'

'Something like that.'

She didn't say anything for a while. We just looked at each other through the thick Plexiglas, our phones pressed to our faces. I wondered who was the last person talking into this phone and if they ever cleaned the mouthpieces. Season Dougherty had a wholesome scrubbed look to her face, pretty in an outdoorsy way. She was about forty, her dark hair straight and thin, but shiny and rich-looking. It was cut a couple inches above the shoulders but bounced whenever she moved her head. She kept it tucked behind her ears like Gloria Vanderbilt. I pictured her squatting in jeans next to a campfire, pouring coffee into a metal cup, a guy in chaps and rawhide gloves hopping off a horse and saying, 'Whattaya want me to do next, ma'am?'

Suddenly Season stood up and peered down through the glass to get a better look at me. 'Stand up,' she said. 'I want to see who I'm dealing with.'

'I don't see how that matters . . .'

'Come on, you've been checking me out since you got here.'

'That's my job. I'm writing a book about you.'

'And I'm supposed to confide in you. Why? Just because Davis sends you over?'

'I think because you signed a contract with him.'

She sat down. 'Right. I did that. You know why?'

I knew this was tricky ground. As tough and self-confident as she seemed, there was something shaky about her. I said, 'To let people know what happened to your daughter, try to keep it from happening to other little girls?'

She laughed outright at this. 'How noble I would have been. How wonderfully good.' She leaned back in her chair and looked around the room. Her eyes glistened. 'I need the money, Ms. Caldwell. I haven't worked in eight months, I haven't a single patient left. My equipment has been repossessed, my office leased to a veterinarian. You think my lawyers are working just for the publicity? Maybe if I were the first case like this. But I'm just some woman dentist from Newport Beach who denied a court order allowing my child-molesting husband visitation with the object of his perversion, my daughter. For a while I had some celebrity status. I photograph well and everyone loves a mystery. "Where is her daughter?" But now my case is as common as mud. And believe me all this costs money. It costs money for lawyers and it costs money to keep my daughter and sister in hiding. I am like a one-woman Witness Protection Program.'

'There are organizations, underground railroads to help women in your situation.'

'I'm not a woman in any fucking situation!'

The young guard looked up from his Scientology questionnaire and made a stern face. He pointed to a sign over his shoulder that said NO FOUL LANGUAGE. She shrugged at him to indicate she would be more careful.

'Look, I didn't kill Philip to make a statement for women everywhere. I killed him because I'd lost too often in the court system and that meant my daughter and sister were going to have to stay in hiding for I don't know how many more years. I knew Philip had hired detectives to find her and kidnap her. It was only a matter of time before they succeeded. What would you have done?'

'How do you know your husband was guilty? A judge acquitted him.'

'Are you a mother, Ms. Caldwell?'

'No.'

She just shrugged, as if nothing she could say to me would matter since I didn't have a child. I resented that maternal smugness. 'Your daughter's testimony was ambiguous at best, that's what the judge said.'

'It wasn't ambiguous to me. It wasn't ambiguous when my five-year-old daughter told me how her daddy took her into the shower with him and how he washed her and washed her and stuck his finger into her vagina and said, "We have to make sure every place is nice and clean, honey." But he kept his finger in her and made her soap his erection and rub it and rub it until he came on her.' She lowered the phone and for a moment I thought she would hang up, the interview was over. She looked around the room again, as if she kept forgetting where she was and had to remind herself. Her right index finger flexed several times, as if she were pulling that trigger again and again.

My own bullet wound ached with sympathy for her and her daughter. Yet, it was not my job to merely chronicle her account of events. I couldn't take her word for things.

302

I'd read the news accounts on the way over here this morning; Davis had the whole file in his car for me. Her daughter, Jamie, testified that she had taken a shower with her father, he had washed her off, but that nothing else had happened. Season Dougherty had testified that the child had come home crying and told her about the sex, but that now she was too frightened by her father to tell the truth. The judge had no choice but to dismiss the charges.

I had no doubt that Season Dougherty was convinced these events were real. But were they? A doctor's examination showed there had been physical penetration, some minor irritation, a disturbed hymen. But Philip Dougherty's doctors had testified that this could have happened a number of ways. Should a man be prosecuted because he showered with his young daughter, because he wasn't ashamed of casual nudity and didn't want his daughter to be?

'He had names for my breasts,' she said. 'Ethel and Fred. You know, like Lucy and Ricky's neighbours on *I Love Lucy*.'

'Why did you divorce?'

She sighed a deep, rattling sigh. 'Why do people divorce?'

'Other lovers.'

'We didn't have any. I know I didn't. I'm pretty sure he didn't, at least no long-term mistresses.'

'Then what?'

She shook her head. 'Erosion. I don't know. I thought I knew then. Then it was so clear. I told all my friends the reasons.' She laughed. 'Maybe you should ask them. Maybe they remember.'

Why had Robby and I split up? Okay, he'd been fucking his professor. But what led to that? What hadn't I given him what he needed, that he now had? Was it just for a change and that's all? A different accent, a different smell, a different taste, to hear different stories from the past? Nothing more?

'How's your daughter taking this? Does she know?'

'She knows.'

I waited for more. None came. 'Will you bring her out of hiding now?'

Season Dougherty looked distracted, like she was thinking of something else. For a moment she reminded me of Wren during one of her inspirational flashes. She sat up, leaned forward, her eyes wide with anticipation. 'What are you wearing?'

'What?'

'You're wearing makeup, aren't you?'

'Some. A little lipstick.'

'And foundation. Eyeliner. I can see it from here. What else?'

'What do you mean?'

'Stand up, let me look.' She smiled. 'What's it going to cost you?'

I stood up, turned slightly. I was wearing a drab brown skirt and a plain white blouse. I dressed more like a prisoner than she did.

'Panty hose, right!' She said it with an accusing bark.

I looked over at the guard, but he didn't look up. 'Yes, panty hose.'

'And heels. You're wearing heels.'

'Short heels. One inch at most.'

'And a tight skirt.'

'A straight skirt. It's not exactly revealing.'

'But it is, Ms. Caldwell. It's extremely revealing. It reveals the kind of mind-set women in this society have. You're a professional woman. Davis tells me you hold several master's degrees.'

I shrugged.

'You are among the élite of women, the educated professionals. Yet you still dress like a slave girl. What exactly is the function of panty hose?'

I studied her eyes, but she wasn't being crazy. Just intense. 'To make your legs look better, I guess.'

'By better you mean sexier?'

'I suppose so.'

'And high heels?'

'I don't know, it's expected. Like bankers wearing a tie.'

'But what's the effect of making you walk tiptoe in heels?'

I didn't want to play this game. 'What's your point?'

'Humor me, Wren. Just answer.'

'The point of heels is to make your calves bulge, I guess.'

'To make them look sexier.'

'Okay, yes. To make them look sexier.'

'Now, why would a professional woman want to make her legs look sexier? You aren't looking to fu . . .' She glanced over at the guard. 'To screw guys when you're out doing your job. Guys don't show their legs, do they? You shave your legs too, right? And your armpits.'

I nodded.

'Why? Why would shaving your body look sexier? Why would putting you in shoes and skirts that inhibit the movement make you sexier? Because it makes you more like a helpless little girl. That's the sexual fantasy we're promoting to the men in this society. We cover our facial lines, shave our bodies, and outfit ourselves in restrictive clothing, all to feed this male desire for young girls. Then when there's an epidemic of child molestation and incest, women start yelling at how this could come about. They accuse pornographers, want restrictions. Hell, we helped it come about. It's our fault for dressing like that, for buying into what we've been told is sexy. If a full-grown woman with hair on her body and wrinkles on her face isn't sexy, then what does that say about our men? You and I are responsible. We're the reason our own children are getting raped.'

'Don't you think that's overstating it a bit?'

She looked at me with a hard gaze, the same look I saw in Byron at times. As if they've seen something I can't even imagine. 'I read this article,' she said, her voice quiet, but intense as a humming power line. 'There're whole parts of Africa where they perform a clitoridectomy on women. You know what that is?'

I didn't know, but my throat constricted at the word.

'They slice off the little girl's clitoris to prevent her from having sexual pleasure, therefore removing her motivation to cheat on him. Then they sew her up so she can pee and have very painful intercourse.'

'Well,' I said, shifting uncomfortably. I thought of my stepmother beating off weasels. 'Primitive tribes have strange customs . . .'

'I'm not talking about some lost tribe in the jungle. I'm talking about eighty million women that have this done. And you know who performs the surgery usually, who talks the girl into this mutilation? Her mother. Her mother and grandmother actually cut it off. You see my point now?' She leaned back in her chair. 'In fact, I can't talk to you anymore until you take off those fucking panty hose.'

'Pardon?'

'Take them off. Right now.'

'I can't do that.'

'The guard can't see you through the partition.'

'I don't care. I'm not stripping down in public.'

'Then I can't talk to you. I have to talk to someone who isn't helping get our children raped.' She got up and walked away.

The hell with her, I thought. Go on and walk, you hairy, flat-footed bitch. I don't need this crap from a shotgun-wielding dentist. I don't need fashion advice from a woman in an orange jumpsuit.

But I did need her, I needed this job. It was my last chance at making something of my life while I still had Wren's identity. If I blew this and went back to being just plain Luna Devon, I had no hope.

'Hey,' I called.

She stopped, looked back. I waved her to return. She didn't.

I looked around the room, no one was on this side of the partition. I reached under my skirt and quickly yanked my panty hose down as fast as I could. My shoes popped off as I pulled them over my feet. I pressed the balled-up panty hose against the Plexiglas partition.

She returned and sat down. 'And please don't wear makeup next time.'

22

'Tell me about the first time you had sex.'

I shook my head.

'Oh, come on. Don't be selfish. What's the big deal?'

'No big deal,' I said. 'I just . . .' I shrugged.

'Just tell me. Jump in, like swimming in the ocean.'

I laughed. 'The very first time?'

'Yes, the very first time. Your first naked penis, long may it wave.'

I thought it over.

'You have had sex, haven't you?'

'Ho, ho,' I said. 'By "first time" do you mean actual intercourse or just sex in general, like just touching it?'

She waved impatiently. 'Whichever is more interesting. Just make it good.'

I thought for a moment. Season sat on the other side of the Plexiglas fidgeting with a yellow pencil stub while waiting for my answer. The phone receiver was pinned between her shoulder and ear. A deep white scratch zagged across the Plexiglas between us as if someone had tried to claw their way through. The scratch hadn't been here yesterday. She licked her thumb and tried to rub out the scratch, but it didn't come off. Out of politeness, I did the same thing on my side of the glass. The scratch remained.

'I'm waiting,' she prodded.

'Shouldn't I be asking *you* these kind of questions?' I said. 'I'm the interviewer here. The book's about you.'

'I'm bored with me,' she said. 'My lawyers talk about me, the shrink they hired talks about me, the news media

308

talk about me, you talk about me . . .' She shrugged. 'I've talked so much about me that I've kind of lost sense of me. I feel like I'm talking about an old friend now, someone I used to be close to but haven't seen for a long time. It's weird. This morning I woke up and couldn't remember what my favorite color was.'

'What is your favorite color?'

'Green, I think. Or blue. I guess I'll have to wait and read your book to find out who I am again.' She smiled crookedly and deep lines that I hadn't noticed before tugged at her eyes. Her body seemed slightly smaller than last time I'd seen her, slightly older. Her orange prison jumpsuit was puffed up around her like an astronaut's space suit. This was my third straight day of interviewing her, and each time we spoke, it was as if, in telling me her story, she were disappearing. As if every word she spoke were organic, a living part of her body. To speak was like tearing off tiny pieces of her flesh and tossing them into the air.

'I look awful, right?' she said suddenly. She tucked a few strands of hair behind her ear.

'No, not at all. You're beautiful.'

She made a sarcastic face. 'Yeah, beautiful in my soul, and I can cook. Shit, I don't want to date you, I just want some truth.'

'You look tired.'

'Tired? Christ, I look like I'm going through chemotherapy.' She gestured around the room. 'This place isn't so bad. They're transferring me to county soon. Now that place is supposed to be a real stalag. You may have to smuggle me in an iron chastity belt.'

'I'm not taking mine off for anyone.'

She laughed. The laughter shook some hair loose from behind her ear. She stopped abruptly to tuck it back. She studied me a few seconds. 'Come on, Wren, tell me something juicy about yourself. Something nasty. A little tit for tat here. Girl talk. Just so I don't feel so damn exposed all the time.'

309

'First sex, huh?'

'That's a good place to start. And feel free to embellish the truth to make it more interesting. I know I have.'

I laughed. 'Don't let Davis hear that.'

'Don't worry, Davis would be the last to care.'

That was probably true. Davis was busy riding a tidal wave of success through Hollywood. He'd made his deal for Season's story to be filmed, and now he'd closed the deal on the woman in Hawaii. A fortyish TV actress who'd once had a hit sitcom bought it for her own production company. Now Davis was in demand, lunching every day with a different studio mogul. Yesterday he'd met Bette Midler about playing Season. Everything was going his way. He claimed that I was his lucky charm, that since he'd met me, great things had happened. He was so happy that he would occasionally burst into song, usually a selection from *The King and I*. He was very proud of his Yul Brynner impression.

But while he sang 'Is a Puzzlement' and lunched at fancy restaurants in Los Angeles, the woman who was the real charm for his success sat in a prison awaiting trial. Of course, Wren, the woman who was my lucky charm, was decomposing in a coffin. Now Season was my new charm. I visited her every day and asked her endless questions about her life. How had a woman who'd accomplished so much come to lose faith in everything she'd believed in, the very values she'd taught her daughter? What brought her to her ex-husband's house with a loaded shotgun? What gave her the courage to pull the trigger? Was it a mother's self-sacrifice for an abused daughter? Or just an embittered ex with a grudge? Sometimes I even forgot I was writing a book and my questions were just the natural curiosity I felt. I was fascinated with how the mundane and the fantastic in our lives merge. How had someone as ordinary as me come to have a gunshot scar on her boob? In some ways, I was like a novitiate studying at the feet of a Zen monk, looking for some truth in the smallest details: What did she wear that day? How did she decide what to wear to her husband's execution? Did she put on her favorite underwear knowing she'd be arrested and strip-searched? Did she wear shoes she didn't mind getting blood and brain goop on?

Davis, on the other hand, rarely asked me personal questions about Season. He cared about her physical welfare, providing her with whatever comforts she was allowed to have in prison. He was like an attentive son. But he wasn't curious about her actions the way I was. He just took them for granted. When I asked him why he wasn't so curious, he said he'd find out everything when he read my book.

Season seemed open with me, answering all my clumsy queries thoughtfully, sometimes even humorously. But I could see she was starting to wane. She'd been under enormous pressure, with bail hearings, media coverage, constant questions from everyone about where her daughter was hiding. Davis coordinated the media interviews and was always present during them, riding shotgun along with Season's lawyer. Some questions, Davis warned the press, were taboo, the answers being reserved exclusively for me and my book. And the trial.

I never wore makeup or panty hose or heels when visiting Season. We debated her 'little girl' theory of fashion a couple times, but she didn't get rabid about it or anything. She explained it all very rationally and I found her uncomfortably convincing.

'Are you an active feminist?' I once asked her.

She'd laughed. 'I'm not a feminist, I'm a mother.'

'What's the difference?'

'Feminist is just a word people use to dismiss the truth. I've never marched or sued or written a political letter. All I did was pull a trigger.'

'You've lost me. I'm just trying to figure out how you expect women to live practically in this world, how can they compete in a male-dominated work force without conforming to some of those male expectations?'

'That's like me tossing a black slave some shackles and

saying, "Here, go lock yourself up for the night."' She'd yawned, bored. 'It doesn't matter. Women know they're wrong, that's why they argue so hard. Every time you take a razor to yourself, you're slicing off a part of who you are, the same as if you were binding your feet, the way Chinese did with their women. It crippled them, you know.' She'd paused, studied her hands. 'Like I said, I was never a political person. I'm just a mother who doesn't want her daughter to end up a prisoner, whether it's inside or outside the bars.'

I continued to shave my legs and armpits, though I always wore slacks and long-sleeved blouses so Season wouldn't know this. Maybe she was right in the long run, but I was no tragic hero willing to sacrifice myself for a cause. Besides, I liked the feel of my skin, smooth and soft. Did that make me a bad person?

The thing is, I'd grown fond of Season, even admired her. Not for killing her husband. I still considered that a little excessive. But at least she had done *something*, she had acted. Even if the action was brutal, even if it was wrong, it was still an attempt to make things right. Even if her reasons were self-delusion, she had acted on her version of reality. What would most women have done in her place? Shrugged, sent their daughters off to their husbands, and hoped for the best. Is that any less a self-delusion?

'Come on, Wren,' Season coaxed. 'Don't be a prig. Spill your guts.'

I shut off the recorder and removed the suction cup from the phone receiver. 'Okay. First sex. Here goes.' I leaned forward toward the Plexiglas. So did Season. Not that we could hear each other any better that way, we still had to speak through the phones. But I appreciated the gesture of intimacy. I hadn't told this story to anyone except Robby and Wren. I don't know why I was telling Season. I mean, I could have told her about Wren's first time with her handsome water polo champion cousin, or Mom's first time with her screenwriter on the set of the

312

giant scorpion movie. After all, what did it matter whose first time it really was I told about. Except that I felt as if I owed Season some little truth.

'I was fifteen. In the ninth grade. My school had a poetry contest—'

'And you won.'

I shook my head. 'Third place. I wrote something about the plight of illegal aliens or something. I just took a Bob Dylan song and replaced all the lyrics with my own. You could've sung my poem to "Mr. Tambourine Man."'

'How'd it go?'

'No. That's where I draw the line. Sex, okay; adolescent poetry no. Leave me some shred of dignity.'

'C'mon. I love Bob Dylan.'

I laughed. 'It went: "Hey, you *bracero*, with the mud between your toes/hardly anybody knows what you've been going through—"'

'You're not going to be this long-winded in our book, are you?'

'Lay off. I'm sharing a moment here.'

She snorted. 'Just get to the good stuff. Naked body parts.'

'Anyway, the three winners from our school got to go to some conference for junior high school poets all over the state. We stayed in a hotel and everything.'

'You boffed one of the other poets when he read his romantic poem.'

'Are you going to let me tell my story or what?'

'Go, go.'

'Right. So, Mr. Bilford, our English teacher who took us to the conference, calls me to his room.'

'Oh, shit, not the teacher.' She laughed. 'I've seen this movie.'

'He starts talking about my poetry and all that stuff, how good I am. Then, suddenly, he's kneeling on the floor with his arms wrapped around my knees telling me how much he likes me, how he's been watching me for a couple years, waiting until I was old enough to tell me his true feelings.'

'Was he cute, at least?'

'He looked like Peter Tork of the Monkees. You remember them?'

She nodded. 'Not my type. Then what?'

'I don't know. I was stunned. I didn't know what to do. Then he starts kissing me and hugging me. I was so scared I didn't know whether to run or what. I didn't kiss him back, but I didn't run either. I guess he considered that encouragement, because then he grabs my hand and places it on his crotch. I'm sitting there with a handful of my English teacher.' I laughed. 'I didn't know what he wanted me to do with it. So he unzips his pants and shoves my hand inside, he wraps my fingers around his penis and holds my hand there, and starts pumping. He came in a couple strokes. Then he gets a washcloth and wipes my fingers like I was a little girl playing in mud. Afterward he cries and begs forgiveness.'

'Christ, could you ask for anything more perfect your first time than a guy who cries and begs you to forgive him?'

'A week later he calls me at home and begs me to start up again with him, he wants to leave his wife, quit his job if he has to. Whatever it takes. I tell him no, I don't want to see him again in that way. He cries and hangs up.'

'What happened to him?'

'He and his wife moved to Florida during the summer.'

'Not bad,' Season said. 'I'll give it an 8.5. Diverting yet with a touch of pathos.'

'Thanks a heap. You got a better one?'

She tapped her front teeth. 'Today I have perfect straight teeth with not one cavity, thanks to the mass of grillwork I wore for most of my puberty. Believe me, the Wonder Years are a little less wonderful smiling through barbed wire.'

I fastened the suction cup back onto the receiver and pressed the Record button.

Season continued: 'I don't think I can blame the braces for any lack of sexual experience. After all, plenty of other girls wore braces and they were sleeping with plenty of cool guys. But I was painfully shy and dating made me physically nauseous. I actually used to throw up before every date. Puke breath doesn't exactly make you popular with the hot hormone crowd. Finally, by eleventh grade, I had a steady boyfriend, Joey Gregson, who did the 400-meter breaststroke for the swim team. We'd been dating for over a year. Mostly we'd done our petting with all our clothes on, though often fully unbuttoned. Usually we finished off these evenings with my no-pregnancy speciality, a one-minute blow job. But he was so afraid of my braces slicing his precious weeny that he made me wax them first. He even gave me something called Sex Wax, which is really for waxing surfboards, but which he'd brought back with him after he'd gone to Los Angeles for a week to visit his uncle. When he'd come back he was crazy to become a surfer, even though there's not much surfing in Flagstaff, Arizona, where we lived. So, I'd wax my braces and do it.' She made a tight circle of her mouth to indicate the act. We both laughed.

'This went on for about six months. Then, during the summer before our senior year, Joey breaks off with me because he's decided to go to L.A. and stay with his uncle for the summer and become a real surfer. He doesn't want any ties, he tells me, he just wants to concentrate on his surfing, not worry about me back here where he can't do anything about it. Here's the part I like: He flies to L.A., goes out surfing the first day, and gets his arm broken by a bunch of surf nazis because he's not a local and he's surfing their waves. He comes back to Flagstaff the next week with his arm in a twenty-pound cast. He calls me up and I end up with Sex Wax permanently embedded in my braces all summer.' She shrugged helplessly. 'Is it any wonder I became a dentist?'

I laughed. 'Why do people talk about sex so much? The

amount of talk about it is disproportionate to the amount
of time actually doing it.'

'I know. It's kind of like you spend so much time fantasizing and analyzing that it's a bit of a disappointment to
actually do it.' She tucked a loose lock of hair behind her
ear again. 'Sex is too complicated. I mean, when do you
know if you're doing it enough to satisfy your partner.
Aren't you always wondering if he wants more than you're
giving him? Or if he doesn't seem to want it as much, isn't
it because you aren't as desirable? Or if you are doing it
a lot, won't it just get boring that much faster. Like each
couple has a specific number of times they can have sex
before it starts to get stale. Then you start wondering if
while he's pumping away on you if he's not picturing that
young beauty he saw in the movie you both attended
earlier that night. How are you supposed to feel knowing
that he's imagining her body and face while he's gripping
your hips?'

'I don't know. I guess you do your own fantasizing.'

'That just seems so pathetic, two people making love,
each thinking about someone else. I mean, I know all the
sex doctors tell you it's healthy and all. I don't know. I'm
probably in no position to talk ethics here.' She crooked
her thumb at the barred windows. 'I haven't had sex since
my divorce over a year ago. I dated, I never had trouble
with men asking me out. I just couldn't get enthused
about it. I tried just doing it to myself for a while. I bought
a huge ole vibrator with more gears than a Porsche. But
that only made me feel lonelier. I kept imagining ghosts
of my dead grandmothers floating around and watching
me, feeling sorry for me.' I noticed tears brimming at the
corners of her eyes.

I didn't know what to tell her. That I'd gone through
the same thing after my marriage broke up. But all that
was behind me now. Now that I'd met Davis. Wouldn't
that just make matters worse for her? After all, prospects
for getting out of prison within the next fifteen years didn't
look promising.

316

'Here's the worse part, Wren,' she said. The tears were flowing freely now. Her mouth was contorting to fight the sobs that had started. There was an urgency in her voice, as if she had to tell me now before she chickened out. When she spoke, her voice was a hoarse whisper. 'I miss him, Wren. I miss Philip. I know it's crazy, but I do.' A loud gasping sob exploded from her as if she'd been punched in the stomach. The guard looked up from his reading, stared menacingly. I smiled at him to indicate all was well. He kept staring for a few seconds longer, then dipped his head back into his book like a cow returning to grazing.

'God help me, Wren. We really were happy once. Philip and I cuddled on Sunday mornings, had lazy sex, read the *Sunday Times*. Jamie would lie on the bed between us, coloring dinosaurs with her fluorescent crayons. Philip would then take us all out to brunch and a movie. I would feel sorry for the rest of the world, that they weren't as happy.' She looked directly at me, her eyes sagging from the weight of tears. 'And the craziest part, Wren, the part that makes me not care what happens to me now, that makes me know I deserve whatever punishment I get, is that I sometimes miss Philip more than I miss Jamie. How am I supposed to live with that?'

I sat there for a moment, watching her sob. She let the phone fall from her hand. I wanted to help her, touch her, comfort her somehow. But the guard was already up and marching toward us.

I turned off the tape recorder. I rewound a little way. I erased.

Davis picked me up outside the jail. 'Get in, babe. I'm breaking ya outta dis crummy joint.'

I got into his station wagon. Davis leaned over and kissed me. I hugged him hard, the way I'd wanted to hug Season.

'How'd it go?' he asked.

'Grim.'

He nodded, as if he already knew what Season had said. He pulled away from the curb. 'Well, forget it for a couple hours. Right now, get in the mood to celebrate.'

'Celebrate what? You sell another project?'

'No, you did.' He reached over and stroked my leg. 'Your book about Season Dougherty has been bought. I finished negotiating the deal a couple hours ago.'

'Really?' I said, excited. 'It's really going to happen then. Jesus, this book is actually going to be published.'

He smiled at my enthusiasm. 'Damn right it is. And it's going to sell a lot of copies.'

'How'd you do it? The publishers don't even know me. I mean, they don't know that I'll do a good job.'

'I sent them some of the tapes of you and Season. They like your interviewing style. Very unorthodox, they said, but effective. Season obviously likes you a hell of a lot more than she likes me.'

'She likes you,' I said.

'Don't bullshit a bullshitter. She tolerates me. I serve a purpose. That's okay.'

I changed the subject. 'You didn't send the publishers

some of my other writing, articles or something? Any of my published works?'

'Nope. Just the tapes.'

I leaned back against the car seat and sighed. That meant the publishers weren't hiring me based on Wren's writing, just my own interviews with Season. My own work.

'They liked the way the two of you interacted. They especially liked the panty hose story I told them, when she made you strip them off before she'd talk to you. Make sure that's in the book. That's the kind of stuff they like.'

Suddenly I wished I hadn't erased Season's confession about missing Philip. That would have made a dynamic passage in the book. Instantly I felt guilty for thinking that. Still, would I do it again, given the choice?

'Based on what they heard so far, they feel confident this will be a major seller.'

'It's nice they have such faith in me.'

'There are lots of writers around, but not everybody can talk to a murderer, get them to open up.'

Murderer. The word startled me. I didn't think of Season as a murderer. She had killed someone, so technically I guess she was one. I just didn't like hearing it. A splinter of anger pulsed behind my right eye.

'It sounds funny hearing you call her a murderer,' I said. 'Cold.'

He looked over at me, frowning. 'You're right. I've been spending too much time in Hollywood. Calling Season a murderer there makes her more valuable to those guys. Sorry, honey.'

It was the first time he called me honey. I liked the sound, I'd missed being called honey and sweetheart and babyface and cuddlebug. I wanted to hear it all again. Yet, I also felt oddly anxious. Season was a murderer, but I was a honey.

'Which brings me to this.' Davis reached over and opened the glove compartment. He pulled out a white legal-sized envelope and handed it to me. 'Wren Caldwell' was typed neatly on the outside. In the upper left-hand corner was a fancy embossed logo and address in red ink: DR Productions. I opened the envelope and pulled out some folded pages. The top page was titled WRITING CONTRACT BETWEEN DR PRODUCTIONS AND WREN CALDWELL. Paper-clipped to the top of the page was a check for $25,000. Made out to Wren Caldwell!

'Jesus,' I said. 'Jesus.'

'I'd have a lawyer look over that contract first. I'm not talking as DR Productions right now, so don't tell that slippery bastard Davis Richard what I'm saying. Have a good lawyer read it. If you think it's fair, sign it and cash the check. Don't cash the check until you see a lawyer, because cashing it constitutes acceptance of the contract. I only included it now because I thought you might need the money and I didn't want any delays later.'

'A lawyer.' I scanned the contract. It was very official. By the second paragraph I was lost in the whereases. 'I don't know any lawyers. You wouldn't try to cheat me, would you, buster?'

'Get a lawyer, Wren. I'm serious.' He took one hand off the steering wheel and laid it in my lap. He squeezed my thigh affectionately. 'We're into something here, you and I. Dating, lovers, a relationship, whatever we want to call it. I just don't want business to screw us up. Money can do that sometimes.'

'Okay,' I said, folding up the contract and stuffing it back into the envelope, then into my purse.

We pulled up to the curb in front of my apartment. I leaned over and kissed him. 'Thanks for the ride, the contract, the check. The new life. Meaning to the universe.' I looked at my watch. 'Now all I've got to do is get some notes together and go teach my art history class.'

'Want me to pick you up after class tonight? We can continue our celebration.'

I was feeling pretty nervous about class. Just envisioning a roomful of students made my stomach shred itself apart. I shook my head. 'I'd better just wait and see how it goes in class first.'

Davis looked over my shoulder at the apartment. 'Is your husband home?'

'I don't know,' I said. Byron hadn't been home since I got bombed three nights ago. I would come home every day after interviewing Season and find Hector had been fed and his litter box cleaned. The phone answering machine had been played, my messages neatly written with time and date. But no Byron.

'Let's check, shall we?' Davis said with a sort of little boy naughtiness. He swung his station wagon into a parking slot and followed me to the front door. A quick search of the apartment turned up a sleeping Hector but no Byron. Hector's litter box had been cleaned and he was wearing a new white flea collar that made him look a little like a priest.

'All clear,' Davis said, coming down the hall.

'The bird's gone,' I said, coming out of the kitchen.

'What?'

'The parrot. Motown. He's gone. The cage and everything.'

'Do you miss him?'

I shrugged. 'No, I guess not.'

Davis put his arms around me and kissed me hard. His fingers dug into my buttocks, lifting me onto my toes. He started unbuttoning my blouse. I nervously looked at the front door.

'I don't know . . .' I said. 'He could come in anytime.'

'He won't.' Another button popped free.

'We don't have time. I have to get ready for class.'

'A quickie. Fast and furious, like in the movies.' He grinned. 'Trust me.' He started singing in his Yul Brynner accent: ' "But unless someday somebody trusts somebody/ There'll be nothing left on earth excepting fishes." '

'Oh, yes, take me, bald stud. Take me now!'

We ran down the hall laughing.

Somehow we ended up in the bathroom. The tiny counter around the sink was covered with colorful cans and tubes and boxes. Deodorant. Toothpaste. Q-Tips. Nivea cream. Davis brushed them all aside and hoisted me up onto the counter next to the sink. The porcelain was cool on my skin and I could feel the faint crust of dried toothpaste. The strip of wall behind the sink was all mirror. But it was back so far that I couldn't comfortably lean against it so I sat there feeling like a little girl at the doctor's office sitting on the table, legs dangling and nothing to lean against.

Davis started kissing me, but he was impatient and left my mouth quickly and trailed down to my breasts, sucking and kissing them while his hand slid between my legs. I was naked except for my panties, which I've always been reluctant to shed during sex until the last possible second. He just slid his hand under the elastic leg and dug in. He bit my nipple firmly, hard enough to cause me to jerk a little, but not hard enough to want him to stop. I pulled his head harder against my breast and scooted my hips forward against his probing hand. He slipped one finger into me, then another, and finally a third. It felt good, but I felt a little like a turkey being stuffed by a hungry chef.

Maybe I just don't relax enough during sex. I think too much about what every action means, its ramifications. Sex makes me feel like the worst softball player on the playground, the last to be picked, the first to drop the game-losing catch. Wren used to tell me of her sexual escapades, the impossible positions, the household objects she used, vegetables and fruits that she and her partners incorporated into their sex. I would gape, which only delighted and encouraged her to tell me more details. Robby and I also had our moments of passion and inventiveness. He liked it when I wore my white socks and hiking boots to bed. We had a modest vibrator that we used on each other sometimes. Once he wore my underwear to bed and I wore his and we pretended to be each other and make love the way the other usually did. There was something exciting about that, though mostly I felt like we were conducting a psychological experiment rather than making love.

My only real sexual experience other than with Robby was my one adulterous affair. Robby and I were going through the usual three-year doldrums that I have since read about in several self-help books. He was studying late all the time and we rarely saw each other and even more rarely had sex. No excuses, I just got lonely and scared and ended up in the sack with a guy who lived in the same apartment complex. He was a Zen Buddhist, though he'd been raised Jewish on Long Island, New York. His father was a copyright lawyer for a record company so he knew a lot of rock 'n' roll stars. He was the calmest guy I'd ever known. His apartment was filled with thick white candles, which he lit every morning at sunrise and every evening at sunset. Sometimes immediately after sex he'd sit on the edge of the bed, his legs crossed, his hands cupping each other, his eyes partially open but unfocused, meditating. He'd practice breathing out. Breathing out was the key, he said, though a lot of people thought breathing in was. You can kill somebody when they're breathing in, that's when we're most vulnerable. He told me about another Buddhist sect in which sex was a symbolic act, very spiritual, having to do with erasing the concept of duality and such. Even though he wasn't a member of that sect, sex with him always seemed kind of spiritual. Also, kind of colorless, odorless, and tasteless, like something that was good for you, though it wasn't especially enjoyable. Like talking to a phone answering machine. After a few times I got to feeling too guilty and I broke it off. He called me a cunt, threw a couple of candles at the wall, and threw me out of his apartment.

I guess that's the point, really, sex has always felt like practice for something better. I read once in a novel where the woman was making love and she felt as if the man were pulling her underwater, dragging her to the bottom of a swimming pool. Sex was never like that for me. I sort

323

of sat on the edge of the pool and dangled my toes in the water.

And here I was again:

Davis lifted my legs up and pulled my panties off. He put his hands on my knees, pushed my legs apart, and knelt in front of me. His tongue lapped at me eagerly. I felt his hand wedge under my buttocks and crawl across my skin until he was at my anus. His fingers were already damp from penetrating me, so he just slid his index finger into me. I yelped from the sudden assault. This was not an area that had much experience. Robby was a little too fastidious perhaps to be much interested there. I tried to squirm away from Davis's finger, mostly out of embarrassment, I guess. It didn't really feel that bad, just a little uncomfortable.

Davis stood up, folded my legs over his hips, and entered me. He thrust hard, fast and furious, as promised. I leaned back until my shoulders were pressed against the mirror. He pounded into me and I wanted him to keep pounding. The skin on my shoulder blades squeaked against the mirror with each thrust like a squeegee against a windshield. He was breathing hard, panting, pumping. His breathing became labored and I opened my eyes to make sure he was all right. His eyes were pressed close with concentration, his face in a pained grimace. For a moment I was concerned he was having a heart attack. But he came and his face relaxed.

After a minute he pulled out of me and turned on the faucet. His penis dripped onto the carpet as he splashed cold water on his face. 'Do you really need to do this teaching?' he asked. 'Can't we just stay home tonight and do that a few more times?'

'They're expecting me.' I hopped down from the counter. My thighs were streaked with his come. My legs were shaky.

He pulled a handful of toilet paper off the roll and wiped my thighs. 'You don't need the money now. Plus, it could interfere with your work on the book.'

'If it does, we'll talk about it then.'

He held up his hands innocently. 'This isn't a male-female issue, Wren. I'm not trying to dominate you here, I'm just showing concern. I can do that, can't I?'

I patted his butt. 'I don't want to go tonight, believe me. But I've made a commitment and it's important that I keep it.' Besides, I didn't want an irate administrator phoning Wren's old university to complain about her and finding out the teacher they hired has been dead over a month.

I started my shower and Davis stretched out on the bed with the newspaper. He looked funny lying there, his naked body pink from exertion, like a pudgy teenager. Yet his face was so adult, concentrating on the articles, scanning for a story to option. I leaned over and kissed his white hip.

'Thanks,' he said.

'How come you're so pale,' I said. 'Where's that Maui tan?'

'I was there for business. For all the outdoors I saw, it might as well have been Kansas. When you and I go, that's when I'll get a tan.'

I walked down the hall to the shower.

The phone rang while I was shampooing my hair.

'I'll get it,' Davis called.

'No!' I shouted. I turned off the faucet, pulled my hair back to keep the soap out of my eyes, and ran to the bedroom for the phone. 'Hello?'

Silence.

'Hello?' I repeated.

Again, silence, though I could hear someone faintly breathing.

I took a wild shot. 'Byron's not here. You want to leave a message?'

'Sure, thanks,' came the pleasant voice. 'Tell him tomorrow's fine. If he's still up to it. I mean, we can postpone if he's not healed by then.'

'Healed? What do you mean?'

'Just tell him, okay? If he doesn't call, I'll be there with the money. Bye.' He hung up.

'Who was that?' Davis asked as I walked back into the bedroom.

'Friend of Byron's.'

'Oh.' Davis returned to his newspaper. I returned to the shower.

When I finished, I wrapped a towel around me and one around my hair. Davis was dressed, except for one shoe, which he was tying.

'That was fast,' I said.

'Fast and furious, as advertised.'

'No, I meant getting dressed.'

'I have some work I should do.'

'Find any potential movies?'

He shook his head and looked at the paper, which he'd left on the bed. 'Nothing I can sell.'

'I've got an idea,' I said. 'I got sick once and they took out my appendix because the doctor thought they had burst. Turned out they hadn't. They charged me for the operation anyway. That's when I got this idea. A doctor, maybe some guy who's lost his license because he did something good, but went against the medical establishment. Anyway, the guy hires himself out now as a medical bodyguard. People pay him to go into the operating room as their representative to make sure everything is done correctly. Like a medical gunslinger or something. People would feel a lot better with someone like that in there.'

Davis shook his head as he slipped on his cardigan sweater.

I'd just said it as a lark, not expecting anything. But I was a little disappointed to get no response at all.

'Of course, it needs fleshing out and stuff,' I said. 'But the idea, I mean, you can have him hired by some mobster who's getting a bypass. Something like that.'

Davis turned his back, pulled something out of his

326

pocket, and started writing. He turned back around and tore a check out of his book. He handed it to me. 'This one you can cash.'

It was for $2,000. 'What's this?'

'An option on your idea. I like it. Possible series, certainly an MOW or even a theatrical. We'll have to spice it up somehow. Something goes wrong during the operation, guy dies. Our hero tries to save him. Turns out he was assassinated and now the mobster's people are after the doc. I dunno, something like that. But I love the idea. It's great.'

I stared at the check. It amazed me how quickly money changed hands, especially for amounts that were more than I'd ever seen before.

'That's my standard option advance,' Davis said. 'I'll have a contract drawn up. If I sell the idea, you stand to make a lot more.'

'How much more?'

'A hundred grand at least.'

Davis left. I watched him drive away, still clutching the check in my hand. First a check for $25,000 and now another one for $2,000. At this rate, I could publish Wren's magazine within the year.

I taped the two checks to the back of the bathroom sink bowl, the last place I thought Byron might look. I wondered what the guy on the phone meant about Byron healing, but decided to ignore it. I scribbled the message down on a scrap of newspaper corner, tore it off, and carried it to Byron's room.

When I opened the door, I was shocked. The bed looked like it had been wrestled into place after a great struggle. The sheets were pulled out of place and tangled in ropy knots. The pillows were scattered across the floor, beaten into unconsciousness. Everything else in the room was in its usual prison neatness. But the bed. The mattress lay askew, a corner flopping off the frame. I inched closer, noticing red smears on the white sheets.

I leaned over the bed. I could smell the sexual activity that had taken place. A few beige stains confirmed that this chaos was the result of some wild coupling. The red smears were mostly lipstick, a tacky shade of reddish orange favored by college freshmen trying to look sophisticated. The other red stains were blood.

I went to his bathroom. The sink counter had a balled-up plastic bag from Thrifty's drugstore. The receipt listed the objects that were lined up next to the sink: peroxide, Band-Aids, cotton swabs. A washcloth, twisted into its wrung-out formation, lay in the sink, still damp, still a little bloody.

I rubbed the blood between my fingertips and sniffed it. As if it were a salad dressing and I were trying to figure out the ingredients. I didn't figure anything out. I had no theory. One of them had been bleeding. This could have happened either before or during sex. That they brought a bag of medical supplies suggests the wound had already occurred, otherwise he would have taken these things from her bathroom and used them. So at least the blood wasn't the result of their sex.

I walked back to my bedroom and finished dressing. Despite Season's philosophy, I applied some makeup. A little foundation, eyeliner. I fluffed my hair trying to make it look bigger. I'd read that elephants held their ears straight out from their heads when charging to make themselves look more formidable to their enemy. I hoped this would work with students.

As I ran the lipstick across my mouth, I noticed tiny spit wads of something on the mirror. The glass was smeared from where I'd rubbed against it during sex with Davis. I plucked one of the balls from the glass and inspected it. Skin. My skin. I felt like a detective at a crime scene. Blood, skin, lipstick, twisted sheets. Definitely a crime scene. All I had to do now was figure out the crime and find the victim.

I grabbed Wren's art book and my notes and drove to school. In the car I noticed I still had some blood on my fingertips. I spat on them and wiped them on the car seat. For no particular reason, I began to wonder what happened to the parrot.

24

'It doesn't make any fucking sense,' he said angrily. 'I mean, I just don't get it. He splits the arrow, right? Correct me if I'm wrong here. He shoots his bow and then his arrow splits the other guy's arrow, right?'

His friend sailed his stiffened index finger through the air like an arrow. He whistled sound effects. 'Thunk,' he said.

'Just answer yes or no, okay? He split the fucking arrow, right?'

'Smack down the middle, Perry Mason.'

'Well, that means Robin Hood put his arrow in the exact same spot as the other guy, right?'

'Technically, yeah.'

'So, technically, Robin Hood didn't really shoot any better than the first guy. So why did he win? Doesn't make any sense. His shot was exactly the same. Explain that to me.'

His friend shrugged. 'Hollywood, man.'

'Great fucking answer. Thanks for the insight, Joseph Campbell.'

'I'm serious, man. It's all part of the master plan. If Robin Hood didn't win, there couldn't have been a Big Speech scene from the evil prince, followed by the Big Capture scene, followed by the Big Chase scene during which Robin Hood escapes. That's the whole point. Everything in movies is directly related to how it affects the chase scene. Like divine intervention.'

'Christ, you make one sixteen-mm film for class and you

think you're Kubrick. My films aren't going to have any chase scenes, ever. Not one. People won't even walk fast. If you ever see me filming one, you have my permission to pound a stake through my heart.'

'Sure, but where you gonna get the heart?'

He didn't laugh. 'Eat shit.'

'Now, *that* you've got plenty of.' He curled his finger into a snail circle and peered at his friend through it as if it were a camera. 'You don't get it, man. Just because something is done a lot in the movies doesn't mean it's bad. I mean, look at sex.'

'You're a moron.'

'At least I'm not trying to be the next Woody Allen. Don't be so pretentious, dude. The chase scene is basically a cool concept. We all dream of having a chase scene in our drab little lives. One sinister moment when all the evil forces that have been secretly fucking up our lives since that first day in preschool reveal themselves for one final showdown. Only then, after years of stamp-licking, stain-removing, toilet-scrubbing existence, does our pathetic life take on any *real* meaning.'

'And you actually believe that shit or are you rehearsing a scene?'

'The chase puts our lives in focus. Finally we have a purpose in which the outcome of something we do actually makes a fucking difference. We're no longer just an average asshole with a million excuses why our life is a failure; we're the Only Hope in some cosmic conspiracy. It's a glimpse of total clarity, maybe the only time in our life when the sides are clear. That's why audiences love it, man. We all live in hope of one day experiencing a climactic chase scene.'

The first guy, who really did look like Woody Allen, made an annoyed face. 'You are hopeless, man.'

'What do you mean?'

The first guy threw up his hands and walked away. His friend followed, repeating. 'What do you mean?'

The two boys discussing Robin Hood had been standing

outside my classroom waiting for the Intermediate Free-hand Drawing class already in there to finish. Now they sat on a bench and continued their animated discussion. Overhearing their conversation made me even more nervous. I wasn't sure I had the nerve to do my Wren act in front of such a large audience. One on one I was okay, but this was the difference between playing Beach Boys tunes on the family upright piano at parties and appearing in concert at Carnegie Hall. Students could be ruthless. My hands were damp with sweat. Some of the ink on the art history textbook I was clutching rubbed off on my fingers.

Other students were beginning to gather around the door now, many of them older than the two filmmakers. Some of the men and women wore business suits and carried briefcases, having come straight from their day jobs. They sat stiffly on the benches provided, smoked cigarettes, or sipped from the Styrofoam cups they'd bought at the campus snack stand. Except for the two boys, the others didn't talk to each other except to make sure this was the right classroom. I'd forgotten that night classes drew an older crowd, one that worked during the day and therefore took their classes more seriously.

My stomach lurched suddenly and I tasted a couple of creamy drops of vomit at the back of my throat. I looked at my watch. Still eighteen minutes before class would begin. I turned and fled down the sidewalk along a row of faculty offices. If I could find a rest room, splash some cold water on my face, hang my head over a toilet, maybe take up meditation, or start smoking again . . .

I ran past an open door, caught a glimpse of a neat row of white toilets, and backtracked. I walked in, but this was definitely not the women's room. I knew a faculty office when I was in one: stacks of art books crammed into the bookshelves, posters on the wall of past student art exhibitions, a Year-at-a-Glance wall calendar with all the school holidays circled in red Magic Marker. I rubbed my nose, which burned a little from the harsh scent of turpentine and paint.

Five toilet bowls were crowded against the wall of the small room. They weren't connected to anything, no plumbing pipes. The lids were off so I walked over and peeked inside.

The inside of the bowls were painted. Not just painted, but each was covered with a replica of a famous masterpiece. I recognized a couple of them by name, the others I'd seen in books somewhere but couldn't recall details. Each toilet contained a completely different artistic style, from Impressionist to Cubist to Romantic. The accuracy was remarkable. I leaned over even farther, holding on to my glasses so they wouldn't fall in.

'Don't squat,' the voice behind me said in a pleasant tone. 'A couple are still wet.'

I turned. She was barely five feet tall, with white-blonde hair that had gone too long between bleachings. The brown roots were starting to gain lost ground. She wore it combed straight down all around, including her bangs, like a vampy imitation of Cleopatra. Her jeans were straight-legged and faded to a pale blue. Her sandals were rubber flipflops, the heel of one had a small bite out of it, the outline of teeth marks still clear. Her sweatshirt said UCLA. Her hair, her jeans, her sandals, her sweatshirt, were all dotted with constellations of different colors of paint. I figured her for about forty, with the distracted look of a woman whose independent life-style has brought her to the verge of either great success, or buying that fourth cat that tips her over the edge from being a cat lover into becoming a cat woman.

She looked at the roll sheet in my hand. 'Adjunct faculty?'

I nodded. 'One course. Art 110.'

'Ohhh, so you're Wren Caldwell.' She smiled mysteriously. 'I thought you'd have bigger tits.'

I nodded. 'So did I.'

She went to her desk and rummaged among loose

papers and art magazines until she found a flat can. She opened the lid, pinched some loose tobacco between her fingers, and tucked the wad into her mouth. The skin next to her lip bulged tumorously, as if she'd just been stung by a bee. 'A tragedy in the making, I know,' she said, tossing the can back onto the desk. 'No excuses. I just like chewing it more than gum. Sue me.'

'Nice meeting you, Sue,' I said. 'Me Wren.'

She laughed. 'Christ, don't make me like you, okay? If I like you, I'll want to spend time with you, if I spend time with you we'll talk, I'll tell you my personal problems, and then you'll pity me and won't like me anymore and we won't spend time together and I'll be terribly hurt. So, just act bitchy and save me the heartache. Deal?'

'Fuck you, slutface,' I said. 'How's that?'

She laughed again and shook her head. 'Too late, I think. Come on, I'll give you the grand tour of my toilets.'

'There's an invitation hard to resist.'

She walked over to the toilet bowls. She picked up a dirty rag and wiped her paint-splattered hands. 'I heard about you from Phil Sanchez, our illustrious department chair. I'll tell you before everyone else does: Phil and I date on occasion, the occasion being when his wife is out of town on business. See, it's started. I'm telling you my personal secrets.'

'I've heard worse.' I thought of Season Dougherty weeping in jail, confessing her love for her child's rapist.

'Anyway, everyone on the Hiring Committee was very impressed with your credentials, though your disappearing act gave Phil another cluster of ulcers.'

'Circumstances beyond my control.'

She snorted. 'That's gonna be the title of my autobiography.'

I didn't say anything. I didn't want to encourage any more personal revelations. I was already overburdened with what I'd heard today from Season.

'I read your article on Ogata Kenzan and his pottery work,' she said. 'Very insightful stuff.'

I had no idea who Ogata Kenzan was. 'Thanks.'

'But I think you underestimate his brother's influence. It wasn't until Korin returned to Kyoto in 1709 that Kenzan really developed his own style. They formed a symbiotic relationship that inspired both of them to go beyond what they were individually capable of. Don't you think so?'

'I think you're confusing inspiration with invention.' I had even less idea what that meant, but I remember Wren saying that to someone at a party who was arguing with her about Tom Wolfe. No, wait, she'd said they were confusing imagination with invention.

'Perhaps,' she said. Apparently she was as baffled by my statement as I was. She held out her hand and we shook. 'I'm Carol Hill.' She pointed to the plastic nameplate on her desk. 'Dreadful name, I know. A young girl with the name Hill and no chest to speak of takes a lot of teasing. "Where are your Hills, Carol?" That sort of thing. I started a rock band when I was in high school. I thought it would make me more popular. I couldn't play an instrument, so I sang. Actually, I couldn't sing either, so I sang like Janis Joplin. I had a sore throat for three years. Anyway, we used to practice every day in the basement, which prompted my father to announce to every guest we ever had that "The Hills are alive with the sound of Carol."' She shook her head. 'Any wonder I'm so screwed up?'

'Did it work? Were you more popular?'

She looked off, as if picturing herself back then, amid the popular crowd. 'Oh, yes, it worked. I was very popular. Disappointing, isn't it? My first lesson in hollow victories, I guess.'

'This is amazing stuff,' I said, gesturing at the toilets.

'Yeah, well.' She pointed to the first bowl, stirring the air with her finger as if cleaning the bowl. 'This one's La Tour's "Magdalen with the Smoking Flame."'

A comely young woman sat in a plain wooden chair. Her hand rested affectionately on a human skull, while she contemplated the flame rising brightly from a jar of what looked like oil. Beside the flame were the Scriptures. A warm glow of candlelight surrounded her protectively like a full-body halo. She looked content, the dark skull of Death cradled in her hand held no fear for her, now that she'd renounced mortality and found the light.

I had seen this painting before in books and always appreciated its simple power. As far as I could tell, this was an exact replication. Subtle and powerful, even clinging to the curved throat of a toilet bowl.

The second bowl's art I also recognized. I couldn't remember the title. A woman sat, head tilted, her enormous rosy-cheeked child propped up on her lap. Impressionist school. The colors soft, muted, but the whole picture somehow bright, clean and hopeful. Again, the duplication was eerily accurate.

'Mary Cassatt,' I said. 'Right?'

'Right,' Carol said. '"Mother About to Wash Her Sleepy Child." The size of that kid scared me off from having any for years. But with my thirty-sixth birthday marching toward me, I've reconsidered. For my birthday, I've decided to give myself a pregnancy.'

I glanced at her finger for a wedding ring, saw none. That could be practical though, not wanting to get paint on it.

'No husband,' she said, fanning out her naked fingers. 'I'm still screening candidates.'

'What do you do with them?'

'The candidates? I fuck them.'

'The toilets. Do you show them in exhibits?'

She went over to the door, walked outside, and spit an enormous gob of brown juice into the lawn. She came back in grinning. 'That's the part I like best.'

'Its charm is alluring.'

She laughed again. 'No, I don't exhibit them. Copying someone else's work isn't really art to me. This is more of a craft. Like making bird houses out of Popsicle sticks.'

'What do you do with them?'

'Sell them. They've got an arts festival every year down in Laguna Beach. I work on these all year and sell them down there during the summer. I make a little more from selling toilets in the summer than I do from teaching full-time the rest of the year. It's a wonderful life, ain't it?'

I studied the toilets again. One of them was a replica of Winslow Homer's 'The Cotton Pickers'. Two young black women wander through an enormous field of cotton, both wearing large bonnets. One woman has a basket of cotton under one arm, the other has a bag of cotton slung over her shoulder. One looks forlornly at the cotton, the other looks hopelessly across the field at her wasted future.

'You pick interesting subjects,' I said.

She shrugged. 'I pick whatever I can forge easiest. It's not that simple to treat the porcelain to hold the paint, then treat the paint so that thousands of flushings don't wash it away with the rest of the shit.'

'Forging. That doesn't sound respectful enough for what you do. You're really good.'

Carol smiled. 'You're mistaking cleverness for talent. I'm a forger, pure and simple. I don't even imitate life, I imitate imitations. I copy other people's work, people who really knew what they were doing and why they were doing it. I take their greatness and magically transform them into kitsch, a curved replica staring up at urinating twats and straining assholes.'

I didn't want to leave on that graphic image. I liked her too much. 'You must have your own work tucked away somewhere.'

She went to the door, waited for a couple of students to pass, then hocked another gob of tobacco juice across the sidewalk. She wiped her chin with the back of her sleeve. When she returned, her hands were dug deep into her pocket. She looked so tiny then, like a penitent child. 'If I could, Wren, then I would. If it's original art you're looking for, talk to Phil Sanchez. He's got showings all the time. Or Tina Lipschutz. She's our performance artist. Terrific gal. Or Zack DuBois, our potter. He's probably

337

just a couple years shy of world famous. Those are true artists. But you want decorated toilets, you come to me.' She leaned over the trash can and spit out the clump of tobacco. She took a swig of Diet Coke from a can on her desk. 'Don't get me wrong, Wren. I'm not having an artistic crisis. Being an artist was never my goal. Teaching was. I love it. But if you want to buy a house and go on vacations, you need another income. That's all there is to it.'

I looked at my watch. 'Gotta go. Class.'

'Have fun. If I haven't scared you off, come see me sometime. We'll have lunch. You're buying.'

I started out of the office. As I reached the door, Carol said, 'Hey, you wouldn't be needing a nifty new toilet, would you? I can make you a deal. You pick your favorite masterpiece, I'll slap it into your toilet.'

I thought about sitting down on a toilet, having someone's face staring up at me. I doubted I'd be able to go. 'I'll think about it.'

I was already ten feet down the sidewalk when I heard her call after me, 'I do bidets too.'

By the time I walked into the classroom, all the desks were full. A few people stood around the door with green slips of paper.

'I'd like to petition,' one hefty older woman said. She wore a tilted black beret as if she thought this were some Left Bank art hangout. 'Do you accept petitioners?'

'I would also like to petition,' a man in an expensive suit and silk tie said. He had a slight British accent.

'Let me do the paperwork here first,' I said, showing them my roster. 'Then we'll see.'

I went to the podium at the front of the class. The room was large and stuffy. The windows and door were open, but that didn't help much. I had the sense that people were breathing the same cubic foot of fresh air, passing it from row to row like a relay race baton. I swallowed dryly.

My roll sheet showed the maximum of forty students had enrolled. At the university in Oregon, English classes never exceeded twenty-five. This was a bit overwhelming. All the desks were taken and there were half a dozen deskless people standing around looking defeated. One wall was all windows, looking out on the sidewalk that fed three other buildings. Students walked back and forth outside and many of my students looked out the windows at them. Keeping their attention was going to be a challenge.

'My name is Wren Caldwell,' I said. 'And this is Art 110, for those of you who have wandered into the wrong classroom.'

'One-ten?' someone said.

'Yes.'

A teen in a white T-shirt and sweatpants that said Ripcurl down the side got up and walked out of the classroom. The old woman in the beret bustled to capture his desk. She smiled triumphantly at those next to her as she sat down.

The rest was administrative stuff, taking roll, signing petition cards to match the number of students who hadn't shown up. Because I had more petitioners than available seats, I did a lottery, pulling names out of a bag. Those whose names weren't drawn were dismissed.

One man whose name had not been selected would not leave. 'I buy lottery tickets every week, the money's supposed to go to education in this state. I've never won a goddamn dime. Now I have to do a lottery to take a stupid art class. This is no way to practice education.'

'I agree completely, sir,' I said. 'However, we are limited by fire laws as to the number of students allowed in each classroom. You'll have to leave.'

'Like hell I do.' He went over to the wall next to the door and sat down on the floor. He wasn't a very big man, under six feet and not especially muscular, but he looked angry enough to start trouble. He was in his fifties, hair longish and streaked with gray. Perhaps an ex-hippy reliving the glory days of sit-ins and taking over the administration building, shaving with the dean's razor, urinating in file cabinets. Actually, I kind of admired him for what he was doing.

The two aspiring filmmakers I'd overheard outside the classroom whispered to each other and gestured at the man. They were probably thinking of ways to film this.

'You do understand, sir, that you will not receive credit for this class?' I told him.

He grumbled something and waved me off.

'Want me to get security?' the man with the British accent offered. He'd been one of the lottery winners. So had the older woman with the beret.

'No, thank you. Let's just get on with class.' I talked about the structure of the class, the number of museum trips required, a diary of all the art works they would see and their critical impressions, the papers due, the number of footnotes, etc. I rattled off due dates as if I knew exactly what I was doing. The attitude I exuded was that there would hardly be enough time in a single semester to cram even a fraction of my vast knowledge of art history into them. I was starting to feel pretty good, in control and confident.

I had them open their textbooks to an abstract work by Willem de Kooning called 'Woman'. It was one of his series on women he did in the early 1950s. I'd picked this one because Wren had tons of notes in the margins about it and I was able to dazzle them with history and interpretation, thanks to Wren's knowledge.

'Notice how the figure seems crammed into a confining space by the placement of the geometric shapes. Yet, despite the confinement, she seems capable of overcoming these limitations by sheer force of will and physical being.' I glanced down at Wren's scrawl. 'This reinforces De Kooning's preoccupation with woman as mother-goddess-fury.'

And so it went until break time. 'Take fifteen minutes,' I said, checking the wall clock.

The man who had lost the lottery didn't move. He sat

hugging his legs, scowling slightly. People filed out past him, some giggling, others ingoring him.

A student blocked my path as I went for the door. She was about twenty, very pretty, wearing bib overalls. 'Wasn't there some concern at the time,' she said, 'that De Kooning might be hurting the abstract movement with these works? I mean, abstract art was only just beginning to gain acceptance in the U.S.'

I remembered one of Wren's notes to that effect. 'That's true,' I said, hurrying past her. I walked quickly down the sidewalk away from the classroom. I felt exhilarated. The class had gone well so far. No one had stood up and denounced me as an imposter. Actual learning had taken place, students knew more now than they had before.

I was practically skipping. I'd never felt so elated. If I'd had any kind of voice I'd have burst into song. It was as if everything in my life had suddenly come together at once. I was writing a book and getting paid. I'd come up with a script idea and picked up another $2,000. I had a boyfriend who was kind, generous, and good in bed. I was teaching, actually teaching a subject I knew little about, yet doing a good job of it. I could do anything. It was as if I suddenly had the golden touch. I was lucky. The way Wren had been lucky. So this was what it was like to get what you want, to feel safe within your good fortune, not to worry about what might happen because it was usually good. I laughed aloud and a couple students passing me gave me strange looks. I was surprised they couldn't see the magic aura surrounding me, like the one around Mary Magdalen in Carol Hill's toilet.

I didn't know what to do. This kind of manic energy shouldn't be wasted prancing around campus. If Davis were here I'd have pulled him into the bushes and jumped him. It would have been the best sex either of us had ever had, I just knew it. But he wasn't here.

Still, I had to do *something*.

Which gave me an idea.

I rounded the corner of the building and saw Carol's office light was still on. Her radio was on and an old Beatles' tune was playing, 'Across the Universe.'

'Carol?' I said, entering.

She was bent over a toilet, spraying an aerosol can. When she heard me, she looked around. She had goggles on and a small mask over her mouth and nose. She lowered the can and pulled down the mask. 'They chase you out already?'

'We're on break. Can I use your phone?'

'Will this involve heavy breathing or the use of cutesy pet names like Bedbug or Cuddles?'

I laughed. 'Not from this end.'

'Okay, you can use it. I've got to go to the bathroom anyway. One of the side effects of chewing tobacco.' She wiped her hands with the same colorful rag and tossed it on the desk. 'Punch nine for an outside line.' She walked out.

I dialed Robby's number.

This wasn't going to be like the other times I called him or wanted to. This was totally different. I wasn't feeling lonely or desperate or bitter. I didn't need his help or assurance. I didn't need anything. I was on top of the world. I closed my eyes and I saw the room as if I were floating fifty feet above it, the way people who have had near-death experiences say they saw the world. Maybe that's what was happening. I was dead. I'd died when BeeGee shot me. Oh, they'd patched and wired me back together, but I was still dead. Or maybe I'd been dead *until* BeeGee shot me. Maybe she'd saved my life.

I opened my eyes and suddenly I was sucked back down into my body like a cartoon ghost into a vacuum cleaner. I listened anxiously as his phone rang. I rocked back and forth, tapping my hand impatiently on the desk. I noticed the paint-spattered cloth, the globs of red. I thought of Bryon's bathroom, the blood, the bandages. What new violence was he involved in? It didn't matter. I could even deal with him now, I had the power.

'Hello?' Helen's genteel drawl.

'Hi, Dr. Jaspers. It's Luna.'

'Luna, how are you?' Solemn concern. Like a shrink.

'"Top of the world, Ma. Top of the world."' I laughed. She didn't laugh. 'How's Dallas? I have relatives there.'

'They send their love. They miss you.' I chuckled giddily. 'I'm kidding. Look, sorry to call so late. I only have a few minutes. My boyfriend just ran down to the drugstore for condoms and K-Y jelly. He'll be back any second. Can I talk to Robby?'

'Sure. Let me get him. You take care, Luna.'

She was gone. I'd passed the first test, getting past the beast that guarded the sacred cavern. I hadn't folded when she'd shown all that concern.

'Hey, Luna, what's up?' Robby said cheerfully. But it was his false cheerfulness, the one he pulled on like a ski mask when he felt nervous.

'Lotsa stuff is up,' I said. My cheerfulness was real. Could he hear it? 'What've you been up to?'

'Same ole shit. I'm doing a paper on architecture symbolism in Chaucer.'

I stifled a laugh. Big deal, I wanted to tell him, I'm interviewing a woman who shotgunned her husband who was raping their daughter. Architectural symbolism in Chaucer? Get real.

'What have you been doing?' he asked. 'How's your dad?'

'Dad's his usual self, traveling. In search of the perfect society, where wives don't die and daughters grow up perfect.'

'Has he tried Vegas?'

I laughed. So did he. I guess that's when we were the most intimate, when we laughed at the same thing together, the rhythm of our laughter falling into sync as if we were harmonizing in choir. It was uncanny. I felt that same feeling now. But I also sensed something else, a sadness in him. 'Are you okay?' I asked.

'Me? Fine.'

'No, really. Are you okay?'

'Really, I'm fine. Well, I've still got that problem of having to strap my dick to my thigh because it's so long, but otherwise . . .' He laughed.

I didn't want to fall into our old Robby and Luna Divorce Show routine where after we split up all serious personal discussions wound up with us joking instead of talking. 'Just talk to me, Robby. Are you happy?'

He sighed. 'Don't ask me those kinds of questions, Luna. What kind of answer could I possibly give?'

'I don't know? The truth, I guess. You left me for someone else, I have to assume because she makes you happier. So does she?'

There was a long silence. I heard some noises in the background coming from Robby's end. Dishes slamming? Then silence.

'Is she gone?' I asked.

'Yes.'

'Then tell me. Are you happier with her than you were with me?'

'Luna, Jesus . . .'

'Don't wuss out on me here, Robby. I'm not the same person you remember. I can take it. Just tell me the truth. You owe me that much.'

'Luna,' he said softly. There was a tone in his voice, that quiet tone he got in moments of intense honesty. Suddenly we were husband and wife again, curled up in our bed at night, talking in the dark. I could smell him through the phone, the scent of warm licorice.

'Tell me,' I said.

'It's different, Luna. My life is different now. It's not better, it's not worse. Fuck!' He was silent for a long time. I didn't rush him. 'I'm happy, but not necessarily happier than I was with you. Like I said, it's different. But then it's not that different either. Not like I thought it would be. It's weird. I mean, I didn't expect to be running around clicking my heels or anything. I don't know what I expected. It's just . . . I don't know.'

My heart pumped faster. 'Do you miss me?'

'Why are you doing this?'

'Do you?' I insisted.

'Yes, of course. I miss you every day. Everything I look at reminds me of you, of something we did.'

I could actually feel the blood washing through my veins like a rain-swollen stream. I looked at my arms, wondering if I'd see the skin rippling from the rush of blood. My bullet wound thumped as if it were a second heart.

'Maybe you made a mistake,' I said quietly.

'Luna, please . . .'

'Maybe you made a mistake. Maybe you could fix it.'

He was quiet for a long time. When he spoke, his voice was barely audible. 'It's not like that, Luna. I love Helen. True, it's not the same as it was with you, and yes, I do miss you. I can't tell you how much. But I miss you the way I miss high school. I'm happy, Luna. I didn't mean to imply anything else.'

'The way you miss high school?' I said. 'What the hell does that mean?'

Another long pause.

'Luna, Helen's pregnant.'

I sagged. BeeGee's bullet probably had less effect on me than Robby's announcement. 'You bastard,' I whispered.

'Luna, listen, I'm sorry.' He started to sob, his voice choked with mucus. 'Luna, Jesus, Luna—'

I hung up.

*   *   *   *   *

The class stared at me. They wanted something.

'Open your books to page forty-seven,' I said.

'What page?' someone asked.

I looked up. 'Forty-seven.'

'What'd she say?' I heard someone whisper.

My head felt hot, feverish. I touched my forehead, but

it was cool. Still, the heat inside me was building, like a dentist's drill held too long against the same tooth. I started to talk, but something doughy at the back of my throat caught all the words before they became airborne. I swallowed hard over and over, but it didn't matter. My eyes burned and I could feel tears trying to squeeze through the pinprick ducts. I blinked them back. I knew I would not cry. All my tears had been spent on my dissolved marriage. Three months of constant crying had dried me out. I hadn't cried once since then, not at being shot, not at Wren's death, not at being suspended from grad school or being fired by the magazine. And I sure as hell was not going to cry now. If nothing else, crying over this crap would be disrespectful to everything I hadn't cried over. Especially to Wren and Esther.

I stared at the David Hockney painting pictured in the book, 'Mulholland Drive: The Road to the Studio.' Wren's notes were lengthy and precise: Hockney influenced by Picasso's spontaneity. Van Gogh's textured brush strokes, Matisse's dominant colors. I could kill an hour on this painting and then assign some reading from the text and send everyone home early.

But when I tried to speak, a throttled sob burst out. I clamped my mouth down quickly to smother it, but the class had already heard me. I looked out at them, their puzzled faces frozen between concern and fear. I forced out a few hacking coughs, pretending that my sob had merely been a throat irritation. I opened my mouth to speak again, but another sob rushed up my throat and trumpeted several sad notes.

'You okay, Ms. Caldwell?' one of the filmmakers asked, the one who liked chase scenes.

I nodded. 'Swallowed down the wrong tube.'

A few people laughed nervously.

Now my eyes were blind with tears. My glasses magnified the tears and suddenly I was looking up at everyone from the bottom of a murky acquarium. Their faces were wavy and bovine, as if they couldn't decide whether or not to reach in and pull me to the surface. I coughed as hard as I could, doubling over a little so I could turn away and blink the tears out of my eyes. I felt a few splash onto my forearm.

I turned my back to the class and went to the blackboard. Maybe if I wrote a question or something on the board, kept my back to them, they wouldn't notice. I could stall until I was back under control. I picked up the yellow chalk and started writing: WHAT ARTISTS' INFLUENCES CAN YOU IDENTIFY IN HOCKNEY'S WORK. I'd ask them to write a list, maybe break into small discussion groups. That should do it.

God, what was I doing here? While my husband was living *my* life with another woman. My life had been stolen! Now I was nothing but a forger with no life of my own. At least Carol Hill had no illusions, no ambitions. I thought about Mom, her thin Polish skin smooth and pale as icing. Except for one mole on her neck, which she monitored the way SAC watches Soviet airspace. She feared that mole, certain it would turn into a fatal melanoma without her noticing. To live in fear that your own body would betray you. What would she think if she knew I was abandoning who she'd brought me up to be because I'd rather be someone else, someone better. She hadn't raised me to become someone else's child. Isn't that the worst betrayal of all to a mother? Dad, on the other hand, would find the whole thing interesting, maybe want to tag along with me through a typical day, take notes for an article. But Mom, she would have cried.

I was only halfway through the sentence on the blackboard when my shoulders started spasming and my hand began shaking. My handwriting turned spiky, like a heart monitor graph. My nose was running. Tears, unstoppable now, streamed wildly down my face. I tried to wrestle myself under control. I pressed my lips together, tightened my shoulders, I even stopped breathing, hoping that would stop the gasping sobs. But nothing worked.

By the time I finished writing this sentence, I would

have to turn around and face the class. When I did, there was no way they wouldn't know I was crying.

I wrote the last word, hooked a giant question mark at the end of the sentence, and dotted it so hard that the chalk snapped in half and bounced back against my glasses. I took the opportunity as an excuse to lift my glasses and quickly wipe my eyes with the back of my sleeve. But the tears were instantly replaced by others. My lips began shivering uncontrollably. They felt numb and rubbery. Fuck it, I finally decided, they've seen people cry before. Now I let the tears stampede down my cheeks as much as they wanted. My face felt sticky, webbed by crisscrossing streams of tears. Plump tears hung from my chin like icicles.

Fuck it, I thought. Fuck it. Fuck them. Fuck me.

I started to turn toward the class.

And suddenly all the lights went out.

25

The room was dark.

'Hey!' someone yelled.

'What the fuck?' someone else yelled.

I looked over at the doorway for the man who'd lost the lottery and had refused to leave. I couldn't really see anything, just a hazy outline of yellow against black where I remembered the door was. The dim yellow lights from outside gave it that spooky contrast. Now I recalled that the lottery man hadn't been there after our break. I started slowly for the doorway. Once outside, I could find security or maintenance.

'Everyone stay calm,' I said, my own voice suddenly calm. 'It's just a fuse or something.'

The darkness was jungle thick. I couldn't really see anyone as I groped with my hands ahead of me. A little light filtered in through the windows and I could see the other classrooms were still lighted.

'Oh, stop it, stop it, you brute,' one of the filmmakers joked in a falsetto. 'Oh, oh, baby, do me, do me!'

Several others laughed.

'This is not funny,' an older woman said.

I took a couple of experimental steps and bumped into someone. 'Please take your seat,' I said, sounding like a flight attendant. 'I'll find some help. Shouldn't take more than a few minutes to restore power.'

Cool hands came up to my face and wiped away the latest batch of tears.

'Excuse me,' I snapped, pulling back. But the hands followed. How could this person see?

'Go outside for a couple minutes,' the voice whispered. 'It's okay, I'll take over.'

I couldn't recognize the voice. Husky. The hands were rough and heavy against my face. A man's.

'Phil Sanchez?' I asked. Who else but the department head would be so bold as to take charge.

'Just step outside a few minutes to collect yourself. It's okay.'

This was ridiculous. I couldn't turn my class over to a voice in the dark. He could be a maniac with an automatic rifle slung over his shoulder and a couple of army surplus grenades in his pocket.

'It's okay,' he repeated. His hands fell from my face and I instantly felt cut loose, like an astronaut taking a space walk whose life line is severed. I reached out, but he was gone.

His voice got to me. Not just that it was soothing or sounded kind. There was something else. An understanding that wasn't just intellectual, like someone who only imagines what you're feeling and coos sympathy. It was more intimate than that, as if he had experienced my same humiliation a dozen times before. Maybe it was Phil Sanchez, maybe it was one of the other art instructors who'd wandered by and watched what was happening. I'd felt a kind of presence outside the door the whole time I was writing on the blackboard. But to turn my classroom over to him? That was a hell of a leap of faith.

I was in a leaping mood, I guess, because I said, 'Okay.' I groped my way out the classroom and I stood outside, pressed flat against the wall so I could peek in and see what was happening. My faith had a short leaping span.

Instantly the lights went back on.

'Let there be light,' Byron said. His hand was on the four light switches, the stub of his missing finger touching one of the switches.

'What the fuck?' someone said. Same guy.

350

'Must you use profanity,' the woman with the beret asked him, scowling.

'One man's profanity,' Byron said, wagging a finger at her, 'is another man's profundity.' He smiled at her and she smiled back, lapping up his charm.

I was hidden by the door so that none of the students could see me. Only Byron could, if he chose. Which he didn't. He began moving confidently around the classroom like a prosecuting attorney with a conviction in the bag.

I noticed for the first time that his face was battered and bruised. His jaw had two small Band-Aids. His nose was swollen, maybe even a little crooked under the swelling. A small cut angled down from his eyebrow. A longer cut near his ear had five or six stitches. The dragonfly earring was still there, though.

'Art, ladies and gentlemen, is illusion. *Art*-ificial. The history of art is like the history of magicians or politicians or just about anything else. In its history is revealed the technique for capturing the minds and hearts of the people, manipulating them so they see what the artist, magician, or politician wants them to see. That's the art part.'

'Where's Ms. Caldwell?' a no-nonsense man in a blue business suit asked.

'Who?'

'Our teacher.'

'What makes you think she's your teacher?'

The man looked confused by the question. 'She had the roster.'

'So every kid wearing a Superman cape can fly?' Byron picked up the roster from the podium where I'd left it. 'Besides, I have the roster now. Doesn't that make me your teacher?'

'That's ridiculous,' the man said. 'She's been teaching this class for over an hour.'

Byron pulled a rolled-up pamphlet out of his back pocket and waved it at the students. 'This schedule of

351

classes says Staff under name of instructor. Perhaps I'm the instructor and she was merely filling in for me.'

'Why?' one of the filmmakers asked.

'Because I asked her to? Because she gets paid to? Maybe I had a car accident that made me late.' He gestured at the cuts and bruises on his face. 'Lots of possibilities, aren't there?'

'This is ridiculous,' the businessman said again and stood up. He grabbed his briefcase. 'I'm going to see someone about this.'

I started to reenter the room. I didn't want to get fired, have any kind of investigation.

'Relax, sir,' Byron told him. 'Ms. Caldwell is fine. This was all part of a little demonstration she and I cooked up. Performance art, you might say, to help you understand the history of art better.' The man didn't sit down, but he didn't walk away, either. Byron swept past him and addressed the rest of the class. 'The history of art isn't just in studying works and memorizing artists. Art movements shouldn't be merely noted, like bowel movements. Art history is understanding the anguish of expression. What social and psychological forces lead to a new movement. Okay, everybody take out a blank piece of paper and draw a geometric design. Something of your own devising. Not too complex, not too simple. Come on. And don't take too long. I'm not collecting them.'

People started taking out paper and drawing. Even the businessman sat back down, removed a single sheet from his briefcase, and began drawing in earnest. His strokes were short and precise, like an accountant's.

'Hurry up,' Byron prodded. 'Just doodle, don't think. Remember, I'm not collecting them.'

I watched Byron pace around the room, looking over their shoulders, chuckling good-naturedly at some of the drawings. Receiving back a grateful smile from the student. I'd never seen this side of him before, the unleashed charm. He hadn't taught them a damn thing, yet in five minutes he was closer to them than I was after an hour of actual learning. But I knew him for what he was, a convict. With emphasis on con.

I took off my glasses. Tears had smudged the lenses, which I wiped on the hem of my blouse. I wasn't crying anymore, I wasn't shaking. I could go in and take over the class again. But I didn't. I was too fascinated watching him gleefully work the crowd, like a pickpocket in a crowded mall. I felt voyeuristic.

He clapped his hands. 'Okay, now fold the papers in half so no one else can see them.'

As they did so, he went around the room and collected them.

'Hey,' the pretty girl in the bib overalls protested. 'You said you weren't going to collect them.'

'I lied,' Byron said. 'Lesson number one. Art is lying. Whether it's a movie or a poem or a painting, it's a lie. That is, the artist uses lies as if they were colors to create something that forms a greater truth. Facts may be true, but they don't reveal the Truth. That's what an artist does. He or she doesn't paint an exact duplication of the subject because that's physically impossible. Instead, the artist presents a likeness. A likeness is what the artist sees influenced by his or her own unique memories and experiences.'

'I don't get it,' a woman said. 'We all see the same objects, no matter what our memories. A chair's a chair.'

I peeked in. She was in her early thirties and about six months pregnant.

'Come up to the blackboard and I'll show you.' He smiled encouragingly at her. 'That's what art is, right, showing not telling.'

She smiled back and stood up boldly. She went to the blackboard. 'How about you, young lady,' he said to the woman in the beret.

'Oh, no,' she said. 'I can't draw. I just like to watch.'

Byron made a leering face. 'Oh, you like to watch, do you? Already we have something in common.'

The class laughed. The beret woman shook her head in mock embarrassment, chuckling the whole time.

'Come on,' Byron said. 'It won't hurt a bit.'

The beret woman went to the blackboard and picked up a piece of chalk with trepidation, as if it were a loaded gun.

Byron quickly looked through the first few sketches he'd collected, selected one, and handed it to the businessman who'd threatened to leave. 'What's your name?'

'Ed Waldman.'

'Okay, Ed, this is what you do. I want you to give them verbal instructions on how to draw the design on this paper. They must follow every direction you give them. Only two stipulations: The artists can't ask questions and you can't use hand gestures, like drawing in the air. Simple enough?'

'Yes,' Ed said.

'Just be precise and clear. It's like you're going to talk down some nonpilot in an airplane after the pilot died of a heart attack.' Byron faced the blackboard. 'Artists, are you ready?' They nodded. Byron clapped his hands. 'Let the art begin.'

Ed studied the sheet. A little grin crept across his face. He looked confident that he would prove himself.

Ed gave directions. They were precise and clear. But by the time he spoke his second sentence, the pregnant woman and the beret woman was already drawing two different objects. Ed tried to guide them back with more complex directions, but that only made things worse. Boxes and triangles sprang up in a jumbled mess. Desperate, Ed started to draw in the air, which Byron quickly reminded him was against the rules. Sweat beaded along Ed's forehead as he continued explaining what was clearly hopeless.

'Okay,' Byron finally said. 'I think that's enough. Artists, thank you, you may be seated.' They returned to their desks. Byron took the sheet from Ed and went to the blackboard. With a few strokes he duplicated the drawing on the paper. Neither of the students' sketches remotely resembled either each other or Byron's sketch. Byron made a diving gesture with his hand, accompanied by an exploding sound. 'Crash and burn, Ed. Those planes are permanently grounded.'

The filmmaker who liked chase scenes laughed loudly.

Byron scratched his head. 'What the heck went wrong? Both artists heard the same instructions.'

A man with a bushy mustache raised his hand. 'They didn't hear what he was saying. They didn't follow his directions.'

'His directions weren't clear,' a woman at the back said. 'I tried to draw along and my picture doesn't match any of them.'

A few more opinions were shouted out, mixed with mumbled debate. Then Byron held up his hands. 'This is the artist's dilemma. To have something to say, but never sure the audience hears what he says, sees what he sees. Ed is the typical artist; the women at the blackboard are the typical audience. Now, all these historic art movements tried to make themselves heard using different techniqes. You'll learn all about that later. For now, it's enough that you understand the problem artists face.'

I walked back into the classroom as if we'd planned my cue. 'With that in mind, I want you to read chapters one through four for next week. I want to see a diary entry on each of the works shown in those pages.'

'Are we going to have two teachers from now on,' someone asked.

'No,' I said. 'This was a guest appearance. One night only.'

Some disappointed groans were heard as they filed out of the room. I didn't look at Byron until they were all gone.

'What happened to your face?' I asked.

'What happened to yours?'

'I asked first.'

He shrugged. 'I lost.'

'You lost? What the hell is it that you play, nude rugby?'

'Their season doesn't start for another month. You want tickets?'

'Do you really know anything about art or was that all bullshit and bluff?'

'Did it make sense?'

'Yeah, some,' I said. 'But then I don't know anything about art. Except for what's in Wren's notes and what I just got out of the library the past couple of days.'

'I know. I was listening. Bullshit and bluff.'

I pointed at his face. 'What really happened to your face?'

'Well, actually . . .' He touched the two Band-Aids on his jaw. 'These two are nicks from shaving. Someone must of run my razor blade through the washing machine.'

I looked away, embarrassed. 'I was drunk. I'm sorry.'

'It's okay. They have company now.'

I didn't know what else to say to him. I wasn't sure what I was feeling. Robby still perched heavily on my shoulders. 'This is weird, what you did. Turning out the lights and all. Very theatrical.' I shook my head. 'What were you doing here?'

'I was in a couple of Wren's art classes in college. That's how we met. At first, I was just meeting my general ed requirements with an easy course. After meeting Wren, though, I took more art classes just to be near her. That little blackboard exercise was one our professor used. He'd been doing it for sixteen years and it always turned out that way.' He sighed, looked around the classroom nostalgically. 'I don't know, I guess I thought seeing you impersonating Wren would remind me of her. Something sentimental like that. I was in an odd mood.'

'Did I remind you of her?'

His face stiffened a little. He seemed angry. 'Did you want to?'

'Look, Byron, I'm just trying to get by here. I don't

want to fight right now.' I backed away from him a couple of steps. 'Thank you for helping me out. Thank you for not pressing me about why I was crying. I'm fine now. I got my mind straight, boss. Won't happen again, I swear.' I gave him a Girl Scout salute.

He stared at me a long time. I couldn't read his expression, it was that prison-yard one he lapsed into every so often. Anger maybe. Or disappointment.

I didn't care. I wanted him to know I didn't care. 'I won't be home tonight,' I said. 'I'm going to see Davis.'

He nodded and walked toward the door, turning to tip an imaginary hat and say, 'Good-bye, Wren.'

Then he was gone.

26

I rang the bell twice. The chimes sounded the first few notes of 'I Whistle a Happy Tune' from *The King and I*.

Davis opened the door. He had a script folded back in one hand and his reading glasses on. His son Mark was standing next to him holding a Nintendo Gameboy. They looked oddly comic, unmistakably father and son. The mixture of bright light and loud sound of the TV emanating from behind them was warm and comforting. A place of families. More than anything else in the world, I wanted to be inside that house.

'Hi, Mark,' I said from the front stoop.

'Hi, Wren,' he said. 'You wanna play with my Gameboy?'

'You bet. But not right now, okay?'

'Okay.' He ran back inside and plopped down three feet from the giant TV screen.

'I thought you didn't want to see me tonight?' Davis said.

'I changed my mind,' I said. 'Is that allowed?'

'Is this the first Monday of a month with a full moon?'

'I have no idea.'

He smiled and kissed my cheek. 'It's allowed.'

We walked into the living room. Mark offered me a bowl of stubby pretzel sticks.

'No, thanks,' I said.

'They're filled with peanut butter. They taste great.'

I took a handful, saw his face gloom over, released half

of them back in the bowl. He smiled and pulled the bowl away before I took any more.

Davis sat on the sofa beside me. 'Mark's mother has a date tonight. Since I didn't have plans, I said I'd watch him.'

'Where's Judy?'

'Girlfriend's house.'

'I don't have any friends,' Mark said casually, his eyes on the Gameboy that he was playing with.

'Sure you do, Mark,' Davis said. 'What about Aaron Bloom?'

'He's a jerk.'

Davis shrugged at me. 'Last week they were best friends. They wanted me to show them how to become bloodbrothers. They were going to cut themselves with a fish scaling knife Aaron found in his dad's tackle box.'

'He's a jerk,' Mark repeated.

'Why is he a jerk?' I asked Mark.

Mark shrugged without looking up from his game.

I looked at Davis. He shrugged too.

I helped Davis put Mark to bed. As we were all walking up the stairs, Mark said to me, 'Mom lets me stay up later.' He wasn't complaining, merely pointing out an interesting fact, as if he had recently figured out that the world's rules weren't all the same, they changed from household to household. And if they weren't all the same, maybe they weren't automatically good rules.

Once Mark was tucked under the covers, Davis took the Gameboy. 'You need your sleep, pal. You've got soccer practice tomorrow.'

'Big deal. I stink at soccer.'

'All the more reason to practice.'

'Dad, if I practice and practice and practice, will I be the best soccer player in the world?'

'Depends how much you practice.'

'Dad, you've seen me play.'

Davis laughed. 'Okay, you won't be the best in the world, but you'll be better than you are now.'

'Well, if I'll never be the best, what's the point?'

Davis looked at me. 'Got an answer I could borrow? Preferably something wise and witty. Something he'll remember fondly years from now.'

'I'm tapped out in the wise and witty department.'

'Sorry, Mark,' Davis said. 'Guess you're just going to have to trust me on this one.'

'You always say that.'

'Have I ever been wrong?'

'About a billion trillion times.'

'Hey, anybody can make a billion trillion mistakes once in a while.'

Mark giggled. Davis kissed his cheek. I patted his chest. I didn't feel comfortable doing anything more maternal. I wasn't yet sure where I fit in the familial structure and I didn't want to confuse the boy.

Davis closed the door to Mark's bedroom. He led me to his own bedroom. I knew the way.

'We have the Gameboy!' he said, cackling like a mad scientist. 'It's all ours, they can't stop us now! Ha, ha, ha!'

Nothing stopped us. We made love with Davis behind me again. I was on my knees, rump in the air, head down on a pillow as if I were praying to Mecca. He had his fingers hooked around my hip bones as he pummeled me, our slapping skin making rude noises. At one point he took my hand and placed it on my vagina, guiding my middle finger to my clitoris. I rubbed it vigorously and we both got so excited we came together shortly thereafter.

'How did class go?' he asked, lying beside me, one leg thrown over my legs.

'Fine.'

I was lying on my back, he was lying on his side.

'Fine?' he repeated. 'Nothing unusual?'

'Nothing to make a movie out of.'

'Low blow,' he laughed. 'Of course, if you're going to blow, low is the place to do it.'

I told him a little about class, the students, the confrontation with the guy who refused to leave, Carol Hill's toilets, some of what I'd taught in class because I knew it made me seem smarter than I was. I didn't mention Robby. Or Byron. Those incidents didn't fit into the image I had created for Davis. My forgery of Wren Caldwell.

Davis reached over and pressed a button on the remote control and the TV clicked on. My head was hanging backward off the edge of the bed, so I watched the screen upside down. A male news announcer was talking about gang violence in Los Angeles. A stray bullet had killed a ten-year-old innocent bystander playing in her yard. Then the female newscaster discussed AIDS testing in local high schools. I flopped over to watch the rest. Davis began scratching my back.

'Don't you get the sports channel?' I said. He didn't answer. I pulled the fluffy down quilt around me like a nest and propped my head up on both hands. Davis's fingernails raked lazily over my back. I started to nod off. What would it be like to wake up in this bed every morning, I wondered.

'Jesus!' Davis said, sitting up in bed.

Startled, I sat up too. I forced my eyes open, but I felt groggy, disoriented. 'What? What's the matter?'

Davis didn't answer. He was watching the television screen. I turned and watched too. A newswoman was standing outside a suburban home. Her face was clenched in a serious expression. A breeze kept whipping a lock of her dark hair across her chin. In the background, yellow police tape could be seen and milling men in uniforms. The words LYDIA ROSS and LIVE flashed across the bottom of the screen.

' . . . family and friends were shocked . . .'

I looked at the clock. I thought I'd just closed my eyes but I'd been asleep for fifteen minutes.

' . . . Denver authorities say the suspect has offered a full confession.' A Denver Police Department spokesperson came on the screen. The name Sgt. Wanda Fueher was on the screen beneath her. 'We have the suspect,

Roger Clemens, in custody. He has offered a full confession in the shooting of Ms. Christine Palmer. Apparently, he'd been stalking her for six months, ever since the operation. Ms. Palmer had gone to court last week and gotten a restraining order against Roger Clemens, preventing him from coming within 1,000 yards of her.'

'Did you know her?' I asked Davis.

'Sshh.' His eyes were fixed on the screen.

A psychiatrist was being interviewed. Dr. Philip Rardin. He was balding and his forehead was knotted in three deep furrows. 'It is not unusual sometimes for a young man to become obsessed with the sister or cousin of a loved one when she dies. He feels such unbearable grief that he must transfer his passion somewhere or explode.' Cut to a reaction shot of reporter Lydia Ross, looking serious again. Back to the shrink. 'In Mr. Clemens's case his wife was killed in a car accident. They both had agreed to be donors and her heart was transplanted into Christine Palmer. Usually the recipient of such a heart would be an older person, but in this case Ms. Palmer was a young woman about the same age as the dead wife. So it was easier for him to obsess on her.'

Cut back to Lydia Ross. She was walking now, slowly strolling down the sidewalk as if, now that the event was over, we should consider it from a philosophical position. 'And obsess he did. Following his wife's funeral and Christine Palmer's release from the hospital, Roger Clemens began following Christine Palmer. He called her at home, sometimes a dozen times a day. He sent her letters, cards, gifts. He offered to take her to Jamaica for two weeks. Apparently that was where he and his wife had honeymooned. Finally, Christine, still weak as she struggled to adjust to her new heart, petitioned the court to keep her unwanted suitor at an arm's distance. Today, the arm's distance proved not to be far enough. Not when there's a gun at the end of that arm.' She arched an eyebrow as if to say, Get it?

'Thank you, Lydia,' the anchorwoman said and introduced the sportscaster.

Davis swung his legs off the bed and picked up the phone. 'I'm sorry, Wren. I have to be going. I'm terribly sorry.'

'Did you know her?'

'No. This is just business. I have to go to Denver.' He started dialing.

'Christ, Davis. You're not going after her family for their story. Jesus.'

'Not their story. His. Roger Clemens.' He held up his hand to indicate he had someone on the line. He spoke into the phone. 'What's the next flight you have to Denver . . . No, it doesn't have to be direct . . . That's too late. What about through LAX? . . . Okay, that's good.' He made a reservation, giving his Mastercard number and expiration date.

When he hung up I said, 'I've never known anyone who knew their credit card number by heart.'

'It's a gift.'

We looked at each other. I squeezed the down comforter. I would not be waking up here in the morning. The bathroom had a skylight. When you showered, the sunlight spotlighted you. I would not be showering here in the morning. The sun would not be spotlighting me.

'I have to call my sister,' he said. He dialed again. His sister agreed to watch Mark for the night and take him back to his mother in the morning. Her voice was very loud and agitated. Before hanging up, I heard her say, 'I wish we were married sometimes so I could divorce you too.'

'See you soon, sis.' Davis hung up and stared at me again. 'I'm terribly sorry. You don't know how sorry. But I have to go. It's business.' He shook his head. 'I know that sounds lame.'

'Do you really think people want to see a movie about a woman who's stalked by the widower of the woman whose heart she received in a transplant?'

'Absolutely. We'll get some too-handsome actor in a

series who's looking to break his nice-guy image and prove he has depth. I expect it will be a big hit.' He stood up and pulled on his underpants. 'The only question now is who will produce this hit, me or some other guy.'

'Doesn't it bother you, flitting from personal tragedy to personal tragedy, like a bee flying from flowers somebody stepped on, trying to suck out the last drop?'

'That's good,' he chuckled. 'Now I remember why I hired you.'

'This kind of thing isn't entertainment, it's tragedy.'

'Shakespeare wrote tragedies, right?'

'Yes, but he gave us some insight into the nature of people. These movies aren't tragedy, they're gossip.' Davis didn't respond. His jaw was clenched as he busied himself looking for shoes. He looked hurt. I felt bad. I softened my tone. 'I don't know, Davis, it all seems so ghoulish.'

'It *is* ghoulish. It's ghoulish, morbid, twisted, and a few other words we could come up with if we put our heads to it. Don't you think I know that? But I do it now so that in a couple years I can see this kind of thing on the news and send some other schmuck to Bumfuck, Egypt, in the middle of the night. Then I can go to sleep with my wife and watch my kid play soccer the next day. What's wrong with that?'

'Nothing,' I admitted. Besides, who was I to be pointing fingers. Talk about ghoulish, I stole my dead friend's identity and now was interviewing a murderer for money. If it weren't for dead people, I wouldn't have a life.

While Davis hurriedly got dressed and packed, I went into the bathroom, closed the door, and sat on the toilet. I had to pee, but sometimes right after sex it takes me a while to get the tap flowing. I picked up a magazine from the stack in the wall rack. An airline magazine. A piece of paper, an old airline ticket receipt, marked one of the articles. I opened it on my lap and started reading. It was about Mark Spitz trying to make a swimming comeback at the next Olympics. He trained very hard every day, swam laps, watched what he ate. I got very excited thinking about training, what it would be like to work out hard every day, how good you must feel about yourself. I decided then I would take up swimming, buy a pair of goggles, and swim laps in the pool at my apartment complex.

I ended up not peeing. I flushed anyway because what would he think I was doing in here all this time if I didn't.

When I went back into the bedroom, Davis was dressed and ready. He wore a blue Polo shirt, khaki pants, and a tweedish sports jacket. His leather overnight bag was slung over his shoulder. 'You almost ready?'

'Take me one minute.'

'Okay, I'll see how Mark's coming along.' He dashed down the hallway.

I was dressed in less than a minute. I made the bed, tugging the fluffy down quilt into place. Then I sat on the edge of the bed and waited, reading the article. I noticed notations in the margins in Davis's handwriting. *Ken Olin as Mark Spitz? Jamie Lee Curtis as wife?*

'Ready?' Davis leaned in the doorway. 'We're ready.'

'Can I borrow this magazine?' I asked. 'I want to finish an article.'

'You have two forms of ID?'

We dropped Mark off at Davis's sister's house in Newport Beach, then we drove to LAX, which took about forty minutes.

'You don't have to wait,' he said. 'You can just drop me off at the curb.'

'I'll wait.'

He smiled. 'Good.'

We had coffee and donuts in the airport cafeteria. We held hands across the table. Granules of salt or sugar from previous customers ground under our wrists. We talked about actresses who'd had breast implants, then we talked about Denver, where he'd never been.

'All I know about Denver is what John Denver sings,' he said.

'Did you know John Denver's real name is John Deutschendorf?' I said.

'Someone gave him some good advice to change it.'

'You don't mind someone changing their name?'

'Hey, that's show business. Who's going to take him seriously if his name is Deutschendorf? Makes him sound like a Nazi collaborator.'

'It means "German village".' He gave me an impressed expression. 'I had two years of German in high school.'

When we got to his gate, he hugged me close. His breath smelled like coffee. 'I'll be back in a day or so.'

'I'll be here.'

'I'll call. God, I don't want to leave you.'

'Don't.'

He sighed. 'Thanks for making it easy on me.'

'I'm sorry, I'm being selfish. Have a good flight. Get everybody's life story while you're there so you won't have to go back every time somebody commits a crime. Say hi to Mr. Deutschendorf. Have a Rocky Mountain high.'

He started to say something, then stopped. He shook his head and said, 'I'm afraid to say anything. I mean anything real. Like you'll have a clever comeback and I'll feel stupid.'

I started to say something like 'If you think what I'm saying is clever, you've been in Hollywood too long.' But I stopped myself. Instead I just leaned against him. He wrapped his arms around me and squeezed hard. It was like being back in that down quilt again, or standing in the shower under the skylight, the hot morning sun warming your face, water washing you clean.

*   *   *   *   *

The drive back to my apartment went quickly. I listened to a talk radio station where they discussed the water shortage in Lourdes. Five million pilgrims visit the city each year to drink from the holy waters or bathe in them. For the first time, Lourdes is rationing the water to protect its 400-million-dollar annual income.

'Try the shower at Davis's house,' I said aloud. 'Same effect.'

Then I started thinking about Byron and how he'd marched into my classroom and taken over. That goofy drawing exercise of his had actually been a good idea. I thought of his face, battered and scarred, my own contributions on his chin. Jesus, what a life. What had he and Wren had in common? What had gone wrong?

I checked my rearview mirror for the white Subaru. Nothing.

Still, what Byron had done had helped me at the time. I had been falling apart. Robby was going to be a father. How many hours had he and I discussed that very issue. When we would have a child, what conditions were necessary for us to do a good job. How often we'd debated as to who would be the better parent. I'd voted for Robby. So had he.

Suddenly, while changing lanes on the 405 Freeway, I realized I wanted a baby. I wanted one right way, right that moment, or at least the inevitability of one. If an all-night insemination clinic were open, I'd have driven right in, spread my legs, and said, 'Okay, shoot me up with a kid.'

I pulled into an all-night drugstore instead. The store was brightly lighted and the aisles were packed with plastic-wrapped goodies. I found a pair of swim goggles in the sports department. They only had one kind, with blue lenses, so I bought it. Then I went to the jewelry counter and looked at the watches. I picked a man's Casio with all kinds of functions and dials. It cost eighty dollars, which I charged. It was a gift for Byron.

I was kind of excited now as I drove into the complex and parked the car. Byron had lost everything, including his watch, gambling. This would show him how much I appreciated what he'd done for me.

As I approached the front door I could hear Ethan's guitar upstairs. His windows were all closed, though, so I couldn't hear what he was singing. I couldn't even make out the melody clearly.

I entered the front door, quietly tiptoeing across the living room. The alarm clock/radio next to Byron's bed was playing some tinny music, jazz, I thought. Good, he was still awake. I could surprise him with my gift.

I sneaked into the kitchen to put down my purse, maybe grab a couple beers to set the spirit. But when I walked into the kitchen I saw the bird cage back in the middle of the floor, one of Wren's designer sheets thrown over it. I hoisted up the sheet and discovered Motown nodding off on his perch. What the hell was he doing back?

Footsteps.

I backed up behind the swinging door just as it eased open. The room was dark so it was hard for me to recognize anything more than a human form moving toward the refrigerator. Then the door opened and the refrigerator light snapped a beam of light on the figure.

She was tall, over six feet, slender through the waist and narrow at her hips. Her skin was dark, her thick braided hair hanging down her back to her waist like a black eel. She looked Native American.

Also, she was buck naked.

27

'Who the hell are you?' I said.

She didn't look up from the refrigerator. She studied the contents a few seconds, reached in for a couple cans of beer, and closed the door with her hip.

'I asked who you are?' I was shouting, I don't know why. I mean, what difference did it make who she was, I had a pretty good idea what she was doing and with whom. Even so, what did I care?

She still didn't answer me. When she turned toward the kitchen door with her beers, she noticed me and jumped back, startled. But she didn't say anything.

The kitchen door swung open and Byron entered, wearing those ratty volleyball shorts I'd first seen him in the day he ambushed Davis and me. The day he stepped on that snail. His shorts were on backward, which indicated the haste with which he'd dressed. His long hair was disheveled, no longer pulled into his ponytail. His dragonfly earring was not dangling from his lobe. He looked at me. 'Oh, hi,' he said.

The woman, more beautiful then I'd realized before, smiled at me. She handed a beer to Bryon and offered the other one to me with a gesture.

'No, I don't want a goddamn beer,' I snapped. 'Christ!'

The woman didn't say anything. She shrugged, popped the tab, and sipped some beer. Her dark nipples seemed enormous, like brown thumbs.

'No point in yelling at Shawna,' Byron said. 'She's deaf.'

'And mute, I suppose.'

'Yup.'

Shawna put her beer can on the counter and made some rapid hand gestures at Byron. He made some back. Shawna laughed. Her laugh was like a dry cough.

'You know sign language?' I said to Byron.

'ASL. American Sign Language.'

I don't know why, but this angered me even more. He had so many secrets. I only had one and he knew it.

'I took it in college as my second language,' he said. 'I thought it would be easier than Spanish.'

'Seems like your whole life has been seeking the path of least resistance.'

'Works for water, doesn't it?'

'How zen of you.' I looked over at Shawna. She drank from her beer can without any display of modesty. Not that she had anything to be modest about. Her body was perfect in ways you never thought existed outside air-brushed magazines. It made me want to put on more clothes. 'Doesn't she want to get dressed or something?'

He gestured at Shawna. She responded.

'What did she say?'

'She wants to know what you're doing in my apartment.'

'Your apartment, huh?'

'I thought I'd explained everything to her. Guess my sign language is a little rusty.'

I looked at Shawna and she smiled again. Her teeth were perfect slabs of light, white marble doors to some exotic palace. A drop of condensation dripped from her beer can, bounced onto her stomach, and rolled into the thicket of black pubic hair. She caught me looking and her smile widened. I looked away, embarrassed.

'What's the bird doing back?' I said. 'I thought you lost it.'

'I did. To Shawna.'

'Then who beat you up? Shawna?'

'Someone else. It's complicated.'

That was it. I was standing in my own home being treated like a child too stupid to understand the big bad world. No more. I grabbed his shorts by the waistband, pulled them open, and stuffed the Save-on Drugs paperbag with the watch and goggles down the front. 'For you,' I said. 'Thanks.'

'Owww,' he jerked away from me. He reached down and pulled the bag out.

I straight-armed the door open and marched out of the kitchen and down the hall toward Byron's room. 'I've had it with all this mystery bullshit. It's complicated? Let me help you simplify it.' I stormed into his bedroom, grabbed a handful of clothing from the closet, and carried it to the front door. I opened the door and tossed everything onto the sidewalk. 'There, does that make things simpler?'

Byron was strapping on the watch to his wrist. 'Hey, a new watch. Thanks.'

'That's okay,' I said. I returned to the bedroom, opened a drawer, scooped up an armful of underwear and socks, and carried them back to the front door. Heave ho. Onto the sidewalk.

'It's got a stopwatch too,' he said with delight. 'Cool.'

'I'm glad you like it.' Back to the bedroom. Shawna was in there now, pulling on her jeans without any underwear. When she hiked the jeans over her hips, her buttocks didn't bunch up around her spine like with most women. The jeans just slid over the dark, solid muscle. She slipped into a sweatshirt, not bothering with a bra. I dug into the next drawer and came up with an armful of T-shirts. She came over, pulled open a third drawer, and picked up a couple of new sweaters.

We formed a mini parade out to the living room. Byron was sitting in the front stoop reading the directions for his watch. His clothes lay scattered across the sidewalk five feet away. 'It's got three alarms and counts laps when you swim. Are the goggles for me too?'

I tossed my armload onto the sidewalk. Shawna did the

371

same thing. On the way back in I snatched the goggles from his hand.

Shawna laughed her hoarse laugh and gestured at Byron. He gestured back.

'What?' I said.

'She says you must know me pretty well to dislike me this much.'

'Did you tell her who I am?'

'Who's that?'

'Don't play zen master with me, okay? Did you tell her I was your wife Wren or your roommate Luna?'

'What's the difference?' he said. 'You afraid she'll talk?'

'You're sick.' I was suddenly exhausted from throwing his stuff out. I went into the living room and flopped onto the sofa. Shawna went to the kitchen and brought me a beer. 'Thanks,' I said.

'This is thanks in ASL,' Byron said, sitting on the floor across from me. He brought his hand up to his lips as if to stifle a yawn, then pushed his hand away and down. 'See?'

I repeated the gesture to Shawna. She extended her hand palm up out to the side and sliced it inward toward her waist.

'That's "welcome,"' Byron said.

I sipped the beer and closed my eyes. What was I doing here? I had been carefully creating a perfect life for myself, sketching in a proper profession, painting a rich background. Okay, so I was borrowing a bit from Wren, not unlike an artist imitating a better artist's style. A homage really. Truffaut imitating Hitchcock. The only problem was my work was being populated with characters from someone else's weird imagination. Byron, the battered gambler. Shawna, the deaf and mute beauty. Motown, the soul-singing bird. And, of course, Hector. The cat.

Byron stood up and closed the front door. He'd made no effort to retrieve his clothing. That made me edgy, as if I'd somehow littered and everyone passing by would know.

'Don't you want your stuff?' I said.

He looked up from his watch, which he was still toying with. 'I know where it is.'

'Someone might take it.'

He shrugged. 'They'd have to be pretty hard up.'

'These are hard-up times.'

He laughed heartily, made some gestures at Shawna. They both laughed together.

'What?' I said. 'What's so funny?'

'What you said. "These are hard-on times."'

'I said hard-up not hard-on.'

He shrugged again. 'Oh. I thought you said hard-on.'

'Aren't you going to tell her?' I pointed to Shawna. I didn't want her thinking I'd said what I hadn't.

'Why ruin the joke?' he said and sat down on the floor next to Shawna.

There's a strange helplessness in having someone in the room with whom you can't communicate. It makes you feel like you need to be on your best behavior because if they can't understand your words, they would try to figure you out by observation. I caught myself gnawing my cuticles and lowered my hand.

The other thing that bothered me was that Shawna and I were both women, but the only way we could communicate was through a man. There was something sinister in that. Something wrong.

'You mustn't think very much of me to have her over and not even close your bedroom door,' I said to Byron.

'You told me you wouldn't be home tonight, remember? What happened to Davis?'

I didn't answer. Hector slinked into the room, walked around rubbing against everyone's leg, then left.

Shawna stood up, gestured, and followed Hector into the kitchen. I heard her opening a can of cat food.

'What is she, some kind of Indian?'

'Italian. But she likes to cultivate the whole Native

373

American image. It's cooler to be Apache than Italian.'

'Where'd you meet her?'

'She's a player.'

I made a skeptical face. 'Why is it so hard to believe anything you say?'

'No one else has a problem believing me.'

'Maybe they don't know you.'

He laughed harshly. 'You don't know me.'

'I know you didn't learn sign language in college. You're too good, too fast for someone just looking for easy credits. That takes years of constant practice, like playing the piano.'

'That's very good. Okay, you caught me. You wanted some truth, okay, here's some truth: My father was deaf. He wasn't born that way, it happened to him in high school. Got an ear infection and that was that. He was an art director for an advertising agency. He died in a hotel fire at a convention because he couldn't hear the fire alarm. Smoke inhalation.' He smiled. 'But I really did take ASL in college. I pretended I didn't know any so I could get the easy language credits.'

'Why didn't you just tell me that in the first place? Why this constant Man o' Mystery act?'

His face got serious. 'You want to know why I don't tell you anything? I'll tell you why. Because my life isn't just background for your impersonation. I'm not just a prop so you can be more and more like Wren. What you're doing is sick.'

'Gee, moral lectures from you really carry a lot of weight. I'm sure your pals at the prison appreciated it as much as I do. Did you hold sermons in the showers?'

'Don't feel so fucking superior to them. One call to the cops and you could be in a cell yourself.'

I jumped up and started screaming. 'Don't threaten me in my own home! You want to make a call?' I marched over to the phone, picked it up, and threw it at him. The receiver flew off and clipped him on the shoulder. 'Then just fucking do it! Do it! Do it!'

I was trembling, knees shaking, eyes burning. I was scaring myself.

He looked at me for a long time. Then a slow grin spread across his face. 'I didn't know you were such a screamer. From what I heard of you and your boyfriend this afternoon, you're more of a moaner.'

I froze, my face flushed. My voice went small. 'You were here?'

'Just for a quick nap. I'd been up all night playing. But how could I sleep with the two of you in the same house. Don't you know that bathrooms magnify sound?' He laughed.

'You're a pig,' I said. 'It's no wonder Wren dumped you.'

His face tightened. I'd hurt him. Good. 'You don't know shit about what happened between Wren and me. You think you do, but you don't.'

'I know she never wanted to see you again. If you're so fucking wise, Confucius, how come you couldn't hold on to her?'

His jaw clenched the way Davis's had earlier when I'd hurt him. Only this time I didn't feel sorry.

Byron unstrapped the watch from his wrist and tossed it to me. 'Here. I didn't come into your classroom to help you. I just didn't want you to ruin Wren's name any more with your pathetic performance.'

My mouth tasted like a toxic waste dump. I was dizzy with anger. 'You don't want this watch?' I said calmly. I put the watch on the floor and started stomping on it. I looked down but I could see it was still working. I jumped on it with all my might, but the shockproof cover wouldn't break. I picked it up by the strap and started whacking it against the edge of the coffee table. Finally the cover shattered. I tossed the broken watch back at him. 'Check your warranty.'

Shawna came back in carrying Hector. Hector was licking his lips.

I put my hands together as if to pray and pressed them

against my cheek to indicate sleep. Shawna laughed and nodded understanding. She waved. I went to my room and closed the door.

I washed my face, brushed my teeth, and peed. I undressed to my panties and climbed into bed. My body was still trembling with emotion. I pulled the covers tight around me, using the edge of my hand to tuck the blanket along the outline of my body. I smoothed out every wrinkle.

I was scared. This wasn't me. I wasn't sure it was Wren either. I had never acted with such manic passion before, not even when Robby left me. It was as if I'd tapped some underground oil well and my bile was gushing all over the wildcatters. Or like a science fiction film. I was the nice scientist trying to create something good for humanity, only to have my creation turn into something horrible: half human/half fly; half human/half wolf; half human/half Luna.

I tried to sleep. But every time I'd nod off some horrible nightmare would jolt me awake. At 3:18 A.M. I was still staring at the clock.

Down the hall I heard noises. Bedboards creaking. Mattress bouncing. Grunting. Strangled cries. I listened, watched the clock. 3:23. 3:35. 3:42. The noises didn't stop.

At 3:45 I reached down under the covers and slipped my panties off. I slid my fingers between my legs. I was a little sore from having had sex with Davis twice today. But I didn't stop. I couldn't have stopped.

28

In my dream, I was walking down a long hospital corridor. But there were no doctors or patients. At first I thought I was alone, but then I felt the pressure of a pair of strong hands holding on to my waist and I knew somehow that Davis was behind me and that Byron was holding his waist behind him and that Robby was behind him. I didn't know who else was back there, but I was certain they went on for several miles like an enormous cha-cha line.

I turned quickly to try to see Davis, but as soon as I moved, they all swung behind me so I couldn't see any of them. I took another couple of steps, pretending to ignore them, then I suddenly whirled around to catch them off guard. But they must have whirled too, because no one was there. I was like the head of a long fat caterpillar, I could never see my body. I looked down at the hands gripping my waist. One was female, the other male.

'Oh, I get it,' I said aloud. 'This is some sort of yin-yang thing, right? Some male/female conflict, right side of the brain battling with the left side? Right?'

'One, two, cha cha cha . . .' someone in line behind me answered. It sounded like Paul Simon.

But then I walked into a hospital room. It was a birthing room, one of the new kind made to look like a bedroom. Wren was there. And Esther. Esther's cat, Sphinx, was on the white bed. They all looked happy to see me.

'Get in,' Wren said, gesturing at the bed.

'Will we all fit?' I asked, hooking a thumb over my shoulder at my entourage.

She laughed and helped me into the bed. The cat curled up on my lap. Esther expertly injected me with a shot in the arm and Wren began attaching tubes to my arms, legs, and nose.

'This is just like the dream sequences on St. Elsewhere,' I said. 'Remember that show?'

'I could never stay awake that late,' Esther said. She stifled a yawn.

'What's going on?' I said.

'You want to be just like us,' Wren said. 'The doctor will help.'

'I don't want to be like BeeGee,' I said. 'No offense, Esther.'

Esther had nodded off. She snored to the melody of 'I Whistle a Happy Tune.'

I started scratching the cat's neck. I felt so happy to be there, like I could relax for the first time. No secrets.

'You guys look good,' I said.

'Think so?' Wren said. She grinned and nodded at my hand that was scratching the cat. I looked down. My fingers were covered with blood and matted fur. I'd scratched the cat's fur off his head as if it were a mask. Sphinx turned and looked at me, his face a bloody clump of muscle and bone. A bullet was lodged in his cheek.

Wren reached up and pulled off her own face. She nudged Esther awake with an elbow and Esther also began yanking her face off. Beneath their rubbery masks were the same wide-eyed bloody messes of bone and sinew, like in an anatomy book.

'The doctor's here, Luna,' Wren said. 'Now you can be just like us. For real.'

Season Dougherty walked into the room wearing a doctor's green operating uniform, only hers had big prison stripes on them. She carried a shotgun.

'Hi, Wren,' she said to me. She aimed the shotgun at my crotch. 'You may feel a little discomfort.'

She fired.

*   *   *   *   *

That's pretty much how the rest of the night went. I couldn't sleep most of it, and when I did manage to drift off for a few minutes, I'd get sucked into another nightmarish horror that shocked me awake with cold sweats.

I tried reading once, finishing that article about Mark Spitz I'd borrowed from Davis. Afterward I managed to kill twenty minutes wondering how my life might have been different if I'd have won a gold medal in something at the Olympics.

About five in the morning I actually got up and put on my swimsuit. I figured that if I couldn't sleep this was as good a time as any to begin my new swimming program. I even tried on my goggles and looked at myself in the mirror. The blue lens made everything seem as if I were already underwater. Anyway, I never made it out of the bedroom. I stripped down and went back to bed.

At 6:45 A.M. I was working on a plan to murder Byron and hack up the body into cat food that I would feed to Hector. Maybe when he was gone I could rent the room to Shawna. When she wasn't fucking like an Amazon warrior-queen, she was pretty quiet. I could learn sign language and she and I could go to lunch and gossip about people at the next table without them knowing. We could 'talk' in the movies and no one would tell us to shut up. We'd be like secret agents, living undercover among the unsuspecting suburbanites, acting like them, eating the same foods, wearing the same clothes. Until our government activated us.

God, is this how BeeGee had lived for so long? All those years without proper sleep, night after night, her mind rambling on and on. I was nuts after only one night.

I guess the question isn't what caused Esther to finally snap, but what took her so damn long?

'"*I saw a stranger with your hair/Tried to make her give it back . . .*"'

I opened my eyes. The music was faint, but distinct.

'" . . . *So I could send it off to you/Maybe Federal Express . . .*"'

I looked at my clock. 7:12 A.M. I must have dozed for a few minutes, I dragged myself to the edge of the bed and sat there, unable to get up or even focus my gritty eyes.

The phone rang. I reached for my nightstand, only to remember that I was no longer living in the bedroom with the phone. Didn't matter. The ringing stopped.

'Hey, Wren,' Byron hollered from down the hall. 'For you. It's the Academy Award people. I think you've been nominated.'

I pulled on some sweatpants and a T-shirt and pattered off to the kitchen phone. When I opened the kitchen door, Motown, whose cage was no longer covered by a sheet, started singing, '"*Baby love . . . baby love . . .*" awwwk.'

I picked up the phone. 'Hello?'

'Tell me you miss me more than anything in the world or I'll kill myself with a rusty razor.'

'Who is this?' I said.

'Very funny.' Davis chuckled. 'You're not very romantic in the morning.'

'Rough night. I didn't get any sleep.'

'At least lie and tell me it was because you were missing me.'

'It's because I was missing you.'

'You're lying.'

I laughed. 'Not entirely. I do miss you. The only time my life has any sanity to it is when I'm with you.'

'If that ain't love, what is?'

'You know what I mean. You run off in the middle of the night, but at least you're honest about it. There are no secrets. I'm tired of secrets.'

380

There was a pause. 'You okay, sweetheart? You don't sound so hot.'

'I'm just tired. I didn't sleep all night. Did I already say that?'

'Yes. Maybe you should stay in bed today, rest.'

'No can do. I've got Season Dougherty sitting in a cell waiting for me to come over and rip her guts out with some of my insightful yet subtle questions.'

'You can take a day off,' he said. 'Lie to your boss.'

'My boss would know. He knows everything.' I was touched by the compassion in his voice. 'When you coming home, Red Ryder?'

'I don't know yet. Negotiations are tricky right now. Lots of lawyers smelling money. State laws prohibiting criminals to profit from their crimes. Et cetera, et cetera. Probably won't be back till tomorrow.'

'Oh.' I let my disappointment come through. He would appreciate it.

Byron walked into the kitchen. He was wearing nothing but those same stupid shorts. As he passed me I could smell the moist scent of sex. A couple of the stitches next to his ear had come out. He stopped at the bird cage, reached a finger in, and started scratching behind Motown's neck. Motown bent his head forward and snuggled up to Byron's finger.

'Say something romantic to keep me going,' Davis said. 'If you can't be romantic, dirty will do.'

I turned my back on Byron so he couldn't overhear me. I lowered my voice. 'Hurry home, okay? I miss you.'

'I miss you, too.' He paused again as if to say something. He sighed. 'I miss you. I really do.'

We repeated ourselves a few more times and then hung up.

Byron was still scratching the bird's neck. Just looking at Byron made me angry again. Certainly he was to blame for my not sleeping. Still, this was no way to act. One of us had to be mature.

381

'I didn't know you could do that,' I said. 'Scratch them like that.'

'They love it.'

'I figured they'd bite your finger off.'

'Only if you do it wrong.' He held up his right hand and wiggled his stump.

'Is that how you lost your finger?' I was just trying to make conversation, be friendly. I didn't even care anymore how he lost his stupid finger.

He ignored my question anyway and started singing to Motown. 'Love child, love child . . .'

'You really are an asshole,' I shouted. 'Why can't you just act like a normal human being for five fucking minutes? Would it kill you, you obnoxious piece of shit?'

Motown sang, '"*Love child . . . love child . . .*"'

Byron opened the refrigerator, took out a carton of orange juice, and walked out of the kitchen without responding to me. I was so furious that I looked around for something to throw at him, a knife or a hammer. All I could see at that instant was the folded sheet that had covered Motown's cage overnight. I grabbed it from the table and burst through the kitchen door in a rage. He was walking down the hall drinking from the juice carton. I hurled the folded sheet at him, but it blossomed open like a parachute and fluttered harmlessly to the ground before reaching him.

He stopped, looked over his shoulder at the sheet, at me. He snorted and went in the bedroom.

I had never in my life wanted to kill anybody. Until that moment. If there'd been a shotgun in my room, within twenty minutes I'd have been in the cell next to Season Dougherty.

I looked around for something to break, but I didn't see anything that I wouldn't later regret having smashed. I went back to my room. It was later than I'd realized so I had to skip my shower and get dressed as quickly as I could. I didn't want to be late for my meeting with Season. I had a feeling that she looked forward to our conversations. I don't know if we were friends exactly, but I think we trusted each other somehow. Maybe because I didn't judge her, maybe because she sensed I wasn't in a position to judge her. I actually felt good sitting there with her, the way I used to feel sitting with Wren and BeeGee, munching microwave popcorn, watching David Letterman on the TV in the refrigerator.

On my way out of the apartment I heard the familiar creaking of bedboards and the muffled throat spasms of Shawna's orgasms. Hector was waiting for me at the door. I noticed the smashed Casio watch I'd bought Byron was fastened around Hector's neck along with the flea collar. He sat next to the door as if he couldn't wait for me to go so the real fun could begin.

I opened the front door. Byron's clothing was still strewn across the sidewalk. I walked on top of it, grinding my heels into the fabrics with each step. That felt good.

When I arrived at the police station, I realized that in my hurry to get out of the apartment I'd pulled on a sleeveless sweater. My clean-shaven underarms, freshly sealed with Arid roll-on, were exposed. Season might balk at them, refuse to see me, demand I drop my pants so she could check the stubble on my legs. That wouldn't do.

I searched the car for another sweater or sweatshirt, something I might have crumpled into a corner unknowingly. I found a muddy white sock and half a pack of Life Savers, a balled-up pair of panty hose from my first meeting with Season. But no shirt.

A red Honda pulled into the space next to mine. A cop in his twenties got out wearing his uniform. He leaned into his car and brought out a hanger draped with freshly pressed civilian clothes still in the dry-cleaning plastic wrapper.

'Hi,' I said to him. 'I know this may sound stupid, but I wonder if you have a T-shirt or something I could borrow for a couple hours while I'm visiting someone. I get so cold in there and I forgot my sweater. I'll give it back. I promise.'

He looked me over. 'You the one who visits that woman who shot her husband? You're writing the book.'

'Yes.' I offered my hand. He shook it. 'I'm Wren Caldwell.'

He nodded. He looked at me as if trying to decide whether or not to make me walk a straight line, touch my fingers to my nose.

'You can hold on to my driver's license,' I said. 'Or a credit card.'

'No need,' he said, laying his clothes carefully across the roof of my car. 'Let's see what I've got.' He popped his trunk and rummaged through some golf clubs, a tennis racquet, a stack of *Newsweek* magazines that were bound with twine. He finally dug out his nylon sports bag and pulled out some wadded clothing: socks, jock strap, shorts, T-shirt. He sniffed the shirt. 'Still a little ripe. I wore it a couple days ago to play basketball.'

'That's fine,' I said, reaching for it. It was damp in a couple places and smelled like the produce drawer of my refrigerator. Season wouldn't notice through the glass. 'It smells like you won.'

'Yeah, we played hard.' He picked up his pressed clothes and pointed at the building. 'You can just drop it off at the desk when you've done. Tell them it's for Hirsh.'

'Thanks, Hirsh,' I said.

'Gary.' He waved and trotted off.

I pulled on the moist shirt and noticed the front said in bold black letters: 'WERE IT LEFT TO ME TO DECIDE WHETHER WE SHOULD HAVE A GOVERNMENT WITHOUT NEWSPAPERS OR NEWSPAPERS WITHOUT A GOVERNMENT I SHOULD NOT HESITATE A MOMENT TO PREFER THE LATTER' Beneath the quote it said: THOMAS JEFFERSON . Beneath that it said: SUPPORT THE FIRST AMENDMENT ACLU.

A cop with an ACLU T-shirt? Was he kidding or what? As I walked into the police station wearing this T-shirt, I felt as if I had a huge red target painted on my chest. I forced a big smile on my face and walked up to the guard, Officer Cooper, who usually brought Season out and sat in attendance while we visited. He sat behind his desk with his Scientology pamphlets open.

I asked him which he'd rather live without, his wife or the carpet. He decided it was petty after all.

'Hello, Officer Cooper,' I said. I nodded toward the door that led to the cells where Season was waiting. 'Once more into the breech.'

He gave me a nervous look. 'Uh, could you have a seat please, Ms. Caldwell. My captain wants to speak to you.'

'Sure,' I said, trying to sound calm, even cheerful.

He turned and disappeared through the door. My stomach felt as if someone were doing heavy spadework inside. What was wrong? My T-shirt? Or maybe they found out about me. They ran some kind of fingerprint check on me, discovered who I was, and were coming out to arrest me. I should run, jump in the car, and keep driving. I knew what I was doing was illegal. Last week I saw on the news they'd arrested some twenty-five-year-old guy in Los Angeles who'd dressed as a girl and enrolled in high school. He even joined the cheerleading squad as a girl. They'd interviewed students at the school. They all said he was very popular and funny. A couple were more suprised that he was twenty-five than that he was a guy. The police charged him with criminal impersonation.

Still, I didn't run. Maybe it was nothing important. They wanted to know how I would portray their department in my book. Maybe something like that. I sat next to Officer Cooper's desk and started browsing through his Scientology stuff. There was a pamphlet. On the cover was a cluster of photographs of smiling well-dressed people, most of them shot through some filmy lens. At the bottom was their motto: Improving Life in a Troubled World.

I opened the questionnaire. You could answer either (1) yes or mostly yes, (2) maybe or uncertain, or (3) no or mostly no. *Do you make thoughtless remarks or accusations that you later regret?* Mostly no. *Is it hard on you when you fail?* Mostly . . . Hmmm. Uncertain. I skipped ahead. *Do you rarely suspect the actions of others?*

The door opened and Officer Cooper and another man came out. The man was in his forties, slightly paunchy. His mustache was thick as my wrist.

'Ms. Caldwell?' he said politely.

'Yes.' I stood up. I watched his hands, expecting handcuffs to come flashing out.

'I'm Captain Hernandez.' His hand came out, but nothing was in it.

I shook it. 'Is there some problem?'

'Well, yes. I'm afraid Mrs. Dougherty committed suicide early this morning.'

I stared at him stupidly. 'She's dead?'

'Uh, yes, the suicide was successful.'

'I don't . . . I'm not . . .' I couldn't think how to finish any sentence.

'Perhaps you'd like to sit down.' He nodded at Officer Cooper, who quickly pushed a chair behind me. I backed away from the chair, but Officer Cooper followed behind me with it. I spun away from both of them. 'I'm fine, really. I don't want to sit.'

Captain Hernandez nodded at Officer Cooper. Cooper put the chair back where he got it.

'How did she do it?' I asked.

'She hung herself,' Officer Cooper said.

'Hanged,' Captain Hernandez corrected. 'Pictures are hung; people are hanged. Am I right, Ms. Caldwell?'

I didn't feel much like participating in a grammar lesson. I nodded. 'Yes.'

'Hanged herself,' Officer Cooper said.

'She used her jumpsuit,' Captain Hernandez said. 'Twisted it into a rope and did it. Very unusual.'

'Aren't there people who watch her? Other prisoners who could see her?'

He shook his head. 'She did it while the others were asleep. Or if they saw her, they didn't bother to stop her.'

I didn't know what else to say. I tried to force myself to think like a reporter. What would I do next?

'Do you want to see her cell?' Captain Hernandez offered. 'I mean, for your book.'

'Her cell?'

'It's no problem. We cooperate thoroughly with the press. We have nothing to hide here.'

'No. I don't think so. Not right now.' I started to leave.

'Just a moment, Ms. Caldwell. Mrs. Dougherty left something for you.'

I turned around. 'She left something for me?' I spoke in slow and stupid tones. I felt as if I were in the next room overhearing our conversation. Who is that idiot woman in the baggy T-shirt?

He opened the drawer to Officer Cooper's desk and took out a manila envelope. Wren Caldwell was handwritten across it.

'She left a suicide note,' he said. 'In it, she stated that she wanted you to have this book.'

I opened the manila envelope and slid the book out. *Modern Plaque Removal Techniques*. I looked at Captain Hernandez with puzzlement.

He shrugged. 'She didn't say anything else, just to give that to you.'

I leafed through the pages, looking for a note she might have stuffed in there, or maybe some writing in the margins. Nothing. The inside covers had been slit and clumsily taped back together.

'We gave it a thorough going over,' he said. 'We didn't find anything either.'

'Thanks,' I said.

'Investigators will be in touch, Ms. Caldwell. They'll just want a brief statement from you about Mrs. Dougherty's state of mind, that sort of thing.'

I nodded and started to leave again.

'See you're wearing Hirsh's shirt,' he said jovially. 'Hell of a basketball player. Can't shoot worth shit, but he's fearless on the rebounds.' He acted as if he thought Hirsh

387

and I were dating and he needed to put in a few good words. 'Can't think of anybody I'd rather have on my team. Pound for pound, he's the best.'

* * * * *

The car was hot. I didn't roll down the windows. I didn't start the engine. I sat there leafing through the pages of *Modern Plaque Removal Techniques* for the fiftieth time. I'd returned Officer Hirsh's T-shirt to the cop at the front desk, but my sweater still retained some of the pungent ammonia odor. The heat inside the car made it worse. Still, I kept leafing.

I didn't know what I was looking for anymore. There were drawings and photographs of teeth in various stages of decomposition. Some very nasty-looking gums. But no code words written on the teeth, no pleas for understanding, justifications for suicide. No nothing.

Then why give me this stupid book?

Maybe this was a professional message. Something was wrong with my teeth. I adjusted the rearview mirror and bared my teeth. I pulled back the lips and studied my gums. They looked fine. Or was that a speck of something cancerous near my incisor? I held up the book and looked back and forth between a drawing and my teeth.

A speck of light flickered through the page.

I pasted the page against the windshield where the sun was blasting through. A tiny pinprick of light flared next to the page number. Page 61.

Again I thumbed through each page, holding each up to the light. I found more pages with pinpricks next to the page numbers. Each page that was marked had a different number of pinpricks, which I assumed indicated the order of the numbers. Page 61 had one hole. Page 95 had two. Page 55 had three. Page 182 had four. Page 9 had five.

6195551829.

A locker combination? Swiss bank account?
A phone number.
Even the dead have secrets.

*   *   *   *   *

When I arrived back at my apartment, Byron's clothes no longer covered the sidewalk entry. The house was clean, the dishes done, the carpet vacuumed. I didn't see anybody, though, so I sneaked down the hallway and suctioned my ear to Byron's bedroom door. I could hear splashing in the bathtub and his laughter, the kind caused by two people being intimate.

I tiptoed to the kitchen, picked up the phone, and dialed the mystery number. It rang for quite a while, ten or fifteen rings. I was about to hang up when it stopped ringing and a little girl's voice said, 'Hello?'

Jesus. Season's daughter.

'Jamie?' I said.

She didn't answer.

I heard rapid footsteps on the other end. A woman whispering harshly, ' . . . told you never to answer when I'm not here . . .'

' . . . thought it might be Mommy . . .' the little girl whispered back.

'Hello?' the woman said firmly. 'Who's this?'

I hung up.

I wandered into my bedroom and closed the door. I dropped onto my unmade bed and pulled a pillow over my face. The pillow smelled like Hector, dank and earthy. I sat up and noticed muddy paw prints across my sheet, a patch of shed hair on the pillowcase.

I did the right thing hanging up, I thought. What did I hope to gain by talking to them? There's nothing that they could say that would make any difference. Season was dead. Why had she bothered going through such an elaborate ruse to give me the phone number? What did she think I would do? Did Season think I would try to figure out why she killed herself? I didn't really care about other people's secrets. I had my own to nurture.

I picked up another pillow, studied it for cat hair. None. I sniffed it. It smelled like Finesse shampoo. I flopped back and smothered myself under its dark softness. I pulled it around my ears.

I tried to imagine Season hanging in her cell. I pictured dangling legs, like they show you on cop shows because it's TV and they can't show you the strangled face, swollen tongue. I read somewhere they vacate their bowels. If Season used her jumpsuit as a rope, what was she wearing? Did she dangle there in her prison-issue bra and panties, her urine and shit dripping down her legs. I pulled the pillow closer against my face. Breathing was very difficult.

Why had Season entrusted the phone number to me when she'd fought so hard to keep it a secret? Did she kill herself because she feared she was cracking, that she might end up revealing her daughter's hiding place? Her husband was dead, why keep the girl hidden anyway?

'Fuuuuuuck!' I screamed into the pillow. The feathered stuffing absorbed my holler like a silencer smothers a gunshot. Fuck sounded like aaaaaawk. I sounded like Motown. Maybe I could take over his life next, sit in a cage and sing Supremes' titles all day. It was bad enough to be tightwire-walking through Wren's life, now I was thrust into Season's.

This wasn't me. I was no crusading reporter, the truth and I weren't even on speaking terms. Now that I thought about it, I never pursued Esther's death, never looked into why she might have killed herself or even why she shot Wren and me? I just passed it off as an insomnia-induced breakdown, visited her grave, and left it at that. Did I even bother chasing down the reasons Robby and I broke up? Not really. I focused on the effects. What it did to me physically, as if the shock were so great that I was

390

actually taking another step in evolution, the way cock-roaches adjust to radiation. I don't look for meaning or insight, just clarity. It's kind of like watching TV; I'm the one who keeps adjusting the contrast, the color, the tint for a better picture, not really caring about the quality of the show. I just take things as they are.

The front door to the apartment opened. I sprang out of bed and peeked out the curtain. Byron and Shawna were walking to her car in the parking lot. Byron was dressed in black jeans, a white shirt, and a black knit tie. His hair was combed and pulled back into his ponytail. He looked like he was going to court. Shawna wore cutoff jeans and a white T-shirt knotted at her belly. Shawna was carrying the iron bird stand, Byron was carrying the bird cage. Inside the cage, Motown kept pacing sideways along his perch to compensate for the rough turbulence. Hector followed them, trotting like a show horse, his tail sticking straight up in the air.

Shawna kissed Byron on the cheek and got in the car. The casualness of that peck seemed somehow more inti-mate than if I'd stood next to their bed and watched them screwing all night. They exchanged hand gestures through the open window, then she drove off.

Byron waved at her until she was out of sight. I watched, waiting for him to come back in. I was going to have it out with him once and for all, no punches pulled.

But he didn't come back. He started across the parking lot toward the street that ran parallel to the complex. Hec-tor didn't follow. He sat on the curb and watched.

I made a decision. I would follow Byron. Get in my car and follow him to where this gambling thing took place. I would find out what he was up to, undoubtedly illegal, then I would have more leverage. I could kick him out and he couldn't talk to anybody lest I do some talking of my own. Maybe it wasn't a shotgun blast to the crotch, but it would be the next best thing.

I grabbed my purse and hurried for the front door. As I rounded the corner into the living room, the phone rang.

I hesitated. It rang a few more times. The machine answered, playing my announcement.

'Sweetheart, I just heard,' Davis's voice said. He sounded breathless, as if he'd just run a couple of blocks. 'Are you there? Pick up, Wren.' Pause. I looked over at the phone. My feet started toward it, but slowly, too slowly to actually reach it. I didn't want to talk, I wanted to follow Byron. I wanted to get the liars out of my life.

'Okay, you must know about Season by now,' Davis continued. 'Jesus, that's terrible. I wish I were there with you. I just don't want you to worry, everything will be okay. The book deal is still on, so you're okay there. I know that sounds very Hollywood of me, but right now I'm more interested in your well-being than anything else.' Another long pause. 'I'll call you later, sweetheart. I don't know what else to say . . .' He hung up.

I walked out the door and jogged to my car. If Byron had walked to the main street, that meant he was taking the bus. The bus stop was at the end of the block.

I nosed my car as far out of the driveway as I could without actually turning onto the street. I saw Byron at the bus stop talking to a Hispanic woman carrying a large shopping bag. The only Hispanics I'd seen so far in Irvine were domestics who came by bus in the morning, cleaned the houses, condos, and townhouses, and left by bus in the afternoon. Some lived in permanently, but they usually wore uniforms.

I waited in the driveway with my car idling. When another car came up behind me to exit, I waved it around me. The drivers would always peer in at me as if I were crazy. Finally, Byron's bus came. He helped the Hispanic woman in, holding her bag for her.

'Count whatever you had inside your bag,' I warned her.

Then Byron climbed aboard the and bus took off.

I followed it with ease for about two miles. That's when I looked into my rearview mirror and noticed that I too was being followed. By a white Subaru.

29

The exhaust from the bus was bitter. I pulled the front of my sweater up over my nose to filter the air, but my sweater still smelled of Officer Hirsh's sweaty T-shirt and last weekend's basketball game. So I alternated between carbon monoxide and ammonia.

The Subaru dropped back a couple of cars, but I could still see him back there, keeping pace, darting in and out of line to see what I was doing. My attitude was surprisingly calm. I wasn't angry at him any more than I was angry at Byron. I simply had a job to do here, some house-cleaning in my life, and I looked on the Subaru and Byron as stubborn stains in the middle of an otherwise spotless carpet. My only concern was removing those stains from the shag pile of my life.

In the case of the Subaru, a little elbow grease was required. And I knew just how to apply it.

Byron's bus grumbled down Jamboree Street like a Rose Bowl float, pulling over to suck up a couple of passengers or belch out a couple. Whenever it stopped, I stopped, pulled my sweater up over my nose like a bandit, and waited. Other cars always pulled around me and sped off, shaking their heads at me or flipping me the bird, something editorial like that. The white Subaru, without the shield of cars, had no other choice but to sit it out right behind me and wait too.

We were all idling there in the slow lane at the intersection of Campus and Jamboree: the bus, me, the Subaru. The car that had been between me and the Subaru, a blue

Mustang, had pulled out with a screech. As he passed me, the balding driver yelled, 'The pedal on the right makes your car go forward!'

I looked in the rearview mirror. The Subaru didn't inch forward the way cars do when someone leaves a lane. Traffic abhors a vacuum. But not him. So I shifted into reverse, eased off the clutch, and stomped the gas pedal. My car rocketed backward twenty-five feet until it smashed into the front end of the Subaru. An explosion of glass and the sound of crunching metal echoed dully through my car. My body snapped forward against my seat belt and rebounded backward into my seat.

I checked the other driver in my mirror. He looked stunned, his eyes glazed and his expression disoriented. Blood dripped down from his mouth into his beard.

I unbuckled my seat belt and leapt out of the car. I ran back to his car. It was the same man Ethan and I had chased away the other night. 'Are you okay?' I asked.

'I bih mah tug,' he said, holding his striped tie against his mouth to soak up the blood.

'You bit your tongue? I'm sorry. You shouldn't follow so closely.'

'Closely. I wass twety-fahv feeh away!'

'Then I guess you shouldn't follow at all.'

He groaned and rubbed his neck. On the seat next to him were half a dozen empty cans of diet Slice and a box of Vanilla Wafers.

The bus carrying Byron pulled away from the curb and lumbered down the street.

'You can wait for the police if you want, maybe tell them why you're following me. Why are you following me?'

'I'b nah followin you. You cwazy.'

I slapped him hard on his sore mouth. He hollered in pain, his eyes tearing up instantly. That's when I reached in and pulled his keys out of the ignition. I tossed them across the street, on the other side of six lanes of steady traffic. Not a bad throw, really.

I ran back to my car, jumped in, and took off after Byron's bus. Something rattled at the back of the car now, but it was worth a little body damage to see myself handle the situation so capably. Just like in the movies. Sigourney Weaver blasting aliens left and right, all the while standing around in her underwear.

But who was I now? Wren? Season? BeeGee? Wild sex, ramming cars, slapping people, following convicts. That wasn't Luna of the lifeless hair and steel-rimmed glasses. Whose life was I leading now?

Eventually Byron transferred to another bus, which I followed down Pacific Coast Highway to Laguna Beach. He got out and walked a couple blocks to a small restaurant that had a few tables corraled outside. He walked up to a man about his age who was already seated and sat down. They immediately leaned close and began talking in a hushed huddle.

I pulled my rattling car against a no parking red curb and spied on them for a while. The new guy wore slacks and an Oxford button-collar shirt. He kept pulling papers out of a battered suitcase and showing them to Byron. Byron studied them, nodded, pointed at various things on the pages, and they talked. What were they discussing? Drug deals? Fencing stolen goods? Blueprints for a house they intended to burglarize?

'Hey,' someone said next to my car.

I turned and looked up at a uniformed cop. 'Hi,' I said.

'You can't park here. It's a red zone.'

'I'm just waiting for a friend . . .' I looked at the stores along the curb. Hardware, bank, frozen yogurt. 'She's just making a deposit in the bank.'

'Sorry, but you'll still have to move it.'

'Okay,' I said. I started the engine and pulled away. He stood in the street and watched me until I was all the way down the block. I circled the block and returned down the same street. Byron and his friend were no longer sitting at the table.

'Shit!' I said. 'Goddamn it!'

But then I spotted them coming out of the bank. Byron handed him a thick envelope. The man opened it and I could see that it was stuffed with money. He counted through it. Byron said something and the man shrugged, looking disappointed. Byron said something else and laughed. The other guy, very studious-looking, laughed too. They shook hands and left in opposite directions.

Now I wasn't sure who to follow. In *All the President's Men*, when Woodward and Bernstein were busting Watergate, Deep Throat told them to 'follow the money'. That seemed to work for them. Maybe I should follow the Oxford shirt and see what he does with the money.

But I stayed with Byron. I had a hunch that he hadn't come all the way down to Laguna Beach just to meet with this guy, not when there were other restaurants and banks more convenient to our apartment.

Since there was no way I could follow him in a car without him spotting me, I crawled along for a few blocks until I found a parking place to tuck my car. Now we were both on foot. I stayed a block behind him, sometimes more depending on the number of other pedestrians I could use to shield myself. I also hung close to the buildings, where I might suddenly duck into a doorway or pretend to window-shop if he got suspicious and turned around. He didn't, though, so I started to feel pretty confident with my shadowing technique. I was surprised at how much practical stuff I'd actually picked up from watching billions of hours of cop shows over the years. I'd disabled the Subaru and now I was following someone on foot.

Byron was walking away from the beach toward the residential area up on the cliffs. The streets were winding higher and higher, with each inclination offering bigger and more expensive houses. The lawns became larger, the gardens more bountiful. We passed several Hispanic gardeners blowing leaves with their loud machines.

Finally, Byron found the house he was looking for, a two-storey mansion with white columns and a brick front, a bizarre architectural hybrid of colonial farmhouse and gothic mansion. Byron marched down the sidewalk to the front door and just walked in the house without ringing the bell or knocking. Apparently, he was expected.

I stood looking at the house for a while. What should I do now? Just stand here all day in the hot sun until Byron came out again? I wouldn't really know anything more about him from the safety of this sidewalk, nothing I could use as counterblackmail. I needed to get closer.

I looked around the neighbourhood. These were million-dollar homes, each with lots of trees and blooming flowers. Fancy mailboxes with iron-stenciled names attached. Cars in driveways: Volvos, BMWs, Accuras, Mercedes. Safe cars. Safe neighbourhood. What could happen to me here?

I started down the cobblestone walk toward the house. I found myself straining to hear a bird chirping. I knew I'd feel better about all this if I could hear some birds chirping. No one would hurt me in a neighbourhood where birds were chirping. I heard something, but it could have been a cricket. Crickets didn't make me feel safe.

I raised a fist to knock on the front door. No, that would be stupid. I was here to spy, not visit. I tiptoed off the front porch and sneaked around the side of the house, stooping next to the well-trimmed bushes that surrounded the house like parsley around lamb chops. I guess the idea of bushes around the edges of a house is to make the building look like it has no edges, as if it just blends in with nature. But it doesn't. A house is just a mixture of cement and wood and plumbing pipes and electrical wires and skylighted showers and down-quilted beds. I didn't know why I was thinking that as I crept around the huge house. Maybe because I was beginning to suspect I was never going to live in such a house in such a neighborhood where cul-de-sacs were plentiful and children let out from school could play unthreatened. This wasn't a house where criminals like Byron should be allowed to just walk in and run whatever illegal activity he was involved in. It was a place for families. Where little Bobby builds a fort out of dirty laundry, or precious Amy traps a spider under a glass and studies it there until it suffocates and she cries all night over the loss.

I felt a yank in the pit of my stomach, a longing to be at a mall selecting wallpaper for the bedroom of my someday-to-be-born child. I made a fist and punched myself in the stomach twice and the longing disappeared.

I heard voices. Men. I raised myself up enough to peek through the window.

'Looking for something,' the voice behind me said. I felt something hard and pointed pressed against my spine. For lack of any other response, I put my hands up.

PART THREE

How To Have a Near-Love Experience

30

'She's mine. I'm gonna take her,' he threatened.

'Go ahead, take her,' Byron said. 'Go crazy.'

'I'm gonna do it, man. You think I'm kidding?'

'Then do it. Time's running out.' Byron pointed to the clock next to him. Two clocks, really, attached to each other in a wooden case. He started tapping his finger against the card table like a metronome.

The other guy sucked his lower lip between his teeth and started gnawing. I could see tiny white scars criss-crossing his lip from decades of gnawing. 'Fuck you, man. I'm not gonna be psyched out by your bullshit. She's mine.'

Byron shrugged. 'Your choice.'

The other guy reached across the wooden chess board between them, picked up his white bishop, slid it diagonally across the board, snatched up Byron's black queen between his last two fingers, and set his bishop down on the vacated square. Instantly he slapped the silver button at the top of the two-faced clock beside the board.

'I just fucked your queen, pal. Stew on that. I humped and bumped and pumped her and she loved every juicy minute, man. "Oooh, yes," she kept saying. "Take me, Willie. Take me." Hey, what's this? Time running out? You got twenty-two seconds and no fat-assed queen. You're as fucked as she is, man. Bye, bye, Byron . . .'

The man kept up his steady stream of patter while Byron stared at the board with a calm gaze, as if this were a meal he was indifferent to eating. Captured chess pieces lined both sides of the board. There were only eight pieces left on the actual playing surface.

'How's this feel, your royal heiny?' the man said, thrusting his hips back and forth in his chair. 'You like a little more of this, queeny?'

Byron reached over, airlifted his castle across the board, and snapped it on a square with a loud smack. 'Check.' Byron tapped the silver button on his clock. He got up and stretched, not bothering to look at the board.

His opponent glanced nervously at the clock and instantly retreated his bishop back between the attacking castle and his defenseless king. He slapped his clock.

From his standing position, Byron jumped his black knight down two spaces and over one into a position near the white king. 'Checkmate.'

'Shit! Where?' The man with the scarred lip studied the board. 'Just a second. Just a fucking second.' His eyes darted from piece to piece, his hand hovered over one, then another, like a fussy hummingbird selecting a flower. Finally, he just tipped over his king, jumped up, pulled a wad of twenty-dollar bills from his pocket, and threw it down on the chess board. Some of the pieces flew onto the floor. He stomped out of the room toward the kitchen. He stepped on a king, snapping off the cross on its head.

Byron counted the money and slipped it into his pocket. He showed no sign of triumphant glee or proud accomplishment. He looked as unmoved as someone who'd just bussed a dirty table.

'I found her outside,' my beefy guardian said to Byron. He gripped my upper arm and shoved me forward. 'She says she knows you.'

'She thinks she does,' Byron said.

'She was spying on us through the window.' He nodded toward the window where he'd caught me. 'Want me to boot her out? When I boot, they stay booted.'

Byron looked me over as if considering that alternative. Finally, he shook his head. 'Not yet. Thanks, Leo.'

Leo shrugged and came out from behind me. He tossed

402

up the sharp object I'd assumed was a knife. It was a pointy-headed bishop chess piece he'd held against my back while he kept me in the foyer until Byron finished his game. He caught it in his palm and closed his fist around it. He walked off into the large living-room. There were about twenty men in the room, all playing chess.

'So, you followed me,' Byron said.

'It wasn't hard.'

He gestured around the room. 'Was it worth it? Did you discover something to blackmail me over? I mean, that is the point, right? To get some dirt on me to neutralize my dirt on you?'

'That's the point.'

'Help yourself. Look around. Talk to people. Pry.'

I looked around the room. Men of all ages huddled over flimsy card tables with chess boards and chess clocks. Cigars, cigarettes, a few joints. A wispy layer of smoke clung to the ceiling. Lots of beer cans, a few coffee cups, one man chugging Evian water. Some of the tables had little piles of money. Over near the sofa was a nineteen-inch Sony TV still in its box. Next to it were a couple of VCRs and CD players, also still in their boxes.

'Well, for starters,' I said, 'there's illegal gambling going on here. That's something the cops might be interested in.'

'So, call the cops,' Byron said. He turned to the other men and announced loudly, 'She wants to call the cops on you, boys. Illegal gambling.'

There was some laughter, some annoyed looks. A 'fuck you, lady' chorused with a 'dumb bitch'.

One of the men who was watching a chess game in progress, gray-haired and overweight, sucking on a stubby cigar, reached into his baggy shirt pocket and pulled out a small black wallet. He opened it and showed me his gold badge. He winked at me. 'Don't worry, ma'am. I'm working undercover.'

Everyone laughed.

'What about those boxes,' I said angrily, pointing at the appliances. 'I bet they're stolen.'

'They are,' Byron said. He pointed at a little man across the room. The man was hunched over his chess game, slapping his pieces down, then smacking the clock. He looked as if he wanted to eat the pieces, the board, the clocks, his opponent. He had a tattoo on one arm that ran all the way from his wrist, up the entire arm, disappearing under his T-shirt sleeve. 'That's Grudge. He stole the stuff from his brother's warehouse. You know his brother, Bonkers Bob, does those commercials where he throws TVs out of windows, runs over stereos with his car because they're priced too high. This is Bonkers Bob's house.'

I gave an appreciative turn. Despite the card tables and hunched men and acrid smoke, this one room was larger than my entire apartment and worth more than everything I owned or ever would own. A white grand piano dominated one corner. Someone had pyramided a dozen Coors cans on top of it. A marble coffee table separated two white leather sofas. The table hosted two different chess games, and a pile of wadded Kleenexes from one of the guys who kept sneezing. I looked down at the carpet, an off-white weave that one usually sees in model homes. The walls were filled with various colorful and abstract art works, all of them originals, all of them undoubtedly expensive.

'Where are the owners?' I said. 'Mr. and Mrs. Bonkers.'

'A cruise. The Mediterranean, I think.'

'How convenient for all of you.'

'Doesn't matter. When they come back, the game moves somewhere else. Last week we were in a movie theater in Anaheim. One of the guys is an usher. Before that we played for two days in a courtroom, I showered in the judge's chambers.' He pointed to a black man slapping his clock. 'He's a security guard at the courthouse. Most of the guys you see around here don't really even appreciate where they are. They don't notice that this place is worth a lot, not unless they're professional burglars or something. They're just here to play chess. Sunny, rainy, doesn't matter. Hot, cold, they don't care. Everything's chess.'

I looked around the room again, this time ignoring the furnishings and concentrating on the men. Byron was right, there was an odd fanatical concentration about them, the same one you see on the faces of computer nerds discussing software. They stared at the boards and slapped pieces down with feverish energy. They looked like patients at a tuberculosis sanatorium, pale and hopeful. Even when they talked it was only about chess, either at their own bad move or their opponent's. There were so many games going on that the room had an odd melody to it, the clacking of pieces snapped against the wooden boards, and the smacking of the clocks next to their games. Games kept ending, payoffs made, new ones beginning, all within a brief time.

'They play so fast,' I said. 'I haven't played much, but I remember it always took us a long time to move.'

'This isn't chess,' Byron said. 'It's blitz, or speed chess. Not the kind you'll read about in the papers or see on TV. Every game lasts from between one and ten minutes, depending upon what the players agree to beforehand. After that, it's a race with the clock as well as against the other player. This is the game where all the big money is made.'

We walked by a table where two men were furiously slapping chess pieces, then their clocks. One of the players wore a white shirt and a tie. His suit jacket was carefully hung on his chair, his briefcase was tucked neatly under his chair. His opponent had a thin blue tattooed line that ran across the top of his forehead like the coastline on a map. There was about two inches between the blue line and his receding hairline.

Byron whispered, 'The suit is a lawyer, represents about a third of the guys in this room.'

'He's young.'

'He's also not very good.' Byron gestured at the other player. 'Billy there had that line tattooed on when he was in high school. Back then it followed his hairline exactly so you couldn't even see it.'

'Why? I mean, why'd he have it done?'

'His girlfriend was worried that he'd go bald someday and wouldn't sleep with him because she didn't want to marry a bald guy. He promised her he wouldn't go bald and to prove it, he had the tattoo done.'

I laughed. 'Did they get married?'

'Yeah. Twice.'

Neither player seemed to notice us watching. They picked up pieces and smacked them down with a crack and instantly slapped their clocks. The pieces on the board were wonderfully ornate versions of cowboys on one side and Indians on the other. I glanced around the room and saw other chess pieces, equally complex and intricate in design.

'The chess pieces are beautiful,' I said.

'Something to show your art class, huh?'

He led me to another table where two men were setting up the pieces. One side of the board was lined with familiar biblical figures, each brightly painted: the king was a carving of Moses with a staff in one hand and the Ten Commandments in the other, his gray hair swept back from an imaginary wind; the knight was a golden calf on a platform; the rock was the Tower of Babel; the pawns were frogs and locusts, representing the ten plagues, I guessed. Across the board a modest Jesus Christ occupied the king's square; a demure haloed Mary was the queen; the bishop was Peter, complete with a fishing net across his shoulder, the pawns were robed beggars, each leaning on a wooden crutch, carrying a Bible.

'Christians versus the Jews,' one of the men said. 'The way it's always been.'

'Karl here's a bit of an anti-Semite,' Byron explained. 'Right, Karl?'

'If that means do I hate the Jews, no, I do not. I do not hate Jews or any other religion. I just think they are misguided.' Karl did not look up at either Byron or myself. He kept his eyes down and chewed frantically on a wad of gum.

'Did you make these?' I asked him.

'Yes, ma'am, every last piece. Made 'em while serving my fifty-eight months for armed robbery and I thank Jesus that he gave me that opportunity. Because it is while incarcerated that I discovered both the Lord and chess.'

'The pieces are very beautiful,' I said.

'Thank you, ma'am. Perhaps you'd appreciate this extra little feature the others only seem to find amusing.' Still without looking at me, he reached over and touched a button at the back of his Christ figure. The arms, which had been at Jesus' side, shot straight out into a crucifixion pose. 'That's for when I lose.'

Byron led me away, pointing out the other chess sets that each man had carved while in prison: Civil War pieces, street gang pieces, movie star sets. One person had one side as the characters from the *Threepenny Opera* versus the characters from *My Fair Lady*. As I looked around at the colorful imaginative pieces, they seemed like what little boys would use as currency if they owned their own country.

'Hiya, Bud,' Byron said, waving over my shoulder.

I turned and saw a red-haired spaniel winding his way under the card tables, sniffing the carpet as he crawled through the room. He had a bandage wrapped around his hind leg and he walked with a limp.

'Hey, Bud,' one of the men said. 'What's shaking?'

'Howya doin', Bud,' another said.

'C'mere and hump my leg for good luck.'

Every person Bud came near stuck out a hand and gave him a scratch or a pat as he passed by. Bud licked up a broken pretzel from the carpet and hobbled out another door.

'Come on,' Byron said, taking my hand. 'I'll give you the ten-cent tour.'

I jerked my hand from his. 'I don't need a crossing guard.'

'I didn't do it to be romantic. I'm letting these guys know you're with me so they don't start hitting on you. Chess players are the most sexually starved species on the planet.'

'Present company excepted, of course.' I didn't give him my hand, but I followed closely. Where else would I go? I suppose I could have just walked out of there, driven home, called Davis, asked him to come home and hold me, make me feel better. But Byron's arrogance nettled me. He couldn't be touched and he knew it. But wasn't this where the bad guys in the movies always went wrong, showing the captured secret agent around their domain like Dr. No and Goldfinger? Maybe there was something he'd overlooked, something illegal I could still nail him for. I still had Detective Diesel's number.

'You play chess?' he asked as we walked down the sun-lit hallway. Overhead skylights let the bright sun spotlight our path to the kitchen.

'Some, like I said. But not *play* play. Robby taught me. He liked to sit there with Bach in the background, a pipe in his mouth, and take two hours to move one piece. I got so bored he finally took to bribing me to play with him. Thank goodness for those computerized chess games. He finally had the perfect partner.'

'Computers are nice toys, but when it comes to blitz, there's not a person in this house today who couldn't cream a computer nine out of ten times.'

'Why? What's so special about blitz.'

'The speed. You don't have time to figure every variation of every move. And there are so many traps and pitfalls. Your opponent is just waiting for that rash move, that's when he crushes you. It's kind of like having a live grenade strapped to your chest that's going to explode in one minute. Now, if you can run across that field to that toolbox, you can disarm the grenade. Only trouble is, the field is loaded with hidden mines. And, oh yeah, someone's shooting at you the whole time. Ready, set, run. That's blitz.'

We entered the kitchen. The appliances were heavy-duty stainless steel, the kind you find in fancy restaurant kitchens. The refrigerator had a sliding glass door so you could see what was inside. Cold cuts, beer, a couple of buckets of fried chicken, potato salad. The kitchen was large enough to include a small family room with complete electronic entertainment center. A couple of guys were eating sandwiches and watching the big-screen TV, reruns of *The Flintstones*. A couple of other guys were playing chess while munching pretzels at the cooking island with their chess board over the butcher block. The rear wall of the kitchen was glass, which looked out onto a large pool and bubbling spa. Two pale guys with flabby guts sat in the spa playing chess. Several white wrought-iron patio tables with umbrellas dotted the poolside area. Every table but one had at least two chess games in progress. At that one table without chess, five men played poker. One chess game ended and the loser pushed his money across the table to the winner. The winner stood up, pocketed the money in his swimsuit, took off his sunglasses, and dove into the pool. He swam across, hoisted himself up on the other side, tossed his soggy money on the table, and started a new game with someone else.

'Who are all these people?' I asked.

'Ex-cons mostly. A cop or two. Leo, the guy who brought you in, he's a retired guard from Chino prison. Not a bad player, though he gets a little cautious when you pressure his queen. No bluff to his game. Cops and guards are like that. They play like they've got something to lose. Makes them easier to beat.'

'Who did you have lunch with at the restaurant?' I didn't care about this chess crap. I was after something tangible. I looked in his eyes for a reaction.

He didn't give me one. 'A friend.'

'And the money you gave him?'

'What beady little eyes you have, Grandma.'

'It's the company I keep.'

He laughed. 'It was a loan.'

'That was a big envelope.'

'It was a big loan.' He grinned at me. 'You need a loan too? Oh, that's right, you've got that $50,000 deal you're working on.'

My skin chilled. 'What deal?'

'I don't know the details, but from what I've been able to piece together from listening to your phone messages and the tapes you bring home every day from jail, you're doing some kind of article or series of articles, though for that kind of money more like a book, about Season Dougherty.'

'You've played my fucking tapes!'

'You figured to take the money, which I suppose your boyfriend Davis is paying you since this is his kind of game, and start Wren's little ego magazine.'

'You went into my room and played my goddamn tapes, you pig!'

'Only Season went and hanged herself this morning and now you're feeling sorry for yourself, so you figured you'd follow me and try to take me out of the picture. What happened, Luna-slash-Wren? Now that Season's dead you've decided to take on *her* identity and come at me with a shotgun?' He pointed at his crotch. 'Fire away, baby.'

I gave him the cold stare, the one he'd been giving me on and off since he'd arrived. But it didn't seem to have any effect. Finally, I just sighed heavily. I felt so tired and heavy.

'How'd you know Season was dead?'

He made a sweeping gesture. 'Look around. We've got cops and lawyers and cons. This place goes twenty-four hours a day, just like a Vegas casino. The only thing these guys like more than chess is gossip. Anything happens to do with prisons, we know about it first.' He slid open the refrigerator door and pulled out a couple cans of Pepsi. He handed one to me. 'No diet, sorry.'

I took it, popped the tab, and sipped. 'I'm living dangerously these days.'

A loud smacking thud nearby startled me. I jumped back, my heart pounding. 'What was that?'

'Jesus Christ,' Byron cursed. He left me and marched over to the sliding glass door that led to the pool. A wet smudge blotched the glass at eye level. He pulled open the door and bent over.

I followed. I stepped outside behind him and watched him examine the still bird.

'What you got there, great white hunter?' one of the cons who wasn't playing yelled from poolside. Those who were playing didn't even look up.

Byron picked up the bird, a sparrow, I think, and carried him over to the plastic trash cans, lifted the lip of the lid, and shoved him in with the beer cans and pizza boxes. He looked at me as he returned to the kitchen. 'This is not going to be one of those broken-wing-nurse-to-health-in-a-shoe-box stories.'

'What happened?'

'They don't see the glass sometimes.' He went over to the sink, opened the cupboards, poked around, then closed them. Next, he tried the refrigerator. He slid open the door, moved some stuff around, and pulled out a can of whipped cream. He shook the can as he walked over to the large glass doors. He began spraying the doors with whipped cream, a zigzag pattern from top to bottom.

'Hey, whatta you nuts?' Grudge said, walking into the kitchen. One fist was filled with money, mostly fives and ones, not the twenties that Byron had won.

'I told you to put some masking tape over the door.'

'A fucking X out of masking tape. You kidding me or what? That stuff leaves sticky shit on the glass when you take it off. My brother's coming back soon. You think I want to be jacking around here scraping sticky tape shit off the glass with my fingernails?'

Byron shrugged. 'One of these birds may eventually crack the glass. You want to replace it?'

'I'll take my chances, okay. Meantime, you shoot your wad on anything else around here and I'll fucking kill you, okay? Am I clear or what?'

Byron aimed the whipped cream nozzle at Grudge's face and squirted a small puff of cream onto the tip of Grudge's nose. 'Kill that.'

Grudge wiped the cream off with one finger and deposited the white glob on his tongue. 'That reminds me, bunch of gay guys sitting in a Jacuzzi, somebody spills some whipped cream in the water.'Nother guy sees it and says, "Hey, who farted?"'

Byron reached over and wiped the remaining dot of whipped cream from Grudge's nose with his palm. Neither man said anything, nor did they laugh at Grudge's joke.

'Prison humor,' Grudge said to me.

I nodded, not really anxious to engage him in conversation.

'Grudge, this is Wren.'

'Yeah your wife. We talked before, right? On the phone?'

I nodded. He acted as if our conversation had been a pleasant discussion of the weather rather than his onslaught of swearing and threats against my life. Again, I noticed the tattoo scribbled across the entire length of his arm. It wasn't the usual dragon or naked woman. It wasn't a picture at all. Just words. I looked closer. They were names. A single column list of names that ran from his wrist up under his sleeve. Daryl Carson. Stevie the Jinx. Swingshift Jackson. Homer Borden.

'Those are the names of the people Grudge has marked for death,' Byron said. 'Right, Grudge?'

Grudge nodded. 'Every single motherfucker guaranteed to die. My word on it.'

I didn't say anything. What could I say? How nice for you?

Byron laughed. 'See, Grudge's whole scam inside was telling people he was mobbed up, connected with the Mafia. Anybody does something he doesn't like, he tells them he'll have them killed. Of course, no one but the new fish took him seriously—'

'Bullshit! Lots of guys took me serious. Lots got outta my way, didn't fuck with me.' Grudge was a head shorter than Byron, about my height. But he had a compacted muscular look, as if he were wound up real tight and one little nudge would send him expanding to twice his size.

'Yeah, right,' Byron said. 'Anyway, one day some guy Grudge threatened actually died. Autopsy doesn't reveal cause of death, but Grudge is strutting around like he knows something. After that, everybody gives him a wide berth, just in case.'

'Just in case, shit. I know what I know.'

'So next, he starts tattooing names on his arm. Names of everybody who he thinks crosses him or who he wants to do him a favor. He tattoos your name on his arm, then you're dead. That's the idea, right, Grudge?'

'Sooner or later,' Grudge said. He pushed up his sleeve past his bicep. Third down from the top of the list is BYRON CALDWELL.

'That's you,' I said.

'Yup. Grudge claimed I bumped into him on the stairs.'

'He wanted to kill you for that?' I said.

Grudge took a step toward me. He smelled of sweet cologne. 'Lady, inside you kill somebody if he stares at you too long. Don't matter the reason, you let somebody get away with something, anything, then soon they got you down on the shower floor and twenty naked guys are kneeling behind you, your asshole the size of the Lincoln Tunnel. You get the picture?'

'Vividly,' I said. But I was thinking about Mark, my old student who came to visit me after I'd been shot. His tattoo. These men around me with their crude tattoos. What were they trying to mark, to measure?

Grudge looked at me in the eyes, stared hard. 'You

413

don't get it.' He looked at Byron and shook his head. 'She don't fucking get it.'

'Give her time,' Byron said. 'She learns quickly.'

'What do I give a shit what she learns?'

I was fed up with this prison mystique bullshit. 'What do I give a shit what you give a shit about?'

'How'd you like to wake up one morning and find your fucking head in the toilet? Huh? How'd that suit you?'

'That's how I do my hair now, so what's your point?'

Byron laughed. He returned the whipped cream to the refrigerator. 'Hungry?' he asked me.

I shook my head.

'I could use a sandwich,' Grudge said.

Leo the ex-prison guard came in and knocked on the counter. 'Hey, Byron. Shawna's here.'

Byron's face changed. He tensed up a little. The smile was still on his face, but it was a prop now, not genuine. 'Business, kids.'

He walked out of the kitchen, following Leo, without waiting for me or Grudge. The guys over watching TV got up and followed. Outside around the pool, men were talking rapidly and those who finished games or were just watching got up and came inside, walking past Grudge and me into the living room. The poker game broke up and the players also came inside.

'What's going on?' I asked Grudge.

'Rematch. Shawna took Byron yesterday three out of five games. She cleaned him out. First time he's lost in a straight-up match.'

'Straight up?'

Grudge sighed impatiently. 'Jesus, straight up. Where Byron don't spot any pieces or time. He's so good that usually to get anyone to play him for money, he's got to take away a couple of his pieces, a rook and a bishop maybe. Or he's got to play with less time, like he's only got two minutes on his clock, his opponent has five or ten.' He scratched his tattooed arm, his fingers digging in around CLANCY ROBBINS. 'But he played Shawna head to head and she kicked his ass.'

'I'd like to see that,' I said.

He grinned at me, his lips kind of crooked, like half his face was shot up with novocaine. 'Yeah, he said you would.'

31

I walked behind Grudge into the living room. Those who were in the midst of a game continued, but once each game finished, the players got up and moved over toward the grand piano, where the crowd was thickest. I couldn't see Byron or Shawna.

Grudge scratched at his tattoo again, stopping suddenly so that I stepped on his heel.

'Sorry,' I said.

'You think my tattoo is stupid, right?' He was angry.

'No,' I said.

'Sure you do. You think I disfigured myself like some asshole just to sound tough. Now I got the names of guys I don't like strapped to my skin for the rest of my fucking life. Am I right? That's what you think.'

'I don't think about it at all.'

'The fuck you don't. First time you saw me you had me pegged as some turd at the bottom of the shit pile.' He shrugged and seemed to calm down. 'Hey, that's okay. What do I care what you think, right?'

'Right.'

He gave me another hard look, eyeball to eyeball. I thought he was going to try to kiss me. Then he took a step backward and just pointed his finger at my face. 'When you're inside, you don't think the consequences your actions will have once you're outside. You follow me? Inside is inside. That's the whole world. And you do whatever you have to to survive. It ain't like the movies, no matter how bad they make it seem. It's worse.' He rubbed his face with his palms, as if his skin were cold. 'Hell, you know. Your husband told you.'

'Like what happened to his finger.'

Grudge nodded enthusiastically. 'Exactly. Jesus, man. I ain't never seen nothing like that. Byron is cornered in the weight room by some 300-pound brain-dead mother-fucker named Connie. I'm not using that description lightly, this guy *really* fucked his mother—after he cut off her head, though. Connie's suddenly decided he wants an intellectual type for his fuckmate and he's got your hubby up against a wall fumbling with his pants.'

I began rubbing my thumb along the seam of my sweater. Grudge's eyes seemed glazed, trance-like as he told the tale.

'Good thing Byron was smart enough not to try to hurt Connie, because then Connie would have killed him and then fucked him. It wouldn't have been the first time since he'd been inside.'

'Where were the guards? Didn't anybody see what was going on?'

Grudge laughed. 'I had a pretty good view, sure. Front row center. Me and about twenty other guys.'

'And you didn't do anything?'

'Yeah, I watched.'

'I mean you didn't help? There were twenty of you.'

Grudge looked annoyed. 'I thought Byron told you how it was inside.'

'He doesn't like to talk about it much.'

'Yeah, that's true. Me, I love talking about it. I'm like one of those old farts at a Veterans of Foreign Wars meeting. Wear some funky hat and talk about all my battles for the rest of my fucking life.'

More people were huddling around by the piano. For a moment I had a vision of Shawna sitting down playing the white grand piano and suddenly singing in a beautiful voice. That whole sign language thing was probably some practical joke they played on me.

'We better be getting over there,' Grudge said, starting away.

I grabbed his tattooed arm and held it. 'Finish your story. Please.'

'Not much to add you don't know. Byron sticks his own finger in his mouth, bites the end clean off, and spits it out on the floor. Then he looks down at Connie's crotch and grins that fucking grin of his. I mean he still has blood all over his teeth.' Grudge laughed. 'You shoulda seen the look on fucking Connie's big face. He's looking at your hubby like he can't fucking believe it. "You're fucking nuts," Connie says and walks away.'

'He bit his own finger off!'

'Sure, what'd he tell you?'

I started toward the crowd. Grudge followed.

'Nobody bothered Byron after that. I mean, nobody wants to fuck with someone like that. Me, I admired his balls. If I'd have thought of it instead of this fucking list, I'd have bit three fingertips off. Shit.' He scratched his arm again.

The crowd was thick as dough around the piano.

'Coming through, assholes,' Grudge said, elbowing ahead of me to break through the men. 'This is Byron's wife. Move it, man, before I have a couple guys come over and chainsaw your flabby ass off, you fucking moron. What're you looking at, fuckhead?'

No one seemed to take Grudge too seriously, but they moved aside just the same. When we got to the front of the circle, Byron and Shawna were setting up their chess pieces on the board. The pieces were simple, carved from wood.

Shawna leaned on the piano with one arm and used her free one to set up her pieces. She looked even more beautiful today than last night. Her black hair dropped straight down the sheer face of a shale cliff. Her expression was serene, as if she were mentally composing a song.

Byron's expression was more intense. His hair, pulled

back and tied at the nape of his neck, seemed more severe than a couple minutes ago. I watched his left hand, studied the stub of his little finger, tried to imagine him biting off his own finger and spitting it out. Was it courage or desperation? The act of a brave man or an animal gnawing off his own foot to be free of a trap?

'What are the stakes?' I whispered to Grudge.

'Whatever they want. They play a series of five games. The first one is ten minutes. Then seven, five, three, and finally a two-minute game.'

Byron reached into his pocket and pulled out the wad of twenties I'd seen him win earlier. Then he reached into his other pocket and pulled out another wad, even larger. He counted out all the bills. Three thousand dollars.

Shawna, not at all impressed, opened her tiny black purse and pulled out thirty crisp one-hundred-dollar bills. She placed them on top of Byron's thicker but dirtier pile and patted them twice, as if assuring them that they would soon all be safely back in her purse where they belonged.

'What does she do to make all that money?' I asked Grudge.

'Well, she wins a lot of it from dopes like us. The rest she makes running her dad's bail-bond business. That's her dad over there.' He pointed to a tall, chubby man with white hair and a kind face. He wore a plaid shirt that yesterday had been one of Byron's. He winked at his daughter and she smiled at him.

'I don't get it,' I said. 'If they want to bet, why not take it to the track or Vegas and put it all on red?'

' 'Cause this ain't gambling. Chess is one of the few games in the world that doesn't have any element of luck. No dice, no cards, no sun or wind. Life within your own control without chance to fuck you up. No new alarm system you're not prepared for, no flat tyre on the getaway car, no snitch who rats you out. Just thirty-two pieces, sixty-four squares, and your skill. It's like . . .' He brought his hands together and squeezed them until his fingers turned white. 'It's like you can hear that clock ticking in your head, like your fucking life is running out, but if you make the right move, the exactly right move, you can win more time. Like you've done something divinely good and you'll be rewarded. That's how it feels to me and I don't even play half as good as Byron. I can't imagine what the fuck he feels like when he's running the board. Like he's a god or something, like he can fucking fly through walls.' He shook his head with envy. 'I don't know. Shit, I'm just a guy who loads appliances in his brother's warehouse, did some time for passing bad checks. Don't ask me to explain nothing.' He scratched his arm.

I noticed that at the same time he was scratching his arm I was rubbing my thumbnail along the seam of my sweater again. We were, in fact, scratching and rubbing at the same pace, matching strokes. He noticed and looked at me, no hard stare this time, more like recognition. He turned away embarrassed at the intimacy.

'Give 'em some room, assholes,' Grudge said, stepping foward and shooing the crowd back a few steps. 'They gotta breathe too.'

Byron looked at Shawna and made some hand gestures. She nodded. They each set the clocks to ten minutes. They leaned across the white grand piano, their butts sticking out, elbows propping up their heads, like mirror images of each other.

Grudge took a light pawn, put both hands behind his back, and brought them out again as closed fists. Shawna tapped his left hand. He opened it and revealed the pawn. She replaced it on the board and turned the board around so the white pieces were in front of her.

The game was rapid, pieces cracking against the board, clock spanked into motion. I noticed a tiny scar on her jawline, which she occasionally touched when it wasn't her turn. Bud came in again, limped around the room, but gained no sympathy, no strokes. He sniffed the pile of tissues the man with the cold had left, found a half-eaten bagel on one of the card tables, grabbed it, and trotted out, his limp much less noticeable now.

'What happened to Bud?' I whispered. 'That limp?'

'Ssshhh,' Grudge said. Everyone in the room was concentrating on the game that clacked off before them.

Byron and Shawna seemed to exchange pieces evenly, so I didn't see that anyone was winning. Plus, they moved so quickly I never got a chance to figure out what I might do.

Suddenly I saw Byron tip over his king. He reached across the board and shook Shawna's hand.

The crowd went into instant murmur mode, discussing mistakes that Byron made, what they would have done, etc. Some ran for the kitchen and returned with cans of beer they distributed to others.

'It's over?' I said, staring at the board. 'But he's not in checkmate.'

'Checkmate in three,' Grudge said.

I looked at the board, confused. He walked over and started moving pieces. 'He moves there, she moves here. Check. He moves there or there, in which case she moves here or here. Check. That only leaves him here or there and she's there. Checkmate. Bam, bam, bam.'

Shawna's father handed Shawna and Byron each a beer, which they began to drink. The three of them gestured to each other, laughing or looking serious. Shawna's father went to the board and arranged the pieces a certain way that I guess they were at during the game. Then he went through some options and they all gestured some more.

'Bud got in a fight,' Grudge said. 'Got the shit clawed out of him from some fucking cat. Jesus, big dog like that let some weasely little cat fuck him up. He's the biggest wuss I've ever seen. Can't fight worth shit.' He started setting the pieces up on the board for a new game. 'Anyways, he comes in a week or so ago, limping like crazy, bleeding all over the place. Byron fixes him up. He's good with animals.'

So that's the dog blood on the money he gave me. At least now I could spend the money and stop holding it as evidence. My case against Byron was slipping away. His big illegal activity was chess, the missing finger was his own doing, the blood was a dog he administered first aid to, the mysterious phone calls involved chess matches. Compared to him, I was the major criminal. Wait, I still had his prison record. He was in there for something, something that involved Wren losing her teeth. I still had hope.

The second game began with seven minutes on the clock. They moved even more quickly this time, but after a while a little flag on Shawna's clock popped up and the game was over. She'd run out of time and lost. The usual post-mortem went on around us and everyone fell silent when the third game started. The clocks were adjusted for five minutes. Pieces were moved with the same mechanical speed, same clacking. Before I even knew what was going on, Shawna tipped over her king.

She made some hand gestures and Byron nodded. Shawna disappeared down the hall.

'Ten-minute break,' Byron announced and everyone scattered. Some went back to their boards to replay the games they just saw. Others threw money on the table and played a challenge game for real. Everyone's intensity made the room swampy with tension. I followed Shawna.

She went into a bathroom and shut the door. After a couple of minutes I heard the toilet flush, the water in the sink run, then she came out. At the moment she opened the door, before she'd prepared for the world outside, I caught a glimpse of her expression. Tired eyes, rimmed with red. She may have been crying. Mouth smeared with fresh lipstick, but the lips tense and frowning. She came out, caught me staring, and smiled. She laid a hand on my arm and squeezed like we were old and dear friends. Then she walked back toward the living-room, shoulders high, head back. Confident.

The three-minute game was played in a flurry of blurred moves. Captured pieces were tossed to the ground in the rush. Pieces were moved so quickly it didn't look to me as if any thought at all was put into the move. Yet some moves brought oohs and aahs from the crowd.

Suddenly Byron slapped a piece down, made a hand gesture, and pushed himself up from the edge of the piano. Shawna studied the board for a few seconds, smiled, and nodded. She curtsied to him and everyone applauded. Byron cut the money into two piles and shoved each pile into a separate pocket. Shawna came around the piano and kissed him on the cheek. He smiled for the first time since the match had started.

The crowd of onlookers rushed back to their games, looking newly inspired. Pieces were set up, clocks adjusted, and suddenly everyone was playing chess. I had to admit, I even felt like pulling up to a board and slamming a few pieces around. The atmosphere was exciting.

Byron walked toward Grudge and me. As he walked, he took a couple Tylenols out of a bottle in his pocket and popped a couple in his mouth. He snagged a beer can from one of the tables, shook it to see if there was anything in it, and washed down the Tylenol with whatever was left.

'Was it good for you?' he asked me.

'From what Grudge says, you just conquered time and space, you were flying, and winning one for the Gipper all rolled into one.'

Byron shrugged. 'It's just a game.'

'Fuck you, man,' Grudge said. 'Just a game. Just a game my ass. It's just a game when some of these patzers play. Not when you and Shawna play. Not when I play neither.'

'Patzer?' I asked.

'A patzer's a hack,' Byron said.

Grudge punched Byron in the arm. 'You can be such an asshole sometimes. If I had room, I'd scratch your name on my arm again.'

'Just don't put a heart around it.'

I looked past Byron and saw Shawna sitting at a card table playing chess with her father. She was plucking one of his pieces from the board and replacing it with her own. She smacked her clock button.

The doorbell rang. No one seemed to notice. Except Leo, who hauled himself off the sofa where he'd been watching a game and marched off to the front door.

'I'm outta here,' Grudge said. 'There's still some money to be made.' He walked off and started talking loudly to some guy returning from the kitchen with a sandwich. 'Don't take a bite, fatso. I'll play you a two-minute blitz for it. What is that, ham and cheese? You put mustard on it, asshole? If I win you go back and put some fucking mustard on it.' They sat down at a table and started setting up the pieces to play for the sandwich.

'Does that make you even with Shawna for beating you yesterday?' I asked Byron.

'No, that puts me ahead. We had a little side bet. She owes me a couple grand for Motown, the parrot, and a grand for the clothes she won.'

I looked at his face. One of his eyes was bloodshot, tiny lightning bolts of red etched through the white. 'You look awful. You okay?'

'Headache. It'll go away.'

'Do you get these headaches often? I mean, are we talking tumor or something?'

'Nothing so romantic. I just get them when I play chess. It's kind of like blowing out your knee in basketball, only there's nothing you can do about it.'

'You can not play.'

He didn't say anything. He looked over at the entrance-way to the foyer where Leo stood with another man, an even bigger man than Leo.

'You must need the money pretty badly to play if it does this to you. What do you do with all your winnings? Other than make loans?'

'I don't give interviews,' he said without looking at me. His eyes were fixed on the man Leo brought in, the man who was now walking toward us, smiling sadly at Bryon. I didn't realize how big he was until he walked by the other men in the room. Their heads barely peeped above his shoulders. It seemed to me that the men in the way purposely moved a little quicker to get out of his way, though no one looked directly at him or acknowledged his presence. Except Byron, who stared into the man's eyes.

'Jesus, Byron,' the man said as he approached. 'Jesus. Why are you making it so hard on yourself? Fuck that, why you making it so hard on me?'

They shook hands. Byron turned the man's hand over to examine the knuckles. 'I guess my face didn't do much damage.'

'My wrist is a little sore. You better not have fucked up my tennis game. Laura and I are in a doubles tournament next week. She'll kill both of us.'

They both laughed.

Byron turned to me. 'This is my old cellmate Jerry Kirn.' He paused, smiled at me. 'Tell him who you are.'

Jerry waited, Byron grinned. What name did he think I'd give?

'Wren,' I said. 'Nice meeting you, Jerry.'

'Aaah,' Jerry said. 'The wife.'

'My current cellmate,' Byron said.

'Am I being dense here or something,' I said to Jerry. 'Did you just say you're the guy who beat Byron up yesterday.'

'That was me,' he said in a chipper voice. He reached out and clutched Byron's jaw in a motherly way, turning it side to side. 'Not bad, not bad at all. Mostly for show stuff, bruises and cuts, but no real damage.'

'I hate men,' I said.

Jerry laughed. He was the most good-natured man I'd ever met. 'We are a dumb bunch of chromosomes, aren't we?'

'Jerry works for Landry,' Byron explained. 'Landry told him to knock me around until I agreed to play a blitz match with his boss.'

'I'm surprised you didn't just chomp off another finger,'

I said. Byron looked startled that I knew. He fired a menacing look across the room at Grudge.

'Wouldn't work,' Jerry said. 'Landry's seen the finger bit already. Hey, "the finger bit", get it?' He chuckled at his own joke.

'So you knocked Byron around and you're still pals, right?'

Jerry shrugged. 'That's my job. Byron knows that. Besides, I could've made it worse. This way it looks like he took a real beating and all I did was throw a few well-placed shots.'

'Jerry's an artist,' Byron said without irony.

Jerry's face went serious. 'Of course, that only works once. Landry was not happy about you refusing him again. I think this time you're gonna have to accept, Byron. I mean it, man.'

Byron shook his head. 'Can't do it, Jerry. The guy's a pig.'

'I don't know. Pig's a matter of perspective. He pays me on time, treats me like a professional. I got no complaints.'

'Can't do it, man. You know that.'

Jerry frowned, looked pained, like he might cry. 'I gotta break something this time, man.'

'Like what?'

'I dunno, he just said not to touch the right arm or hand so you can play.'

Byron looked down at his own body. 'It would be hard to get to a bus on crutches, so how about my left hand? That sound good?'

I couldn't take it any longer. 'Are you two crazy? You're discussing which limb to break because he doesn't want to play a game of chess with your boss. What's the big deal? Play the guy!'

'I think she's right, Byron. It were me, hell, I'd just play him. You know he's not gonna stop hounding you till you do. You know why.'

Byron looked at me. I don't know what he thought he

426

saw, but there was a sadness and gentleness in his expression I'd never seen before. For a moment, I thought he was waiting for me to do something or say something. And, crazy enough, I wanted to, maybe touch his face, smooth his hair, pat his hand. Some gesture as simple and clear as the sign language he spoke with Shawna, the movement of a chess piece. I wanted to do something.

Then the moment passed and he said to Jerry, 'Tell Landry I'll play him.'

'Don't dick me around, Byron. That would only make things worse.'

'Tell him I'll call with details.'

Jerry looked both relieved and disappointed, like he saved a friend but lost a hero. 'I'll tell him.' He turned and walked away.

Before Jerry was out the front door, the room was loud with discussions of what had been overheard. There was excitement and awe and a kind of nervous anticipation.

'Let's get out of here,' Bryon said.

Somehow I got the feeling that he'd taken the match because of me. Somehow I got the feeling that was a big, big mistake.

32

'Where are we going?' I asked. I'd been driving about thirty minutes along the 91 Freeway toward Riverside.

'Keep going. I'll tell you when we get there.'

I'm not the kind of person who generally accepts that as an answer. But this time I didn't argue. I drove.

'Why is Landry so hot to play you?'

'There's a McDonald's. Pull off.'

'Sure you can afford it, big spender?'

He looked at me. 'Who said I'm buying?'

We coasted through the drive-thru lane and picked up our bag at the second window. The girl in the headphones said, 'Four thirty-eight.' I refused to reach for any money. So did Byron. 'That'll be $4.38,' she repeated nervously. I didn't budge. The car behind us nosed closer. A car behind them honked twice. I stared out the windshield. Finally, Byron dug into his pocket and handed me a twenty, which I handed to the girl. 'Keep the change,' I said to her and sped away. I saw her puzzled look in my rearview mirror as she hung out the window, the twenty-dollar bill clutched in her hand.

'Guess they don't get tipped much here,' I said.

He reached into the bag and handed me my iced tea. He shoved a few shoestring fries into his mouth.

'Landry's a loan shark,' Byron said. 'He was in prison the same time Jerry and I were. He fancies himself as something of an intellectual. A gentleman crook, like David Niven or Cary Grant.'

'He was part of your little chess club?'

Byron shrugged, popped a McNugget into his mouth.

I laughed. 'Prison isn't what I imagined. I mean, I envisioned sweaty guys with bad teeth settling arguments with the sharpened end of a toothbrush.'

'Yeah, that's the rule generally. Everything you've ever imagined it to be. Only worse. The gangs, the murders, the rapes. You tell a joke and somebody doesn't get the punchline, he may just kill you for the insult. But even within that there are little groups of aficionado. The weight-lifting group is out there every day pumping iron until their necks look like inner-tube mutations. You know what the Hillside Strangler and the Freeway Killer and those mass murderers do every day? They play bridge. Swear to God, the bastards have a little bridge club, mass murderers only need apply.'

'Sounds cozy.'

Byron slurped his root beer. 'It passes time. More than that it gives meaning to time, structure to what seems like an endless stream of minutes passing you by. They take their games very seriously.'

'But you don't, right? Like you said, it's just a game.'

He looked over at me and smiled. 'That's right. It's just a game. For me, a way to pick up some money.'

A couple of cars coming the other way had their headlights on and I noticed it was starting to get dark. I switched on my headlights too. 'Landry. You were telling me about Landry.'

'No big secret. He's a loan shark looking to step up in the world. Like I said, he fancies himself an intellectual, a mastermind. He's very ambitious and something of a publicity nut. He'd like to be planning major heists, the kind of stuff that makes headlines, like the Brinks job, or the Lufthansa heist, or the Great Train Robbery. Naturally, only those in the very top positions would know he's responsible, but that's enough for Landry. Thing is, to do something that size you need to get permission from the local organized-crime heads. And that you can't get unless they think you've got a hell of a good chance of pulling it off.'

'Are we still talking about chess or did I take a wrong turn somewhere?'

'Be patient, Luna.'

When he said my name, I felt a strange tingle across my scalp. I hadn't heard it in so long it felt kind of nice. Luna. Say it again, I wanted to say. Luna. Luna. Luna.

'For the crime bosses to give Landry permission, he needs to convince them he can do the job and not bring any heat down on them. To do that, he needs top talent, the kind of professional talent that is hard to come by. Why would any of them hook up with a loan shark like Landry? Unless he can convince them he's a smart guy. He thinks beating me at chess will be favorable P.R. for him among the criminal community. First step on the thousand-mile journey.'

'Is that as stupid as it sounds?'

'What, you think crooks are wise old men who spout proverbs and play boccie ball? They're criminals. If he were such a genius, why'd he go to prison in the first place?'

'Why'd you?'

He didn't answer. He finished his root beer and started chewing his ice. So did I. For a couple miles there was no sound in the car but the crunching of ice.

'Pull over,' he said, pointing to the side of the road.

'You sick?'

'Yes.'

I snapped on my turn signal and eased across two lanes until I was able to safely pull off the freeway. Cars whooshed beside us, the force of their speed rocking the car a little. Byron sat straight up staring out the windshield.

'Don't you want to get out or something? Hang your head out the window?'

He turned in the seat and flicked on the overhead light. He reached into his jacket pocket and pulled out a little

430

wooden box, which he unfolded, releasing tiny black and white chess pieces onto his seat like bombs.

'What the hell are you doing? I thought you were sick.'

'I am sick of listening to you talk about things you don't know shit about.' He quickly stuck the pegged chess pieces into their holes and set the board between us. I was white. Then he snatched up from his side a rook, a bishop, two pawns, a knight, and his queen. 'Fair enough?' he asked.

True, I didn't play chess that much with Robby, but I wasn't an idiot either. By the time we were divorced, I played well enough to beat Robby a few times. Head to head, I knew there was no way I could beat Byron. But with half of his pieces gone, especially his queen, I figured I had a better than even chance.

'How about this,' he said. 'You can have one full minute for each move, I'll move within three seconds. That better?'

His arrogance dug into my chest, making my bullet scar ache. 'Yes,' I said. 'That's better.'

'Your move.'

I did, playing a basically sound game, moving my queen's pawn out, then developing my knights to control the center of the board, then castling to protect my king. I moved cautiously but deliberately, showing him no lack of confidence. He moved like a robot, his eyes never leaving the board, but as if he knew all of his moves ahead of time and that none of my moves interfered with his plan the least bit. I started to panic a little, watch the clock when it was my move.

'Time,' he said.

'What?'

'Your minute is up.'

'No it isn't.' I looked over at the car clock but I couldn't remember when my time had started. I moved a piece and he took my rook. My heart was pounding in an unnatural rhythm, like reggae steel drums. My thumbnail was sore from being rubbed against the edge of the seat. I moved again and again he took my piece, a knight.

'Check,' he said. 'Mate in two.'

I studied the board, tried to see the mate in two. I put my hand on my queen, then on my rook, back to the queen.

'Time,' he said.

'Jesus, stop it.'

'You want another minute?'

'Fuck you.' I moved my queen to cancel his check.

He unpegged his knight and pegged it so that it could take either my king or queen. 'Check.'

I had no choice but to move my king, which I did without taking much time. He slid his rook across the board into the same file as my king.

'Checkmate.'

I stared dumbly at the board, looking for his error. Impossible that I could be checkmated so rapidly by his crippled army. Sweat thickened my skin. My throat felt ashy, my teeth were coated with something gritty that hadn't been there before the game started.

He sat back and stared straight ahead out the windshield. 'You feel humiliated, right? There's nothing you'd rather do right now than crush my skull with a hammer. Except maybe play me again. That's the only way you can get a little shred of self-respect back, isn't it? I mean, think about it. I had no queen, for God's sake. One rook, one bishop, one knight, and only six pawns. I moved in three seconds. Three. One thousand one, one thousand two, one thousand three. Pow. Checkmate, stupid.'

'It's just a game,' I said and started the car. I pulled back into the traffic. But the thing was, he was right. I felt stupid, humiliated. And the fact that I knew it was stupid to feel that way only made it worse. I wanted to hurt him for putting me through this.

Byron swallowed another Tylenol. 'Now you know how Landry feels.'

The sky was completely dark now. Headlights crawled by in an ominous procession.

'I came out here with you because I felt kind of sorry for you before,' I said. 'I don't feel that way any longer, so I'm turning around.'

'We're almost there,' he said.

'Almost where?'

'You want to know where the money goes, right? My winnings?'

'I couldn't care less. Why would I care?'

But I kept driving and we kept chewing ice.

33

The man was running toward us yelling before I'd even braked the car to a stop: 'What the hell are you doing here? Who is she? Were you followed?'

I recognized him from his lunch with Byron earlier that day, the guy to whom Byron gave the envelope stuffed with money. He was short and thin, with wire-rimmed glasses similar to mine. He wore an orange T-shirt and baggy shorts that hung to his knees, making him look a little like an over-age skateboarder. My headlights spotlighted him jumping up and down and waving at us so that he looked like he was doing a kind of crazy dance on a stage. Byron laughed at the sight.

I parked next to the dusty black Jeep in the gravel driveway. A thick cloud of road dust that the tyres had kicked up rose up around the car like smoke. Byron got out and stretched.

'Byron. Christ.' The man shook his head as he trotted toward us, distraught. He peered back down the deserted road that we'd just driven on. 'Are you sure you weren't followed?'

'Relax,' Byron said.

'I'll relax when I'm sure you weren't followed.'

'I don't see any headlights,' I said. I was just trying to calm him down.

'Their headlights wouldn't be on if they were following you,' he snapped. 'That's the whole point. Stealth.' He shook his head. 'Shit!'

'Gee,' I said, 'maybe we should sweep the car for hidden transmitters that might be beaming back our location to a secret helicopter.'

'I've already taken care of that. I've planted four electronic tumblers out there—' he pointed in four compass directions at the vast desert around us— 'that scramble any low-frequency signals for a five-mile radius. Kills bugs dead.'

I looked at Byron for some explanation of what we were doing here and how dangerous this guy might be, but Byron was walking toward the ancient two-storey white house next to the driveway.

'I have to use the john,' he announced. 'Zeno, that's Luna. Luna, Zeno. He knows all about you, so relax.'

Zeno and I watched him walk away, then we looked at each other like children abandoned in a supermarket. We quickly hurried after him.

'This is crazy, Byron,' Zeno said. 'You shouldn't be here and she *especially* shouldn't be here. You're jeopardizing everything. I want that to go on record right now.'

'So recorded.' Byron went up the splintered, sun-dried stairs, across the porch, and into the house. The screen door clattered behind him.

Zeno held the screen door open and waved me impatiently inside. He stared out into the darkness one last time for stealthy cars before closing the door behind him.

Byron stood in the bathroom with the door open and pissed into the toilet. Zeno averted his eyes. I didn't. I could see the steady stream shooting down. The sound was loud and kind of soothing. 'I brought some more money, Zeno.'

This perked Zeno up. 'How much?'

'Not enough. Six thousand.'

'That's not enough. Not nearly enough.'

'That's what I just said.' Byron finished, shook himself, zipped up, washed his hands, and flushed. I thought it odd that he flushed *after* washing his hands. I guess I even thought it odd that he washed his hands at all.

'Where are we exactly?' I asked.

'You don't need to know,' Zeno said.

'Forty miles past Palm Springs,' Byron said. 'Desert all around us for hundreds of miles.'

'Christ,' Zeno slapped his hip. 'Why not take an ad out?'

'We can trust her.' There was something in the simple way he said it that made me ashamed. After all, I was here for dirt, not trust. But Byron knew that. Why then did he bring me here, to the lair of his secrets?

'So far there's not a whole lot to trust me with,' I said. 'An old house in the desert. Did you guys find some gold or uranium or something?'

'Better,' Byron said.

'Much better,' Zeno added. His attitude seemed to change suddenly. Now that he accepted my presence, he got excited and talkative. 'This is bigger than precious metals, and potentially worth a lot more. We're talking about something that will change the world for centuries to come. Nothing will ever be the same.'

I sighed. 'Desert desert everywhere, but not a decent shrink.'

'What's that supposed to mean?' Zeno asked.

'It means you two need some professional help. Byron's playing chess every day, taking an occasional beating to his head. You're holed up here in the thousand-degree heat working on some secret formula or something. Didn't I see this movie already? Jeff Goldblum plays both of you.'

Byron laughed. 'Let's show her, Zeno.'

Zeno looked petulant. 'Screw her. Let her believe whatever she wants. Who cares what she thinks?'

'I care.' Byron led the way through the house and out the back door where we stood in front of a large makeshift greenhouse covered with clear plastic sheets. The building was the size of a barn.

Oh, Christ, I thought, drugs. They're growing some new potent marijuana. The feds probably have the place surrounded and now they think I'm part of the gang. Any second now guys wearing jackets with DEA AGENT in big white letters on them will come rushing in waving heavy rifles.

'Come on, don't be scared,' Byron said. 'It's all very legitimate.'

He held the door of the greenhouse open and I entered. The air was thick and moist, it smelled somehow tropical, the dank-sweet scent of decaying leaves. Warm flannel air clung to my skin like Velcro. I found myself breathing deeply to make sure I was getting enough oxygen.

The room was laid out very simply. Three rows of wooden troughs filled with plants lined the greenhouse. They didn't look like marijuana.

'Bamboo,' Zeno said.

I walked up one aisle and down the next. At the back of the greenhouse was a laboratory bench with all kinds of chemicals and tools and microscopes. 'Bamboo,' I repeated, nodding. 'Just bamboo.'

'Yes,' Zeno said sarcastically. 'Just bamboo.'

'And this is what's going to change the world? I hate to tell you boys, but bamboo already grows in a lot of the world. They been sticking bamboo splints up people's fingernails for centuries. Accept no subsitute.'

'There are over 500 species,' Zeno said. 'Throughout south-eastern Asia, through India, all the way across to Korea and Japan. Even though it's technically a grass, it can grow over 135 feet tall. Amazing, isn't it?'

'Stupefying,' I said. 'What's the point?'

Zeno shook his head and looked at Byron. 'God, you were right about her.'

I looked at Byron too. 'Oh? How so?'

'I told him you sometimes confused being a smart-ass with being smart.' I started to protest, but Byron waved at Zeno to continue.

'Anyway, bamboo isn't just a convenience, millions of people depend on it to literally stay alive. Bamboo hay has four times the protein content of hay from fodder grasses, which means the entire livestock population of most of those countries is dependent on bamboo. No bamboo, no food. The paper made from bamboo in China is far superior to newsprint. Even more significant, bamboo is responsible for much of the housing material in these countries. They depend on it for food and shelter.'

Byron hopped up on a shaky wooden table stacked with bags of soil. 'Problem is, most bamboo has a very long period between flowerings—fifteen years, thirty years, sixty years, even 120 years. This makes it very difficult to use consistently and can cause famine and homelessness in some countries.'

'That's true,' Zeno said, looking annoyed with Byron's interruption. 'Because you have whole stands of bamboo flowering at one time, they also die at the same time. This leads to the collapse of entire forests at once, which often results in vast forest fires as well as rat infestations as they gather to eat the seeds. That means disease and thousands of deaths.' Zeno began tucking his T-shirt into his shorts, assuming a more professorial appearance. He adjusted his glasses. 'Scientists all over the world have been trying to quicken the gestation period of bamboo to make it flower faster.' He looked at Byron and grinned. 'I found a way.'

'Not entirely on your own,' Byron reminded him.

Zeno looked embarrassed.

Byron continued, 'Zeno and I met in prison. He was tutoring illiterate prisoners, teaching them how to read in exchange for cigarettes and whatever other prison currency he could get.'

'Were you a part of the chess club too?' I asked.

'Me? No way. Chess is a stupid game. Waste of time.'

Byron didn't seem to take any offense at that. 'Before prison, Zeno was a lab assistant at a university, doing some key research in plant genetics.'

'The guy I was working for, Dr. Palomar, is one of the big shots in plant genetics. He pioneered acceleration of flowering of the loblolly pine and day lily as a result of tissue culture. Quite fascinating methodology if you—'

'Keep it simple, man,' Byron said.

'What were you in for?' I asked Zeno.

Zeno looked confused, as if he didn't remember being in prison. 'I stole library books and sold them to collectors.'

'You stole books? You went to prison for stealing library books?' I laughed.

'How much did you make a year stealing library books, Zeno,' Byron asked, but he was looking at me.

'Depends. I mean, I had to travel a bit to various university libraries, so there were travel expenses to deduct.'

'Net profit.'

Zeno shrugged. 'Fifty to seventy-five thousand dollars a year.'

'Impossible,' I said.

'Not really,' Zeno said. 'There's actually quite a market for antiquarian books. You'd be surprised.'

'Surprised? I'm dumbfounded. Seventy-five thousand dollars a year for used library books. Christ.'

'Not just any book. They have to be rare, that's the challenge.'

I sat down on a couple of burlap bags of soil. 'Why'd you do it?'

He looked surprised. 'Money, of course. Dr. Palomar abandoned the bamboo project because he was afraid he couldn't get another government grant. Everything is run on grants in the university. So, always sensing grant opportunities, Dr. Palomar applied for a grant to create a smokeless, nicotineless, cancerless tobacco for cigarettes. The money poured in and the bamboo was scrapped.'

'So, Zeno here saved what papers he could from the project, and stole library books to finance his own experiments.'

I looked at Byron. 'And now that he has no more income, you play chess to make enough money to finance this whole thing.' I gestured to encompass the greenhouse.

'We're very close to success,' Zeno said excitedly. 'The idea is adding cytokinin and coconut milk to the tissue-cultured shoots. The coconut milk supplies the inositol and cytokinin oxidase inhibitors that then allows the cytokinin to promote the plant maturation.'

'That's good?'

'Good? Jesus, I've already gotten them to flower after only three subcultures. This is an innovation equal to the Salk vaccine, discovering penicillin . . .' He waved his hands, his mouth open chewing air, searching for an appropriate metaphor.

'Refrigeration,' Byron offered.

'Exactly!' He pointed at Byron. 'Refrigeration. We're talking about not only eliminating one of the world's greatest plagues, but actually increasing food and building supplies. Within a couple generations, a heartier, faster flowering species of bamboo will be growing everywhere.'

I stood up, brushed the loose soil from my pants. 'Thanks for the tour. Your secret is safe with me. I'd like to go home now.'

Byron hopped off the table. 'Zeno, can we borrow your Jeep.'

'Sure, yeah. What for?' He tossed the keys to Byron.

'I want to show Luna something.'

'I don't want to see anything else,' I said. 'I've seen so much. My eyeballs are on full. Really.'

'You want to know about Wren, don't you? What happened to us? About my evil criminal life? Her missing teeth? I mean, isn't that the mystery piece of the puzzle, the information that will make your performance, your impersonation of her all the more complete?'

I looked at him for a while. His face didn't reveal anything, just stared back with that blank wall expression while he fingered his dragonfly earring. All around us mutated bamboo shoots were growing unnaturally fast. That made me nervous, as if I expected them to suddenly shoot a root thick as a cable out of the sod, wrap it around my neck, and drag me back under the ground until I was mulch.

Did I really want to know what happened between

440

Byron and Wren? If Wren had wanted me to, she would have told me. Besides, I was getting out of the Wren business. Out of the Season business. Just as soon as Davis came back, I was telling him everything. I owed him the truth. I owed someone some kind of truth.

'Never mind,' Byron said. He tossed the keys back to Zeno and started walking back to the house. 'She's just talked herself out of it.'

I marched over to Zeno and grabbed the keys from his hand. 'Let's go, bucko. Show me what you've got.'

34

'Insects,' he said.

'Insects? As in bugs?'

He smiled. 'One and the same. Technically, Insecta.'

'Insecta? Sounds like a Japanese movie. Some giant mantis head crushing a lot of cardboard buildings.'

We were bouncing through the cool night air across a dirt path through the desert. Byron drove what seemed to be much faster than was safe, given the low visibility and lack of clearly defined road. He didn't look worried. He wrestled the steering wheel through turns and curves like someone who knew this land by heart. Every bounce cinched my seat belt tighter against my bladder and I was wishing I'd gone to the bathroom back at the house.

'Insecta is a class of the largest animal phylum, Anthropoda. They used to be called Hexapoda because of the three pairs of legs at the thorax. There are over one million known species and they constitute about eighty three per cent of known animal life on this planet. Impressed or should I babble on?'

'Impressed,' I said. 'Okay, so you were a bug major in college.'

'Entomology.'

'Did you have a specialty, like an English major might specialize in the nineteenth-century British novel?'

'You mean did I have a favorite bug?'

'Right.'

'I was partial to the Hymenoptera.'

'Why, because it had hymen in it?'

He laughed. 'I hadn't thought about it, but you may be right.'

If I concentrated on staring up at the stars, the bouncing of the Jeep didn't bother me as much. Even though we were zipping around like a drunken jackrabbit, the stars overhead stayed in one place and that made me feel better. 'So what is the hymen bug?'

'Hymenoptera. It's an ant. I like ants.'

Now I laughed. I don't know why, it wasn't especially funny. But I felt suddenly giddy, like I had a secret pact with the stars to keep me safe. Or maybe it was the pressure on my bladder.

He must have interpreted my laughter as a response to his love of ants. 'Ants are more complex than people realize,' he said defensively. 'There are 8,804 species of the family Formicidae. They do things we can't fully imagine. For example, they build nests that can go twenty feet deep and have over a thousand entrances. The weaver ants use silk thread from larvae to bind leaves together for penthouse suites. A species in Malaysia keeps livestock in the form of mealybugs. Get this, the mealybug eats sap rich in amino acids and sugar, then passes it on to the ants in the form of drops of excrement.'

'Jesus.' I made a face and swallowed dryly.

'In exchange for this service, the ants protect them from other predators. And when the sap dries up, the ants use their jaws to carry the mealybugs on to new plants. Kind of like being carried in a shark's mouth.'

'Fascinating, Byron,' I said, hoping that would end it.

'It's more than fascinating, it's fucking cosmic. You've got a carpenter ant that has no reproductive organs. You know what it has instead?'

'Cable TV?'

'That space instead holds poison-filled glands. One of these ants gets into a fight, in order to protect the nest, it will purposely rupture this gland, exploding its own body so it can spray the poison on the enemy. God, that's interesting.'

I turned in my seat to look at him. His face was boyish and happy. 'I just realized,' I said. 'You're the same type of nerd as Zeno back there. His face looked just like yours when he was talking bamboo sprouts and coconut milk. I mean, you play chess and wear an earring and bite off your fingers, but basically you guys are a lot alike.'

'I don't take that as an insult.'

'It wasn't meant as one. It's just an observation, that's all.'

'Do you have any insight to go with your observation?'

'I don't do insight. I'm not Wren, as you so often point out, just an imposter.'

We were silent for a while. Except for the stars, there were no other lights. I had no idea even what direction the house was. Hell, what direction Los Angeles was. All around us was desert dirt and wiry bushes and a crisp smell that was almost sharp enough to slice your lungs.

'So how did you go from bugs to prison?' I asked.

'I was working for the U.S. Department of Agriculture, developing a program to match beneficial insects with specific crops as an alternative to insecticides. We were trying different breeding methods to make enough insects to keep up with the demand.'

'Like a bug bordello, huh?'

He ignored me. 'We were raising the green lacewing, the cryptolaemus, certain predatory mites. And with the pesticide scare going on, we were in demand.'

'Where does Wren fit into all this?'

'Wren,' he said softly. He shook his head as if he were having an internal discussion.

'Wren,' I repeated.

'I worked with the bugs during the day, but I worked with EarthWorth at night. Secretly, of course.'

'EarthWorth? You mean those guys who chain themselves to the redwoods so the loggers don't cut them down, that sort of thing?'

He frowned at the reference. 'Yeah, that sort of thing. We were a monkey-wrench activist group, like Earth First or Greenpeace. That means we didn't just talk about the environment, we took some corrective action.'

'Like chaining yourself to a tree.'

'I didn't chain myself to a fucking tree, okay? I wasn't a tree hugger, I was an environmental activist. We did things like hammering spikes into trees so the loggers would break their saws. Once we dug a trench across a logging road, filled it with quick-drying cement, and stepped into it to form a human severe-tyre-damage line.'

'Sounds like tree hugging to me.'

He sighed. 'We sabotaged some heavy equipment when they wanted to build condos out here and ruin the ecosystem balance.'

'None of this sounds like Wren.'

He stopped the Jeep. The headlights shone against a sheer rock wall of mountain. We'd been following the hills for a couple miles but I hadn't noticed us getting so close. He jumped out of the Jeep and started foraging in the back. He found a blanket and some matches. 'Go over there,' he said, pointing at some gnarled bushes. 'I'll build a fire.'

'Why do you want me to go over there? So I won't learn the secret of fire, Prometheus?'

'So you can take a leak. You've been squirming in your seat for twenty minutes.'

I walked over behind the bushes, pulled down my pants and panties, and squatted.

'Watch out for scorpions,' he called. 'They're all over the place.'

I looked down at my exposed opening only inches from the ground and lifted myself a little higher. When I finished, I dressed and returned to the Jeep. A few feet away Byron was tossing wood onto a pleasant little campfire.

'Doesn't this destroy the ecosytem balance?' I said, sitting on the blanket next to him.

'Yeah, but I plan to sacrifice you to the god of the desert and spill your blood into the sand, so it all evens out.'

We both stared into the fire the way people always do,

445

like they've never seen one before, dumb expressions on their faces as if their life forces were being extracted by the wiggling flames. Sitting there, not knowing which direction was which, how far we were from civilization, only twenty feet from a wet spot on the ground where I'd just urinated, I felt relaxed. I wasn't even anxious to hear about Wren.

'Wren didn't like my nocturnal activities. Neither did the Ag Department. They fired my ass as soon as a photo of me appeared in *Time* magazine with my feet stuck in cement.'

I tried to imagine Wren with her feet stuck in cement. Somehow I couldn't.

'She thought our behaviour too extreme. We fought about it.'

And you popped her one, right? I thought. Knocked her teeth out, then fell to your knees begging forgiveness.

'Wren liked to watch, to observe. To judge. She was good at it. Analyzing what people did, why they did it, what they meant by it. But she didn't really *do* anything. Did you know she wasn't even registered to vote?'

I shook my head. That surprised me. She always had very vocal opinions about every political issue and candidate.

'For all her articulation, Wren didn't really want to participate. She didn't live life in the fast lane or the slow lane, she lived in the bus lane. Safe and above the others, with someone else driving.'

'That's bullshit,' I said. 'Wren didn't let anyone drive her. She did what she wanted, she was in complete control. Everyone knew that, everyone who really knew her.'

He shrugged. 'She was a better actress than you.'

I stood up angrily. 'You really piss me off. You come out of the woodwork without even seeing her for two years and you start telling me what she was like. Well, maybe you didn't know her as well as you thought. Maybe you didn't know her at all.'

'Maybe,' he said quietly. He tossed a rock into the fire

and some sparks flew up. 'One evening I'd talked her into going on one of our little raids.' He pointed out into the darkness. 'Just a few miles over there where people came here to drive their all-terrain vehicles, chewing up the land and killing off a lot of necessary wildlife. I guess I shamed her into it, calling her a fence sitter, a moral Peeping Tom. That sort of thing.'

I sat back down and watched him. He looked right at me, not with his cold prison-yard face, but with lost eyes and a sad turn to his mouth.

'We went in at night to plant some big deep rocks in the paths where they usually did their racing. Wren and I were digging a hole when we heard loud engines suddenly start up and bright flashlights shining on us. Somehow they found out about our plan and had come down and hid out, waiting for us. They started chasing us in their ATVs, armed with baseball bats. I dragged Wren out of there. We were running together when some yahoo drove by us and swung his bat into Wren's face.'

'Jesus.'

'Yeah.' He flicked a small rock from his thumbnail and it sailed over the fire. 'I took her to the hospital. The cops arrested me while I was waiting there. I got two years.'

'For what? Did you kill the bastard who hit her?'

He laughed wryly. 'We never found out who did it. I was sent up for destruction of property and trespassing. I was an example.'

I laid down on my side and propped up my head with my arm. 'That's it, huh? You didn't smack her around?'

'Sorry to disappoint you. Anyway, she wouldn't speak to me after that. She blamed me for what happened, for talking her into going in the first place.' He looked at me. 'I guess she was right.'

Staring into the fire and listening to Byron's voice made me sleepy. Now that I knew there was nothing sinister about him, I could relax even more. But part of me was disappointed. I had set him up as my adversary, the man

I would defeat. I guess it was a lot like having a chase scene, the way my student described. Having Byron as the villain gave some meaning to what I did. Without him in the garden, what good was paradise?

'Why did you tell me all this now?' I said. 'I asked you plenty of times before.'

'I told you. I wasn't going to help you impersonate Wren. And that's the only reason you wanted the information, to add to your shrine.'

'What's different now?'

He flicked another stone from his thumbnail. It arced up high and dropped into the fire. 'You're different.'

I didn't see any difference. As far as he knew I was still pretending to be Wren. Nothing had really changed. So I had to think of some other reason he was telling me all this. It didn't take me long. Money. I had some and he needed some.

'How long before your bamboo project is done?' I asked.

'Hard to tell. We're still running experiments. That takes money. So, as long as I keep winning, we're still in business. But that's going to get harder. I'm going to have to give away too much from now on just to get someone to bet money. Too many pieces, too much time. That will catch up to me.'

'How much money do you need?'

He shook his head. 'Zeno figures another hundred grand. But, considering we're going to make millions, it's worth the investment.'

I sat up. 'Is that what this is about? Making millions?'

He laughed. 'You mean, am I in this for the bucks or to carry on the altruistic spirit of tree hugging?'

'Yes, that's what I mean.'

'Can't I do both? Save a tree and still make a few bucks?'

'A few million bucks.'

He leaned forward and gently laid another piece of gray wood on the fire. 'You're making $50,000 writing a book pretending to be Wren. Does that mean you cared any less for Wren?'

'It's not the same.'

'Sure it is. I hugged trees, you hugged Wren. We both got burned, now we're both in it for the bucks. I can accept that, why can't you?'

I had a mental image of Byron and I standing side by side in a clearing. He had his arms wrapped around a skinny sapling of a tree. I had mine wrapped around a white pine coffin. Inside I could feel Wren's weight pulling the coffin toward the ground, but I wouldn't let it fall.

'You sure must see things a lot different than you used to,' I said.

'Two years in a small cell helps you see the big picture. Two years of looking at things through a snitch mirror you hold outside your bars changes your perspective a little. After you see things in reflection long enough, when you see them without the mirror they look funny, fake.' He whistled a couple notes. 'Yeah, I see different. More clearly.'

'What about EarthWorth? Maybe they'd be glad to invest for such a worthy cause?'

He looked up from the fire straight at me. 'What are you trying to say?'

'I'm saying that I have no intention of giving you any of my money. I'm saying that this whole trip to the desert to meet your wacky pal and see your little greenhouse doesn't mean shit to me. And this cozy chat around the campfire won't get you a cent.'

'That's what you think this was about? Getting your money? Jesus, you're worse than I thought.'

'Right. Like you don't want my money. Were you after just part of it or the whole fifty grand. Did you really want the money for your project or just to keep me from publishing Wren's magazine and making it a success?'

'That magazine is a failure no matter how popular it becomes.'

'Yeah, right. More prison parables from the Monk of C Block.'

He stood up and brushed the dirt from his pants. 'Forget it. I don't weep at the extinction of species, I don't wince at dolphins in tuna nets, I don't lecture passers-by on smoking. The whole world is dying anyway, heading toward extinction. That's as inevitable as the sun flaming out.' He kicked dirt onto the campfire, smothering half the flames.

'Is that your big insight? Two years of looking through a mirror and that's it? Maybe you should have Windexed your mirror, pal. We already know the sun will nova. In a few billion years. Meantime, I still plan to keep up my subscription to *People* magazine.'

'Under whose name? Or is Luna Devon an extinct species.'

I don't know, something about the way he said it, phrased it maybe, I don't know. My skin tightened as if I'd just stepped inside a freezer. I threw a couple more pieces of wood on the fire and blew the flames back to life. I needed warmth.

'Let's go,' Byron said. 'Now that you know I wouldn't take your fucking money, there's nothing to stay for.'

His moral tone bugged me, so I marched back to the Jeep, snagged my purse, and returned to the campfire. I dug out my checkbook and wrote a check for a thousand dollars. I tore it off and handed it to him. 'Here. For your bamboo. No strings. Consider it payment for information received about Wren. For her sake, it was worth it.'

He studied the check a moment, then smiled. He folded it in half as if he would stick it in his shirt pocket. Then, still smiling, he reached the check into the fire, let a flame jump to the edge of the paper, and held it between us while it burned. The flames ate across the paper to his fingers, but he still held it. Finally he just crushed out the flames in his hand and tossed the scrap of check and black ash into the fire.

'Not enough?' I said. I wrote another check for two

thousand dollars. He tossed it into the fire without looking at it. My face was burning with anger as I scribbled another check, now for five thousand dollars. He balled it up without looking at the amount, put it on the end of a stick like a marshmallow, and roasted it to ash in the flames.

Before he was even done roasting that check I was writing another one for ten thousand dollars. I was so furious, my penpoint cut right through the paper as I signed my name. 'You might want to look at this one first.'

He didn't. He balled it up, stuck it on his stick, let it catch fire, then flung the burning ball at me. The flaming paper struck my breast and bounced onto my lap. I quickly brushed it away. I attacked my checkbook again. I was practically choking with hate as I scratched twenty-five thousand dollars into the amount line of the check. I knew this bastard could be bought, and I would buy him. That would prove something. I tore the check from the book, crumpled it up, and threw it in his face. It caught him in the corner of the eye because that eye teared up instantly. He rubbed it, but didn't pick up the check.

'Go ahead!' I shouted. 'Let's see you burn it. Let's see you burn $25,000.'

He picked up the crumpled check, looked at the amount. His smile widened. 'This one I think I'll keep.' He smoothed it against his thigh, folded it neatly in half, and stuck it into his shirt pocket.

'You lying cocksucking motherfucking son of a bitch,' I said.

He nodded. 'But then, you knew that.'

35

After he stamped the fire out and scattered the ashes, the darkness seemed too loud. Just standing there my ears seemed to pick up some night melody from the darkness. Or else I was going crazy. Certainly sitting around with Byron could drive one over the edge.

I could barely see him, just a shadowy gray ghost moving about. From the sound, he was shaking out the blanket, folding it. I leaned against the Jeep, let the cool metal anchor me. In this kind of darkness, one was liable to float away.

'Here,' he said, suddenly behind me.

I turned quickly, my head smacking his chin.

'Ow,' he said.

I didn't say I was sorry. 'What's here.'

'What?'

'You said "here". What's here?'

'Here, take this.' His hand touched my arm, felt its way down to my hand, opened my fingers, then stuck the folded piece of paper that must have been my check in them. He closed my fingers around the check. 'I wasn't looking for your money.' He paused. 'You're more like Wren than I thought.'

'You don't sound like that's a compliment.'

He didn't answer. But he didn't move away either. I could hear his breathing, see a blotch of face, a glistening in the eyes. His shirt smelled like the campfire. His breath rhythmically puffed into my hair.

Then I saw the darkness around his face shift and suddenly he was kissing me and I was letting him and I thought about Davis and I thought about Robby and I thought about Wren, but I let it happen anyway. And then I was kissing him back and I didn't think about anything else but how that kiss felt. I imagined our lips pressed against each other magnified a billion times. The crevices and lines were craters and gulches. Then I saw our giant tongues leaping over our lips into each other's mouths like thick pink whales at play. Or plump dolphins bumping bellies. And while I thought of this I felt my blouse come undone and my bra open and strong fingers pulled at my nipples like little mouths. Then he was gone and I heard the snap of the blanket opening up like a flag. And somehow we were naked and on the ground, the rough texture of the blanket scratching my skin.

Even without his clothes he smelled like the campfire and I liked that. I buried my face against his chest. His skin was moist with sweat. I heard a noise in the distance.

'What if we're attacked by a pack of wild coyotes?' I said.

'Maybe we'd better work fast.'

'Not too fast,' I said.

He laughed, his head thrown back looking a little like a coyote, I thought. Then his head disappeared and I felt the nuzzling between my legs, the soft attention of his tongue. I opened my eyes and looked straight up into space. The stars were so clear and sparkling, like they just came out of a dishwasher. What I didn't understand was how I could stare off into space and see things billions of miles away so clearly but the man who was nibbling between my legs was only a dark ink blot. I couldn't even see my own hand, though I could still feel the crumpled check in it.

He lifted my legs up over his shoulders so he could plunge his tongue into me. His hands slid up my side and I winced when he hit a ticklish spot, but he went past that until he was cupping my breasts. He unsheathed his tongue from my vagina and licked his way up to my clitoris. His tongue swirled in circular motions like he was trying to keep an ice-cream cone from dripping. I liked thinking of my clitoris that way and smiled as he continued. Soon I was gasping and bucking and I could feel myself being dragged toward climaxing. But I didn't want to come without seeing him. I grasped his head and pulled him up on top of me. I reached down and planted his penis at my opening and he thrust forward and into me.

I looked right at him, our faces not more than six inches apart, as he rocked back and forth, first slowly, then gathering speed. I still couldn't see his face clearly, though having the stars behind him at least made the outline of his head sharper. He made love differently than Davis or Ethan or Robby. I hadn't realized this before, but there had been something familiar about the others, as if they'd all read the same sex manual. It wasn't that Byron did anything especially different, there was still only the obvious combinations of tongues and vagina and penis. Yet, it was different. More personal. Like someone making you a birthday card rather than buying one.

Then he was ramming into me hard and I wanted him to do it even harder. I dug my nails into his hard buttocks and pulled him into me. Images burst into my mind as I felt myself nearing climax. The darkness exploded into white, like an old-fashioned flash bulb that blinded me at first, then the white drained away and I could see things. Flash! Me ramming that white Subaru, crunching his fender. Flash! Me smashing Byron's watch against the table, jumping up and down on it. Flash! Me throwing checks at Byron. All the moments of passion I'd been accumulating. And then the flashes stopped and I was moaning and my hands were gripping Byron's hair. He was grunting in my ear and he pumped against me and I didn't give a shit about anything else in the past, present, or future except what would happen in the next couple of seconds.

'Luna,' he said. 'God, Luna.'

I was so close, so close, so close, soclosesoclose. I flung my hands out to the side to arch myself better. One hand hit the blanket, the other hit the sand, and the one that hit the sand suddenly caught fire.

'Aaaahh!!' I screamed. I looked over to see why my hand felt as if a nail had been pounded through it. But I couldn't see anything. 'Goddammmmmmmn!'

And Byron, thinking I was coming, I guess, pumped even harder.

'No!' I said, hitting him on the head with my good hand. But I felt him spasm and his come shooting into me. 'I'm hurt!' I cried. 'Something bit me.'

He pulled out of me instantly. His penis was still leaking sperm, because I felt the trail drip down my thigh all the way to my knee as he sat up. 'Where? Where are you hurt?'

'My hand. Jesus, it feels like it's burning up.'

'Don't move,' he said. He stood up and ran over to the Jeep. He started up the engine and for a moment I thought he was just going to drive away and leave me here, yelling something like 'Hold on, I'm going for help.'

But all he did was turn the Jeep around so it faced us and switched on the headlights. The light bounced off my naked body making it look even paler than it actually was. I didn't care. My hand hurt too much to care about anything else. I sat up and examined the hand. There was a red hole on the back of my hand and serious swelling around it. The veins stood out and looked kind of bluish. I looked around the blanket I was on for what caused it. I didn't see anything.

He stood up on the driver's side and leaned over the windshield. His penis was mashed against the windshield. 'What's it look like?' he said.

'Like a flattened worm,' I said, pointing.

He looked down and smiled. 'I'm talking about your hand.'

'Red and swollen.'

'Teeth marks?'

'A little hole.'

He nodded and sat down. He switched off the engine

and the headlights. I heard him rooting around in the back of the Jeep.

'What the hell was it?' I asked.

'Scorpion.'

'Scorpion?' I pulled my legs tighter and hugged my knees. I let my wounded hand lie on the blanket as if it weren't a part of me. It throbbed horribly.

'Shouldn't we keep the lights on so we can see them?' I suggested.

'Lights won't help,' he said. 'At least not the regular kind.'

Apparently he found what he'd been looking for, because he climbed out of the Jeep, or at least that's what it sounded like.

'Shouldn't we be rushing me to the hospital or something? Don't people die from scorpion bites?'

'By the hundreds,' he said. 'The symptoms resemble strychnine poisoning. The tongue gets thick, muscles twitch, you start sneezing and frothing. Then convulsions and a bluishness in the extremities.'

'What the fuck are you doing? Get me to a hospital!'

'But those symptoms are rare and you would already be slurring your speech if it was going to affect you that way. Mostly people experience a sharp burning sensation, followed by a needles-and-pin tingling like when your foot falls asleep. At least that's how it affected me when I was stung.' I heard his voice coming closer, but I couldn't see him.

'Where are you?' I asked.

'Here,' he said. 'I'm shining a flashlight so I can see the scorpions without stepping on one.'

'Either one of us is crazy or you need some fresh batteries, because I don't see any flashlight shining.'

'It's a black light. You can only spot them under an ultraviolet beam.'

'Look, my hand is doing the samba on hot coals and you're doing your Dr. Frankenstein number. Let's just get out of here, okay?'

'There!' he said. From his voice, I could tell he was standing right next to me, but I still couldn't see him and I didn't know where 'there' was. Then I felt his hand on my arm. He was kneeling beside me, his arm around my shoulder. 'There,' he said softly and I turned.

'Jesus,' I said. 'Jesus, what the hell is that?'

His ultraviolet flashlight was aimed at the cliff wall fifteen feet away. The entire face of the rock was covered with neon greenish-blue outlines of scorpions. 'It's just a photochemical reaction to the black light,' Byron said. 'Beautiful, isn't it?'

That struck me as off, because I expected him to say, Scary, isn't it. That's probably what I would have said. But it wasn't what I was thinking at that moment. I was thinking, Beautiful, isn't it. Though I didn't know it until he said it. Gazing at the cliff wall was like seeing hundreds of zodiac signs. In fact, they reminded me of stars, so clear and precise.

He shifted the flashlight away from the cliff and shone it on the ground around us. Nothing. He aimed it at our pile of clothes. Nothing.

'They're very shy,' he said, as if describing a pet. 'They like to hide.' He picked up a stick and poked my panties. A neon blue-green scorpion scuttered out from under them.

'That's sick,' I said.

'Just be glad he wasn't in them when you put them back on.'

We got dressed—carefully—and drove back to the house. Byron took all of Zeno's ice and packed my hand in it for the drive home to Orange County. We didn't speak much during the trip. He asked how my hand was. Better, I said. Did I feel okay? Fine, I said.

I was busy thinking. Thinking about Davis. I had betrayed him. What did I know about Byron except what he told me. How could I trust that? Even if it was true, even if it was true, so what? I had feelings for Davis. I knew who he was, what he did, what he was about.

'What are you thinking about?' Byron asked me after a long stretch of silence.

'Nothing.'

'Come on.'

'Scorpions,' I said. 'How we could be out in the middle of hundreds of scorpions doing what we were doing without knowing they were there.'

'I knew they were there.'

'Then you should have warned me.'

'I did, earlier. I said watch out for scorpions.'

'Yeah, but you said it like "Watch out for falling meteors." Like it was only a remote possibility.'

He shrugged. 'If I'd have shone my black light around beforehand, would you still have made love?'

'I don't know what I would have done.'

He didn't say anything for a while. 'That's not what this is about. The guilt's set in. You're wondering if this has been a mistake. You followed me in the first place to get rid of me and now that you fucked me, you're wishing you'd just gotten rid of me instead. Right?'

'Don't tell me what I think, okay?'

He didn't speak the rest of the trip. We arrived at the apartment and he carried the dripping icepacks to the kitchen sink and tossed them in. There was an envelope under the front door mat addressed to Wren and Byron. I opened it. Inside was a note from Ethan asking us to call him. The phone number was a Los Angeles area code. I tossed the envelope on the sofa and went to the refrigerator for a soda. I was dying of thirst.

'Drink water,' he said. 'It'll flush your system out.'

I popped the Dr Pepper and drank.

He just smiled sadly and sighed. 'Okay, I've been debating about whether or not to tell you this. Before I figured it was none of my business. Maybe it still isn't.'

'What?'

'You know the bookmark you use in that flight magazine?'

I thought for a moment. The magazine I brought home from Davis's. 'Yes. What about it?'

'Nothing. If you know, you know.' He turned and walked down the hall to his room and shut the door.

I went to my room, holding the cold can of soda against the back of my swollen hand. I found the magazine on the back of the toilet where I'd left it. For Byron to have known about it, he must have searched my room again. Like I had done to his room, I reminded myself.

I opened the magazine and looked at the bookmark. It was Davis's boarding pass. But I already knew that. So what? He'd just gone to Hawaii last week. But I looked at the boarding pass more closely. Destination: Los Angeles. Departure: Denver.

I sat on the toilet. My hand throbbed and burned even more suddenly, as if my heart had somehow been washed out of my chest and got snagged inside my hand. He hadn't gone to Hawaii, he'd gone to Denver. And if he'd gone to Denver, he'd gone before this man had shot the woman. What if Davis had made a deal with the guy based just on his hounding of the poor woman who'd received the transplant? What if the man, knowing he had a deal, decided to do something more dramatic, something to make the story even better? We're not talking about a stable personality here, we're talking a disturbed man trying to get back to his wife's body parts. He views this woman as a surrogate, as if his wife were growing inside of the other woman. But he can't get back to his wife until he kills the surrogate that's in the way.

I didn't really know what had gone through the man's mind. Any more than I'd known what had gone through Davis's mind. He'd signed a contract with Season Dougherty and she'd killed her husband. That had become his big break. Did he now go searching for people on the verge of exploding and signing them up before the violence so he had exclusive rights? Jesus, think about it.

I stood up and walked out of my room. I didn't bother to switch on the lights. I knew my way through darkness by now. I imagined scorpions lining the walls, the floor. I didn't care. I knew one thing was for sure, I was throwing Byron out. He had always picked at my scabs, tried to lift the corner of my mask, shine his white and black lights at me, expose my neon self. But now he had taken away the one thing I had left in my life. Davis. I hadn't asked for the truth and I wasn't grateful for it. Byron was out of here. Tonight.

I turned the knob on his bedroom door and flung it open. The room was empty. I walked around it, opened doors, the closet. Everything was gone. I searched the apartment for Hector. He was gone too.

36

While waiting for Davis, I sat on the park bench next to the artificial lake and watched an old man shoot baskets. The old man was thin and bony, his pale legs sticking out of his baggy shorts seemed wobbly and coltish. His hair was thin and white and lifted with each puff of wind. He stood at the free-throw line, made sure his toes were lined up, bounced the ball once with both hands, and lofted it at the basket. I'd watched him toss at least twenty shots and he'd missed every one of them. The ball usually bounced off the rim and rolled into the grass that surrounded the small cement court. He walked in slow small steps after it, picked it up, and carried it right back to the free-throw line. He didn't dribble the ball or spin it on the end of his finger. He carried it in front of him as if it were a fragile globe. Bounce. Toss. Miss. Retrieve.

'I'm not late, am I?' Davis said. He came up behind me and kissed me on the neck.

'You're not late.' I was still watching the old man. I knew that once I took my eyes off him and faced Davis, everything would change. 'He doesn't dribble.'

'What?'

'Watch. He never dribbles the ball.'

Davis watched the old man for a minute. 'He's a lousy shot, that's for sure.'

'Yes, but he doesn't dribble. Have you ever known anyone to walk across a court with a basketball and not dribble it a couple times. You can't help yourself.'

'That's true. I hadn't thought of it before.'

We watched the old man shoot a couple more times, never making the basket, never dribbling the ball.

'God, he's a bad shot.' Davis laughed.

I turned to face him. 'My name's Luna Devon, not Wren Caldwell. Wren and I were best friends. She died.'

'Pardon?'

I told him everything. About Robby, the Bat-Faced Girl, my father, Byron. I didn't tell him about the bamboo. When I was done, I leaned back against the bench and sighed. I'd expected to feel somehow different. Purer, maybe. I didn't. I looked around for a sign that the world had changed because of my great revelation. Perhaps the old man would now sink a basket. But his shot ricocheted off the rim, bounced over the top of the backboard, and rolled off until it hit a water fountain.

Davis laughed. 'Is this a pitch for a script? Because I love it. Kind of a Jane Austen meets *Twin Peaks*.'

It was funny to think of your life as a synthesis of two works. As if your life isn't real unless it can be compared with two unreal things. I tried to think of what movies or novels I'd have picked. *Anna Karenina* meets *Attack of the Killer Tomatoes*?

I flexed my hand, which was still sore from the scorpion sting. 'Not a pitch, Davis. Just my life.'

'Jesus,' he said, slumping. His face went pale as the old man's legs. 'Jesus, Wren.'

'Luna.'

'Luna.' He nodded. 'It may take me a little while to get used to.'

'Davis, when you went to Denver this time, you'd already had a contract with this guy who killed that woman, didn't you?'

'With Roger Clemens?'

'Yes, the murderer.'

'Well, that hasn't been proven. I mean, Roger did kill Christine Palmer, but whether or not it's murder, that's going to be the tough call. Legally speaking.'

462

'Davis, this isn't a press conference. We're talking, that's all.'

He chuckled. 'Right. Sorry. Yes, I had a contract with Roger. When I read about the restraining order last week, I flew to Denver to talk to him. He was very lucid, very intelligent. No blithering madman. He said, yes, he'd been trying to contact Christine Palmer, at first, out of grief over his wife's death, but later, as he got to know more about her, for Christine herself. He made quite a convincing case.'

'So, you had no idea he was capable of anything like this. Of murder.'

Davis shook his head. 'No, not really.'

I stared at him for a minute.

'What?' he said.

'I'm not sure whether you're lying to me or to yourself. Either way, it's a lie.'

'What are you talking about?'

'You go to some guy who's emotionally unstable and you give him money and tell him you're going to make a movie out of his life—'

'Whoa. I didn't promise any movie. I optioned the rights to his life story, but I made it clear that any movie was a long shot.'

'And you think he heard that? He's not in the business, for chrissake, and you know it. Average guy has a movie producer fly in to make a contract and give him money, they expect a goddamn movie. Real people don't expect to get paid money for nothing.'

Davis held up his hands. 'I explained everything to him.'

'Come on, Davis, at least play fair with me. You know what I'm talking about. He was unstable, no matter how lucid he sounded. You went to this unstable man who was already overwrought about his wife's death and you offered him immortality. On the screen. And you don't think that affected him? You don't think that somewhere in his confused mind he didn't come up with a plan to

463

ensure the movie would be made. Hell, he decided to write the ending himself. With a gun.'

Davis looked off at the old man for a couple of minutes. 'I've never seen anyone miss so many shots. It must be mathematically impossible to miss that many, don't you think?'

I didn't answer.

'So, what are you saying? I'm to blame here? I'm responsible for Christine Palmer's death because I wanted to make a movie? Jesus, Wren . . . Luna . . .' He shook his head.

'Why'd you lie to me about going to Hawaii?'

'Shit, we're not going to start comparing lies, are we? I mean, I'm a tadpole in the pond compared to you.'

'I'm not bitching about you lying. I only want to know why you did it.'

He looked off at the old man again, cupped his hands, and shouted, 'Bend your knees. Bend your goddamn knees.'

The old man stopped in midshot, looked back at us, waved, and shot again. He did not bend his knees. He missed the shot.

'Jesus, is that guy stupid or what?' Davis rubbed his hands together and glanced over at me. His face was sad and he looked tired. 'I have tax troubles. And I'm being sued by another video company I did business with over some ridiculous crap.' He waved his hand, dismissing it. 'I was a millionaire before I was twenty-eight, and I did it legally, without selling drugs, junk bonds, or anything like that. I just worked hard. Everything I dabbled in was a success. Then things started going wrong, nobody's fault. Lawsuits, tax problems, depressed economy.' He smiled at me. 'Baby, I need another success.'

I slid over and touched his hand. He saw the bandage on the back of mine.

'What happened?' he asked.

'Scorpion bite.'

He started laughing, laughing loudly. The old man

shooting baskets turned around with an annoyed expression, as if we were throwing off his game. He threw the ball up, it missed, and he looked at me and scowled as if it were my fault.

'I don't know, Luna,' Davis said, still chuckling. 'I still say you sell me your story and we both clean up. Jesus, scorpion bite.'

I didn't say anything. I kept my hand over his. I didn't know what I was feeling then, I wasn't even sure what I was going to do. I had no plan, no ultimatums, no speeches. I was winging it.

He sighed heavily. 'Gaaaaaawwd. Shit. I don't know. I didn't think he'd kill her. I really didn't. I figured he'd do something crazy, I guess, and she'd have him locked up and I'd have my story.'

The old man picked up his ball and started walking away, around the edge of the lake. I expected him to do something dramatic, like throw the ball into the water, but he didn't.

'I thought he was going to chuck the ball into the lake,' Davis said. 'He didn't make one basket the whole time we've been here.'

I was startled that we'd had the same thought.

'You want to say something,' Davis said. 'The suspense is killing me.'

'I don't know what to say. I guess, I'm going to say something high schoolish, like we should stop seeing each other.'

'Something like that or that exactly?'

I hesitated, uncertain. I groped ahead through the darkness of my feelings, looking for scorpions. 'That exactly.'

'See, I don't think that makes sense. Not really. Not when you think about it. We still care for each other. Okay, I didn't tell you because maybe I felt guilty and you didn't tell me because you felt . . .' He stopped, unsure what I felt. 'What? Inadequate? I don't know.'

'Inadequate sounds right.'

'Whatever the reason, that's past. That's gone. Isn't

465

that what relationships are all about, adjusting, making some mistakes, readjusting? Right?'

I shrugged. 'You're asking the wrong person for definitions of relationships.'

'Well, help me out here, Luna. What would it take to make things right? Tell me, I'll do it.'

I took my hand off his and leaned forward, my elbows on my knees, my head in my hands. I tried to imagine myself under Davis's warm quilt, showering under his skylight, braiding his daughter's hair, teaching his son to clean his room. I looked good in that picture. 'Thing is, Davis,' I said, 'you fell in love with me as Wren. It's kind of like a kid falling in love with an actress on the screen. Wren's a role I play well and now that I know how effective it is with you, I may resort to it without even trying. I'm not sure I'd ever get out of it.'

He didn't say anything. He looked around for the old man, but he was long gone. He turned, saw some Asian kids playing on the swings, their young mothers sitting nearby talking rapidly and laughing. 'People from other countries, they laugh differently. Did you ever notice that? Like laughter was part of their language and had to be pronounced just so. You wouldn't think there'd be a difference.' He stood up. 'I talked to New York this morning. Our deal is still good on the Season Dougherty book. You think you can handle it?'

I looked up at him, shielding my eyes from the sun. 'Yes.'

'Okay, then. You might want to interview the cops who found her, some of the inmates who knew her, that sort of thing. Her attorneys, maybe the prosecuting attorneys. You know what to do.'

'Yes.'

He stood there, hands in pocket, nodding. He didn't seem to know what to say or do. 'You need any help, any doors opened, call me. Or call me just because you want to. I'm not convinced this identity crisis thing won't just blow over.'

466

'Yes.'

He took a deep breath. 'Meantime, I got some writers to hire for the Roger Clemens story. Paramount has already offered me a preemptive bid. Looks like this one's going to the big screen.'

'Congratulations.'

'Thanks.' He leaned over and kissed me on the mouth, our lips barely touching. Then he walked off. I didn't watch him. I stared out at the lake and listened to his shoes shoosh against the thick grass with each step. Shoosh, shoosh. Shoosh, shoosh. Shoosh . . .

37

'I shouldn't be talking to you,' she said.

'You don't have to,' I agreed.

She studied me from behind the crack in the door. She started with my face, my hair, then down to my clothes and my shoes. I was wearing jeans and black Keds, a blue jersey; my hair was straight and limp, still a little damp from the shower I'd taken before driving down here. I didn't look too threatening.

'Okay,' she said. 'Come in. But when I say leave, I want you to leave. Got it?'

'Yes.'

'I mean it. I'm serious.'

'I'll leave.'

She opened the door and I entered her apartment. The name on the mailbox said Wendy Clove, but her real name was Carla Lasher. Season Dougherty's missing sister. I'd called her after my meeting with Davis and she'd agreed to see me.

'I don't know why Season gave you this number,' she said. 'But if she did, she must have trusted you. I guess I owe it to her to talk to you.'

'How do you like Del Mar?' I said.

'It's fine. Nice beach community. Jamie and I go for walks along the ocean every evening after dinner.'

'Does she go to school?'

'Every day.'

'Aren't you afraid someone will recognize her? Her photo's been on TV a lot.'

Carla shrugged. 'I cut her hair into a bob and dyed it brunette. She wears those contact lenses that change the color of your eyes to brown. They're all looking for a blond, blue-eyed girl with pigtails. Anyway, now that Season's dead, they'll stop looking.'

She sat on the sofa and I took the nearby armchair. The apartment was neat and very clean, but the furniture looked worn and the walls needed paint. The neighbourhood had probably once been a lovely place with cottages and bungalows for the inland wealthy to spend their summers near the shore. Now there were a lot of FOR RENT signs in dirty windows and a general atmosphere of decay.

'Our neighbours are mostly surfers, five of them renting one apartment, or stable hands working the racetrack. So don't mind the noise.'

'Okay,' I said, though there wasn't any noise.

'It's not bad now, but the moment the sun goes down . . .' She shook her head. Carla was about five years younger than Season, but not nearly as attractive. Every feature that had made Season beautiful seemed to have the opposite effect on Carla. Her face looked somehow underbaked.

'Where's Jamie now?' I asked.

Carla hesitated. She looked out the window, thinking. Finally, she sighed. 'Well, Season's dead, isn't she? I guess there's not much left to be secretive about.' She turned and faced the hallway. 'Tanya, come here, sweetheart.'

'Tanya?'

'We had to get used to calling each other our madeup names so we didn't slip in public. I guess I'm still used to it.'

'Who picked Tanya?'

'Season. Her little joke. It was the name Patty Hearst used when she was kidnapped and inducted into the SLA.'

'I remember.'

'Our last name, Clove, she got from clove oil, one of

the main things dentists use to take away pain. She had a sense of humor, my sister. Oh, here's my little angel.'

Maybe because of the Tanya name and the image of Patty Hearst, I half expected Jamie to come out dressed in army fatigues, a beret, and brandishing an AK-47. She didn't. She wore red shorts and a T-shirt with a drawing of crayons arranged to spell out Kid's Club.

'Hi, Jamie,' I said.

Jamie looked at Carla.

'It's okay, Jamie,' Carla said. 'This lady knew your mother.'

'How are you, Jamie?' I said.

'Fine.' She hopped onto the sofa next to her aunt and stared at me, waiting for the questions to begin. She was used to being asked questions by adults.

'She knows her mother's dead,' Carla said, hugging Jamie. 'She knows her mother's gone to a better place. No more jail, no more pain. That her mom's waiting there for her.'

'In heaven,' Jamie offered.

'Of course,' I said. I rubbed my thumbnail along the cushion seat of my chair. 'I'm writing a book about your mother. About how she took care of you.'

'She sent us down here to live.' Jamie pointed out the window. 'The ocean is two blocks that way. I can go there anytime I want.'

'What will you do now?' I asked Carla.

'Go home. Believe it or not, I had a steady job and a house mortgage. I lost the job, but I still own a house in Mission Viejo. My ex-husband still keeps making the payments on it since I went into hiding, bless him. He calls me almost every day to make sure we're okay.'

'Maybe you two will get back together now that this ordeal is over.' I smiled encouragingly.

Carla laughed loudly and I could hear the echo of Season's voice in that laugh. 'Why would I want to do that? Larry's a great guy, but we can't stand being married to each other. That much hasn't changed.'

I guess I'd been looking for some happy endings. Fat chance.

'Jamie will come live with me, just as we've been doing. I suppose the district attorney could bring charges against me, but my attorney doesn't think that will happen now.'

Jamie pointed at my bandaged hand. 'What happened?'

'Scorpion bit me.'

'Cool!' She smiled. 'Did it hurt?'

'Lots. Kind of like scraping your knee and squirting onion juice in the wound.'

'Yeeeech.'

'That's what I said.'

Carla kissed Jamie's cheek. 'Honey, why don't you go off to your room and play for a little while. I want to talk to the lady alone.'

Jamie slid off the sofa and walked to her room.

'Bye, Jamie,' I called after her.

'Bye.' A door closed behind her.

Carla faced me with a stern expression. 'Go ahead and ask what you came here to ask. Let's just get it over with.'

I didn't know what I'd come there to ask. I guess I was trying to figure out why Season wanted me to come here. Why she thought it was so damn important.

'You must have loved your sister very much to go through all this,' I said. 'Uproot your life, go into hiding.'

'I was a legal secretary at a title search company. Doesn't sound like much, especially when compared to Season being a dentist. A dentist, a mother, beautiful.'

'That's a hell of a legacy to live up to.'

'Actually, it was quite easy. No one expected me to do as well. I mean, she was after all Season. So whatever I did, no matter how lame, it was celebrated as if I'd won the Nobel Prize. Lots of parties when I was a kid. Plenty of encouragement. And no expectations. I think my parents thought it unfair to expect much from me when God had given them such a winner in Season.' She laughed. 'Some kind of Catholic voodoo, I guess.'

'Where are your parents now?'

'Arizona. My mother has Alzheimer's. She's in a home. My father has an apartment nearby. He has his little routine. Visits Mom once a day, visits the church once a day to pray for her, and plays golf the rest of the time. He just won his club's championship for the second year in a row.'

I was thirsty, but since I hadn't been offered anything, I didn't want to ask. Carla was fidgeting with a loose threat on the sofa cushion. She glanced at her wristwatch, holding the pose long enough for me to see and take the hint.

'Look,' she said, 'you seem like a nice person. I'm sure Season must have trusted you or she wouldn't have given you this number. She didn't even give it to Dad. So, go ahead and ask.'

Ask what? I wondered. Why was I missing what was so obvious to her?

She sighed impatiently. 'Christ, maybe I'm not Season, but I'm not made of glass. You want to know about the molestation, right?'

I nodded.

'Well, it never happened. There wasn't any.' She'd said it quickly, like a secret she'd been holding in too long. Now that she'd said it, her face relaxed in such a way I could see a resemblance to Season again.

I guess I wasn't really surprised by what she said, because once she said it, I just kept nodding. 'No sexual contact at all?'

'None. Philip wasn't a bad guy. He and Season had their problems, but he adored Jamie and he was always very good to me. I should be so lucky to find a guy like Philip.' She looked up at me quickly, like someone who'd just dribbled her soup down her blouse. Then I knew. The sexual contact hadn't been between Philip and Jamie, but between Philip and Carla. She continued, 'Philip used to give Jamie baths when he had custody. They played volleyball on the beach and they'd come home sandy and hop in the tub, take off their sandy bathing suits, and wash off. Philip wasn't embarrassed by nudity and he didn't

472

want Jamie to be either. It was all harmless enough.'

'And Jamie testified to that?'

'About a hundred times. But Season was convinced she was lying because she was afraid of her father. I tried to talk her out of it, but she got caught up in the whole martyr business and she just couldn't see straight.'

'So, out of loyalty to your sister, you followed her wishes and went into hiding with Jamie.'

Carla's mouth twisted into a bitter smile. 'Yeah, out of loyalty and guilt.' She looked me in the eyes and knew that I knew about her and Philip. 'And because there are millions of women who are fighting a real battle for their children and if people knew the truth about Season's case it might screw it up for a lot of authentically molested children.'

Why had Season sent me down here? To find out the truth she wasn't able to admit, even to herself? What good did this truth do me? I didn't need it or want it, except to write it down in a book that would sell at grocery store checkout stands along with *TV Guide* and *Soap Opera Digest*.

I left Carla's apartment and walked numbly down the sidewalk. I had to be the worst journalist in the world; I hated truth. I didn't want to write a book that would make Season out to be a monster, Carla an adulterer, Jamie molested more by her mother's delusions than her father's innocent showers. Shit, maybe I wasn't the right person for this job after all.

A bearded man was leaning against my car, a big man in a foam neck brace. I looked around for his white Subaru but didn't see it.

'You follow me on foot?' I asked as I nudged him away from the driver's door.

'New car,' he said proudly. He swept his hand toward the car parked behind me, a white Honda Prelude. 'Subaru was a piece of shit. But this baby is luxury and speed.'

'You like white.'

'People don't notice it as much when you follow them.'

'Guess not, I didn't notice you.'

'You probably would have on the way back. You're more paranoid than most, which usually means something to hide, but you're not who I'm after. That's why I'm approaching you like this. I don't want any more accidents like the last time.' He patted his neck brace. 'You know how much these things cost? Don't ask. I'm still dicking around with my insurance company over medical costs. I'm thinking of suing the whole fucking bunch, make enough to fish for the rest of my life.'

I got into my car and closed the door. He rapped on the window with his knuckle. I rolled it down an inch and locked the door.

'I'm not after you. Like I said, I was just following you because you're shacked up with Byron Caldwell. And he's a known associate of the guy I'm after, Zeno Harris. You know Zeno?'

'If you're a cop, let me see your ID.'

'Hey, lady, if I were a fucking cop, I'd have shot you by now, okay? I used to be a cop, but I'm retired. Nerves.' He held out his hand to show me how it shook a little. He grinned like a man who'd put something over on someone. 'Now I do some consultancy work. Private investigation stuff. Like on TV.'

'For whom?'

'Whom? Whom, I like that. For the University of California Library, that's whom. Seems our boy Zeno stole a few rare books since he's been out and they want me to track him down and get the books back so other patrons of the arts may also enjoy them. That *whom* enough for you?'

I started the engine.

'Hey, come on,' he whined. 'Help me out. It's not like you wouldn't be doing a good deed in helping a library.'

'Why not follow Byron? He's the known associate.'

He shook his head. 'I tried. Half a dozen times. You know how easy it is to follow someone who takes a bus?

But the son of a bitch always spots me and always shakes me. He's just one of those guys you can't follow unless you've got a team of three cars.'

I closed my eyes and leaned my head back against the headrest. Why hadn't it occurred to me before. Byron had let me follow him. He'd wanted me to. What for? To show me his bamboo sprouts so I'd invest money? To fuck me? Both?

I could just tell this man where Zeno was and let him sort out the ethics of who's doing what to whom. What did I care?

'Just tell me where Zeno Harris is, okay? Then you never see me again.'

I didn't say anything. He waited, but when it became clear I wasn't going to speak, he started back to his new Prelude. I watched him in my rearview mirror. I beeped my horn. He looked up, grinned, walked back to my car.

'Yeah?'

'You work for the university, right?'

'Right. The Board of Regents.'

'I have their phone number. Who's your boss, the guy who hired you? I want to call him first.'

'Tanner. Dr. Felix Tanner.'

I looked up into his wide face. His expression was serious and honest. 'There is no Dr. Felix Tanner,' I said. 'I just did a story on the university and I know every person on the Board of Regents and the administrators.'

He shrugged, looked confused. 'Maybe he's new or something.'

I'd been bluffing, but now I knew he was lying.

He was undoubtedly with some corporation out to steal or destroy Byron's bamboo experiments. So what? What did I owe to Byron, really? Nothing.

I shoved the shift into reverse, stomped the gas pedal, and popped the clutch.

'*Nooo!!!*' he hollered.

My little Rabbit flew backward into his Prelude and

smashed the front end with a chorus of shattering glass and crunching metal.

'You fucking cunt!' he said.

I drove off. Finally, I knew where I was going and what I was going to do.

38

'I'm Luna Devon,' I said. It was the first time in so long I'd introduced myself by my real name, I felt as if I should follow it with, 'And I'm an alcoholic,' or something equally confessional.

'Yes?' the woman said, meaning 'so what?'

I looked over her shoulder, down the hallway. I saw no one, just Bud sitting there with a fresh bandage. I heard no snapping of chess pieces, no rumble of men's voices. The room behind her was clear of hazy smoke. A man came down the hallway carrying a bowl of ice cream. I recognized him from his TV commercials. Bonkers Bob.

'I'm looking for Grudge,' I said.

Bonkers Bob came to the door, spooning chocolate ice cream into his mouth. He was tall and good-looking, so was his wife. They had deep tans. They were both in their mid-forties, both dressed in tennis outfits.

'Hi,' he said.

'I'm looking for Grudge,' I repeated.

They both seemed startled, looking me over as if searching for obscene tattoos. Mrs. Bonkers slipped away without saying anything.

'Jimmy's at work today.' He stood in the doorway, making it clear I was not going to be invited inside.

'Do you have a number where I can reach him? It's important.'

He held his bowl and stared at me. 'I don't know. Jimmy's on parole, you know.'

'I'm not a convict, if that's what you're getting at. He

won't be breaking parole talking to me. I'm a reporter with *Orange Coast Today* and I'm doing a story of the local chess scene. I was told he knows something.'

Bob relaxed, spooned another glob of ice cream into his mouth. 'Hell, yes. Jimmy's a chess whiz. Plays all the time. Belongs to some chess club, bunch of retired folks, I guess. Helps keep him away from those punks he used to hang around, keeps him out of trouble. Sport is our best defense against crime, I say.'

He gave me the phone number of his warehouse and I drove to the nearest gas station and called him.

'I'm looking for Byron,' I said.

'I'm not his keeper, babe.'

'When I hang up, I'm going right to the parole office and telling them everything I know about you. Gambling is certainly a violation of your parole, so is associating with known felons. All cops can't all be chess players who are willing to turn their backs.'

'You go there,' he growled, 'and I'll have your fucking heart cut out and stuffed in your cocksucking mouth, you bitch. Then they'll fuck the hole in your chest. You hear me? You're dead!'

'Is that a no?'

There was a long pause.

'Twelve-eighteen Baker Street. Pick me up at midnight.'

'Midnight? Give me a break.'

'Hey, that's when I finish my shift. I can't just walk off, my brother would fire my ass and then I'd be back in the joint.'

'Why don't you just tell me where he is?'

'Because I don't know where he is. But I do know where he'll be at one A.M.'

'Where?'

'Playing chess with Landry for all the marbles. I gotta go. See you at midnight.' He hung up.

*   *   *   *   *

478

'You sure this is the place?' I said.

He gave me a disgusted look. 'Feel free to drop me off and look somewhere else by yourself.'

I turned off the engine and stared at the synagogue. It was dark. The entire neighbourhood was dark, no lights anywhere except the outside lights of the synagogue that shone on the large stained-glass window.

'I didn't know synagogues had stained glass,' Grudge said. 'Aren't Jews against that sort of thing?'

'Guess not,' I said. Theological discussions seemed out of place right now. 'I don't see anybody.'

'Well, if you saw them, then this wouldn't be a good place, would it?'

We got out of the car. I found myself tiptoeing down the sidewalk.

'Don't be a jerk, okay?' Grudge said. 'Just walk normal. We're not here to rob the place, for chrissake. Just to watch some chess.'

'It's still illegal entry,' I whispered.

'What're you, a fucking lawyer? Don't sweat it so much. It's not that big of a deal. The Jews probably wouldn't press charges even if they found out. They're a pretty sporting bunch, I hear.'

The name of the synagogue was carved in the stone archway around the front door. Ohev Sholom. Grudge knocked on the heavy wooden door. The door opened a crack, a face studied us, then the door opened the rest of the way.

The doorman was close to seven feet tall but couldn't have weighed more than 150 pounds. He wore coveralls and a khaki shirt underneath. A black skullcap sat on his head.

'Hey, Blinky,' Grudge said.

'Don't start with that Blinky shit, you got me?' The man quickly closed the door behind us and locked it. The foyer and hallway was dark. 'I don't know you,' he said to me.

'She's with Byron.'

'Oh, she's the one.' He nodded and gave me an extra

appreciative look that stripped me naked, bent me over, and had me begging him for more.

'How's the eye, Blinky?' Grudge said.

'Very funny.'

'I once tossed a glass of 7Up in Blinky's face and told him it was acid. You shoulda seen him screaming and blinking.' Grudge laughed, blinking his eyes rapidly in imitation.

'Very funny,' Blinky repeated. He handed Grudge a white skullcap from a wooden bin. On the inside, in gold letters, was written: *On the occasion of the bar mitzvah of Barry H. Levinson, October 12, 1991.*

'What am I supposed to do with this?' Grudge said.

'You wear it, moron.' He pointed to the one on his own head. 'It's a yarmulke.'

'I'm not Jewish, asshole.'

'Neither am I. But these people think it's important that you wear one and they gave me a job when no one else would, so I'm gonna make sure everyone else wears one. You don't put it on, you're not getting in.'

Grudge's face twitched at the challenge. He didn't actually move, but his body seemed to crouch under his clothes. Blinky looked more than happy to oblige and even an old score.

'You boys settle it,' I said. 'Meantime, can you point me toward the chess game?'

Mentioning chess seemed to remind them what they were here for. Grudge put the skullcap on his head and struck a model's pose. 'How do I look? Jewish enough for you?'

Blinky pointed down the hall. 'Go through those doors.'

I walked off toward the doors with Grudge following. 'The guy's a fucking janitor, right away thinks he's Moses or something.'

I pushed through the door into what looked to be a gymnasium. The floors were hardwood with the painted stripes of a basketball court. But there were banquet tables set up in long rows, all facing the far wall, where three long tables were elevated on a platform. All the tables had white tablecloths on them, though they were all dirty, stained with various foods and wine. Crumbs sprinkled the tops of many tablecloths. Men and women were sitting at the various tables, some brushing the crumbs away, others just talking. Most of the people were still milling around, discussing intently.

'They had a bar mitzvah here Saturday,' Blinky said behind us. I hadn't even heard him come up. Next to me, Grudge jumped slightly, also startled. The grin on Blinky's face indicated that was why he'd done it.

'Jesus, Blinky,' Grudge barked. 'Nice way to get yourself killed.'

Blinky ignored him and spoke to me. 'Name's Terry Dern,' he said. 'This jerk's the only one who calls me Blinky.'

'Hi, Terry. I'm Luna.'

'Gotta go. This is a conservative synagogue, which means they're kind of strict about all their religious mumbo jumbo. Still use mostly Hebrew in their services and such. Problem is, they've been losing a lot of customers to the looser reform bunch. That means less money for expenses. That's why I'm the only janitor.' He smiled proudly at his knowledge of the intricacies of Judaism.

'You a chess enthusiast?' I asked him, but I was scanning the crowd for Byron.

'Play every day with the rabbi here. He hates blitz, though. Says it ruins your game, keeps you from becoming a grandmaster.'

'Like you really need to worry about becoming a grandmaster, Blinkmaster.' Grudge chortled. 'Yeah, I think I'm gonna have you killed by having chess pieces shoved up your ass until your colon explodes. How's that sound to you?'

'Like your sexual fantasy, jerkoff.'

Grudge spun around with his fists clenched. 'Right now, asshole!'

Terry made fists and went into a crouch and I realized these two men were about to start swinging. I was surprised at how quickly they had escalated from insult to action.

'You guys start something,' a calm voice said, 'and I'll be forced to finish it.'

The three of us turned around. Jerry Kirn, Byron's ex-cellmate and Landry's current strong-arm man, stood there smiling. He was a surprisingly handsome man, and dressed in his knit shirt with a fashionable cardigan sweater blousing over his huge chest, he looked very much like a successful athlete-turned-entrepreneur. He patted Grudge on the shoulder in a friendly but firm way. 'Make it easy on yourselves, boys.'

Fists were relaxed into empty hands.

'I'd better check on some things,' Terry said and drifted off.

'Nice seeing you again,' Jerry said, nodding at us and disappearing into the crowd.

Grudge watched him wend through the men and women, staring but not saying anything. I'd expected a threat, a description of the death he planned for Jerry Kirn. But then, maybe Jerry Kirn wasn't the kind you threatened without being able to instantly back it up. His presence here gave the whole atmosphere a dangerous tinge. I felt like I was in an old speakeasy and a rival mob might come busting in at any second and start shooting.

'Where's Byron?' I asked.

'I don't see him.' Grudge pointed at the three tables on the platform. Two men were setting up chess pieces. A third was sitting down, cleaning his glasses and smoking a pipe. 'That's Landry. Son of a bitch just started smoking a pipe. Thinks it makes him look smarter. Same with the glasses. Guy told me they're just regular window glass.'

I studied Landry. He finished polishing his glasses and put them on. They did make him look smarter. He puffed on the pipe and waited patiently, looking every bit the thoughtful fortyish economics professor rather than the bone-busting ex-con loan shark. He didn't dress in the shiny suit I'd expected, or the dark shirt and darker tie I'd envisioned. He wore pleated khaki pants and a button-down cotton shirt straight from a Land's End catalogue. His hair was longish on top, mussed strategically. If I'd seen him sipping cappucchino at a café, I might have found him attractive. I asked Grudge, 'How good is he?'

'He's good. Not as good as me, maybe half as good as Byron.'

'Then Byron can beat him?'

Grudge laughed. 'That's not the point. The point is, Byron's not going to beat him. They'll play five games of blitz, all two-minute games. Byron will win the first one, lose the second one, win the third, and lose the next two.'

I looked at him. 'You already know this? Did Byron tell you?'

'He doesn't have to. This whole thing isn't about fucking chess. He told you that much, didn't he?'

'Yes. Landry wants to start moving up to big heists. He's hoping to prove himself the mastermind by beating Byron at chess, thereby attracting more quality thieves. That about it?'

He stared at me. 'Yeah, but you can drop the fucking sarcasm. Sure, it sounds stupid to you. You want a job, you just apply. Doesn't work that way out in the organized crime world. See, Byron has a reputation, not as a criminal but as a bright guy. I mean, let's face it, all that monkey-wrench bullshit he pulled was fucking amateur hour. Cementing your feet in a ditch?' He laughed. 'I crack up every time I think about that. Anyway. Byron's a yutz when it comes to real crime, okay? But he is the guy who thought up all those raids where they broke into places and damaged the logging equipment, stuff like that. And no one from his group ever got caught. The guys respect that kind of brains. Now do you see? Landry kicks Byron's ass tonight and he gets the rep.'

'But don't people know it's fixed?'

'Sure, but it doesn't matter how you win. If you win through brains, fine; if through intimidation, even better. The fix part will be forgotten anyway. Crooks just remember who wins and who loses. The details don't fucking matter.'

'So this is just a show, like professional wrestling.'

'Basically. More like a ceremony.'

'Doesn't anyone remember that Byron got caught? That's how he wound up in jail.'

Grudge waved a dismissing hand. 'Sure, but that's only because his old lady needed help. He could've made a clean getaway, instead he took her to the hospital. Even after he took her there he could've split, but he just sat there and waited for her, waited with her, even though he knew the cops were coming. Yeah, it's stupid, but crooks got a romantic streak in them. They don't hold it against a guy if he does something like that.'

I thought of Wren lying in the hospital, her teeth knocked out by a baseball bat. Probably unconscious from sedatives. Byron sitting next to her while she slept. I thought of myself in the hospital bed, a bullet tunnel to my heart, waking up to the nurse I thought was my mother.

What was I doing here? Earlier, when I'd been driving home from visiting Carla and Jamie, everything had seemed so clear. I would find Byron and . . . And then what? What had I been thinking would happen? I closed my eyes, felt my head throbbing. I put my hand on my aching bullet wound and felt my heart beating. My head and heart were synchronized, pounding a message of sympathetic pain to each other. What was my plan again?

'There he is,' Grudge said excitedly. It was odd to hear the excitement in his voice, as if he didn't already know the outcome.

I opened my eyes. Byron walked up to the platform, shook Landry's hand, and took a seat opposite him. The chess clock was placed between them so it faced outward. Everyone began swarming toward the platform.

'What does Byron get out of all this?' I asked Grudge as we moved forward with the crowd. 'Except not beaten up anymore?'

'He places a bet on the game, something nominal like five grand. When he loses, Landry keeps the money, but turns around and loans him, interest free, a hundred grand. Landry gets his reputation boosted and Byron gets to finish whatever he and that asshole Zeno got cooking. You know what it is?'

He asked in such an offhanded way I almost told him. But I stopped myself, remembering Zeno's hysterical face when he saw me invade his little nest. 'No, I don't know.'

He turned and grinned at me. 'You're getting the hang of this, aren't you?'

I saw Shawna at the front edge of the crowd. She was gesturing to the man next to her, her father. Their gestures seemed more frantic than usual. I recognized others from the Laguna Hills house yesterday. But there were a lot more people here tonight. Some people were standing on chairs, on tables, angling for a better look. People were genuinely excited, bouncing with anticipation. Even Grudge seemed edgy. It was as if, even knowing there was probably a fix in, maybe things would turn out differently than they knew it would. Perhaps the more certain the outcome, the more excited people get at the potential for an upset. Futility seems to fuel hope more than anything else.

With all the people surging around me, I could hardly see Byron or Landry. I pulled a folding metal chair out, brushed off some bread crumbs, and climbed atop it. Now I could see them clearly. I also saw a table at the front where people were betting money on the game. Thousands of dollars was stacked up.

I stuck out my leg and tapped my toe against Grudge's shoulder.

He looked back and up, annoyed. 'What?'

I stooped down and whispered, 'If it's common knowledge Landry's going to win, why would anybody bet?'

485

'They're giving good odds. Thirty to one against Byron.'

'But they know Byron's going to lose.'

He shrugged. 'You never know. Not really. Besides, it's hard for gamblers to pass up good odds, doesn't matter what they know.'

I shook my head and stood back up. The colors had been chosen and the game was starting. Byron had white. He shoved his piece out. The game took less than a minute, with Byron handily crushing Landry. Landry smiled, shook Byron's hand, and started polishing his glasses. There was a break while more people made bets.

'God, he's good,' Grudge said. It sort of just popped out and he looked around embarrassed to have said anything so envious. He noticed me looking and slouched into his usual cynical attitude. 'Forget this next game, it'll be a snooze. The only interesting thing will be how Byron manages to lose without making it look too obvious. He has to be careful not to humiliate Landry by lying down too easy. Landry'll bust his legs for that too.'

The second game started and lasted almost the entire two minutes. They seemed neck and neck, swapping pieces evenly all along. For a moment I thought Byron was going to win, but toward the end of the game he made a bad move and allowed himself to get pinned. Landry won.

'They'll make it go all the way to five games,' Grudge said. 'Just to give the boobs their money's worth. This game could go either way, but I figure it's a better show if Byron wins.'

Which is exactly what happened. Byron rolled over Landry's pieces like an avalanche, snatching pieces left and right while Landry faltered and seemed confused. The game was over and Landry just kept staring at the board. Byron got up and went to the bathroom.

'He'd better cool it,' Grudge said. 'That's just the kind of thing that'll get him a permanent limp.'

Bets continued to be made at the table in front of the

platform. The white tablecloth on the table had a long purple stain splattered across it where someone had probably knocked over a wineglass.

Byron returned, took his seat across from Landry. Landry's face was no longer the calm expression of professorial detachment. He looked angry.

I climbed down from my chair and pushed my way to the front of the crowd. 'Excuse me,' I said, hacking my way with forearms and elbows through the thicket of people. Finally I made it to the betting table. 'A thousand dollars on Landry,' I said loudly and looked up at Byron.

He stared down at me, his face tight and grim. He shook his head at me in disappointment.

I took out my checkbook.

'This is a cash kind of business, lady,' the guy behind the table said.

'All I have are checks. They're good.'

'Right. They always are.'

'I don't have any cash.'

'Sorry, honey.' The man taking bets shrugged.

'She's okay, Mike.' Jerry Kirn appeared out of the crowd, signaled Mike, the bet taker, and floated away again.

Mike sighed heavily. 'Fine, fine. Everybody knows my business. Fine.' He waved me in impatiently. 'You got a credit card number we can take your check.'

I wrote the check for a thousand dollars and handed it to Mike. 'Kind of a stupid bet, lady,' Mike said. 'You're risking a grand when all you can win is $300 plus your grand back. That's not smart. You bet Byron there you stand to win $30,000. And he's already two games to one ahead. I mean, it's none of my business, I'm just trying to help you out.'

'Put it on Landry,' I said. I glanced up at Byron. I didn't know what was in his face or in his head. He just stared at me.

I didn't know why I'd bet the money exactly. I thought I had a reason when I'd started for the table, but by the time I'd made my way through the crowd, all I remembered was my goal, not the reasoning. Still, it seemed like a good idea to go through with my plan. At least it was a plan, I was doing something.

Then the fourth game began. Smack, smack, smack. Pieces were flying again. Sometimes they didn't bother to pick up a captured piece, they just knocked it off the board. I had to admit, watching them attack the board like that had my adrenaline thundering through my body. My headache and heart pain were both gone. Smack, smack, smack. I felt the vibrations of each move pass through me like an earthquake aftershock.

Then it was all over.

Landry won.

'Two games apiece,' Mike announced.

Their was a marked letdown in the crowd. Few people bet now. Most looked disappointed, defeated themselves. Anyone who had doubted the outcome of the match before now knew what would happen.

'Come on, come on,' Mike encouraged people. 'Thirty to one. One more game, one more game. Thirty to fucking one.'

Jerry Kirn swam up out of the crowd, whispered to Mike, then drove back into the crowd and disappeared.

'Forty to one! Jesus, forty to one odds, folks.' Mike acted as if he couldn't believe what he was saying.

A few more people stepped up and placed some small wagers.

Landry looked more relaxed now, beneficent. He puffed on his pipe, looking down on the gathered throng as if they were here to pay their respects to him. I guess in a way they were. They had come to acknowledge their role in the grand scheme of the food chain. Like that scene in Robin Hood my students had talked about.

Yes, I thought, just like that scene.

I stepped up to the betting table. 'Five thousand more on Landry, Mike,' I said. I wrote a check and handed it to him.

He groaned. 'The odds have changed, lady. You bet this on Byron and you could win $200,000. You have any idea how much money that is? Better odds than the goddamn lottery.'

'Five thousand. On Landry.'

He took the money, handed me a receipt. Then he went back to trying to drum up more business. No one else bet.

Byron glared at me, his look no longer confusing. I had touched him all right, touched him deep and hard. Now that I thought of it, I guess that was my plan all along.

The final game began.

39

Smack, smack.

Smack, smack, smack, smack.

Smack, smack, smack, smack, smack, smack.

Smack, smack, smack, smack, smack, smack, smack, smack, smack, smack, smack, smack, smack.

And it was over.

No one said anything at first. They just watched the two men on the platform stare at each other. Watched Landry reach for his pipe, light it, sucking the flames to life. Watched Byron, face grim as a gravedigger, rise, shake hands with Landry. Watched Landry paste a phony smile on his face and raise Byron's hand in the air.

The winner.

Then everyone spoke and moved at once. The betting table was swarmed by people waving receipts. Others pulled out pocket-sized chess games and began replaying each game. I could see the triumphant look on everyone's face, as if they had all just come out of an uplifting movie.

Byron took the money that was stacked in front of the board and quickly shoved it into his pants pocket. With his glum expression and bulging pockets, he looked like he'd just won the marbles championship but was about to be scolded by his mother for coming home late. Landry, still smiling sharkishly, whispered something to him. From the way Landry's lips flexed. I could tell it was not something pleasant. Byron shrugged and walked away. As he entered the crowd, people closed around him, slapping his back, shaking his hand. He nodded politely at them, accepting their adulation without encouraging it.

'Jesus fucking Christ,' Grudge said, sidling up beside me. 'I can't believe he did something so stupid.' He was counting a handful of money.

'Where'd you get that?'

'I won it.'

'But you knew it was fixed.'

'Like I said, the odds were too good to pass up.'

Byron broke through a ring of the loyal, their hands reaching out to touch him as he brushed by them. He snagged my arm without slowing down and trawled me alongside him.

'What are you—?'

'Do you have your car?' he asked. People talked to him, offered their hands. He ignored them now, picking up speed as we headed toward the exit. I was trotting to stay up with him.

'Let me go,' I said, trying to pull away. His grip was too strong. I felt a pain shooting up my arm as he tightened his grip more.

'Do you have your car?'

'Yes, I have my goddamn car.'

'Show me.'

We shoved through the gymnasium doors and were hustling through the lobby. Blinky was polishing a glass showcase that displayed fancy skullcaps, candle holders, and such. A little white sign said AVAILABLE AT B'NAI B'RITH SHOP. Blinky hooked the spray container of Glass-Plus onto his waistband and reached for the large ring of keys clipped to his belt.

'You were great, man,' Blinky said. 'Great.'

'Thanks,' Byron said impatiently. We stood in front of the exit door waiting for Blinky to find the right key.

'I wish the rabbi could have seen you. He's a pretty cool guy. I think he might give you a game. Not in blitz, of course, but like a regular game. You wouldn't think a guy that old, being so religious and such, would have such an

491

aggressive game.' He unlocked the door and Byron pulled me through it.

'Where?' he said. 'Where's your car?'

I pointed.

'Get your keys out. Now.'

As we jogged toward my car, I dug through my purse for my keys. I slowed down to rummage.

'Hurry up,' Byron urged. He was already standing at the car, pulling on the locked door and looking nervously at the synagogue doors.

I stalled, pretending to not be able to find the keys. Things were going just as I had planned, I had to keep them that way.

Byron ran over, yanked my purse from my hands, and dumped it on the hood of the car, emptying it completely. The keys clattered out among tissues and my wallet, a movie ticket stub, lipstick. He snatched them up and ran for the driver's side.

I took as long as possible shoveling my stuff back into my purse. When I had everything in it, I slung my purse over my shoulder, marched over to the driver's side, pulled open the door, and said, 'I'm driving.'

'Just get in,' he said, hooking a thumb at the other door.

'It's my goddamn car and I'm driving.'

'Get in or I'm leaving you here.'

I climbed into the driver's side on top of him and gripped the wheel as hard as I could. He tried to push me aside, but I hugged the wheel to my chest and ground my butt into his lap.

'What the hell's wrong with you?' he said. 'Are you crazy?'

'It's my car and I'll drive.'

I had to drive if I was going to make this work. And we couldn't leave yet, not until the rest of the cast had assembled.

'Fine!' he said. 'You fucking drive.' He wiggled out from under me and scooted over to the passenger seat. 'Okay? Happy? Can we get the hell out of here now?'

'Whoa there, pardner,' I heard.

My stalling had worked. Jerry Kirn and another man ran up to the car. Byron sighed and swore under his breath.

'Byron, buddy, you weren't leaving already?' Jerry asked. 'The party's just starting. You're the man of honor.'

The man with Jerry was even larger, no more than twenty-three, his round face set in a permanent scowl of a football lineman trying to intimidate his opponent. Somehow the white skullcap still sitting on his head looked like a dunce cap on him.

'Hell of a game you played in there, buddy,' Jerry said. 'Hell of a game.'

Byron said nothing.

'You mind?' I said. 'We want to celebrate alone.'

Jerry looked at me with a curious expression. 'You lost some bucks tonight betting against our boy here.'

'The check's good. I'm not stopping payment or anything.'

He laughed. 'No, I know you aren't.' A sharp threat was sheathed in his tone. 'I'm just impressed with how well you take losing that kind of money. Not only that, but then you go off with the guy who you bet against. I don't know, it just looks funny, I can't figure it out.'

Byron angrily flung open his door and jumped out of the car. Jerry Kirn's partner tensed for action. Jerry just stood there, hands in pocket, completely calm.

'Look, Jerry,' Byron said. 'It just happened. I didn't plan it.'

'You double-crossed Mr. Landry,' Jerry's partner grunted.

In a blur of motion, Jerry's hand snapped out and slapped his partner in the mouth. The calm, almost bored expression never left Jerry's face. 'I do the talking, Trent.'

Trent nodded, then touched his fingers to his lips. When he took them away he saw the blood on his fingertips.

Jerry took a couple steps toward Byron. Byron didn't flinch or move. Jerry put his arm around Byron's shoulder and spoke quietly. 'Christ, Byron, what do you have against me that you keep putting me in a position where I've got to hurt you?'

'What are friends for?'

Jerry laughed. 'See? That's what I mean. I consider us friends.'

'I do too, Jerry.'

'Yet you back out on your word and you stomp my boss to pulp in front of all the people he's trying to impress.' He shook his head. 'Tell me, at least, it's not because of her.' He pointed at me. 'It's not because she goaded you by betting all that money against you. Please tell me it's not that stupid.'

Byron looked over at me. 'It wasn't because of her.'

Jerry laughed. 'Shit, even Trent here doesn't believe that and he's stupider than his own fist. Aren't you, Trent?'

'Yes, sir, I am.'

'Well, where does that leave us? You know I'm going to have to do some damage this time.' Jerry looked up at the sky, his face suddenly angry. 'Jesus, you make me mad sometimes, Byron.'

'Go ahead and do it, man,' Byron said. 'What's it going to take to satisfy him?'

'A broken limb, at least. Maybe two. Probably a concussion, though a coma would be better. You know, it's got to be visible enough that people, the people who count, can spread the word about what happens when you fuck with Mr. Landry. I can leave your face alone, I suppose, though a nice deep scar would sure be to my benefit. You mind a scar on your face?'

Byron shrugged. 'I'll leave it in your capable hands. Go ahead.' He braced himself.

'Not here, putz,' Jerry said. 'Not now. We got a nice quiet neighbourhood, we got a synagogue full of witnesses. The potential for getting snitched out is too great.' He patted Byron on the arm. 'But it'll happen, don't worry. I'll find you later.'

'Excuse me,' I said. 'Which is your car?'

Jerry looked confused. 'My car?'

'Yes, I'm curious what kind of car you drive.' Most men have an instinctive reaction to that question. If it's a clunker, they shrug and talk about how sick and tired they are of a culture that places so much value on something as shallow as a car. If they have a hot car, they can't wait to point it out, their chests all puffed up like an adder.

He pointed across the street. 'That red Miata.' His chest puffed up.

'You like it?' I asked.

'What's not to like? She handles great, is fast as a bullet. It's the perfect car.'

'Get in,' I said to Byron.

Byron didn't move. He and Jerry exchanged sad looks.

'Go on,' Jerry said. 'I'm getting stinking drunk tonight. Then I'm going home and catch hell from my wife. But tomorrow, Byron . . .' He let the threat hang. 'Don't make it harder on me by running, man. You know that's only going to cost you more pain.'

Byron got into the car and closed the door. Jerry and Trent started walking slowly back to the synagogue. Jerry reached over and straightened Trent's skullcap.

'That was close,' I said, starting the engine.

'What's the difference, tonight or tomorrow? Same results.'

'Well, if there's no difference, then there's no time like the present.' I gunned the motor, popped the clutch, and squealed away from the curb. I shot across the street and sideswiped the red Miata hugging the curb. The metal collapsed in a dent that ran the entire length of the car.

'What are you doing?' Byron shouted, grabbing for the steering wheel.

I pushed Byron's hands away and looked over at Jerry's incredulous face. His eyes studied his car, the dent, the scraped paint, then swung over to fix on me. I idled the car in the middle of the street, waiting. Jerry and Trent suddenly dashed for my car.

'Go, go, go!' Byron yelled. 'This isn't the mood I want him in when he catches me.'

I waited until Jerry and Trent were almost on us before peeling out down the street. I waited at the intersection. In my rearview mirror I could see them jumping into the Miata. Byron was twisted around, watching them.

'Either you're completely deranged or this is the most serious case of PMS I've ever seen,' Byron said. 'Let's get the hell out of here. These guys aren't going to be so polite now. And I wouldn't count on your being a woman as any protection.'

'It never has been,' I said. 'Anyway, I'm just raising the stakes.'

'What stakes?'

'For the chase, Byron. We can't have a chase if there's nothing to lose.'

'Oh, God,' he said, clutching his head. 'I knew better than to sleep with a woman who pretends to be my dead wife. I know the Golden Rule of Males, never sleep with a woman who has more problems than you do. I know it, I broke it. But isn't this punishment worse than the crime?'

The Miata was rocketing toward us. I pulled away from the intersection.

The chase was on.

40

Byron tapped his finger against my gas guage. 'Maybe next time you engineer a car chase, you can remember to fill up the tank first.'

We were empty.

'I didn't engineer it. I was inspired, like an artist.'

'Oh, come on. You hunted Grudge down and blackmailed him into bringing you, right? I mean, that's the only reason he'd have done it unless you had sex with him.'

'I didn't have sex with him.'

'Okay, then it was blackmail. Then you bet against me in the chess match, knowing it was fixed. Grudge would have told you that much. You goaded me into winning that last game. Now, I don't blame you, that's my own fault for letting you affect me. That's the part I still don't get myself. That, and why it was worth six grand to you to see me win. Do you want me dead that much?'

'I don't want you dead.'

'Well, you enraged Jerry back there, forced him into following us. Tomorrow he would have found me, broken a limb or two, put me in the hospital for a week. Nothing worse. Hell, he would even have driven me to the hospital. Now . . .' He turned in his seat, saw the Miata racing behind us. 'Now he's going to do worse. Much worse.'

'We won't let him. That's the point of a chase. We outrun them.'

'Without gas?'

'An oversight. I didn't exactly plan this ahead of time.'

'No shit.'

I didn't tell him, but I was forming details to my plan as we drove. Okay, maybe the chase stuff was a last-minute revelation, but everything I'd done since leaving Carla and Jamie had been leading to this. A white whale hunt, only we were the whale. Driving an empty Rabbit.

'What did you hope to accomplish?' he said. 'In fucking up my life like this.'

'I'm not fucking up your life. I'm fixing it.'

'Jesus, If it's not broke, don't fix it. Haven't you ever heard that before?'

'Is that one of those guy sayings?'

'I'd like to give you a couple good guy sayings,' he grumbled.

'Look, one of us has to be authentic. One of us has to be the genuine article, the person we really are. I'm too far gone, but you aren't.'

He laughed. 'Luna, I've been a prisoner for two years. A convict. That's not who I really was, but I learned to adapt, to live like one, be one. Because, to everyone else, that's who I really was. So I became what they saw me as. Same as you.'

'You don't understand,' I said.

'Yes, I do. And you know it. That's what bugs you.'

I saw a gas station and pulled in. The Miata pulled in behind us, then veered into another slot beside a different pump. Trent hopped out of the Miata as I got out of my car. I walked to the cashier inside the glass booth. He was a kid, maybe nineteen with a series of moles on his cheekbone. A cigarette burned in a glass ashtray next to the cash register, filling the interior of the booth with white smoke. I could smell the bitter scent seeping through the pay slot. It made me want to smoke again. I gave him a twenty and told him the pump number. He took the money and nodded, then looked up at me. Something behind his eyes shifted, because he smiled slightly and said, 'Thank you.' I looked at my blouse to make sure it wasn't unbuttoned or something. It wasn't. I guess he just liked my looks, the way guys used to react to Wren.

Trent walked up behind me, stood there breathing like a bull. I didn't look back at him, just walked back to my car. I heard money being slid into the pay slot, Trent saying, 'Pump three.'

When I got back to the car, Byron was already pumping the gas.

'Give me Zeno's phone number,' I said.

'Why?'

'Just give it to me. We don't have time to argue, Ike and Tina are on our butts.'

He looked over at the Miata. Trent pumped gas and glared at us. Jerry sat behind the wheel reading the newspaper in the dim yellow light of the station, not even looking our way.

Byron gave me the number and I ran over to the phone booth and made a call. Zeno finally answered after the eighth ring. He complained, argued, grumbled, but in the end, he listened.

I ran back to the car and found Byron sitting in the driver's seat. I climbed in on the other side. 'Did you get the change?' I asked.

'Sure,' he said. 'I'm just waiting for our free Star Trek glasses and Dick Tracy coloring book.' He shook his head and pulled out of the station.

The Miata was right behind us.

'Okay, what's the plan?' he asked.

'Drive, she said.'

'Where?'

I gave him a look. 'Follow your heart.'

He laughed. 'God, if only you weren't crazy, you'd make a good convict.'

'If only you weren't stupid, you'd make a good man.'

We looked at each other and did an exaggerated Laurel and Hardy nod.

'Head out to the desert,' I told him. 'It's time for a little nature trip.'

'That's your plan? Head out to a desolate place and make it easier to hide our bodies?'

'Pretty good plan, huh?'

He kept driving. I didn't offer any more explanation because I didn't want him to know how half-cocked all this was. Even using the word plan seemed to give too much credit to my idea, as if I'd thought it all through or something. I was improvising, adapting to the circumstances, like some form of rapid evolution. I had a notion that we could lose these guys if we pulled a quick switch of cars with Zeno down the road. They'd end up following Zeno, eventually realize their mistake, and just go back home. If I told this to Byron, he'd find things wrong with it and probably come up with a better plan and talk me into using it. But this wasn't his chase scene; it was mine. He was just part of the cast, a featured player, perhaps, but not the star. That was me.

I found a tape in the glove department. I thumbed it into the cassette player. The music started in the middle of a song.

' . . . Wash your hands in dreams and lightning
Cut off your hair, and whatever is frightening . . .'

Byron stabbed the Eject button and yanked the tape out. He opened the window and tossed it out. 'I'm sick of Paul Simon. You know how much Wren used to play him?'

'You know how long it takes for a plastic cassette like that to decompose? You know what it does to our environment?'

He rolled his window back up. 'You're right, I should go back for it.'

'That's not the point, Mr. EarthWorth, Mr. Monkey-Wrench Gang, Mr. Tree Hugger, Mr.—'

'I get the point, subtle as it is.' He drove without speaking, though after a couple of miles he started humming the

Paul Simon song he'd thrown out. He caught himself and started humming something else, Crosby, Stills & Nash, I think.

'Don't you feel guilty?' I asked.

'About what?'

'About throwing that tape out. Forget that it was my private property. But what you did, littering like that. I mean, you just spent two years in jail for protecting the environment.'

'Ecology is the new civil rights,' he said. 'The earth as nigger. It's the perfect middle-class cause, it can't resent us later for our help.'

'Well, it's effective. I feel guilty about everything my body does. If I eat I'm killing something, if I shit or piss I'm spoiling something else. I have a period, my tampons are adding to the landfills. I'm either consuming or polluting.'

'Yup, that's the cycle all right. And no way out of it. Even dead, your body feeds the undertaking industry, also polluters. At least the corpse feeds insects.'

'So I have to wait until then to do some good?'

He looked over at me with a strange expression, like he'd noticed something different he hadn't seen before. It kind of reminded me of the gas station attendant's look and I thought once again maybe I should check my blouse buttons. 'I haven't thrown anything out of a car window since I was thirteen. When I saw you betting that money against me, I wanted you to lose it so bad I went against my survival instinct, an instinct that I honed through two long fucking years in prison. Every day for 730 days I was scared shitless. But I played it cool. No emotion. I had guys three times your size, guys who carried razor blades in their mouths try to get a rise out of me and fail.' He shook his head. 'You bring something out in me, Luna, I'm not sure what. It can't be good. Not if it means being chased by Jerry Kirn through the desert at three in the morning.'

'You give me too much credit.'

'You know what I think? I think people haven't given you enough credit.'

I had no idea what that meant. I didn't want to pursue it, either. 'Turn off that same road we took to where you have your greenhouse.'

'I'm not taking those guys near the house. Forget it.'

'We're not going there. Just do it, okay?'

He did. I directed him, giving him the same route Zeno had given me on the phone.

'So tell me, Byron. Once you and Captain Zeno perfect your flowering bamboo, then what? Sell it for millions and retire to a pollutant-free biodegradable life-style on Maui?'

'This conversation is a little too predictable. You looking to trap me into confessing some hypocrisy? Reveal me for a burnt-out radical who's caved in to the system, trying to get my piece of the pie and split? Or crap to that effect.'

'Yup, that's the effect.'

'Forget it. That's some bullshit yuppie mantra: "What have you done for the revolution lately?" Hey, nature isn't all it's cracked up to be, anyway.'

'Here it comes, the speech of the disillusioned. Dim the lights, dust off the Judy Collins albums.'

'You know me so fucking well. As well as you knew Wren?'

He had me there. I thought I'd known her as intimately as a sister, but I hadn't at all. Only what she'd revealed, not what was in her heart.

'You ever hear of the cuckoo bird?'

'Like in those Swiss clocks, right? They pop out all night and keep you awake.'

'You want to hear this?'

'Turn there.' I pointed.

He turned. We were off the freeway and driving down a dark road. In the distance, a faint cluster of lights. 'Cuckoo birds lay their eggs in other birds' nests. The cuckoo hatching is usually bigger and more aggressive than the hatchling that actually belongs to the nest, so the little cuckoo pushes the smaller bird out of the nest. Then, when the parents return, they feed the cuckoo and ignore their own child because he isn't in the nest. In essence, they're feeding their own children's murderer.'

'Bullshit,' I said. 'You saying that these birds don't notice the difference?'

'Or they don't care. They have a set rule: feed what's in the nest, ignore what isn't. Every creature marks its territory. Like the booby bird. Sailors named it that because they were so tame you could walk right up to one and catch it for dinner.'

'It's straight ahead,' I said. 'When we get there, we're going to have to move fast, so just follow my lead.'

'What lead? What are we doing?'

'Just relax. Tell me about the booby. It's tame. Sailors ate it.'

'They have something called the guano ring.'

'Guano,' I said, thinking. 'That's birdshit.'

'Exactly. They use it to make a circle, then they hatch their young inside the circle. If there's plenty of food, the baby birds leave each other alone. If there isn't, the biggest chick pushes the other chick out of the ring. Once the chick is outside the ring, the mother ignores it and won't feed it. Her child can cry and cry only a foot away, but she'll let it starve to death.'

'Is there a point to all this, Bwana Jim? Other than to depress me?'

'I'm saying, people make their own circles, they draw a circle in the dirt and say, "This much I care about. This is my family, my home, these are my friends in here. Anything outside is not my problem." It doesn't matter the type of dirt, the size of the circle, everybody does it. The rest of their lives is just keeping an eye on the perimeter.'

'Are you saying that's good or bad?'

'Neither. It just is. A person has to recognize their own perimeter, the edge of their own circle. You try to extend that circle or step out of it, there's no way back inside because the perimeter goes on forever. You're up to your eyeballs in birdshit.'

'I think you've been looking at the world through a snitch mirror too long, pal. It's just as distorting as looking at it through mall store windows.'

He didn't say anything for a minute. He looked over at me with an odd expression. 'You miss my point. I'm talking about love here, too. Two people get together, they draw their own circle in the dirt, say to everyone, this is our life. This is where we make a stand against the world. In here we combine our concerns, our goals, our lives. That's love. A circle in the dirt.'

I snorted. 'You're a hell of a romantic.'

'I'm not talking romantic love. I'm talking reality. Think of the most repulsive man you can, both physically and spiritually. His eating habits are gross, he has no personal hygiene, and he thinks women are pigs. We stick the two of you on a desert island for the rest of your lives. You and I both know that sooner or later you two will learn to love each other as much as, if not more than, you have loved anyone before. I've seen it in prison: two men who outside the walls would have killed each other over a ball game, inside are living like man and wife. Love is circumstances, nothing more.'

'Christ, I should've left you back there for Jerry and Trent. You deserve each other.'

'You think you did me a favor here? Fuck, before they were just going to bust me up a little. Now they're going to bust me up a lot.'

This whole thing wasn't working out as I'd planned it. The significance of the chase scene is to have the stakes high enough so that it matters if you're caught. I'd done that. But you also need a little cooperation from the co-chasee. There has to be a feeling of shared worth, like living actually is desirable. After listening to Byron, I'd lost some of my spirit for the adventure. Maybe he'd just sobered me up, made me aware that this whole thing

wasn't a game, after all. Those guys were serious. For the
first time, I was scared.

'Up there,' I said.

'That's a minimart gas station.'

'Right. It's open all night.'

'We still have gas.'

'We're not stopping for gas.'

He sighed. 'Just trust the Force, Luke.'

We could see Zeno standing in front of the minimart
eating a donut. As soon as he saw us, he jumped into the
Jeep and started the engine. He left his door open.

I turned to Byron. 'Okay, as soon as we pull in, you put
on the emergency brake and hop out. Leave the motor
running and the door open. You run into the Jeep and
duck down out of sight.'

'And what happens? Zeno gets in this car and the two
of you drive away, hoping Jerry will follow?'

'It'll work,' I said. 'You just turn down that street and
circle behind the station before turning into it. While
we're making the switch, Jerry and Trent will be blocked
by the building. By the time they clear it, Zeno and I will
be driving away and they'll have to follow. It'll work.'

He thought about it. 'Yeah, it probably will.'

'Thanks.' I smiled, feeling some of that chase spirit returning.

'Except I'm not doing it. When they catch up with you
guys, and they will catch up, they'll just take it out on you
and Zeno. You can take it, but Zeno can't.'

'You sweet talker, you.' I pointed. 'Okay, turn here,
then circle around the building as fast as you can. This has
to be done fast.'

'I told you, I'm not doing it.'

'I can take care of myself. I'll take care of Zeno too.'

'Goddamn it!' he said and stomped the gas. The car
squealed around the curb and shot the length of the quiet
desert road, then he turned to circle the gas station. 'I'm
not going without you, Luna.'

I looked at him. He kept his eyes on the road, but I

could see the glint in them, the soft sadness. 'What are you saying, we're the two most repulsive people on the planet and we've just been marooned on a desert island?'

He yanked the steering wheel and we slid around another corner. One more corner and everything would happen fast. Too fast to make any mistakes. No turning back.

'I'm saying this is my circle in the dirt, my guano ring, baby.' He glanced at me. 'And you're on the inside.'

I laughed. 'See, you can be romantic after all.'

He laughed too and I felt a sudden lightness about me. A happiness, I guess. But not like any happiness I'd ever known before. Maybe because it didn't seem like a shared happiness as much as just my own, like eating a whole pint of ice cream by myself. Like I knew who I was and where I was and what I was doing for the first time. I mean, for the first time ever. I had always lived in someone else's house, someone else's routine, someone else's life. I thought of Robby then and there was no longing, no sense that I was missing a part of me. I suppose I had always been missing a part of me, since way before Robby.

The man by my side had seen me do some pretty crazy stunts, had lived with me while I pretended to be his dead wife. He had seen me smashing watches. He had made love to me while I'd been stung by a scorpion. He had seen me at my most extreme. I had no secrets left to hide from him.

I popped open the glove compartment and searched through the shreds of old parking lot tickets and gas credit and receipts and broken eyeliner pencils until I found a tattered book of matches from the days when I used to smoke. I stuffed them into my pocket. I leaned over the back seat and rummaged through the magazines, newspapers, empty Butterfingers wrappers. Finally I found what I'd been looking for, my old balled-up panty hose that Season had made me strip off that first day. I crammed them into my other pocket.

'Okay,' I said, plopping back in my seat. 'I'm in the

circle. Anyone else comes in, we peck the shit out of them. That the deal?'

'That's the deal.'

We screeched into the gas station and both of us leapt from the car. Zeno ran out from behind the idling Jeep and jumped into the car. 'Hey,' he said to me. 'I thought I was taking you?'

'Change of plans,' I hollered over my shoulder. 'Drive on home, they won't follow.'

He took off, missed the driveway, and shot over the curb, bouncing my car onto the street. He disappeared into the darkness.

Suddenly the red Miata was sweeping around the curb and shooting into the gas station. By now Byron and I were strapped into the Jeep. Byron jammed the gas pedal and we swung aound in front of the Miata and blasted out of there, flying off the curb and blasting down the street. Jerry Kirn did a neat spin with his car and was right on our tail the whole time.

'We're not going to lose them,' Byron shouted because the wind whipped around us so loudly. 'And we sure as shit can't outrun them.'

'We're not going to try. Just take us to that place where we had sex. Remember?'

'The place or the sex?'

I swatted his arm. He laughed. His laughter sounded different now, somehow richer. Edgeless. As if before he'd always laughed in mono and now he laughed in stereo. Hearing him laugh was like listening to a song that made you want to sing along or drum against the steering wheel or do something to be involved with that sound.

'Okay,' I said. 'I guess we need a plan now.'

'It's your chase. I'm only the bait.'

I hadn't thought about that, but I guess he was right. I had wanted them to follow, but if it hadn't been them, it would have been someone else. Maybe I would have sped by a police car and given them the finger. Or sideswiped a car with six gangbangers cruising around. I don't know, something. I liked that he recognized that and didn't try to interfere or reshape what I was doing. My art.

'How's this sound?' I told him my plan, every crazy detail. When I finished I smiled and said, 'Simple and direct.'

He looked over at me. The wind was tugging at his hair, flipping his ponytail around like a floundering fish. His dragonfly earring twirled like a weather vane. I leaned over and kissed his cheek. He leaned into me. It was the smallest of gestures, yet it felt so damned complete, just that little kiss, his light nudge. The sex had been consuming and heated, but it had been missing something. Whatever that something was, I felt it then.

'Your plan doesn't call for us to pull over to the side of the road and make love, does it?'

I shook my head.

'Then you need a new plan.'

We drove through the dark desert, leaving a plume of dust to wag in the Miata's face. I looked behind us and saw only the dim headlights surrounded by the gritty fog of brown dust. Up ahead were the rocky cliffs where Byron and I had made love.

'Ready?' I asked.

'Are you?'

We exchanged looks.

'Go!' he shouted. I unfastened my seat belt and climbed into the back of the Jeep. I found the ultraviolet flashlight but I couldn't find a container. I emptied the small toolbox, dumping everything on the floor. I returned to my seat.

'Got it,' I said.

Byron began zigzagging the Jeep, kicking up even more dust. Then he slowed just enough for me to leap out with the empty toolbox and ultraviolet flashlight in hand. I hit the ground at a run and kept running, veering away from the dirt cloud. Then I dropped to the ground, face first, and waited for the Miata to drive by. Once it had, I walked over to the cliff face and shone my black light on it.

The constellation of green-blue scorpions lit up the rock face the same as it had the night before. Some scuttled across the rock like shooting stars arcing across the sky. Most just sat there, clinging, waiting for something. Whatever they were waiting for, it wasn't me. I wondered if one of them was the one that stung me. I looked for a guilty face. They all looked sufficiently guilty, their eyes staring blankly.

I opened the small silver toolbox and began scooping scorpions into the box. I scraped the lip along the cliff and brushed the reluctant ones in with the tip of my flashlight. When I had about thirty or so piled three deep in the box, I closed the lid and waited. I could feel them moving around inside the box and that made me feel creepy. While I waited, I kept pointing the black light all around my feet, making sure there was no scorpion rescue squad heading for me.

About five minutes later, I heard Byron's Jeep returning. I ran out and waved at him. He pulled off the dirt road and hopped out of the Jeep.

'Ready?' he said.

I nodded. But I was scared. I hadn't felt scared up until now. I'd felt excited, elated, nervous, depressed, all kinds of things. But scared was new.

The Miata braked to a stop and Jerry and Trent got out. They walked slowly toward us.

Jerry's face was grim and menacing. 'You know, Byron, from everything you ever told me about your wife, she was supposed to be smart. A real genius.' He gestured at the Jeep, the Miata, the desert itself. 'This was not genius. This was dumb.'

'This isn't my wife,' Byron said.

'Thanks for that resounding defense,' I said.

Jerry gave me a look that said I wasn't even there yet, but when he decided I was there, I'd better watch out. I had a feeling his wife experienced that look a lot. 'Thing is, Byron, now I've got to make things right, not just for Landry, but for me. Christ, you know I don't want to. Why couldn't you just stick to the rules? You know the goddamn rules.'

'I figured we were out of prison.'

Jerry shook his head. 'Unh-uh, I'm not getting suckered into one of your fucking philosophical discussions. Let's just get this over with, okay? I'm pissed, I admit that. That's why I'm going to let Trent do this job.'

Trent, face arranged into his most intimidating scowl, started toward us.

'Don't you know karate or something?' I said to Byron.

'I wrestled in high school until some guy dislocated my shoulder. If I take him down I can get two points.'

Trent stomped closer.

'Do something, Byron,' I said. 'Bite off a finger or something.'

'Fine. Give me your hand.'

Now Trent was within a couple yards. Close enough.

I opened the toolbox and displayed the contents. 'Trent's liable to get a face full of scorpions. And they're pissed.'

Trent halted, his scowl melting as he stared at the writhing tangle of scorpions. I shone the ultraviolet light on them to make them look even scarier. Trent blanched and took a step backward.

Jerry looked disappointed. 'You don't think that's going to stop us, do you, Byron? You've seen me eat worse shit than that in the prison cafeteria.'

'Then come and get 'em,' Byron said. 'They're the fresh catch of the day.'

Jerry started slowly toward us. Trent, nervous but taking his boss's cue, also started toward us. It was like having a pair of pliers closing on you. Byron and I backed up a couple steps until we were pinned against the fender of the Jeep.

Jerry walked closer, rolling up his sleeves with each step. Trent was snorting again.

'I think they just entered our guano circle,' I said.

'You do have a backup plan, right?' Byron asked.

'Yup. Dine and dash.' I heaved the toolbox's contents and half of my scorpions became airborne. Trent covered his face and backpedaled. I tossed the rest of the scorpions at Jerry. He casually sidestepped the flock. They belly-flopped to the ground and scuttled away.

I dropped the light and the toolbox and ran like hell. Byron jumped into the Jeep and tried to start it, but they were on him before he could escape. I heard the crunch of knuckles against bone, the thump of fist against body. And still I ran.

I dashed around the big rocky cliff, circling all the way around the thing until I came out next to the Miata. I crouched down so they couldn't see me crawling up to the little red car. The gas lid was locked, but I managed to jimmy it open with my keys. I tried not to listen to the thumping and cracking of the two men beating on Byron. I had to concentrate on what I was doing. I pulled the ball of panty hose from my pocket, shook them loose, and stuffed them part of the way down the gas tank. Then I removed the matches and stood up.

'Hey, boys,' I called out.

Jerry and Trent turned and looked at me. Byron, who was slumped over the hood of the car, slid to the ground and lifted his head. His mouth was bloody, but otherwise not too bad.

'What kind of bullshit is this?' Jerry said, annoyed.

I lit a match and waved it near the panty hose hanging out of his gas tank. 'Now we see why panty hose are a fire hazard.'

'Don't be stupid. You're even stupider than I thought. You light that and you'll get blown up with the car. You'll die.'

'I've been dead before. It's not that bad.' The thing was, I meant it too. I mean, I wasn't trying to be dramatic or even threatening. I was actually being honest. Dying wasn't part of my original plan, but I didn't mind. That's when it occurred to me that I wasn't afraid anymore.

Jerry appealed to Byron. 'Tell her, man. This isn't a life or death thing we're doing here. I don't carry a gun. Trent doesn't carry a gun. We're not killers. We're just going to bust you up a little so people know how to do business with Landry. We're not out to kill you, either of you.'

I thought about that a moment. 'Maybe you should.'

Byron wiped the blood from his mouth with the back of his hand. 'The opinions expressed do not necessarily reflect those of the management.'

'I mean it, Byron,' I said. 'These guys want to hurt you as a lesson. And you are willing to let them. Some lesson. Life and death. Maybe if more things were life and death, things would have more value. I don't know.'

Trent looked at Jerry with confusion. Jerry stared at me, trying to decide how far he was willing to go, how far he thought I'd go. He looked at my face, my matches, his car. He shrugged, pushed his rolled-up sleeves down. 'Fuck it. It's not worth it.'

Trent whispered something to Jerry, his face puffed up with deviousness. Jerry shook his head. 'Forget it. This isn't the right time, that's all.'

I stayed next to the panty hose, a match pressed against the sandpaper stripe, ready to strike it to flame. Jerry and Trent didn't even look at me as they got in the car, started it up, and drove away.

Byron and I watched their red taillights fade into the night.

'Think they'll be back?' I asked.

'Not tonight.'

'Whew.' I sat down on the ground and breathed deeply. Now that they were gone, the old fear curdled my stomach.

Byron limped over to me, holding his side and wincing. He stooped beside me. 'You okay?'

'I feel as if someone had scraped his feet across three miles of thick carpet and just touched my heart with his fingertip.'

'Is that fear? Or something else?'

I shook my head. 'I don't know.'

Byron kissed me on the cheek and stood up. He walked around to the front of the Jeep and popped open the hood. He lifted the hood up as high as it would go. 'You meant that whole thing, didn't you? About life and death and stuff.'

'At the time. Don't ask me to repeat it.'

'I was impressed,' he said.

'Really?'

'Yeah. It sure wasn't Wren saying all that.'

'I'm not sure it was me either.'

'Must have been you. Your lips were moving.'

I laughed and looked over at him just as he gripped the edge of the heavy metal hood of the Jeep and slammed it down as hard as he could on his forearm.

41

The emergency room wasn't very busy. When I brought Byron in, they seemed relieved to finally have something to do. Nurses and a woman doctor fussed over him as they ushered him to a back room. I waited in the lobby, reading *National Geographic* and sipping diet Pepsi. I looked for familiar faces in the *National Geographic*, booby birds, cuckoos, dragonflies, scorpions, bedbugs, any of the creatures great and small that had scuttled through my life lately.

When they gave Byron back to me, his left arm was in an orange plaster cast. He was groggy from sedation. The doctor handed me a prescription.

'That was a bad break,' she said. She was about my age but her eyes were so close together she seemed to be constantly staring at the tip of her own nose.

'He was fixing the car,' I explained. 'The hood came down.'

'Hell of a hood,' she said. 'Caught him in the mouth and eyes too. And I think one of his ribs is cracked.'

'You know guys, they always think they're more mechanical than they are.'

She nodded. 'Handy is to men what sexy is to women.'

I drove Byron to Zeno's. Zeno gave us his bedroom and he took the couch. During the next day, Zeno worked in the greenhouse. Byron mostly dozed. I made some lunch for Zeno and me and we chatted while Byron slept. Zeno was a pretty funny guy actually, now that he wasn't afraid of me. He chattered enthusiastically about bamboo for over an hour, with digressions to the art of stealing rare books from libaries. He went back to work in the greenhouse and if I hadn't pulled him out for some dinner, he probably would have just kept working through the night. After dinner he went back to the greenhouse to 'make a few notes'. I went to bed at eleven o'clock and he was still in there.

Byron was awake when I went into the bedroom. He was stretched out on the bed in his underpants. His broken arm lay at his side like a club. He was watching the news on the tiny black and white TV Zeno kept on a chair near the bed.

'Feel better?' I asked.

'A little drugged.'

'The doctor might have gotten overzealous. She thinks you're either accident prone or I've been beating you up.'

'I forget. Which is it?'

I laid down next to him on the bed. I could see his hardened penis straining under the white underpants. 'Apparently she didn't sedate you enough.'

'I'm just excited, the weather forecast is about to come on.'

I put my hand on his good arm and stroked him. 'I've been thinking real hard since last night. I mean, I know I'm no genius, but I'm not an idiot either. Still, I can't figure out what the fuck you think you were doing by breaking your own arm. Some sort of delayed stress syndrome? What? Tell me.'

He watched the weatherman point at a projection of the California coast, poke his finger at a cloud mass moving toward southern California. Expect rain, the weatherman said, but not enough to dent the drought we've been having.

'I mean,' I continued, since Byron wasn't answering. 'I mean, after all we went through to keep you from taking a serious beating. It's like it was all for nothing.'

He didn't take his eyes off the TV. 'It wasn't for nothing. Don't think that. I probably have never been happier or more in love in my whole life than the moment I saw you standing there next to Jerry's Miata, your panty hose hanging out of his gas tank. It was the most perfect moment. Everything you did, everything you said, was just right.'

'I was babbling.'

'No,' he said, reaching over to hold my hand. 'You weren't.'

'The panty hose in the gas tank, you knew about it. That was part of our plan.'

He shrugged. 'I knew, but I didn't know how it would feel. You know, like sex with someone new. You know how it's going to feel, but sometimes it surprises you, it feels better than you'd ever imagined.'

'Does it?' I said.

'Sometimes,' he said. 'If everything is just right.' He reached over and pulled me on top of him. We kissed. The kiss lasted a while, I'm not sure how long. Long enough to make my skin ache to be rubbing against his skin. We broke apart. He lifted his broken arm the way a lobster with a pegged wrist might. 'This,' he said, 'this is the payment for witnessing that perfect moment. Jerry won't have told Landry anything about what happened. Neither will Trent, he's too afraid of Jerry. Jerry didn't have to leave last night, he could've stayed. He probably could have even taken away those matches and yanked out the panty hose without any damage to his car.'

'You knew that going in?'

'Sure. I've seen him take out three guys at once. He's not afraid of anything, certainly not us.'

'Then why'd you go along with my plan?'

'Because I didn't care if it worked. That didn't matter.' He sat up more adjusted his pillow. 'Besides, I knew Jerry. He wasn't going to risk anything over us. We're not worth it. He knows he'll find me later and finish then. That's how it is. By breaking my own arm, I allow him to save face with his boss, because now everybody sees me walking around in a cast, they know why. Now Jerry doesn't have much reason to do anything more to me. In that way, I've probably saved myself a lot worse pain. Just makes sense all around.'

We both stared at the TV screen. Some time during our conversation, Johnny Carson had replaced the news team. Johnny was sitting behind his desk. Loni Anderson was sitting next to him. We watched them talk for a few minutes, then Loni left. She wore a tight dress that clung to her hips and her exit drew a lot of applause and a few whistles.

'Here's a bright new comedian,' Johnny said. 'Very funny guy. Ethan Brand.'

'Jesus,' I said. 'Look. It's Ethan. Our Ethan.'

Indeed, it was Ethan emerging from the curtain, carrying his guitar and smiling at the audience.

'It's Ethan,' I repeated, sitting up. I remembered the note he'd left us to call him. Probably about this.

Ethan began talking about the TV shows he grew up on and how the theme songs weren't appropriate to the way he perceived the characters. Which is why he'd written some more pertinent lyrics. Like this, he said, and began singing: '*It's the story of a dork named Brady . . .*'

'That's your song,' I said to Byron. 'Cleaned up a little, but otherwise the same.'

But Byron was laughing. 'He's very funny. I didn't realize.'

Ethan did a couple other songs, takeoffs on the '*Beverly Hillbillies* Theme' and the '*Love Boat* Theme'. He was funnier than he'd ever been the times I'd heard his other acts. Byron and I laughed until Zeno came in to see what was going on. He sat on the bed, watched Ethan, and laughed too. When it was over, Zeno looked at us, grinned, and returned to his greenhouse.

I shut off the TV.

Byron and I kissed. He had a slight medicinal taste in his mouth, probably from the sedatives. I didn't mind. During that kiss I could suddenly see the future again, the way I had been able to when I was with Robby. Only it wasn't the same. I didn't see me old, I didn't see Byron old. I didn't see a quiet house, tucked safely away somewhere. I saw us making love in about five minutes. I saw me slipping his underpants over his hips and burying my head in his lap. I saw me finishing my book on Season. I would tell the truth about her, because that was the truth about me, about many women. I knew the future, not because of Robby being there or Byron or anyone else. I knew it because I knew *I* would be there: I couldn't be sure exactly who I'd be in the morning, part Wren, part Season? I couldn't remember who the old Luna was, what she liked, how she felt. It's not so wrong being someone else for a while. We're always in the state of becoming something or someone else. Like shedding skin, evolving into some other creature altogether. Yesterday I was a fish, today I suddenly have legs and scurry across the mud. Tomorrow I may walk upright.

I guess I'd just have to wait and see.

LARAMIE DUNAWAY

HUNGRY WOMEN

They want it all – love, riches, success – and to be at the mercy of no man.

Four women: Raunchy, passionate and ambitious. At work or at play, each is determined to get all she can from life.

Strong women: They will make the most of every weapon at their disposal – sex, intrigue and the power of their own femininity.

Fast-lane women: Giving their all. They stop at nothing in their drive to the ultimate heights.

Hungry women: Crave the satisfaction that all women need yet few dare to demand.

'You'll recognise their dreams, feel their pain, and root for them to the last riveting page'
Elizabeth Villars, author of *Lipstick on His Collar*

A Royal Mail service in association with the Book Marketing Council & The Booksellers Association.
Post-A-Book is a Post Office trademark.

JESSICA MARCH

OBSESSIONS

As long as she could remember, beautiful Niki Sandeman had been fighting back. Fighting against the stigma of illegitimacy. Fighting to redeem the legacy of her glamorous but ill-fated mother.

Now she is engaged in the most perilous fight of her young, defiant life.

The challenge is to beat at their own game the arrogant, powerful Hyland dynasty – her own family, which has always refused to acknowledge her. The prize is control of a mighty business empire.

But if she wins in business, she may lose in love. Only if she can break free from her own hunger for recognition and revenge will she be able to give her heart to the one man who can mean more to her than any of life's obsessions.

HODDER AND STOUGHTON PAPERBACKS

JESSICA MARCH

TEMPTATIONS

Once she had been the international jet set's most glittering cover girl. Throwing herself into an ecstatic whirl of love affairs, fueled by the most potent pleasure drugs of an era of abandon, Stevie Knight had emerged as a rare survivor from her generation's dizzying, devastating trip into decadence. Survived because she was as strong as she was beautiful.

Now, America's richest and most glamorous women come to The Oasis – the haven she has set up in the New Mexico desert. There they are helped to overcome their addictions, repair their shattered lives.

But even as she uses all her strength and her hard-won insights to help her clients, Stevie is facing her own greatest challenge. She has fallen in love with a passion greater than any she has experienced before. Fallen in love with a man who demands a commitment she is too proud to make, who demands the one thing to which she has never surrendered. Surrender itself.

HODDER AND STOUGHTON PAPERBACKS

JESSICA MARCH

ILLUSIONS

Marriage was not for Willa Dellahaye.

Love to her was surrender, and Willa would never surrender. Tough, glamorous and successful, still she could never forget the pain and helplessness of her childhood. Never forget her father's brutal betrayal of her mother.

A brilliant divorce lawyer, she had built up an unmatched reputation for fighting and winning for the women she represented.

Now, en route to Saudi Arabia by private jet, she was heading for the greatest challenge of her life – and about to discover that the ultimate battle would be fought within her own heart . . .

'Power, passion and well-reasoned philosophy'
Annabel

'A must if you enjoy Hollywood-style blockbusters'
Manchester Evening News

HODDER AND STOUGHTON PAPERBACKS

BELVA PLAIN

BLESSINGS

Life was at last going well for Jennie. Her recent engagement to Jay promised happiness beyond dreams. Her legal work in the poorest parts of the city was profoundly satisfying. And now she had the extra challenge of protecting a thousand acres of wilderness from the developers.

Just that one phone call changed everything.

Long forgotten memories awaken a hurt so deep, they threaten the loss of the man she loves. In danger both at home and at work, Jennie finds she must face the hard decisions she evaded so many years before.

'The suspense is real enough. And so are the emotions'

New York Daily News

HODDER AND STOUGHTON PAPERBACKS

MORE TITLES AVAILABLE FROM
NEW ENGLISH LIBRARY PAPERBACKS